SECRETS AT ROSE ARBOR

by Gail Gaymer Martin

Forget Me Not Romances, a division of Winged Publications

ISBN-13: 978-1-947523-45-6
ISBN-10: 1-947523-45-7

"Can anyone hide in secret places
so that I cannot see him?" declares the Lord.
"Do not I fill heaven and earth?"
Jeremiah 23:24

Chapter One

Home.

Susan Boyd stood in the dusky light and gazed at the small Louisiana plantation cottage where she'd been raised. Inside the clapboard house, she knew her mother waited. Whether she was pleased or not was an unanswered question. All Susan knew was she had come home.

With a sigh, she turned and opened the trunk of her small sedan. She shifted the boxes and dragged out her luggage. Coming back to Devereaux weighed heavily on her spirit. She'd hoped that time and maturity would have healed the wounds that happened seventeen years earlier when she was sent away, but it hadn't.

She shifted her gaze toward the plantation manor next door, barely visible through the oak trees dripping with moss. The manor's imposing lines were only a silhouette in the failing daylight. One bright thought about coming home had excited her—Libby Taylor, owner of the estate, but tonight instead of Libby's welcoming lights, she saw the manor's dark windows. Though disappointed, she looked forward to running next door later to say hello to the wonderful woman who'd meant so much to her.

Libby had been a bright spot in her life. From her, she'd learned so much. Yet... No need for melancholy now.

Edging around to face her mother's house, she drew back her shoulders, ready to face the world. Really to face her mother. At times, Margaret Boyd seemed as encompassing as the world.

She stacked her luggage and rolled it toward the back door. A light burned in the kitchen, and her hope lifted knowing her mother was anticipating her arrival.

When her luggage wheels struck the wooden porch steps, the back door opened, and Margaret pushed aside the screen. "Welcome home, Susan."

"Thank you, Momma." She surprised herself using her childhood endearment for her mother.

Though her mother had spoken a welcome, Susan heard a restive undertone that made her question whether or not welcome was the word. In spite of the tone, age had softened her mother's determined chin. With time, gravity had loosened her taut skin and tight lips to an easier expression. Yet the old resolve shone in her mother's eyes.

When she'd struggled her luggage onto the porch, Margaret stepped forward and relieved her of one suitcase. "I wondered how late you'd be. I didn't keep dinner."

Susan nodded, not surprised.

Margaret walked ahead of her, rolling the medium suitcase while her heels smacked the hardwood flooring with her purposeful steps. "I dusted and vacuumed your old room."

"Thank you." The comment raised the hope she was truly being welcomed.

Ahead of her, Margaret opened the door and vanished inside while she maneuvered the other luggage to make the turn from the narrow hallway. As she crossed the threshold of her childhood bedroom, a lamp sprang to life, spreading a soft glow over the pure white walls.

Memories flooded back, and she stood a moment to accept her decision to come home to make amends and to find herself after so many years.

"I'll leave you be," Margaret said. "There's a cold plate in the refrigerator if you're hungry." Without waiting for a response, she left the room and closed the door.

Susan sank to the edge of the mattress and studied the room. A mahogany dresser, a single bed and a large wardrobe with a mirror so filled with patina she looked speckled. A round rag rug covered part of the plank flooring and sheer curtains hung at the windows with the shades already drawn. The only adornment on the walls was a picture of Jesus knocking at a door. Susan had spent many youthful nights, wondering if anyone had answered.

She rose and moved to the window to lift the shade. The dusky light did little to brighten the room. Seeing the quickening night, she pulled down the shade again and set about unpacking her luggage.

When she'd finished, she checked her watch. Eight-thirty. She hoped Libby had returned home by now, so she could run over to say hello. At the manor house, she would be greeted with open arms. Libby's demonstrative love was a given.

After a last look around the room to make sure everything had been put away, Susan opened the door and stepped into the hallway. The television sounded from the living room as she headed for the kitchen to check the cold plate her mother had mentioned.

When she looked inside the refrigerator, she saw cold cuts and salad. She owed her mother a thank you for her thoughtfulness and few moments of conversation before she visited Libby. She strolled into the living room and settled on the edge of a chair, waiting until a commercial began before interrupting.

The program flashed off and focused on a tube of toothpaste. Susan drew in a breath. "How have you been?"

"Good as can be expected."

Their eyes met in undefined emotion.

Susan brushed her moist palms against the upholstery. "You seem better than the last time we spoke."

Her mother's eyes narrowed. "Did you come home because you thought I was dying?"

"No. I came home because I need a change. I need to find myself."

"Find yourself? Isn't it too late for that? You should have given thought to that years ago."

Susan controlled her instinct to wince. "So, what's happened in

Devereaux? Anything new?"

Margaret gestured toward the side window. "Libby Taylor died. Funeral was yesterday."

The news struck her like a slap. Susan's lungs collapsed, then with a gasp, she breathed. "Libby died?" The words were unbearable and unbelievable. Death. Libby had seemed eternal. So filled with life, death could never stop her. The TV blatted while her mind struggled to accept what she'd heard.

Hoping to hide her emotion, Susan swallowed the lump. "What happened?"

Her mother shrugged. "Stroke, I think."

"But why didn't you let me know?"

Her mother frowned. "Don't look so startled."

"I am startled. You know I thought a lot of Libby."

"You worshiped her and her evil ways. That's what got you in trouble."

The lump in Susan's throat grew. "Blame me. Not Libby." She studied her mother's expression. "You could have called me to let me know."

Margaret looked toward the TV commercial. "I figured he would let you know."

He. "I haven't spoken to Justin since I left Devereaux. I haven't had contact with anyone from here except you."

"Me?" Her mother's voice shot to a grating pitch. "I rarely see you."

The tone of her voice took Susan back many years when she'd neglected her homework or forgot to do the dishes. "I know, Mother, but I'm here now. I want to—"

The TV program had begun again, and her mother's interest had returned to the television.

The age-old problem. The eternal bitterness. Susan feared she'd made a terrible mistake coming home, but as the thought entered her mind, it sagged and died. Where else would she go? Roads always seemed to lead home. For better or worse, but she'd hoped for better.

She left her thoughts and eyed her mother's stoic profile. "I'm going out for some air." She rose, not waiting for a response.

Her legs felt unsteady as she hurried to the back door and stepped outside. The pleasant spring evening washed over her, and she sucked in the fresh air while memories tore through her like the sorrow that wracked her frame. Libby had been a source of joy, her mentor. Coming home meant seeing Libby again. Now—

Swiping at her tears with the back of her hand, she felt beckoned across the grass. Her feet carried her to the property line and through the stately trees guiding her into Libby's garden and to the rose arbor.

The arbor. Memories prickled down her neck.

She stood in its shadow and looked across the moon-flecked lawn where the plantation manor sat shrouded in darkness. The fragrance of roses and honeysuckle hung heavy on the air—as heavy as her heart. She ran her fingers along the wooden bench, feeling the rough, weathered plank, the white paint fading to a gray ghost.

She sat, leaning her back against the hard wood and stretching her legs, as her mind drifted to her youth—fresh scrubbed and innocent. Since she'd been a child, Libby had entertained her with lemonade and wonderful stories. Even in later years on Susan's rare visits home, Libby had opened her door and her arms in a warm greeting.

Susan pictured Libby sitting on the gallery, her auburn hair lightened by sun and age, wisps curling from her natural waves. Sometimes the curls formed a halo around her face, and she would brush them back with long fingers, so pale and delicate they reminded Susan of her grandmother's China doll that sat on a shelf in her mother's living room.

Libby had the look of a Southern belle from the days of ruffled hoop skirts and gracious living. In her mid-sixties, she'd been too young, too full of life and hope to die.

And now what would become of the plantation manor? A single woman, Libby had doted on her handsome nephew. Justin Taylor Robard. Even his name sent a shiver along Susan's spine. Justin had caught her interest with his dark brown hair and eyes gray as a stormy sky.

He'd beguiled her, not by his own efforts, but by her imagination. Her young girl fantasy wove around his brooding good looks, and without knowing it, he'd caused her deep grief.

Tangled in bittersweet memories, Susan brushed her finger over her locket which held two miniature photographs—portraits from a different time, a changed world, but the same place...as if time had stood still. She pushed her hair behind her ear, rose and stepped away from the arbor for another look at the silent manor before heading back to her mother's.

The dew-laden grass spotted her sandals and dampened her toes. Her footfall swished on the lawn, and the silence wrapped around her until a faint sound drifted from the gallery. She faltered, then held her breath to listen. The squeak of a rocking chair. Frissons prickled her arms.

The creaking stopped, and footsteps thudded on the wide gallery planks. She held her breath and narrowed her eyes, peering into the darkness.

Tales of a ghost's presence had been a legend at the manor since she could remember, but her good sense and Christian upbringing told her it was only a myth. But the eerie sounds sent her imagination on edge.

Bathed in hazy moonlight, a tall masculine form surged toward her. She swallowed her fear, pushing the foolish ghost notion out of her mind. The tangible shape had to be a realtor or another neighbor paying tribute to Libby's memory.

"May I help you?" His voice rolled from the shadow.

"Sorry." She restrained the anxiety from her voice, "I didn't know anyone was here." She extended her hand to the broad-shouldered figure. "I'm Susan Boyd. A neighbor. I grew up next door."

The form twitched, and she heard an intake of breath. "Susan?"

Her pulse coursed to her temples. She lowered her arm and moved closer. "Justin?"

He gave a faint nod.

She longed to embrace him, but good sense won over instinct. For once, she would act on her honest sympathy. "I'm so sorry about Libby." Justin's shadowed face couldn't shroud his matured good looks. Susan steadied herself. "No one let me know, or I would have been here."

"I looked for you at the funeral." His voice sounded deep and heavy. "I thought your mother would have told you."

Glad the dark hid her expression, Susan kept her voice even. "She didn't. I've been living out of town and got back this evening." She took a step closer, needing to feel his presence. They had both lost someone precious to them. "I loved your aunt more than I can tell you. I'll never forget her."

"I won't either." His voice resounded with so much meaning, it made her heart ache.

He glanced over his shoulder toward the house. “I’ve been trying to find the courage to open the door.”

His candid remark whooshed through her chest. “You’ve been sitting outside all evening?”

“For a couple of hours.” His gaze searched her face. “Would you come in?”

Her thoughts tumbled, recalling the last time they were together before he left for college. She’d spent years clinging to her anger at Justin, even though she told her mother she hadn’t blamed him, and tonight she wanted to refuse his invitation, but seeing the sadness in his eyes and his drawn look that almost pleaded, she couldn’t refuse.

“It won’t be the same here. Ever.” Justin ran his fingers through his moonlit hair. “Libby brightened the manor even when she didn’t have the same spring in her step.”

His sadness washed over her. “Things change,” she said, repeating the same words from long ago on a night like this one. He was going off to college and she...she was staying in Devereaux. But this time her sadness was different.

His eyes searched hers. “You’ve said that before.”

He’d remembered. Time had never been gentle for either of them.

Motioning toward the gallery steps, Justin held back.

She hesitated, yet out of shared grief, she moved ahead of him. Silence hung between them except for the brush of their footfalls in the grass and the slap of their shoes on the wooden stairs. While he located the key and unlocked the door, Susan waited, washed in memories.

Justin swung open the door and reached inside to snap on a light. He motioned her forward.

Squinting at the brightness, she stepped through the doorway, overwhelmed by the sweep of nostalgia. Her feet moved on the worn oriental carpet...from Madagascar, if she remembered correctly. Libby had a story for everything in the manor.

“Let’s sit in the parlor.” he pointed as he backed away. “Let me find us something to drink.”

He moved with purpose through the broad foyer and vanished toward the kitchen.

Susan passed the curved staircase winding to the second floor and entered the family parlor. Gazing around the familiar room, she wandered to the secretary desk to eye an old photograph, then to the mantel saddened by the floral bouquet that had passed its prime. Finally, she settled against the toss pillows propped on the beige settee. The room smelled of dust and age, but a stronger scent of Libby's potpourri...or perhaps her floral perfume still clung to the upholstery.

She drew in the sweet scent, reliving the many evenings she'd sat in this room with Libby. Her mind soared back, and a smile eased her tension as she remembered her dear neighbor.

Driven by nostalgia, Susan rose and strolled to Libby's bedroom door off the parlor. The sweet scent seemed stronger there. She pushed back the door and stepped inside, her gaze sweeping the room—the towering armoire, her dressing table, the half-canopied bed. She caught her reflection in the cheval mirror, a silhouette backlit be the parlor's light. Sadness overcame her as she moved forward and snapped on the vanity lamp.

She stood a moment, longing to talk with Libby. She'd anticipated Libby's wonderful advice and her spirit. Looking down, she gazed at Libby's comb and brush. White hairs still clung to the bristles, and she touched one, realizing that was as close as she could get to the woman who'd filled her life with so many good things.

She moved away, then turned back with her gaze settling on a ledger tucked beneath a jewelry box. Susan lifted the box. A journal. Her breath hitched. She grasped the volume, almost afraid to look inside. Replacing the box, she moved closer to the lamp and opened the cover. Her eyes scanned the dated pages in Libby's neat script with her fancy flared capitals.

Susan clutched the journal to her chest and glanced into the parlor. Would Justin mind that she'd wandered into Libby's room? She had no right to nose into Libby's belongings.

She lifted the box to return the diary, then faltered. She could ask Justin if she could read it. What would be the harm? Drawing up her shoulders, she snapped off the light and returned to the settee, tucking the journal alongside her on the cushion. She heard Justin's footsteps and tensed.

"Do you still drink sweet tea?" Justin stepped through the doorway, carrying two tall slender glasses. "I can probably find lemonade in the freezer if you prefer."

"Sweet tea is perfect," She took the drink and watched him head for the chair and felt hopeful for the first time. Perhaps she and Justin could be casual friends again. Forget the kisses of their youth. Forget their mistakes. They could start again as friends.

Justin sank into a wingback chair across from her, its tall back rising behind him. He leaned his head against the cushion for a moment before rousing himself to take a sip of the drink. He studied her over the glass rim. When he lowered it, his expression changed. "You look good, Susan. It's been a long time."

"About seventeen years." Her gaze held captive, she tasted her drink. "I've been thinking about those days."

Discomfort flickered across his face. "About Libby?"

"Libby and Rose Arbor."

"She loved this house." He settled back, looking more at ease.

"We did, too."

He gave a faint nod.

"Remember when Libby took us to New Orleans for the day? I'll never forget how far we walked in that horrible humidity."

He chuckled. "The hottest day in the summer...to visit the above ground cemeteries. Libby's strange idea of fun."

"But it was interesting, and later we went to Jackson Park. I loved the music and the carriages."

"You loved the beignets. We couldn't get you to leave Café Du Monde."

The image of powdered sugar drenching the chairs, tables and floors shot into her thoughts. "I remember Libby trying to teach me how to eat beignets without getting the sugar all over me."

"You're a slow learner." A faint grin touched his lips.

Susan opened her mouth to offer a jibe, but his expression halted her. His grin faded as if he'd suddenly remembered Libby was gone. He lowered his head.

"Justin, how is your mother handling Libby's death. It must be hard on—"

"Mother and Aunt Libby were never close." A ragged breath rumbled from his chest. "My father, if he were alive, would have shown more emotion, I'm guessing. He showed his feelings so much more than my mother."

"Was your dad a storyteller, like Libby?"

Justin grinned. "Oh yes, he did when I was young. I think he gave up when my mother told him so often that no one cared about his stories."

"I'm sorry, Justin. I wish I'd known your dad. I would have liked him."

"Yes, you would have. My dad knew how to entertain his company." His grin faded. "Libby's stories were something we both enjoyed."

"We did." The pressure of the journal against her leg made her uneasy. She tried to ignore it as she sipped the tea, wanting to say something comforting, but his quietness reminded her too much of their past together. Justin had a way of laughing one moment and turning sullen the next. She'd often wondered if that was the attraction. He seemed a mystery to her. An intriguing, tempting enigma.

Finally, he lifted his head. "You don't live in Devereaux?"

"I've been in Baton Rouge for a number of years, but I've—"

"Baton Rouge?" He leaned forward, resting his free hand on his knee. "My partner and I own a business there. My condo overlooks the Mississippi River not too far from the university."

Her chest tightened realizing how near he'd been. "I worked at the Museum of Art. We were probably neighbors—"

"The Museum of Art." His eyes widened. "What did you do there?"

"I began as a technician. I worked with the curators doing research on objects in the museum collections. Finally, I was promoted to a specialist and worked with exhibit designs. I liked working with textiles."

"I'm impressed. I admire your getting away from Devereaux. So many people stay here. I see them around, and wonder why they have no impetus to leave."

Her expression twisted to concern. "I came back, Justin."

His brow furrowed as he leaned forward. "Why?"

She pressed her spine against the cushion. "I have my reasons. It seems good being here."

"Then I'm glad you came back." He eased back and studied her. "You've always impressed me, Susan. You've always been able to make good out of bad. You find a bright spot in even the darkest night." He seemed to sail away in thought, but soon his gaze returned to hers. "Although I'm impressed, for some reason, I can't picture you working in a museum. I always thought you'd be teaching school or—"

Admiration glinted in his eyes, and a moment passed before she managed to speak. "I'm a people person, you mean."

"You always were." His gaze softened. "You listened to people with intensity. You came to life with Libby's stories. I can still hear your laughter."

"I do like to work with people, but the museum didn't give me that chance. I was behind the scenes. I've decided to rethink my career. That's why I moved home for a while."

"Home."

The single word sounded like a eulogy. Yet, he seemed to come around as a questioning look settled on his face.

"How will being in Devereaux help? Work's not as plentiful here as in Baton Rouge."

"It's not just the employment. I have a number of reasons for returning." Her shoulders tensed while she struggled with how to explain without revealing too much. "I've had some issues with my parents for a number of years. When my dad died a few years ago, we hadn't resolved the problems. I vowed to do something about it."

A curious look filled his face, and she sensed he wanted to ask her more. Instead, he only tilted his head and waited.

"My mother's dealing with some health problems, and I would never forgive myself if we don't settle our differences."

"I'm sorry about your mother."

"Thanks. She seems to be doing better now." She hesitated, uncomfortable talking about her relationship with her mother. "I have other reasons, too. I want time to think about my career. Maybe try something new. I don't know... I want to make my life more meaningful. I'm ready to step out in faith."

"Faith. That's always been important to you."

Her heart skipped. Justin had a minimal grasp of faith and received only a glimmer of the Lord from Libby's occasional comments. "Faith. You can call it taking a risk."

"We all need to do that sometimes." He ran his finger around the lip of his glass, his expression distant. Finally, he lowered his hand. "You vanished from Devereaux. I always wondered why, and I feared it was because..."

His gaze caught hers, and she held her breath.

"When I came home for Christmas vacation my first year in college, Aunt Libby told me you'd decided to live with relatives and finish school there."

She wanted to leave his statement unanswered and prayed he wouldn't press her. She'd never told anyone the reason she left, not even Libby. Susan studied his face, wondering if she could ever tell Justin the whole truth. "It was my parents' decision."

His gaze clung to hers for a moment before it glided to her ring finger.

When he looked up, she read the question in his eyes. "I've never been married."

A frown shadowed his face again.

Motivated by her own curiosity, she sidled a look at his left hand and found it free of jewelry. Only a wristwatch peeked from beneath his sleeve.

"I'm single, too" he said, answering her question. "Never thought marriage had much to offer. I always pictured Aunt Libby—free, content and happier than most people. Being single seemed safer and less trouble than marriage."

Safer? Less trouble than marriage? The words twisted in her mind, recalling his teenage depression. She'd always questioned why.

Contrition settled on his face. "This conversation is boring you."

"You've never bored me."

His expression drew Susan back to the young Justin with the same brooding eyes and petulant turn of his mouth—his lips, the kisses that had changed everything. Now time had supplied a matured look that added character. "You've aged well, Justin."

"Hard work. Can't get into much trouble that way."

She weighed his comment and let it pass. "How long will you be here?"

"A few days."

The mundane conversation had become strained, and she became more aware of the journal against her leg. She lifted her glass and took another drink, then placed it on the oval coffee table in front of her, thinking she should leave, then wondering how he would react when she mentioned the journal.

Before she moved, a strange sensation settled in her chest—a deep longing to tell him everything, to renew their friendship despite the impossibility. No matter what the past had held, she felt a connection to Justin. They'd shared so much. Too much. She wanted to learn more about the matured man who still sent her pulse rising.

"Justin, what about you? What happens now to the plantation?" Seeing his expression, she knew she'd asked the wrong question and wished she could retract it. "I'm sorry for asking. I'm sure it's difficult to even think of selling the manor. It's been in your family for years. I shouldn't have said a thing."

Justin lifted his shoulders as if he'd caught a second wind, and he aimed a direct look at her. "Selling the manor isn't the problem."

"What do you mean it's not the problem?"

"Aunt Libby left the manor to me."

Her pulse skittered. "But that's wonderful, Justin." As if her hand had been pulled by a magnet, she raised it and fondled her locket. "Think of all the happy times—"

"You didn't let me finish." He lowered his eyes. "She left it to me...with stipulations."

"Stipulations?" Her mind reeled. Libby never posed conditions on anything. She had always been so open and spirited. She studied Justin's dark eyes. "What kind of stipulations?"

Air drained from his lungs before he spoke. "Rose Arbor can never be sold. I either live here or give it to the historical society."

Images swarmed her mind. Justin walking in the garden and sitting on the gallery. Justin home at Rose Arbor. Her thoughts twisted. "But what's wrong with—"

"Susan, my business is in Baton Rouge. I'll have to donate the property to the historical society. I could never live in Devereaux."

Chapter Two

Justin watched Susan's sky-blue eyes grow as wide as the Mississippi while his own vision blurred with the weight of his statement. He could never live here. Yet how could he give away Rose Arbor?

"Never? I don't understand." Her voice faded to a whisper.

Never seemed so final. The word that rattled him. Yet, since he'd heard the reading of the will, options had wavered through him, going nowhere. He grasped his glass and brought it to his lips, his senses yearning for something real and refreshing like his mint tea.

Susan moved to the edge of her seat, and he knew she was anticipating his response.

He slid his empty glass onto the small side table and drew in a lengthy breath. "It's impossible to live here."

"But why?"

He watched a frown mar her smooth forehead and reined in his frustration with her lack of understanding. "Baton Rouge is a long drive every day to come back here to a—to a lonely house filled with memories and nothing else."

Her dark lashes flickered against her pale skin, and he wished he'd bitten back the admission. He'd been rocked by a gale-force wind since he found Susan in the garden.

When she first had come to visit his aunt, Justin recalled Susan's admiring eyes watching him like one observes a hungry baby bird. Her eyes had been filled with tenderness and concern—just as they were today. Those eyes and the hero-worship had undone him years early, and they were doing the same today.

"It'll be your home, Justin." Susan's urgent tone knotted in his chest. "You'll fill the house with your own things. With friends, and perhaps one day a—"

"A wife. Not for me." He startled himself with the quickness of his response. "Marriage won't work for me, Susan."

Sadness shuffled over her countenance, and she sank against the seat cushion. She appeared in thought, and he waited, trying to formulate words to defend his statement. Finally, she focused on him again.

"So, you're going to donate the manor to the historical society." She blew out a stream of air. "I can't believe you're giving up that easily."

The unexpected change of topic hit him hard and knotted in his neck. He lifted his hand to work out the stress from his shoulders. "I'm overwhelmed. You know how the historical society restores many of the old plantation houses and opens them as museums for tourists. It makes sense."

"Yes, they do that, but—" She faltered, pressing her fingers against her temples as if trying to sort out her thoughts. "Why would Libby do that? She was so giving. Why would she make you heir and then bind you with conditions?"

"I assumed she would leave Rose Arbor to my mother, so I was startled she left it to me and more surprised with the no-sale specification." His chest tightened watching her follow his every word. "But I've given it thought, Susan. That's what I did for two hours tonight sitting on the gallery. I know the answer."

"You do?"

"Aunt Libby loved this house. That's the whole of it. The house, the plantation, its history. These buildings have been in the Taylor family for generations. I suppose she didn't want strangers owning the house even though some of the property had already been sold."

"Like my folks house," Susan said. "My father said it had once been servants' quarters."

"Yes. Like your house. That happened before Libby became the owner."

"Then you must choose." Her face weighted with uncertainty.

Though questions filled her eyes, he couldn't find a response. The decision seemed impossible. He couldn't see himself living in Devereaux, yet giving away Rose Arbor ate at his soul. "Too much has happened these past couple days. I can't think."

You must choose. Her comment sent him on a backward journey, envisioning the special times he'd spent in this house with Aunt Libby and many times in Susan's company. The house gave him life. Libby had given him life. She reminded him of flowers and springtime—always full of life despite her years.

He'd learned about flowers from his aunt—about planting and appreciating them. He could picture Libby's tapered fingers holding a bulb before setting it in the moist soil. Then she would mound the earth, telling him that life was like a bulb waiting to birth beautiful things.

Beautiful things? Libby was right. Amid the thorns and brambles, life had blossomed around him in a strange way. His first such memory was Susan.

"I know you love this place. We've had...you've had wonderful times here. How can you give it to anyone?"

Her questions—even her expression—unsettled him. "I have the memories." His defensive reaction startled him, and his chest ached when he saw tears welling in her eyes. She brushed them away, seeming as confused as he felt. "This is a bad time for you, too. Libby saved both of us in a way."

She lowered her eyes, and when she lifted her gaze, she rose.

"Take your time, Justin. Don't force a decision."

A book had fallen onto the chair cushion. Justin eyed it wondering where it had come from.

Susan's face had lost its glow. She turned and picked up the book. "Do you mind if I take this home? I believe it was Libby's." She clasped it to her chest. "I'll return it tomorrow."

Justin studied the cover, confused by her request. He wanted to ask what kind of book, but he stopped himself. Libby loved poetry and he guessed it was a small volume of verses. "By all means. Don't rush."

Relief spread over her face as she grasped her glass from the table.

"I'd better get home. Mother will think I ran off."

Justin stepped toward her, but seeing a guarded look in her eyes, he stopped himself and took the goblet from her hand. "It was good to see you." The words sounded empty and impersonal in light of their hour together.

She extended her free hand, and he grasped it, feeling her slender fingers against his larger ones.

"Thanks for the tea." She glanced down at her hand. "And for loaning me the book."

"You're welcome. I'm sure we'll see each other again." Though he said the word, he flinched with his uneasiness as to how she affected him.

Still tonight he felt grateful for her surprise appearance in the garden. Emotion had nailed him to the gallery chair. He'd learned from childhood not to cry, to be a man, to let hurt and disappointment roll off his shoulders. Yet he'd sat so long on the gallery, fighting his emotion and hating to enter the manor without Libby's cheerful voice greeting him.

Susan put her hand on the doorknob and paused. "Good night, Justin. I hope you sleep well."

"I'll be fine. Thanks for coming inside with me."

"You're welcome." She opened the door and stepped onto the gallery.

He stood in the doorway and watched her walk down the steps into the night's shadows. She turned toward the large red oak and her house beyond. He stepped to the gallery stairs, and when she moved from beneath the tree into the moonlight, she looked at him over her shoulder before vanishing again into the darkness.

He strode inside surrounded by silence. His head ached, and he hurried into the kitchen, searching the cabinets for a remedy.

Though Susan had offered him company and the impetus to enter the house, she had given him a headache and worse left him puzzled and sentimental. She'd set him on edge with her questions and compassion. Now she'd left him alone to struggle with a difficult decision and merciless memory.

His mind wandered back to an evening so long ago. Susan's sixteenth birthday. They'd had cake on the gallery, and he remembered a locket. He'd wondered if it were the same one she'd worn tonight.

He rubbed the back of his neck again and opened another cabinet door. Inside, he found the aspirin. He grabbed the bottle and filled a glass with water. Tossing two pills onto his tongue, he swilled down the liquid and set the tumbler in the sink.

Turning off lights as he went, he wandered back into the parlor and crossed the worn carpet toward Libby's bedroom. He would sleep there tonight.

He stood in the doorway and surveyed the familiar room with its Victorian bed on the red and gold Tabriz carpet. The armoire and dressers still held Libby's clothing. He'd deal with that another day.

He strode across the room and dropped his jacket over the chair of the vanity. His reflection in the cheval mirror startled him, and he caught his breath, feeling idiotic like a frightened child in a carnival spook house.

He snapped on the small vanity lamp, then retraced his steps to extinguish the parlor light. In the dim glow, he undressed and sank onto the high mattress. Folding his arm over his eyes, he left the lamp burning.

♥

"What kept you?" Margaret asked from her chair in front of the TV. "You've been gone for over an hour." Her back had stiffened, and she looked at Susan with suspicion.

"I walked to the manor," she said, wishing she could lie and tell some wild story of abduction or anything to stop the questions. She nestled Libby's journal close to her side.

"He was there I s'pose."

She could play games and ask her mother who she meant, but what was the point. "Yes. I saw Justin." She sank onto the sofa, tucking the book between her and the arm.

Her mother gripped the chair. "So, it starts again."

"Nothing's started again. We're adults, Mother. We share a common grief. We both loved Libby."

Margaret dropped back against the cushion and closed her eyes. "Libby. You'd think she was the Queen of Sheba."

Susan winced. "She was a good woman. That's all."

"You doted on her. You'd skedaddle out of the house to go there. I always wondered how she managed to charm you."

"Charm me?" Susan felt her jaw drop. "She offered me kindness. She listened to a young girl's naivety without complaint or questions. She made me laugh. She made me feel welcome."

Her mother's eyes snapped open, and her mother's look nailed her to the cushion. "And I didn't make you feel welcome in your own home. I wasn't kind."

"I knew I was welcome in my home. Yes, you were kind." Her mind reeled with unbidden thoughts. Shouldn't a mother be more than kind? Shouldn't she love her child without conditions. She dug deep for a response. "You are my mother. Libby was a...a friend."

"She was a woman who gave you wild ideas and who encouraged you—"

"Libby encouraged nothing. Libby was a Christian woman who lived her faith. No, she didn't attend church often, but she knew Jesus was her Savior. She followed the golden rule. Please don't blame Libby for anything I've done. The sin was mine."

"And Justin's." Her tone punctuated his name. "He's the one who got you pregnant."

"It wasn't just him, Mother. It takes two. I loved Justin, and I was stupid."

"And you'll be stupid again if you let him have his way now that you know the consequences."

Susan couldn't respond to that. She'd learned her lesson the worst way a young girl could learn. Hairs pricked on her arms as she knelt beside her mother, praying God would guide her words. "Momma, I've come home to live for a while. I'm a woman. Thirty-three. I'm still naive, I suppose, and still a sinner as we all are, but I want to spend time with you and see if we can make up for the years we were apart." She waited until her mother's eyes met hers. "Please."

Margaret remained silent a long time until finally she gave a single nod.

"I'm tired, Mamma. It's been a long day. I'll see you in the morning."

Without waiting to hear if her mother would respond, Susan slipped the journal into her hand and strode toward the hallway.

"What's that in your hand?"

Susan froze. “A book.”

“What book?”

Her fingers pressed into the leather, wanting to halt the interrogation. “It was Libby’s. It’s Bible verses.”

“Bible verses? Libby?”

“Yes. I’m returning it tomorrow.” Susan turned away from her mother’s dark look,

strode from the room and down the hallway before her mother said any more.

Inside her bedroom, she dropped onto the mattress. Her mother’s accusing words rattled her. She had loved going to Libby’s. Not that her mother’s home wasn’t comfortable and safe. It had been. Her father worked hard tending the farm while her mother stayed home with the chores. Libby’s house was different. It encompassed history and prosperity. It captured her imagination, allowing her to be a young woman of wealth and charm.

Susan had been raised a farmer’s daughter. Clothes mended and worn, shoes resoled, and hands that knew how to scrub a sink or pass a mop. But at Rose Arbor, she learned about gracious living from a woman who was as hospitable as her tales were exciting. Though single and alone, Libby’s life seemed filled with passion.

Leaving the journal on the bed, Susan rose and slipped off her clothes. She hung her pants over a hanger and folded the top, then pulled out her gown. Her mind swelled with emotions, her mother’s accusations, Libby’s death, and seeing Justin.

She pulled back the blankets and propped the pillow against the headboard, her thoughts turning again to Justin. They’d stumbled into a relationship, each seeking love and a sense of worth. She never understood why Justin didn’t feel worthy. He seemed to be raised with so many advantages, but she guessed he needed love more than he wanted material things. She had been loved by her parents, but in a different way, a way that was more meat and potatoes, than roses and lockets.

The locket. Her hand shifted, and she let her fingers touch the pendant still around her neck. She wore it always, remembering her birthday and Libby’s generosity. Libby. Tears flooded her eyes and she shifted her hand across the sheet to grasp the journal. Her fingers brushed the soft leather as she opened the cover and gazed at a Bible verse written in Libby's hand.

My health may fail, and my spirit may grow weak,
but God remains the strength of my heart; he is mine forever.
Psalm 73:26
For you are my hiding place; you protect me from
trouble. You surround me with songs of victory.
Psalm 32:7

Beneath the two verses, Libby had written, "Lord, mistakes and all, I am yours." She stared at the words, touched by her poignant statement. Had Libby known she was ill? No date. No other explanation.

She turned the pages, reading similar verses, ones dealing with trust and faith, but nothing personal, nothing to give Susan a hint of why Libby had chosen the verses.

As she flicked through the pages, she noticed more than half the journal was empty. She turned back to the last entries, tensing as she read the verses.

God has purchased our freedom with his blood
and has forgiven all our sins. Colossians 1:14
He heals the brokenhearted, binding up their wounds.
Psalms 147:3

Susan studied the scripture—sin, brokenhearted, forgiveness. Her eyes shifted to the words beneath, and her jaw dropped. Libby's poignant prayer pierced Susan's heart, and tears swelled in her eyes. She turned the pages, longing to understand Libby's cry for forgiveness. She found nothing but empty paper as empty as she felt. What did it mean? Libby had been a believer, and she led a wonderful life. What had happened to cause her the anguish that emanated from the journal's pages?

After closing the cover, Susan wiped the moisture from her eyes. She set the journal on her nightstand and fell against the pillow. Libby? Her mind swarmed with questions, until good sense took over. Libby may have been ill. She may have sensed death was near. A Christian would ask the Lord for forgiveness. She'd asked her own forgiveness each day in her prayers.

She brushed away her concern, realizing how foolish it was. The emotion of learning of Libby's death had knocked her senseless, and then seeing Justin...

She ran her fingers over the pendant against her neck, her mind soaring back to the day Libby had invited her to the manor for a birthday surprise. While Libby slipped the locket around her neck, Justin stood by and scrutinized the event. That had been his way.

That night, Libby had invited them to sit on the gallery for birthday cake. Susan chose one of the cane rockers. She'd leaned back, sipping her lemonade and watching the moon wash its soft glow over the spring blossoms.

After Libby had retired inside, she and Justin remained on the porch talking about many things, but mainly the future. Justin would graduate from high school that year and attend college. Susan's spirit had darkened knowing she'd see little of him after that.

Saddened, she had risen and ambled down the gallery steps onto the lawn. As she moved across the damp grass, she heard Justin's footsteps on the stairs and his woodsy scent mingled with the rose's perfume.

"What's wrong?" he'd asked, stepping beside her.

"Things change, Justin. Time makes things different."

"What things?" He clasped her arm.

She faltered in the center of the rose garden and turned toward him. She tilted her head, her gaze captured in his dark, shadowed eyes. "Life. You'll be in college. I'll be here. We'll forget our talks. Maybe...we'll even forget each other. It feels lonely."

He cupped his hands over her shoulders and drew her against him. "No matter what happens, Susan, I'll never forget you." When she lifted her eyes to his, he lowered his mouth and pressed his lips against hers. The tender feeling enveloped her. It had shivered down her arms and wrapped around her heart. Her first kiss. A moment she could never forget.

So many wonderful things had been her firsts at the manor. Her first locket. Her first kiss. Her first taste of romance. Her first—she let the memory of her first child fade. Justin didn't need to know. Never.

Unbidden tears blurred her eyes, and she brushed them away. Crying over her sin had long passed. she had learned to be strong, to close her heart...she thought, but seeing Justin again awakened her.

Rising from the bed, her spirit drained. She may have made a grave error coming home and thinking time could heal wounds. Her parents had been so hurt by her pregnancy, and so had she. After being sent away, she had felt lost and alone even though she stayed with relatives. They pitied her. She saw it in their eyes. She didn't want pity. She wanted love and forgiveness. Apparently so had Libby.

Susan gazed at the picture of Jesus, knocking on the door. Right now, she was knocking on the door of her mother's heart. Would her mother answer?

♥

The next morning, Susan woke early. She'd spent a restless night, tossing, thinking, and praying that God would walk with her through the next weeks. She needed help and the only One who could give her strength was the Lord.

Not only her mother, but Justin had filled her nighttime thoughts. Her mother's bitterness. Justin's indecision. The more she thought about Justin, the more she wanted to stay clear of him, afraid she'd be caught up in his vulnerable charm, just as her mother feared. She couldn't continue as she'd been.

She rose and thought about a scripture she'd read recently from Lamentations that had clung to her mind. *The steadfast love of the Lord never ceases, his mercies never come to an end; they are new every morning; great is his faithfulness.*

The Lord's love never ceases. Love never ends. She knew that in her heart. She wandered to the window, and when she raised the shade, she saw the first visages of daylight hanging above the horizon. The sun rose every day. It never ceased just as God's love never ceased nor His mercies. *They are new every morning.*

The words gave her hope. If God's love changed the world, love could make a small difference in her life. Whatever might happen between her and her mother and her with Justin, she set her mind to demonstrate love and compassion. Her mother needed understanding and Susan's patience. Justin needed a friend. She could be those things with God's help.

With her decision strengthened, Susan headed to the kitchen. She would make orange muffins for her mother. Margaret loved them.

By the time Susan pulled the muffins from the oven, the sun had risen. She set the cakes on a cooling rack, then made a pot of coffee. If her mother were the same as she'd always been, she would sleep another hour. By then Susan would be back home.

She poured a cup of coffee, and being as quiet as possible, she opened the door, stepped outside, and crossed the dew-speckled lawn to settle again on the bench beneath Libby's rose arbor.

As she sipped the coffee, a pink dewy rosebud caught her eye. She pulled the flower closer and smelled the rich fragrance in the morning sun. The aroma swirled in her memory, recreating the days and evenings when she and Justin would sit on the bench, their romance blossoming as sweet and warm as the roses.

She remembered exploring his youthful whiskers, the feel of his hands against her back, his lips against hers. She'd lost herself in the emotion, and she gave without shame.

But disgrace followed on the heels of bliss. Pregnant, she was sent to Natchez to live with well-meaning relatives who reminded her daily of her sin. She went to school, trying to hide her bulging belly, her spirit sinking from the looks of teachers and students she didn't know and never could understand. The trauma, the scandal had overwhelmed her.

But she grasped her courage and went on with life. Her thoughts drifted to the day she graduated with high grades and received a scholarship. With a past she didn't want to remember, she delved into her college classes and drowned in knowledge. The past, history, the pride of the south filled her and helped to cover the sorrow she'd felt for what she'd done.

She'd never blamed Justin, but he was to blame as much as she. They both knew better. Yet she suffered alone.

"Good morning."

Susan bolted upward, startled to hear Justin's voice. "Sorry, I hope I didn't disturb you. I wandered over here without thinking."

"You don't have to apologize." He settled on the bench beside her. "I was awake before dawn."

"Do you remember playing blindman's bluff with Libby when we were really young?"

He nodded. "She always hid in here because we were afraid of getting pricked by the thorns."

"But that didn't stop you." Susan laughed remembering his determination.

He raised his hand and stared at his palm. "I probably have scars to prove it." He reached over and plucked a rose from the stem, using his fingernails like pincers. "I'm in your debt, Susan. You were more help than you will ever know last night."

His expression rattled her, and she grasped her mug and held it in her hand, fastening her attention to the swirl of milky brown within the rim. "Please don't feel in my debt, Justin. We're. . .old friends."

"Very old," A hint of irony settled in his voice. "That's how I feel today."

She wanted to remind him that they weren't as old as Libby or their mothers, but the humor seemed pointless. "Old is a matter of the heart."

His head tipped upward, and he studied her without response.

"Look at Libby. She found something new around every corner." Susan paused, thinking of the journal, then looked at Justin's stressed face, the lines that furrowed his forehead and his mouth. "You're too young to feel old. Life is what you make it...and so is age. I'm trying to learn that, too."

"You're like springtime, Susan. Bright. Sunny. Awakening to a new day." He closed his eyes. "Some of us don't greet the morning with the same excitement." His lips tightened like a bank vault. "Libby's death has been a blow, and I'm not handling things well."

"Each day will get better until life seems normal again." Her own life loomed in her mind. Losing the baby had taken time to heal. Even her fear of God's punishment had eased.

"That's the difference between us, Susan."

His voice jerked her from her reverie.

"You're optimistic, Susan. I've spent much of my life hanging on to the negative, because it's more realistic. Then when something positive happens, it's a pleasant surprise."

His comment jarred her.

"I've startled you."

"Apparently, we both had lives that lacked something, and Libby came to our rescue, but I'm here to make things better. I'm looking at it like a hope-filled venture. I sense you're willing to just settle for whatever, and that disappoints me." She grasped her coffee mug and rose. "I'll let you be with your misery, Justin."

Before she took a step, he rose and placed his hands on her shoulders, his face so close she could feel the heat of his breath. Her gaze riveted to his mouth, and when his lips seemed to draw near, her heart stopped.

"You're right, Susan. I can't argue with you. I need to think and get a grip."

"And I need to get home." She pulled away and stepped from beneath the arbor.

Justin lifted the rose from the bench and handed it to her. "Take this with you. When you look at it, know that I'm trying to change. I realize it's better to smile at life than grumble about it. It's just difficult to change."

Susan grasped the rose, unable to pull her gaze from his eyes.

He slid his hands into his trouser pockets. "I hope it doesn't take too long." He looked away and stepped past her.

"I hope so, too." Her whispered response struck his back as he headed toward the manor.

She stood for a moment, then lifted the rose and pressed it to her cheek as her mother's accusing words filled her mind. She'd be stupid to fall for him again.

She moved across the lawn, trying to sort her thoughts. As she headed home, her gaze drifted to the oak trees heavy with Spanish moss. Its spidery fingers clung to the leaves just as Justin had fused to her heart.

Chapter Three

Justin sat in front of the attorney's desk, his hands gripped in his lap. He searched the man's face, longing to see a flicker of hope appear as he looked over the will again.

"I really can't help you, Mr. Robard," he said, studying him over his bifocals.

Justin felt the jolt of his response. "You mean no loopholes. Nothing?"

The lawyer lowered the document to his desk. "I wrote the will the way your aunt requested. You can talk with another attorney, but you'll find no loopholes. She wanted the house to stay in the family. I should say it her way. She wanted you to have Rose Arbor."

The emphasis stung Justin. Libby wanted him to have the plantation house. The situation curled in his stomach like milk on a hot summer day.

"But, I explained my dilemma. I own a business in Baton Rouge. How can I..." The attorney's stoic expression drowned any fleeting hope he'd had. His plea meant nothing to the lawyer.

Justin bowed his head, realizing he wasn't fighting this man. The lawyer had only done what Libby had asked, and it was too late to talk it over with her.

"You have an option," the man said, breaking into Justin's thoughts.

The words jerked his head upward. "Option?"

"Give the property to the historical society, and you'll have yourself a tax break."

Tax break? He didn't want a tax break. If he couldn't have Libby, he wanted the plantation. "That's not an option the way I see it." He searched the lawyer's eyes.

The man shrugged and folded his hands over the will. "Then you'll have to work out the kinks. Libby's property belongs to you."

Grasping the leather arms, Justin scooted the chair away from the desk, rose and extended his hand to the lawyer. "Thank you, Sir, for your time."

"You're welcome. I'm sorry I don't have better news. I followed Libby's wishes."

"I know." Justin shoved his hands into his pockets as he turned toward the door. "I'll think of something."

Justin didn't wait to hear if the attorney made a comment. He hurried through the waiting room and out into the spring air. Inside his car, he turned on the air conditioner and sat a moment before grasping the steering wheel.

Thinking of Susan's determination to make life better, he pulled away from the lawyer's office and headed toward his mother's. He hadn't talked with her since the funeral, and he hoped to ease the tension between them. His life seemed on the same plane with Susan's. She'd mentioned resolving issues with her mother. Apparently, children spent part of their lives repairing damaged relationships with their parents. He'd been blessed with his aunt's undaunted love.

Love. The word squeezed against his heart. He'd felt unquestionable love twice in his life—Libby and the girl Susan. Libby's was a given. She adored him, and he loved her back with interest. But Susan? She slipped into his life like a sunbeam, silently brightening his life, adding dimension to his world, filling in the dark places with happiness.

He'd taken advantage of Susan then. He hadn't meant it to happen, and for a long time, he'd dismissed it with male hormones and zeal for experience, but later he realized the scope of what he'd done. They'd kissed and kissed again. They'd held hands in the moonlight beneath the rose arbor covered by darkness and the fragrance of roses. Their kisses deepened, and she yielded with abandon. He lost himself in the wonder of her giving, a kind of giving he'd never experienced.

Then Susan had vanished. He believed his aunt knew where she was, but she vowed she didn't know. Susan had moved away to live with relatives was all he'd heard. Susan's parents had never liked Justin, and when he asked them about her, he received no response. He felt lost and wounded with her disappearance.

To compensate, he decided to sow—what his father called—wild oats. No one touched his life like Susan, Susan with her faith in God and her faith in joy despite life's downfalls.

And now she'd touched him again, and he'd been so thoughtless. She'd given him her time and interest. Yesterday he'd acted terribly unkind during their conversation, and he couldn't blame her for walking away.

The sunlight glinted off his car hood, and he squinted. His hands tensed as he turned down the avenue toward his mother's home, and he pushed his agitation inside, letting his mind fill with Susan. Her fair skin, eyes as blue as the sky framed by dark lashes, a peeked chin and full lips that he still longed to kiss. Was that why he felt so troubled when he was near her?

Women had been the least of his worries. He'd let romance slide from his life after college. He'd dismissed marriage as easily as setting out the week's trash. Instead, he kept himself busy with his business and tending to his mother's needs and finances. He let those things fill his time.

Fill his time. That's what his life had become. A time filler. Shouldn't it be more than that? Susan said she'd come home to make things better, to face life anew. "Life is what you make it," she'd said. Nothing profound, but filled with truth.

Justin refocused as he pulled into the driveway of Robard Hall, his mother's expansive home. Houses like hers dotted the landscape on the west side of Devereaux. Even in his youth, the house seemed cold and empty while his father worked long hours and his mother Caroline ran the home and servants with a firm hand.

Justin slid from his car, prepared for the visit. His feet crunched on the loose gravel, and when he reached the brick walkway, he stood a moment and drew in a lengthy breath, then rang the bell.

The door opened. Clovis' face broke into a grin. "Mista Justin, *bon jour*. It's been too long. Come inside." He waved Justin through the door, then closed it, shutting out the sun. Only an arc of light fell to the floor from the transom window above the door.

"*Très bien*, Clovis. It's good to see you." He motioned toward the parlor. "Is my mother at home?"

"She be havin' tea in the garden." He led Justin to the French doors leading to the garden patio and flung it open. "Mista Justin come to visit, Ma'am."

Justin stepped outside, watching his mother's face turn from surprise to curious. "How are you, Mother?" He strode across the sun-sprinkled tiles to the umbrella table.

"Justin." She lowered her teacup, then raised her head. "I wasn't expecting you."

"I didn't call. This was a spur of the moment visit. I haven't spoken with you since—"

"The funeral. I know." She lifted her hand and brushed imaginary wrinkles from her black dress, the color he assumed was to show her mourning for Libby, but in truth, he knew his mother had a dislike for her younger sister. They had never seemed close, and he had always wondered why.

"May I sit?"

"Certainly." She motioned toward a chair.

As he pulled the chair from beneath the table, he heard a chuckle from the doorway. He looked behind him and saw Clovis' wife, Rèmi, heading toward him with a tray.

"So good to see you, Mista Justin," she said, lowering the tray so she could hand him a teacup and a plate of sweet biscuits and jam, his favorite. She gave a slight nod.

He responded with a wink as she backed away with another chuckle.

Justin poured the tea and refreshed his mother's cup while using the pause to gain control. His mother's greeting had sounded stressed, and he knew the purpose for his visit would add to the tension.

Justin sipped from the cup, then managed to open the conversation. "You've made no comment about Aunt Libby's decision to leave Rose Arbor to me." The umbrella's shadow fell across her face, but a faint flinch didn't escape him.

She lifted her chin. "What do you want me to say?"

He took a moment to sort his thoughts. "I don't know. I hoped that you weren't upset, I suppose."

"Libby always made her own decisions, Justin. I'm not surprised she left you the property. It's appropriate."

Appropriate? Perhaps. She always doted on him, but he doubted his mother really accepted the decision. "I feared you might be disappointed."

"I don't want the plantation. I have Robard Hall. That's enough for me. You know Robard Hall will be yours one day, too."

Her comment whacked him in the chest. He'd never given thought that one day he would own his parent's residence even though he was their only child. A response stuck in his throat.

His mother's gaze pinned him.

"Thank you, Mother. I'm assuming you'll live many more years."

"Assumptions aren't reality."

"I know, but you're healthy and—" The expression on her face caused his chest to tighten. "Is something wrong?" He studied her face, looking for a glimmer of truth. "Are you ill?"

"I'm fine."

"Please don't evade my question, Mother."

"I've had a few little problems. Nothing serious."

"You should let me know when you're ill." He wanted to reach out to her, but his mother would never accept physical contact. "What kind of problems?" His mother's little problems never were small. "What are your symptoms?"

"It's nothing. A little disorientation. Numbness in my arm, but it passes. Don't make something out of it that it isn't."

"All right," he said, biting his tongue. When she closed a subject, it was closed. He'd ask Rèmi later. He'd learned more about his family from her than anyone.

"Will you be moving into Rose Arbor?" She'd changed the subject as he suspected she would.

"I don't know what I'll do. The drive from Baton Rouge to Devereaux would be difficult, yet—"

"Your dear Aunt Libby gave you another option." A wry look flickered on her lips. "The historical society."

He cringed. "That's a choice, but not one I want to make."

"Then she's put you in a bad position, hasn't she? Libby often did that to people."

He searched her face, but like most things, she would never explain the innuendo. He let the discussion slide and talked about the weather.

♥

Susan stood inside the office building, reading the flyers posted on the bulletin boards. She pulled a brochure from the display stand nearby and scanned the plantation photos on the front. Rose Arbor was lovelier than the glossy images she viewed in pamphlet. *Spring Plantation Tours* the heading announced. She gazed at the schedule of events during the week-long May event. The photographs inside beckoned tourists with women dressed in elegant hoop-skirted gowns and amazing bonnets or wide-brimmed hats. She'd had to wear one of these dresses for an event in Baton Rouge, and she would never forget the corset. It had been torture.

"Miss Boyd."

She lifted her head. "Yes." She folded the brochure and tucked it into her handbag.

"I'm sorry. Mr. Burford, can't see you today." Her lips opened as if she had more to say.

Susan waited to hear the "but."

"But, we do have a full-staff at this time." She offered a meager smile. "Mr. Burford did ask me to say he's impressed with your experience and training, and he said he'll be happy to hold onto your résumé." The woman's smile brightened.

"Thank you," Susan said, as she backed away, knowing she should be pleased that the man was impressed, but the kudos didn't help her find a job.

"If anything changes, we'll be in touch."

Susan nodded and turned toward the door, reining in her disappointment. She'd already known finding work in Devereaux would be near to impossible. Still she'd hoped.

Outside, a sweet, yeasty scent drifted on the air from down the street. She turned in that direction, and when she passed the bakery, she looked into the window, fighting her temptation to buy a glazed donut or a pecan pastry, but she forced herself to pass. Without work, putting on weight would be too easy. She needed to be active, to be busy. She needed a constructive way to spend her time instead of wading in the nostalgia of Rose Arbor.

With the thought of Rose Arbor, Justin's image rose in her mind. Too good-looking, she'd decided, too intriguing, and he'd never change. He'd spend his life leaning from one emotion to another, from a smile to a frown without a moment's notice.

Why did she worry about his problem? Why did she care? The words filled her mind, but the reason filled her heart. Justin had changed her life. He'd made an indention that could never be filled by anyone else, just as she knew no one could ever replace Libby. And now even Libby had left her curious. The Bible verses and comments in her journal bounced into her thoughts since she'd read Libby's troubled entries.

Susan closed her eyes. She had problems of her own. Not finding a job meant she'd have to leave Devereaux without resolving the issues with her mother and without— Without what? Without settling things with Justin. The thought seemed stupid. She couldn't resolve things with Justin unless she told him, and she couldn't tell him. The past would become too real again, too sad, too disappointing.

Wanting to lift her spirit, Susan tried to put a bounce in her step as she strode past the shops, but she failed. She only scuffed along the sidewalk lugging her disappointment like a child dragging a deflated balloon home on a string.

She wanted to do something purposeful and positive. Her mother's negativity weighed on her at home, and Justin's moody manner stung her when she was there. She should let his comments roll of her back, let him be miserable if he chose misery, but she couldn't stop herself from wanting to make a difference in his life, wanting to put a smile on his face, a smile that stayed there without fading away too soon. Justin deserved more out of life, even if he didn't know it.

She stopped at a newspaper box and slipped out the *Devereaux Daily*. She hadn't noticed a paper in her mother's home since she'd arrived. The television seemed to serve as her mother's connection with the outside world.

With the newspaper under her arm, she pushed open the door of a coffee shop and strode inside. A seat-yourself sign stood at the entrance, and she spotted an empty booth along the front window.

She ordered a lemonade and opened the newspaper to the Help Wanted ads. Scanning the column, she passed over waitress jobs, clerk positions, childcare workers, secretarial situations while her discouragement grew.

Maybe finding a job shouldn't be her priority. She and her mother had made little progress. At night as she tried to sleep, her frustration found an answer. How could she make amends with her mother when she refused to stay away from Rose Arbor? If she avoided the manor, she might take a giant step forward with her mother.

But that seemed impossible. It was part of her past and now her present. And her future? She couldn't see beyond today. If she could help Justin find a solution to his dilemma, at least she would have done a good deed. What would solve his problem? How could he keep the plantation and still live in Baton Rouge?

The question hung on the air.

She turned to gaze out the window, then let her focus shift upward to the sky. If only her life could be as clear as the cloudless blue expanse that spread before her. She released a sigh while her mind toppled back into its topsy-turvy struggle. Make amends with her mother. Be Justin's friend. Find a job. Move away again.

He has made everything beautiful in its time. The verse made her smile. *Lord, I'm a mess. Smooth me into something beautiful.*

♥

Justin left the grocery store and headed home, his thoughts filled with the visit with his mother. She'd left him bewildered as she so often did. He'd noticed her sardonic look and her cryptic comments about her health and his inheritance.

She always left him muddled, but today he felt more concerned. When he asked Rèmi before he left the house, she'd said his mother had experienced a couple of mini-strokes. Mini or maxi, a stroke of any kind sounded like bad news. He would have to keep a careful watch on her.

When he turned onto Melrose Avenue, his pulse quickened. Rose Arbor stood before him bathed in sunlight and shadows of the stately live oaks. Its white wide clapboards, black shutters and white Federal columns rose along the expansive front gallery welcoming guests as warmly as Libby herself.

Pressure increased behind his eyes, and he closed them to squeeze away the emotion that caught in his throat. Libby would be the first to tell him to make his decision and get on with life. . .and he would.

As he parked beside a blossoming magnolia and opened the door, he drew in the lemony sweet fragrance as he gathered the grocery bags. He climbed the sidesteps to the gallery, then unlocked the entry door to the kitchen and propped his sacks on the counter.

He peered at his watch and realized he hadn't eaten since breakfast except for Rèmi's biscuits and jam. He stored the groceries, then marinated a steak to grill for dinner. With a glass of lemonade in his hand, he stepped onto the gallery and looked ahead at the rose arbor, remembering his conversation with Susan the night before. He wished he'd handled things differently.

A movement caught his attention, and veering from the arbor, he headed toward the large oak, his gaze drawn to the Boyd house and to Susan's car pulling into the yard. When she climbed out, his chest tightened, and he took a step forward, driven by the desire to apologize and to talk about his frustrations with the attorney.

She looked up and noticed him, but she stood still a moment before lifting her hand in a faint wave and continuing on.

"Susan," he called, taking quicker steps toward her.

When she faced him, he was taken aback by her appearance. Standing in the sunlight, her slender frame looked delicate, though hidden beneath baggy pants and an oversized top. With her large eyes and fair complexion, she seemed beautiful, glowing with an inner radiance that rattled him.

"Did you need me?" she asked as she strode closer, yet still keeping her distance.

Did he need her? His stomach tightened. "I'd like to talk with you if you have a moment."

She drew back. "Talk? About what?"

"I saw the attorney today."

Her expression changed, and concern replaced her aloofness. "Bad news?" Her step quickened as she approached.

He nodded. "I'm still in a muddle."

"I'm sorry Justin. I wish I could help."

She appeared to be anxious to leave, and he knew last night was still on her mind. He wanted to keep her there so they could talk, maybe smooth things out, and then the steak marinating in the refrigerator fell into his mind. "Have you eaten? I picked up a couple of steaks, and—"

"Mother's cooking for us. I'm making dessert."

He felt like a kid missing the ice cream truck. "Too bad. I grill a mean steak."

"Sorry, but thanks for the invitation."

He nodded, hoping he'd covered his disappointment.

She stood a moment, her eyes squinting from the sunlight flickering through the trees.

Justin stepped back, feeling awkward and sensing she had nothing more to say, but her expression changed.

Her jaw relaxed. "How about dessert?"

He rocked on his heels. "Dessert?"

Susan's taunt expression faded. "You'll like it."

"Sure. I'd love dessert."

With a swift nod, she turned and headed home while he watched her, irritated with unwanted feelings she aroused in him.

After Susan vanished, he lit the grill, returned to the house and brought out the steak. He threw it on the grate, then shoved his hands into his pockets and wandered toward the back of the yard.

On each side of him, azaleas bloomed along the wings of the house, stretching away from the main rooms of the manor. At the end of the wings, Libby's flower beds struggled to blossom. He bent to pluck an invading weed. Dying daffodils stood in the lowering sunlight. Beside them were irises and foxglove ready to bloom. And as always, the roses.

Beyond the arbor, the scent of honeysuckle drifted on the air, bringing back images of his childhood when he played beside Libby as she worked in the garden. His gaze swept the colorful beds, brightening his hope.

The steak's aroma drifted past him, and Justin returned to the grill, turning the meat and waiting until it was medium rare. He made a salad to go with it and when he'd finished eating, he wandered outside again to the gallery and waited for Susan, his focus drifting periodically to the oak tree before returning to the quiet of the setting sun.

He looked up, surprised he hadn't noticed her arrival until she spoke. "You look pensive."

She stood on the grass, carrying the book she'd borrowed along with a container in one hand and a glass of what appeared to be lemonade in the other.

"What's in the dish," he asked, not wanting to talk about her observation.

"The surprise. Now or later?"

"Let's talk first," he said.

"I'll put this in the fridge."

She vanished inside and returned in a moment, settling on a cane chair beside him.

His concerns rattled in his head, multiplied by his confusion over Susan. Why had she come back at a time he felt most vulnerable. She seemed like a balm to him, a familiar remedy to heal his wounds.

"You're quiet, Justin," she sipped the lemonade and watched him.

"Just thinking." He couldn't tell her she was also on his mind.

"About Rose Arbor again."

"Rose Arbor and my mother."

"Your mother? What's wrong?"

His stomach knotted as he relayed what Rèmi had said about his mother's health. "Now I have to add that to my worries."

"I'm sorry, Justin. Life seems to be made up of worrying about one thing or another."

In his case, one thing and another. "I'm so up in the air with everything."

"This is a lovely home, Justin. I know turning it over to the historical society would be difficult." She paused as if in thought. "Things may change for you one day. You might want to move back to Devereaux. Could you rent the manor until then?"

He couldn't control his deep sigh. "I double checked on that with the lawyer today. I wanted to be positive, but the stipulation is definitely that I live in the house." He looked away, deep in thought.

She remained quiet and thoughtful beside him. The setting sun played on her dark hair, and his longing grew, remembering so many things.

"If you had a real choice, Justin, how would you want things to be?"

Her question hit his stomach like a rock, but the answer came without reservation. "I don't want to lose Rose Arbor. I have too many mem...I don't think Libby really wanted that, but if I can't live here, what's my option?"

An idea flew into his thoughts. A foolish idea but worth a shot. "Unless the renter was a boarder who could keep an eye on things. Someone I knew. Someone who'd let me keep a room here, so I'd meet the will's terms. This could be my permanent residence, and I could stay as often as I could arrange it." He rocked forward in his chair and searched Susan's face to see if she understood.

She gave him an uneasy look. "That's a wonderful idea. Do you have someone in mind?"

His hopes sank with her lack of awareness. "What about you, Susan?"

"Me?" A frown cut across her face.

"I-I thought you might like to live near your mother, and it seemed at Rose Arbor you'd be close yet independent." Her expression wrought defeat in his voice.

"I'm sorry, but I haven't found a position yet." She tucked her hair behind her ear. "I had a disappointing job interview today. I took a chance, but it didn't work. I need to see what's available locally before I make any commitments for living quarters. I may have to move after all."

Move? The word trudged across his chest. "Don't apologize. The idea was farfetched at best." He didn't know what else to say. How could he beg her to stay? For what purpose? What hope could he—

"You must know someone." She reached across and touched his arm, sending a sensation waltzing to his chest. "The idea's perfect. Think, Justin."

His concentration failed while his thoughts shifted to her slender fingers resting against his arm. "I can't think of a soul." He forced his mind back to the topic.

"That's the perfect solution."

Her optimism sank in his confused mind. "Susan, I'm—"

"Good." She clapped her hands and smiled. "You're ready for dessert. I thought so."

She'd plowed his comment beneath her perfect solution, and though his appetite had dwindled, the dessert had roused his curiosity. He dragged his spirit upward. "What's the surprise?"

"Your favorite." She rose and headed toward the kitchen.

His favorite? He heard the refrigerator door open and close, followed by the clink of china. He had no idea what his favorite might be. He'd rarely thought of anything as his favorite, so how would she know what he liked and didn't like?

His thoughts slipped into the familiar brooding he'd felt for so many years. His career had taught him to cover them with a plastic smile, but the darkness only sank to the recesses of his mind.

Another sound from the kitchen drew him back. If anyone could find a positive in his life, his Aunt Libby could. And Susan. He waited, and in a moment, she came through the doorway carrying two crystal bowls.

"I hope the sauce is warm enough. I put it in the microwave for a minute."

When she slid the dish into his hand, his chest tightened. He fought the emotion rising to his throat and making it difficult to speak. "Aunt Libby's bread pudding."

"With white chocolate sauce," she said, her voice ringing. "I remember how much you loved it." She handed him a spoon. "I'm sure it's not as delicious as Libby's but...I tried."

While she watched, he dipped the spoon into the rich pudding and raised it to his lips. Her mouth responded in unison with his as he slid the dessert between his teeth. The delectable sweetness rolled on his tongue, and he held it there, remembering how many years he'd enjoyed the special dessert. Susan's surprise surpassed his memory. "Aunt Libby would be proud."

"Do you think so?"

"Try it yourself." He motioned for her to taste it.

Susan dipped her spoon into the dessert and slid it between her lips.

Triumph spread across her face, and his belly tightened, leaving an ache that caught him by surprise. He pulled his gaze away as they finished the dessert in silence.

When he looked up, Susan rose.

"I'll leave the rest for you to have tomorrow." She strode to his side and collected the bowls.

He sat, unable to rise. His legs felt weak as the scene washed over him. Susan and he together like old times, except for the empty chair that would have been Libby's.

"You're thinking again," Susan said.

He jolted to attention. "Thinking of Libby."

Susan stepped past him and paused. "I know. I've been thinking of her all evening."

He forced himself to rise and took the bowls from her hand, not wanting her to know that it wasn't only Libby filling his thoughts. "I'll take care of these."

"If you're sure."

He nodded.

"Good night, Justin." She squeezed his arm. "I'll pray that God helps you find the solution."

"Thanks," he said, being struck again by her strong faith.

She gave a wave as she turned and strode along the gallery, bounced down the steps and vanished behind the house.

Staring into the shadows where she'd disappeared, he stood still, smothered by emptiness.

A moment later her voice ebbed from the distance. "We'll think of something, Justin. You can count on me."

You can count on me. Hadn't he always counted on her? Susan giving. Justin taking. It always seemed to come down to that.

He turned away and strode inside, rinsing the dishes in the sink, then reached to shut off the light. As he did, his gaze lowered to the book Susan had set on the counter near the door. Libby's book. Curious, he lifted it and opened the cover. His heart clenched. A journal of some kind. He flipped through the pages, most empty.

He closed the cover, paused, and opened it again and gazed at Libby's neat script. Bible verses and an occasional comment. He had never known her to be so religious, but he knew she had faith. Fingering the pages, he opened to her last entry. He scanned the verses, sensing some kind of struggle. What had bothered Libby?

His stomach tightened, as he read her final words. He read them again, bewildered. "Lord, forgive me for my sins and for my silence all these years." Silence? Silence all these years? His pulse throbbed in his temples. What did she mean?

Chapter 4

Trying to fall asleep, Susan had tangled in her bedclothes thinking about Justin. She'd watched his jaw tighten with tension. His thoughtful eyes clouded like a coming storm. Then her mind shifted to Justin's proposition for the rental. He'd caught her by surprise. The thought of living at Rose Arbor thrilled her, but circumstances made it unwise.

She'd awakened in the night and lay there while sleep evaded her. She wanted to help Justin, but all ideas that settled in her thoughts were too difficult. They involved her help, and she couldn't make that kind of commitment to him. It would be too dangerous for her.

Finally, she climbed out of bed and sat on the edge of the mattress, pondering her day. She had so much she should do. First, she needed to find employment. She knew with persistence she'd find the perfect job.

After her career was back in gear, she wanted a place of her own. Justin's offer came to mind—perfect yet impossible. By the time she could rent Rose Arbor, Justin's dilemma would be settled.

While dressing, she decided to head into town and pick up a newspaper. Finding a job prospect would keep her busy, and if she stayed away from Rose Arbor, she could be free of Justin. Free of Justin? Seventeen years of separation hadn't accomplished it.

She left her room and found her mother in the kitchen. "Good morning." She didn't miss her mother's accusing look. "You went to bed early last night."

"I waited up for you until ten."

Fire smoldered in her mother's eyes, and her unspoken bitterness knifed Susan as it always did. "I'm sorry. I didn't realize you were waiting up."

"You were with him again."

Susan swallowed the untruth she wanted to utter. "Yes."

Margaret slammed a cabinet door. "At least you didn't lie to me."

"I don't lie, mother."

"Then I did one thing right in raisin' you."

"You did more than that." Susan crossed to the coffee pot, then decided better of it. "I'm going into town. Do you need anything?"

"You haven't had breakfast." Margaret said, really looking at her for the first time.

"I'm not hungry." Susan walked to the kitchen chair where she'd dropped her handbag the night before. "Can I get you anything in town?"

Her mother eyed her for a moment, then sighed. "I have a prescription waiting at Conner's Pharmacy if you don't mind pickin' it up."

"I'd be happy to." Susan wished with all her heart she could find a way to heal the wounds between her and her mother. The tension had begun so many years before.

Susan said goodbye and drove the mile to town. When she reached the pharmacy, she picked up a copy of *The Chronicle*, then walked to the drug counter at the back of the store.

"A prescription for Margaret Boyd," Susan said.

The pharmacist returned and placed the pill bottle in a small white bag. She paid for the medication and newspaper, then returned to the sidewalk. Curious, she opened the sack and eyed the medication. A rush of concern shot through her.

A heart medication. Her mother had never mentioned she had a heart problem, and that was just like her. Susan tossed the bottle back into the bag. Her mother's favorite role was to be a silent martyr. Susan felt she couldn't win. She couldn't even tie.

Whose fault was this tension anyway? She pondered its beginning. Jealousy, she decided, because of Libby. But it had been more than jealousy. Susan had caused the ultimate schism by breaking her parent's' hearts. But time had passed, and wouldn't it seem reasonable to have it end?

She walked half a block and stopped at the bakery to buy a donut and coffee, then crossed the street to a shaded bench outside a fruit market. The scent of fresh fruit and potted flowers drifted on the air from the nursery nearby, and seeing the colorful display brightened her spirit.

The sugar donut vanished, and while she sipped her coffee, Susan used her free hand to flip open the newspaper. She turned the pages to the want ads, but her eyes didn't register on the employment section. Instead her mind flew back to the previous evening and Justin's predicament. She'd had a thought that had lingered in her mind all night, but she kept pushing it aside. Yet the idea seemed so natural. Owners of old plantation houses had turned them into tourist attractions or a bed and breakfast where the owner could still live in the house. Why not Rose Arbor?

Why not? Because Justin didn't have the time or inclination to handle such an endeavor. Her pulse skipped with anticipation, and she knew that's why she had been pushing away the idea. She definitely had time and knowledge after working with historical homes. Before her full-time employment at the museum, she'd been involved in historical research in Baton Rouge. Though she had the experience to help Justin, getting involved in the project would mean spending time—

"Gracious goodness. Could it be?"

Hearing the voice, Susan's hand jerked, slopping coffee from her paper cup. She brushed the spill from her pants and looked up at the stranger.

"Susan Boyd? Is that you?"

A frown tugged at Susan's face as she eyed the stranger who seemed to know her. "Yes, I'm Susan Boyd."

As Susan stood, the woman opened her arms. "Well, bless my heart." She embraced Susan with a powerful hug, then leaned back and faced her nose to nose. "It's me. Clarissa. Clarissa Pradat. I'm Clarissa Melacon now."

"Clarissa!" Susan looked at her old high school friend who'd actually grown more attractive with age. Her crooked teeth were now straight, her thick glasses were gone, and her mousy hair shone with reddish tints in an attractive style. "Clarissa, you look wonderful."

"Why, suga' you look awesome yourself. Time has been good to us both." She drew back but kept one arm wrapped around Susan's shoulder. "How long has it been?" She tapped a slender finger against her pursed lips. "You vanished into nowhere when we were high school juniors, if I recall correctly."

Susan felt her heart kick and pick up pace. "Yes, about then. I moved away." As she said the words, her mind grappled for the old story that her parents had concocted to cover her absence.

"But I saw your momma in town. She said you'd gone to live with an aunt in..."

"Natchez." Susan hesitated, trying to catch her breath. The story had to be only slightly altered from the truth. "Momma thought I should have new experiences. She didn't want me growing up stuck in this little town all my life. I graduated from high school in Natchez and then went on to college."

"Really. How exciting. And I suppose you're married."

Noticing the large diamond on Clarissa's finger triggered Susan's discomfort. "No. Still single."

"My, that's hard to believe. I remember you had such a thing for that young man. What was his name?"

"Justin Robard." His name caught in Susan's throat.

"That's it. You made him sound so mysterious. I just envied you." She paused a moment, then her eyes widened. "I figured when you vanished, you'd run off and eloped with him."

Grease from her donut rose to Susan's throat, and she tried to swallow the bitterness, fearing somehow Clarissa knew the truth of why she'd left Devereaux. "Nothing that exciting."

"That's too bad. You seemed so in love?" She squeezed Susan's shoulder.

"I was only a girl, Clarissa." But she had been in love.

Clarissa raised her hand and brushed a stray hair from her cheek. "How long will you be in town?"

"A while. I'm staying with my mother." Susan's mind spun, and she longed to escape.

"Then we have to get together one day." She dug in her handbag and pulled out a card. "I'm the motha' of two little girls. They are so precious."

"I'm sure they are, and I'll try to give you a call one day."

"Please do, and if not, then I'll call you. I'm sure your momma's in the book."

"She is," Susan said, anxious to get away.

Clarissa handed her the card, said goodbye and moved off while Susan crumpled onto the bench. Her mother, Justin, and now inquisitive Clarissa. Susan rubbed her temples, questioning her wisdom coming back home.

♥

"Why didn't you tell me you had a heart problem?"

Her mother looked at her with blank eyes. "I didn't think it made a difference."

Susan shook her head as she lowered her gaze. "Mother, please. It does make a difference. Haven't I been punished enough?"

"Ask the Lord, Susan."

Tears stung Susan's eyes, but she held them back. "I have, Mother, many times. God says we only need ask. I've asked for forgiveness, and the Bible says if I repent, I am forgiven."

"How do I know you've repented?" She gestured toward Rose Arbor. "I don't see it in your behavior."

"It's not what you see. It's what God sees. I answer to the Lord, and He knows the truth."

Her mother shrugged, "It's on your shoulders not mine." She opened the pharmacy bag, drew out the medication and tapped the container. "It's nothing anyways. I have angina. It won't kill me."

Susan longed to embrace her mother, but years had passed since they'd shown any affection. Instead, she rested her palm on her mother's arm. "I'm sorry that you're having problems. I didn't know."

"Like I said, it won't kill me."

Defeated, Susan let her hands drop to her sides. "I'll be in my room for a while," She hugged the newspaper against her side while feeling a driving need to get away.

Her mother didn't respond, and Susan headed up the stairs, discouraged. Inside her room, she plopped on her bed and slipped off her shoes. She plumped her pillow and rested her head against it, pondering what had just happened again between her and her mother. Could this be

God's way to tell her to leave Devereaux?

The question simmered until a new insight struck her. Why did she always assume God motivated everything in her life. Satan also had his way in the world, and if she were going to give up with every small defeat, she'd get nowhere. If she gave in to Satan's wiles, the evilness could win out over God's love.

She lowered her head. "Lord, give me patience. Tell me what I need to do to make amends." As the amen fell into her thoughts, she rolled over and opened the newspaper to the want ads. Susan studied the job opportunities, but everything seemed so similar to the position she'd left. She longed to work with people and not just behind the scenes. She folded the paper and tossed it on the nightstand.

The bed and breakfast idea returned to her thoughts. That could work for Justin. How much would it entail? How much would it cost, and did Justin have enough ready cash? And if Justin wanted to open the house for tourists, he'd need help.

Feeling the strong pull of interest, Susan closed her eyes, but moments later, they snapped open. Her friend Georgia was employed in Natchez, Mississippi, working with the organizations that planned the Spring and Fall Pilgrimage Tours of the antebellum homes each year. Georgia would have the answer.

Slipping her feet over the edge of the bed, she used her elbow to raise herself. Her handbag lay across the room, and she stretched to reach it. She dug into her purse and pulled out her cell phone. She hit menu, selected Georgia's phone number and pushed the button.

Georgia sounded out of breath when she said hello.

"Have I called at a bad time?"

"Susan." Her voice lifted with pleasure. "I'm so glad to hear from you. I just finished a meeting, and I'm walking back to my office. How are you?"

"Fine."

Georgia hesitated before responding. "I know you too well, Susan. Things aren't fine."

"You know my problem. Getting along with my mother is like trying to herd cats."

Georgia's chuckle echoed over the line.

"But I'm fine, really. I called because I have some questions for you." She explained Justin's situation and her idea. "Do you think it would cost a fortune? He owns another business, so I don't know how much he has to invest."

"It depends on the condition of the manor, the furnishings already on hand, and the amount of staff he'll need to run the business. If he pursues it, he'll need someone to oversee the project."

A ragged sigh left her. "I don't know what he'll want to do, but I thought it could be a solution."

"If I can find some time, Susan, I'll come down to Devereaux and take a look at the estate. You know I've helped restore so many antebellum homes, but then, you have, too."

"Not recently and not with your expertise, and this is different. I have an attachment to Rose Arbor. I don't know if I can see it with clear eyes, and I'm afraid if I suggest the idea, he'll ask me to help him or I'll volunteer. I know that's not wise." Susan winced, wishing she'd not been so blatant.

"Not wise? Why?"

Susan had never shared her past with Georgia, and she didn't plan to now. "I need to get on with my life. I want a permanent position that'll be long term."

"I understand that, but it might be a great interim job. You know enough about renovating antebellum homes. If he considers your plan and you need another opinion, let me know. I'll be there and look over the idea with you."

"Thanks," Susan said, wishing she could let the whole thing slide from her mind. She disconnected and sat on the edge of her bed, considering Georgia's offer. After a few minutes, she rose, knowing she couldn't spend hours alone in her room without upsetting her mother worse. She dropped her cell phone back into her purse and went into the kitchen.

The room was empty, so she grabbed a coke and strode to the living room. Her mother wasn't there either, but Susan noticed her head bobbing up from the flower beds along the front window.

Susan took a sip of the drink, then stepped onto the veranda. Her mother didn't look up but continued to dig into the bedraggled flower beds, pulling weeds and plucking spent blossoms of the sparse beds.

An idea struck Susan, seeing the meager flower garden. Instead of forcing more conversation, she slipped back inside, grabbed her handbag from her bedroom, and headed for her car once again. Earlier she'd admired the display of potted flowers at the nursery next to the fruit market. Working in the garden might cheer her and her mother.

When Susan headed for her car, the late April air felt heavy with humidity, and the sun burned in the sky. Another muggy evening faced her as weighted as her dampened spirit.

As she drove toward town, her thoughts centered again on Justin. They shared a past, and even though time had ebbed away, they once again shared a common emotion. They shared grief—not for the loss of their child since Justin had never been told, but for the loss of Libby who'd been their source of joy and dreams.

Like a shadow, Libby's journal fell across Susan's thoughts. Repentance. Forgiveness. Those weren't the words of the Libby Susan knew.

A car braked in front of her, and her mind jerked to the present. She came to a stop at the light, concentrating on her present task and wondering if she would ever let go of those memories.

In town, she passed the bakery, then parked in the next block and made her way to the nursery. She stopped to view an outside display of annuals and perennials.

Susan winced as she faced her motive. She was trying to please her mother with a few colorful pots of blossoms. The thought of buying her mother's praise with flowers marred her intention.

After selecting some potted lantana plants, then a few salvia and impatiens to plant around the back veranda, Susan paid for her purchases, then pulled her car forward to load.

When she returned home, she unloaded her trunk, but as she stepped toward the door, her gaze drifted next door. Through the trees, she noticed Justin studying Libby's flowerbeds, a look of concern on his face.

Susan watched him, admiring his chiseled features, the deep cleft in his chin and his full lips that always enthralled her. Today her heart wrenched seeing him alone, staring at Libby's neglected garden.

She left the pots on the veranda and crossed the yard. "Is something wrong?" she asked when she was close enough for him to hear.

He shook his head. "Just thinking about this mess." He gestured toward the thirsty plants and growing weeds.

Susan stood beside him, smelling the heat of the sun against his bare arms. She noticed dirt on his hands, then eyed the Louisiana iris beds.

"Weeding?" She motioned to his hands.

He looked at the telltale dirt and brushed his fingers against his jeans. "Everything's out of hand."

His comment triggered an immediate response. Things were out of hand. She pulled her mind back. "When I'm finished planting my flowers, I'd be happy to help. I hate to see the flowers die." Spoken, she couldn't withdraw the offer.

"You don't have to do that, Susan." His gaze swept across her face. "I need to hire someone to take care of a few things while I decide what I'm going to do." He drew in a rattled breath. "No matter what my decision, I want the property to look good."

She heard despondency in his voice and decided not to press the point. His tight jaw and distraction alerted her to his struggle. "It's wise to hire help. You can't do everything."

He didn't respond, and feeling uneasy with her desire to help him, she pulled her gaze away. "I'd better head home and leave you to your weeding."

His eyes searched hers. Then slowly, he lifted his hand and brushed a strand of hair from her cheek.

The unexpected touch sent her pulse skipping. "Thanks," she whispered barely able to move the words from her mouth. She drew away and headed back to her pots of flowers that now seemed unimportant in light of her confusion.

♥

"Would you like tea?" Margaret asked as Susan stepped from her bedroom where she'd spent the past half hour in prayer. Useless prayer, it seemed. She flinched, knowing the Lord sometimes said no or waited for His own time to respond, but she needed an answer fast.

Her mother's question returned. Tea. She glanced at her watch. Three-fifteen. "That would be nice."

She followed as Margaret headed toward the kitchen, but instead of stopping there, her mother continued through the doorway to the back veranda. Susan trailed behind her, wondering if the tea offering was her mother's effort to apologize for her earlier silence.

The porch roof shadowed the table where Margaret had laid out the tea things, and a needed breeze drifted past as Susan sank into a chair. The new lantana pot swayed on its hook, its cerise pink and yellow blossoms fluttering with the brief gust of wind.

While her mother poured, Susan admired the flower beds highlighted by the new colors that brightened the yard.

"Here, Susan." Her mother held up the teacup. "You can add your own sugar."

Susan's thoughts fluttered away. She grasped the cup and placed it on the table, feeling sadly strained.

"Thank you for the flowers. They look pretty," Margaret said, stirring sugar into her tea.

"I thought they would cheer you."

"Cheer me?" She turned her attention to Susan, her face pulling into tight lines while she continued to stir the life from her tea.

"You seem tense when I'm here." Her stomach tightened into a knot.

"What do you expect, Susan? I thought perhaps you'd learned your lesson, but your feet no more'n hit the floor and you headed back to Rose Arbor. You came home for that uppity woman, not for me."

"That's not true." Libby's death smacked Susan in the chest. "I came home because I—" Why had she come home? "I came home to make amends."

"You've done a poor job. If you aren't headin' across the grass like a dog in heat, you're hidin' in your room thinking about him."

"Mother, let's back up." Susan realized she was headed for trouble. Her common sense spiraled into an abyss as her mother's dark words battered her. What could she say? How could she explain? "First, Libby was not uppity. You never gave her a chance. Libby was spirited and kindhearted. She believed in the Lord and never did anything to lead me astray."

"You can't prove it by me. Look what you did by hangin' there. Shamed us and brought your father to an early grave."

Nausea rolled up Susan's throat. How many times had she heard this from her mother? "Papa died from an aneurysm twelve years after I left home. And did you ever think your nagging all those years might have had some—"

Susan stopped, her heart in her throat. *Lord, forgive me. I can't honor my mother when she's so unforgiving.* A voice inside Susan's head disagreed with her thought. *Forgive as the Lord forgave you.* She could argue no better with the Lord than with her mother.

"I'm sorry, Momma. I'm being hurtful."

"Yes, you are."

Susan looked into her mother's face, seeing the years of hard work and unfilled dreams. Her leather skin looked dried and taut from too much time in the sun. She'd spent her days cooking, cleaning, and canning, and when she was needed, she'd tended the fields by her father's side during planting and harvest.

As the thought left her, Susan reached across the table and touched her mother's crepey hand. "You worked hard for all of us. I never appreciated all you did."

"That's part of bein' a farmer's wife." She lowered her gaze, then raised it. "But I loved your father, Susan. Our life was hard, but workin' side by side connects people. It binds them together for better or worse."

For better or worse. Sadly, Susan seemed to have both with Justin. With her palm still resting against her mother's hand, Susan captured her gaze. "Momma, I promise you. I will not get involved with Justin—not like you mean. I won't let my emotions get carried away." Too late for that, she faced, but she promised herself she would never act on her feelings.

"You should have thought of that years ago before you acted like trash and got yourself in the family way."

Her mother's words churned through her, riling the past like gritty swill in a drain and dragging her into a cesspool of thought. Her action had been one of innocent wonder—naive, stupid and sinful, yes—but not rubbish. But it had been wrong, and she'd reaped the punishment. Her life had changed. She would never be the same.

"Does he know?"

Her mother's question pricked her heart. "No." And that's the way she wanted it.

"Well, keep it that way. I don't want him fallin' all over you out of pity."

Pity? The word stung. "I don't want that either."

"You hurt us all, Susan, and the Lord punished you."

Susan winced with the blow. When she'd been younger, her mother's words had sent her into the depths of despair. She felt unclean and unloved. But she'd worked through that, and now the comments could only remind her of where she'd been and where she no longer wanted to be.

"Momma, will you ever find forgiveness in your heart? You've hung on to this too long."

Margaret's neck jerked back. "The Bible says forgiveness comes with repentance."

Startled, Susan's head drooped. What could she say that hadn't been said already? She had repented. No man had touched her since Justin, and none would. How could a woman offer her defiled body as a gift to her Christian husband, and Susan would have no one less.

Though she knew her words would fall on deaf ears, she tried again. "I've repented, and God's forgiven me."

Sorrow washed over her. God had forgiven her, but had she forgiven herself?

Chapter Five

Justin wandered onto the gallery and looked at yesterday's handiwork. He'd weeded the flower beds, loosened the soil and watered. Maybe they'd have half a chance. He wished he'd fared as well.

The house weighted on him like the restlessness that filled his nights. Sleep evaded him, and if he wanted a good rest, he'd need to go back to his condo and away from his thoughts. He couldn't think logically, bombarded by Libby's image each way he turned. His aunt had been his solace—the only family member who truly loved him, faults and all.

He ambled to the gallery steps and let his gaze travel to the elm and beyond. A pang of regret rolled over him. Susan had offered to help with the flowers, and he'd discouraged her, but he needed to steer clear of her. She was a woman who deserved a loving husband, someone with a strong faith in God and someone who could be a warm, loving father to her children. He could never meet either of those attributes.

Justin pulled his attention away from the cottage next door and wandered into the yard. Yesterday he'd pruned the roses, and today the scent of the flowers took him back to a different time. He rubbed his neck, recalling the night he'd first kissed Susan. She'd looked so forlorn he couldn't stop his eagerness, but it had opened doors and made promises he'd been too young to keep, and Susan had been so naive. So trusting. Yet for years that first kiss had lain in his memory as sweet as honeysuckle. Now her return had refreshed those feelings, and he didn't want that to happen. If he didn't watch his step, he'd—

"Justin."

He turned and looked into Susan's tender gaze.

She strolled nearer. "The flower beds look good. I can smell the roses all the way over here."

Justin drew in a deep rasp of air as her personal fragrance covered the flower's aroma. She smelled of citrus, as fresh as a spring rain.

Susan's eyes glistened. "There's something so refreshing about flowers growing and the scent of the earth. I suppose that's part of spring. It's all so real."

It's so real? He no longer knew what was real and what was dredged up memories. His connection with Susan felt maddening, and he knew he had to get away for a while, take a break from his wavering thoughts.

She became quiet, and when he focused on her, she'd turned away, gazing at the house as if waiting for something. He'd often stood outside expecting to see Libby open the kitchen door and beckon him inside for lemonade or warm beignets.

After a moment, Susan looked at him and then glanced toward the gallery. He watched her eye the rooms running the length of the wing. "I don't remember seeing inside the rooms in that wing, but I suppose I have."

Justin swung his arm to the right. "They're mainly bedrooms on this side and closed for years. Some of the Taylor ancestors had many children, and other times relatives came to stay. It's the oldest wing."

"I've been thinking about your quandary."

"And?"

"I'm not sure, but I'd like to see the rooms."

Her comment made him curious. What had she been thinking that they hadn't already talked about?

"I'll be happy to show you if you'd like." He took a step closer and motioned to the furthest wing on his left. "The wing over there was added last. Actually, the portion closest to the gallery is old, too. It's the original kitchen. You know they didn't cook inside the plantation house in case of fire. That's why it's not attached."

She nodded, eyeing him with interest.

"In the early 1900s," he said, "when relatives modernized, they added a kitchen to the main wing."

Susan's attention seemed riveted to his words. "So much history...and all of it your family's. This house is a fitting memorial to Libby. Have you thought of that?"

He had, and that didn't make his decision any easier. "What's your idea?"

"I'd rather look first."

More time with her meant more temptation, but he looked at her eager face and felt in his pocket. "Now?" he asked, pulling out the key ring.

"Sure, if you have time."

He motioned to the steps near the garden, and she moved ahead and waited at the top of the stairs. The key ring jingled as he followed behind her. He stopped at the first door, opened the screen, and tried a key. It didn't turn. He tried another. This time the door swung open. He pushed it inward and beckoned Susan inside.

He gazed at the white walls and the four-poster bed with a canopy. The bed was so high, a three-step stool stood beside it.

Susan moved forward. She gave him a silly grin and climbed the first step, then the second, and swung around sinking into the bed. "It's firm." She bounced against the mattress.

Justin watched her, so full of enjoyment for something so simple. He'd never slept on this bed, opting for one inside the main part of the house.

Susan rose and stepped onto the stool again, but before she climbed down, she fingered the bed draperies. "Fine linen. That's nice. So much better than velvet. They hold dust." She exited to the floor.

She knelt and ran her hand over the large rag rug that lay on the wide planks. "It's in good condition. I have one like this in my bedroom at home." She rose again and continued her inspection.

Justin studied her with interest as she lovingly ran her hand across a small table, lifting an empty vase, then placing it down again.

"The room's a little dusty but other than that it seems in good condition. Almost ready for use."

Ready for use? He opened his mouth to ask about her plan again, but she turned her back and ran her finger along a cherry circular table.

"Lovely antiques in here," she said, halting at the end of the bed, "and look at the trunk." She checked for a lock. "I wonder what's inside." She reached for the latch, then seemed to think better of it and withdrew her hand.

"This is the room where the Rose Arbor ghost is supposed to live." Justin grinned.

"Ghost. Pooh." She faced him with a chuckle, waving her hand as if to brush away the idea. "You know me better than that. Christians don't believe in those tales."

He rested his hand on her shoulder. "I don't either. Never saw one. Never expect to."

She shifted away, letting his hand drop back to his side. "Are the other rooms as nice as this one?"

Justin shrugged. "I haven't been inside them for years. Aunt Libby had a housekeeper who came in a couple days a week. I think she cleaned the rooms every couple months or so."

He opened the door, and Susan stepped outside. Her curiosity piqued his interest. He'd been surprised at Susan's desire to see the rooms and even more surprised at what he recalled Libby telling him about the rooms and their family history.

He led her along the gallery, and as he passed a table sitting beneath the next window, his focus settled on a potted plant with its leaves drooping. He fingered it and realized it needed water. The sad looking plant reminded Justin of himself. Wouldn't it be nice if life could be revived and freshened by a little water?

Susan followed him to the next room, and Justin watched her face as she scrutinized the decor and sparse furnishings. Her attention darted from one corner to another as if calculating. "What are you thinking, Susan?"

"Just some disjointed thoughts, but the rooms seem to have potential."

"For what?"

"I'm surprised the rooms have their own bath. That seems so modern."

"The Taylors went in for all sorts of luxuries," he said. "They modernized Rose Arbor before most other people in this area." Justin figured she would have heard enough, but Susan's enthusiasm seemed to grow.

When they left the bedroom, Justin opened the doors of the other two rooms along the wing but found them empty, except for a couple of chairs and a small table.

Susan took a cursory look. "That's enough, I suppose, but I'm disappointed."

Her comment surprised him as they strode along the gallery to the main wing of the house. He'd had enough after the first room. Watching her finger through items in the rooms with excitement, seeing her bound along the gallery filled with curiosity, only reminded him that she was too much a part of him.

"I'd hoped the other rooms were furnished," she said.

"You shouldn't be surprised. No one's used them for years."

"I know, but—"

He waited, yet she didn't continue. When they reached the doorway near the kitchen, Susan halted and he turned to see why.

She'd stopped to look at the vase Libby must have left on the table outside the door. He hadn't noticed it, but today a pink rosebud rested inside the cut glass. His mind flew back, wondering when Susan could have put the rose there. She gave him a questioning look, and he supposed she expected him to say something. "Thank you." He tilted his head toward the vase.

She lifted it and lowered her head to smell the flower. "The rose is lovely, Justin." She drew back and returned the vase to the table.

"It was thoughtful." He nodded, a grin growing on his face. She studied him, appearing confused, and he felt totally confounded. What had he said? What had he done? What had Susan expected. He had already thanked her for the rose.

Susan searched his face, then eyed the rose again. Her expression addled him. She seemed to think he was joking. He had no idea what she'd meant by his being thoughtful?

She looked at the vase again and then eyed him. "Do you think I picked the rosebud?"

He sent her one of his rare grins. "You? No."

She shook her head. "Good, because I thought you'd picked it."

"Me? No." His grin faded, but then he cheered up. "It was the Rose Arbor ghost."

His grin made her laugh, and this time, she shook her head. "Never mind."

His face darkened as he clasped the doorknob, his manner edgy.

"Justin, is something wrong?"

He evaded her eyes. "No."

"Do you have a minute to talk?"

"Now?"

When else? He'd obviously withdrawn again, like a snail hiding in his shell. "I thought you might like to hear my idea." She took a step backward. "It can wait."

He faltered, and she could see he struggled with something.

"Did I tell you I'm heading back to Baton Rouge in the morning?" He remained a statue, his hand on the doorknob, his shoulders blocking the doorway.

She faltered, trying to control her disappointment "But I thought you were staying for a while."

"I need to check on some things at the office." He turned his back and headed inside.

Her chest tightened as she grasped the screen door and stepped behind him. "If you're leaving, then I'd like to talk. It'll only take a minute. Can I come in?"

From the look on his face, she wondered. He studied her a moment, his expression unchanged, then backed away and widened the opening.

"I thought you'd be excited," she said, puzzled by his urgency to return to Baton Rouge and as bewildered by her own desire to help him.

She strode into the family parlor and sank into the smaller wingback. Justin passed her and stood in front of the fireplace, resting his arm on the white mantle.

"Can you sit for a minute?" Susan felt rushed by his attitude.

"I'm fine. What's your idea?"

He seemed strange, totally disinterested. She rose, irritated at herself for letting Rose Arbor possess her. "Never mind."

"Susan, please." He stepped toward her. "I'm sorry. I'm distracted today. I'd like to hear your idea."

She pushed a strand of hair behind her ear, trying to decide if she should stay or leave as her commonsense told her to do.

His shoulders lowered. "Tell me what's on your mind." He stood beside the settee, his expression contrite.

"A way you can keep the manor...keep both places if you want," she said.

He sank into the cushion. "You mean Rose Arbor and my condo?" He rubbed the back of his neck, but a look of interest settled on his face.

"Yes." She watched his mouth soften, yet his expression remained guarded. "Do you want to hear it?"

"Yes."

She looked toward the chair where she'd been sitting but decided to remain standing. "You can turn Rose Arbor into a bed and breakfast."

"A what?" A mixture of disappointment and surprise jarred his face.

"Don't look so startled. They're very common in the south. Baton Rouge is loaded with them. So is Natchez, Mississippi. I have a friend who works there, and the business is thriving. Tourists love staying in plantation houses."

"A bed and breakfast." He slowly repeated the words, his gaze scanning the parlor, then returning to her. "I know nothing about the business. That's a lot of work and—"

"And it's worth it, if you want to save the house." She shifted, closing the distance between them. "Once you have the manor ready and everything in place, you don't have to run it. Hire someone to do that."

She could almost hear the gears creaking in his mind.

"What does this entail?" He searched her face, his frustration evident. "I have no idea how to run a business like that."

She settled beside him on the settee. "You'd need to bring original antiques into the house. Right now, the formal parlor is nearly empty, but I'd guess Libby has furniture packed away in some of the upper rooms...or the attic."

"And then what?" He shook his head. "So, I refurbish all the rooms to 1800s."

"Get a license to run a bed and breakfast, and hire help—a hostess, part-time cook and housekeeper, and solicit publicity. Brochures and ads. The hostess could do that or a business manager if you could afford it."

"That depends," he said. "What's the time frame? And what about me? I still have the same problem."

"You'll keep your bedroom here. It wouldn't take that long to get the house ready, and my friend, Georgia Fanchon from Natchez said she'd come for a weekend and offer some suggestions if you'd like."

Though his expression relaxed, Justin still looked dubious. "But I still don't know one iota about that kind of thing, and I don't know who to trust to handle a production like this."

Susan drew in a deep breath, fighting her good sense. She wanted Rose Arbor to live for Libby. She stopped herself. Was it really a memorial for Libby or for herself—a way to memorialize her relationship with Justin? He'd fathered her child. He'd been a part of her life, and the memories haunted her. Could she help him without being hurt? She lowered her head and closed her eyes. Lord, tell me what to do. Let me act with wisdom.

"You may not know anything, but I do." The words left her mouth, and she prayed they were truly directed by God.

"But do you know about running a bed and breakfast?"

"I can help you get the place put together while I'm looking for a position. You'll have an initial investment, but a bed and breakfast should pay for itself, Justin. You'll be able to keep the house and not have it drain your finances."

He fell back against the settee and stared at her without comment.

Anticipation shot through her like an electrical volt. To have a purpose again, to make Rose Arbor a showplace, to keep the house alive—a multitude of meaningful purposes soared through her mind. "I'd had the inkling of an idea, and after seeing the gallery bedrooms, everything fell into place."

"Are you up for the job?"

"I am, I think. I've been dreaming about what wonderful antiques and surprises I might find in the attic hidden beneath a drop cloth or enveloped with dust." The Taylor family history, the thought charged through her. "I'm a historian of sorts, Justin. A designer of museum displays. Artwork, textiles, furniture. I love it all, and I'd be working with people to get the job done."

"I couldn't ask that of you," he said finally.

"You didn't ask, Justin. I volunteered."

He drummed his fingernails against the cherry table as if struggling with the idea. "I would pay you."

For the first time in minutes, his gaze captured hers.

"That's not necessary, Justin. I'll enjoy—"

"I would pay you." His voice filled with determination.

Today, she didn't argue. Susan only wanted him to take her plan seriously. She knew it would work.

Silence hovered over the room. She opened her mouth to speak, then closed it. Let him mull over the idea. That's what he had to do. Weighing decisions seemed to be Justin's way.

"It's possible," he said finally. "I need to give it more thought." He rose and circled the room, then paced from one side to the other. "The project will take money."

"Yes, until it's in business, but I think that it can pay for itself."

"I need to check with the attorney again. The will said I had to occupy the manor, but I don't recall that I had to be here every night."

"If it's still your residence, Justin, it should work. You'd spend weekends here, and any other time you could spare. It would be your home."

"Yes, but I-I need to give this thought." He looked desperate.

"What's wrong, Justin?"

"Wrong?" His deep frown returned.

"You seem upset. Something at work, or is it—"

"I'm fine. It's nothing."

Susan shook her head. "I know you well enough to know something's wrong." She rose and crossed to him. "If you want me to stop interfering in your business, I will. Just tell me."

"It's not you. It's me." He pressed his palms against his eyes, cupping his head in his hands.

Susan's chest tightened, seeing his despair. She rested her hand against his shoulder and felt a shudder run through his body.

He lifted his head, his eyes glazed with emotion, and he pressed his palm over hers. The warmth shot up her arm and into her chest. Her lungs refused to draw in air until she forced a calming breath. "That's fine, Justin. Take your time, and I'll scribble some ideas while you think." She headed toward the doorway, then turned to face him. "You'll let me know?"

Without waiting for his response, she yanked open the door and stepped outside, filled with turmoil.

Chapter 6

The music resounded against the arched roof, and Susan rose with the congregation to sing another hymn. Though the post-Easter message reminded her of God's loving promises, she struggled to concentrate. She'd missed Justin this past week, and the longer he stayed away, the more her disappointment heightened. He couldn't handle Rose Arbor or her offer. She feared he would let the lovely manor go to the historical society.

The hymn ended, and though her lips had formed the words, she could have been singing nonsense. She sank to her seat and lowered her head, needing forgiveness for her distraction. In her peripheral vision, she eyed her mother, wondering where her thoughts were. They'd arrived at the last minute, and though Susan saw heads turn when she and her mother headed down the aisle, she felt safe from their greetings and questions for now, but after the service, she had prepared herself.

In the dimmer light of the service, her mother's face looked tired and stressed. A twinge of regret prickled through Susan, knowing that she had caused the deep grief.

Thinking back, her mother had surprised her with her comments about Susan's father. 'I loved your father, Susan. Our life was hard, but workin' side by side connects people. It binds them together for better or worse.'"

The words tugged at Susan's heart. She'd never thought of her parents as being in love. They toiled side by side, they ate meals at the same table, they slept in the same bed. She'd seen their for-better-or-worse part, and mostly the latter. But romance? Love? Susan had never seen it.

She couldn't imagine her mother's heart beating in her throat as it had for Susan when she loved Justin. She'd clung to Justin's every word. Her emotions fluttered at the sight of him, every look, every touch. To her, that was love. Working side by side? That didn't fit her parents' picture, even at her age.

Still her mother's words stuck in her mind.

When the prayers began, the congregation rose, and Susan joined them, forcing herself to listen to the petitions spoken by Pastor Ralph and others who voiced aloud their needs and struggles. Her lips pressed together, unwilling to utter one word, unwilling to admit she had problems that needed prayer. She could send her prayers heavenward alone, and she did.

"Let us close with the prayer that Jesus taught us," Pastor Ralph said. "Our Father which art in heaven, Hallowed be thy name."

Voices rose around her as the congregation spoke the Lord's Prayer. Kingdom come. Will be done. Daily Bread. The familiar words marched from her lips without thought. "And forgive us our debts, as we forgive our debtors..."

Our debts. The words caught in her throat. Debts are sins. Forgive us our sins as we forgive. As we forgive. The phrase repeated in her head. She'd tried to forgive. She'd thought she'd forgiven, but maybe she hadn't. It was so hard to overlook the pain she felt, the feeling of abandonment she'd suffered, the weight of shame she still carried.

Tears filled her eyes, and she brushed them away with her fingertips.

Be patient. She lifted her head, wondering if the thought had come from something the pastor had been saying. As she listened, she knew they hadn't. Patience—one of the fruits of the spirit. She needed patience. She needed so much. She needed to open up to someone, but who could she trust?

"Susan."

Her head jerked upward as she looked into her mother's questioning eyes. "Is something wrong?"

She sat a moment, knowing many things were wrong, but not wanting to go there. "I was thinking." She rose and clasped her purse. "It was a wonderful service. I'm glad I came."

A faint smile loosened her mother's mouth. "Good." She waved to Susan to begin the trek through the row of seats.

Susan turned and saw Clarissa waiting for her in the aisle with two little blond girls in tow, and Susan managed a smile.

"I've been lookin' for you," Clarissa called. "And here you are, bless your heart." She beckoned as Susan made her way past the people pausing to chat or gathering their belongings.

"Hello, again," Susan said, turning her gaze to the two little girls. Clarissa had been right. The girls were precious. Their smiling faces were upturned, gazing at her with wide eyes.

"How old are you, honey," Susan asked.

"I'm four," the child said, holding up her fingers.

"This is Honour," Clarissa said, resting her hand on the child's golden hair. "And this is my oldest, Mellie Kay."

Susan smiled at the girl who looked to be about nine or ten. "You have darling girls, Clarissa."

"It's good to see you, Mrs. Boyd," Clarissa said, looking at Susan's mother.

Margaret clasped her hand. "I keep hoping Susan will marry one day—" She gave Susan a knowing look. "—so I can have my own grandbabies."

"Why I'm still surprised when Susan told me she was single. You're certainly missin' out on the good life, Susan."

Susan winced, waiting for her mother to say something horrible, but the only sound Susan heard was the buzz of other conversations.

"We need to get along," Susan said, trying to ease away politely.

"I truly want y'all to come by for tea one afternoon." She lifted her hand to her chest. "Or better yet, you must come to our *cushon de lei*. I'll send you an invitation."

"Thank you," Susan said, knowing the last thing she wanted to do is go to Clarissa's pig roast.

After they said their goodbyes, Susan noticed the pastor heading for the hallway. A need gripped her heart, and she touched her mother's arm. "I'll catch you in a minute. I want to talk to someone."

She darted past the clusters of people, apparently catching up on the latest news. During the service, she'd been moved to talk with Pastor Ralph. She needed to talk with someone—someone uninvolved, someone she could trust. She longed to lift the burden from her heart. She'd worked on patience, and part of patience also meant being open to God's direction. She needed that desperately.

♥

Monday morning, Justin stood in the office hallway, trying to take the step. He'd thought about talking with his partner, Rod LeFaive, but he'd avoided it for the past week. With so many decisions to make, he needed a clear mind because his was far from it.

He'd spent the week weighing his decision. Could he afford Rose Arbor? Did he have the time to run two businesses? Could he spend time with Susan without getting involved?

He pushed his hand into his pocket as if he might find something there to help him get a grip on himself. He pressed his chin downward and closed his eyes, forming the sentence, then tapped on the door and gave it a shove.

Rod's head lifted as Justin pushed open the door. "Just the man I want to talk with," Rod said.

Justin drew back surprised and curious. "Shoot." He grasped the back of a chair, shifted it and sat in front of Rod's desk.

"Super-Tech wants to talk with us about a project. Do you want to handle it, or should I?"

The answer rose to Justin's tongue, but he paused. He needed Rod's cooperation and jumping to a response without hearing all sides of the story wasn't wise. "What's your preference?"

"I know you've been under stress with your aunt's death, so I'm happy to handle it myself, but I want to give you the option."

A chuckle flew from Justin before he could stop it. "I'd be relieved, Rod. I stopped by to get your take on decisions I'm struggling with. I need someone with a sound mind, because mine certainly isn't."

Rod erased the air as in disagreement. "You have a good head on your shoulders, Justin. If you hadn't, I wouldn't be your partner." He opened a candy dish and popped in a green and white mint, then offered one to Justin.

Justin shook his head.

He put the lid back on the dish, then leaned back. “How can I help you?”

Justin dragged in a breath and reviewed his situation. He’d already told Rod about the will, but not about Susan’s ideas.

Rod listened, occasionally picking up a pencil to jot a note to himself, then lifted his gaze again.

“What do you think?” Justin asked when he finished.

Rod glanced at his notes. “What kind of financing would you need?”

“I don’t know. Susan said she’d come up with a game plan while I was deciding what to do.”

“What’s the condition of the place?”

Justin described Rose Arbor, noting the pride in his voice and he described the steps that Susan had laid out for him—inspections, license, staff.

“So, if it’s not finances, what’s the problem?” Rod tilted his head as if trying to read Justin’s mind.

“The time. It means spending more time there. I doubt if weekends will be enough, and that puts our business on your shoulders.”

“It’s not like you’re hundreds of miles away, Justin. Until you get settled, we have the phone, email, and it’s an hour or so drive back when you’re needed. If we’re talking short term, I can handle that.”

“Thanks. I don’t want to dump my share of the work on you.”

“When Carrie had Roddy, I spent time with her and the baby. You didn’t grumble so why should I?”

As Justin shrugged his response, he recalled Rod’s jubilation when he announced the birth of his son. Justin knew he would never enjoy that thrill. He would never have a child of his own, and the awareness left him empty.

“And what’s the next problem?”

Justin’s pulse tripped. “I don’t have one.”

“What about this Susan? Do you want to talk about her?”

Justin longed to avert Rod’s gaze, but he knew it would give him away. “Not really.”

But Rod pressed the issue and Justin gave him a brief summary of his relationship with Susan, her background, and why she'd volunteered to help him.

Rod tilted back in his chair and scrutinized him. "What's in it for her?"

"Nothing." The question hit him hard. "She offered out of kindness, but I'll pay her."

Rod's arched his brows. "Is this finally a romance?"

"Never."

Rod's brows arched even higher. "How can you be so sure?"

"Because I have no interest in marriage, and she's not the kind of woman to—" He stumbled over his words. "And I'd never take advantage of her." Like I did once, he thought.

Rod straightened and rose. He dropped the note pad on his desk, then rounded the corner and rested against the desktop facing him. "What's wrong with falling in love, Justin. I've never understood you on that."

"I don't want the commitment. I wouldn't be a good husband."

"Pooh! Why would you say that?"

"Role model, Rod. My dad worked his life away. I do the same."

Rod shook his head. "I'd suggest you rethink that. Maybe Susan isn't the woman, but one of these days, Justin, I'll enjoy seeing you eat your words."

♥

Monday afternoon, Susan stood in the church parlor waiting for Pastor Ralph. He'd agreed to talk with her, and now that she'd come, she had no idea what she wanted to say. Her courage from yesterday afternoon had shrunk to the size of a pea.

"Susan." The pastor's voice came from the doorway. "I'm off the phone. Sorry to keep you waiting."

"That's okay," she said, wishing he'd stayed tied up longer because she may have been able to make her escape.

"How have you been? You've been away a long time."

"I'm fine. Thanks."

"Good." He gave her a smile. "Come this way." He beckoned her to follow.

She trailed behind him into the hallway, then to his office where he pulled out a chair and motioned for her to sit. "So now, how can I help you?" His wry smile made him appear to know something she didn't.

"I don't know quite where to begin."

His smile fizzled to concern. "I thought you'd come to talk about a wedding perhaps."

Susan managed a smile. "No wedding plans for me." Her stomach tightened at the impossibility. She delved into her mind deciding where to begin. "I'm concerned about my mother, really. I should say my relationship with my mother, and—" She paused scuffling with words. "And forgiveness. I just need someone to listen."

"Then you've come to the right place. Please go ahead. Anything you say here is confidential."

She drew in a breath and described the tension between her and Margaret without giving him the details that had caused the rift between them. "I know God wants me to honor my mother, and it hurts at my age not getting along with her. We're two grown women acting like children."

"Sometimes we still are in our parent-child relationships, Susan. But God can heal them. You have to pray and believe, and then take the first step."

She felt a frown settle on her face. "What do you mean take the first step? I've taken so many steps."

"First, have you truly forgiven your mother? Remember, I said you have to believe that God works with you. And if you're confidant you've forgiven her, then the next question is, have you forgiven yourself?"

Forgiven herself? The question chaffed her mind. Had she forgiven herself? Had she really forgiven her mother? She lifted her downcast eyes and saw the sincerity in Pastor Ralph's eyes. "I don't know."

"Then that's where you begin." He reached to the corner of his desk and picked up his Bible. "Did you bring your Bible?"

He looked at her empty hands, and Susan felt embarrassed that she hadn't thought to bring the scripture along. She shook her head.

"Then let me share some things with you." He flipped open the cover and ran his finger along the verses before looking at her again. "Psalms is wonderful for dealing with our relationship with God. When we get that straight, our human relationships seem to fall into place so much easier."

His words struck her. Had she not been right with God? The answer came quickly. Probably not. She'd tried to hide from the Lord, but he saw her in her darkest moments.

"Listen to these verses from Psalm 139. 'Search me, O God, and know my heart; test me and know my anxious thoughts. See if there is any offensive way in me, and lead me in the way everlasting.'"

He lifted his gaze and looked deeply into her eyes as if he were trying to search her soul. "Let those verses be your prayer, Susan. You must ask God to search the secret places of your heart and help you carry all the baggage that's piled there."

He closed the cover, keeping his finger inside to mark the spot. "That's the first step."

She nodded. "I know I need patience. I've prayed for that."

"Patience for your mother and for yourself. Nothing is worse than stressful relationships with our loved ones. No matter what the situation, it comes from both directions. The offender and the offended are damaged by the infraction—whatever it may be. A little child is put to bed or gets time out. The parent is offended by the child's action and the child is offended by punishment. That's a simplistic example."

Susan lowered her eyes, struck by how far her sin had been from a naughty child. "And the older we get the worse our sins."

"Yes," he said. "And you're not alone. We all sin. We all fall short of God's glory. Each of us break commandments daily, and that's why we must pray the verses I just gave you. We have sins we know and sins we don't even realize. Those that are overt—our actions and words—and those that are covert—those inside us like envy and pride."

"And being unable to forgive."

"Yes, that, too."

They sat in silence a moment while his advice rolled through her, thinking of what she had to do and wondering if she could.

"Thank you. You've given me something important to think about. Yesterday during the Lord's prayer, the words hit me. We're to forgive as God has forgiven us.

"And I know scripture tells us to forgive others, so that the Lord will forgive our sins."

"It's a big task," Pastor Ralph said, opening the Bible and searching again through the pages. "What do you say?"

"I'll work on it. I will." But the task seemed too difficult.

"Here's one more verse from Ephesians for you to think about while your relationship is healing. Think of it as a guide. 'Be completely humble and gentle; be patient, bearing with one another in love. Make every effort to keep the unity of the Spirit through the bond of peace.' You'll find it in chapter four. You might want to read the whole verse. It talks about speaking the truth in love. Sometimes we forget. We speak in anger, but remember love can do so much more."

"Thank you," Susan said, sensing that their time had ended. "I'll do some heavy praying."

He rose and extended his hand.

Susan grasped his fingers, but instead of a handshake, he didn't let go.

"And if you ever want to talk about your real struggle, Susan, I'm here."

The awareness in his eyes startled her, and she caught her breath, realizing he'd seen too much in her face.

He gave her hand a squeeze and released it. "This is between us, as I said."

She nodded and rose, her hands trembling as she hung her purse on her shoulder. "I appreciate everything you've said." She spoke the words as she backed toward the doorway, and when her foot hit the threshold, she darted down the hallway.

Chapter Seven

Susan leaned her back against the rose arbor bench and tucked her legs beneath her. The heavy floral fragrance surrounded her in the May afternoon heat. She'd come to the arbor for quiet. In her mother's house, the television blatted with soap operas and game shows until she wanted to scream.

She didn't know if her mother actually watched the programs or just lost herself in the noise. Susan also realized that staring at the TV gave her mother an excuse not to talk with her.

The supposition flattened her. Why would she think something like that? As she drove home from her appointment on Monday, she had reviewed the verses Pastor Ralph had shared with her, and she'd prayed that she would find the answer that she needed to renew her strained relationship with her mother. She'd also come to one meaningful realization. Until she could forgive herself, she may never be able to forgive her mother.

And as forgiveness filled her thoughts, she became aware that she'd never forgiven Justin. She'd been angry but mainly at herself. She'd been hurt by his absence, but it had been her fleeing Devereaux that caused the separation. Would Justin have stepped up to her plight if he'd known? Seeing his strange behavior now made her question the possibility. Still she'd never given him the chance, and now it seemed useless. He had enough to struggle with, and as her mother reminded her, she didn't want Justin's pity.

Back then Susan's longing to be loved and to be wanted had won out over her wisdom and morals. A girl of sixteen might be forgiven for her lack of wisdom but never for her lack of morals. Her mother had drenched her in good moral conduct from the day she'd realized Susan had begun to blossom. Perhaps that's why her curiosity had been so stirred. What hidden secret—what unspeakable urge—would motivate her undemonstrative mother to fill her with warnings of young men's desires?

Susan had never given romance a thought until Justin came along. His dark look intrigued and beguiled her as a spider's web entraps the unknowing fly. He'd had nothing to lose. She'd had everything to lose, and she did.

The spider and fly image gave her pause. She'd convinced herself that Justin hadn't been the spider, and that she had been. She'd imagined that she'd used her feminine wiles to draw him into her web, and that had been her shame.

But her reasoning had been so wrong. Even today, she found herself drawn to Justin, and for what? To die again in his web?

"Forgive me, Lord." The prayer whispered past her ears. "Keep my thoughts straight and true. Right and wrong, who's to blame and who's not doesn't matter anymore. Forgiveness is the key—to forgive my mother, Justin and myself."

Her prayer and her thoughts drew her back to Libby's journal. Why had Libby written down her thoughts? She'd never considered Libby as a writer, but she'd always been a great storyteller. But the journal hadn't been one of Libby's delightful stories. Instead it was scripture and prayers for forgiveness. She couldn't believe she and Libby struggled with the same need.

Unable to think about it any longer, Susan flipped open her spiral-bound memo pad and reviewed her notes. She'd tried to organize a list of what needed to be done at Rose Arbor to make it a viable tourist attraction, whether a bed and breakfast or guided historic tours, if Justin preferred.

The bed and breakfast appealed to her more. The homey comforts of the manor couldn't be enjoyed without spending time on the gallery or eating an old-fashioned southern breakfast in the dining room with its punkah fan over the table once moved by the servants.

As she jotted another idea, a sound caught her attention. She slipped her legs from beneath her, realizing they had fallen asleep. She took a moment to get her balance, then walked from beneath the arbor. When she looked at the gallery, Justin was opening the door to the manor.

She stood in the arbor's shadow, willing her legs to awaken so she could make her escape. She wouldn't grovel for Justin's attention any longer. That was one decision she'd made. She was no longer a girl longing for attention. She no longer needed to learn the hidden secrets of her mother's fear. She'd experienced and found it a weight around her neck. Forgiveness was one thing, allowing herself to be hurt again was another.

The tingling in her legs lessened as she waited for Justin to vanish inside the house. She wanted him to make his decision without any pressure, and she feared just seeing her might trigger it. Sometimes she wondered if he ran off to Baton Rouge to get away from her and her ideas. The possibility hurt.

She clasped the note pad and stepped from behind the arbor. The house seemed quiet, and she assumed Justin was occupied enough for her to make her escape. As she headed across the grass, she heard the door opening, and her plan slipped away.

"Susan."

She stopped and turned to face him. "You're back."

He stepped closer and leaned against the gallery railing. "For a while."

She remained where she was. "I didn't mean to disturb you. I was working in the arbor. You know how I love it in the afternoon sun."

He gave a faint nod. "I want to talk with you if you have time."

"Now?" Her chest tightened.

"Sure, if you're free."

The comment seemed ridiculous. She had been so free it made her sick. No position had opened to her, and now she wondered if she were playing games with herself. Had she been dismissing career opportunities because she'd offered her services to Justin?

Justin remained on the gallery, his shoulder supported by the ceiling column as he studied her.

She hesitated a moment to get her bearings, then crossed the grass and climbed the steps.

Without a word, Justin pulled his weight from the pillar and opened the door, motioning her to go inside.

"It's cooler here," he said. "I bought some cold drinks at the store." He pointed to the refrigerator. "Would you like something?"

She shook her head.

"Let's sit in the parlor then." He passed through the dining room into the parlor and waited in the archway for her to find a seat.

Today she sank onto the settee and laid the notepad on the coffee table.

He settled in the wingback near the window. "Have you found employment yet?"

His question pierced the silence. "Not yet."

He dropped his gaze. "Good." His comment was almost inaudible.

"Good?" A tight frown settled on her face.

"I've been thinking about your proposal. In fact, I talked to my partner about it. I think it will work."

Surprised, she studied his expression to make sure she'd heard him correctly. "It'll work? Did you check with your lawyer?"

"I spoke to the attorney this morning. Legally, he saw it as a possibility. I would claim Rose Arbor as my residence as you suggested. I'd have a room here and would have to spend time in the house, but I could live at my condo during the week."

"That's good, then."

"My partner's agreeable. He knows I'll have to split my time, but I can resolve that."

He quieted a moment gazing at her as if expecting her to say something, but she found nothing to say. And now that she'd struggled with her mother's hard words about tempting herself, she wondered if that's what she was doing. Would her behavior reflect her repentance if she allowed her life to revolve around the man who participated in her sin?

"You don't look happy, Susan." His brief smile had faded. Now he gave her a puzzled look.

"I'm happy for you, Justin."

"Then you're willing to work for me?"

Work for him? The reality of his question knotted in her stomach. She'd proposed the plan, made it sound as if she were willing to help, but now that he'd agreed, fear needled through her. Would she be asking for trouble from her mother and disappointing God.

He studied her. "It's too difficult to do this without you. You know that? It was your idea. You have the vision and knowledge."

His pleading tightened the knots in her belly. "Justin, I said I would, but—" But what? Yes or no? "I need to pray about this Justin. I can tell you what needs to be done but to work with you, I don't know. I'm giving that second thoughts."

He leaped from the chair, tucked his hands into his pockets and closed his eyes almost as if he were praying. She knew he had been a believer, but he'd always prided himself on never asking God for help. Justin never asked anyone for help that she could remember until today. She guessed he wasn't praying at all—only angry.

Finally, he turned his back on her and braced his hands on Libby's open secretary desk, turning his face toward the window.

Silence hung above her like a guillotine ready to drop.

But then he spoke. "I'm disappointed and confused, Susan."

"I'm confused, too." His downhearted voice rent her heart, and she clenched her teeth, wondering how her mother would react when she told her, and if helping Justin went against God's will. She'd let her enthusiasm for Rose Arbor overshadow what might be best for both of them.

"I've felt relieved, Susan, since I made the decision to take you up on your idea. Please don't drop it now."

"I didn't say no, Justin. I said I needed to give prayerful thought to working with you. I'll give you all my notes, all the things I've thought about. We can talk about them and see if you really need me."

He didn't move for a moment, then turned his head from the window and looked at her from his bowed position at the desk. "It's me, isn't it?"

His question startled her.

He straightened and strode to her side, then knelt at her feet. "It's what I did all those years ago? I'm sorry, Susan. I didn't mean to take advantage of you. I didn't realize you were a virgin. I suppose I should have known."

A ragged breath shuddered through her.

His head lowered as he shook it. "I probably didn't care. I was young and intrigued by you. Charmed, I suppose. I've felt guilty every time I think of you. I was nearly as naive as you were, but I'm not anymore, and I promise you I won't touch you again, Susan. I would never try to—"

Never. Though his words should have filled her with comfort, they decimated her. "No, Justin. It's not you. It's me. Please. We're adults now. We're not children any longer. We know the repercussions of making bad decisions. We won't do that again."

He clutched her hands and looked so deeply into her eyes, she felt he could read the truth in her soul. "I will never do anything to hurt you," he said. "I promise on my honor."

She wanted to scream. His promise hurt her, not that she should want him anymore, but that she didn't know what she wanted. "I still need to pray on this, Justin. I thought I could do it, but I'm uncertain. My relationship with my mother is strained. I don't know what will happen if I stay at the house."

"Then move in here. You can have one of the rooms in the wing."

How could she tell him that would totally undo any hope of resolving the tension with her mother? "I'll let you know by tomorrow, Justin. I promise."

He rose from his knee and sat beside her on the settee. "I suppose I have to accept your decision."

Her back straightened, and she felt her hands knot. "Justin, the problem is you're spoiled. Libby doted on you, but don't expect me to."

He looked startled. "Susan, I can't believe—"

"I won't leave you in a lurch. I'll call Georgia—my friend from Natchez—and see when she can come down. She'll give you good advice, and I have my notes." She touched the memo pad.

He gave a faint nod, his attention on her notes. "Can I see what you've written?" He tilted his head toward the pad.

"Sure." She lifted the notebook and flipped to the first page. "I was working from memory, but here's a list of furniture we still need." *We.* She heard the word like a foghorn. It vibrated through her. "You'll need the walls washed and perhaps painted. If I recall the draperies and window treatments are in good condition. They'll need to be cleaned. The rooms on the wing may not be. You'll have to check.

"You'll want a plumber to check the plumbing and make sure everything's in good working order. Add fresh caulking to spruce up the bathrooms."

Her excitement grew as she talked about what needed to be completed, but guilt rose again. She'd said she would pray, and yet in her heart, she knew what she wanted to do. This needs to be indented to match the other paragraphs. Justin flipped the pages. "I'll need a license."

"License for sure, and you'd want to get the approval of the historical society. They will be a great supporter and promoter if they're involved."

He closed the notebook and handed it back to her. "What should I do now?"

"You could contact an inspector first, to make sure the building is sound. That's the first step since you'd need an inspection for a license anyway."

"I can do that." He rose and turned to the fireplace, his back to her. "And what will you do?"

"What I said, Justin. I'll pray."

♥

Susan brushed the moisture from her face and squinted her eyes in the afternoon sun. Though she wore a wide-brimmed straw hat, it didn't keep the bright glare from giving her a headache.

She knelt beside her mother's back yard flowerbeds, pulling out new weeds and plucking off the dead blossoms. She'd promised Justin a decision, and she'd yet to find the answer. Justin seemed to think the world revolved around him. She hoped her words gave him something to think about.

Last night she'd wanted to talk with her mother, but her rationalization sank into a pool of antiquated debris. Her mother would dredge out the past, and her only lifesaver would be her promise to not get involved with Justin, which, to her mother, would seem like airless water wings.

In her room during the night, she'd searched God's Word. In 2 Corinthians 7, she found it. *Godly sorrow brings repentance that leads to salvation and leaves no regret.* Yes, she had been eager to rid herself of the guilt. She'd been filled with indignation at herself for hurting her parents and bringing shame on her name. She'd accepted that God's forgiveness could cover her sin and make her innocent. She had no regret that she'd promised the Lord she would never again repeat her infraction. She'd never allow passion to overcome her love of God. She would keep her promise.

Even if she spent time in Justin's company on this project, Susan knew she would not change her decision. God had promised to wash away her sin, but she couldn't ask Him to do it again. She would never allow that guilt and shame to find her again. Now all she had to do was convince her mother of that.

She thought of Justin's admission. "I will never do anything to hurt you. I promise on my honor." Could she trust his honor? She wanted to for the sake of Rose Arbor and for the sake of forgiveness. She could never forgive Justin if she didn't trust him.

Pastor Ralph had reminded her to be patient—patient with herself and patient with her mother. Could she do that with a whole heart? Day by day she would chip away at the wall between them, and eventually she knew the Lord would send the wall tumbling to the ground.

She rose and stretched her legs to relieve her cramped knees. She pulled off her hat and used it as a fan. The artificial breeze felt good on her damp skin. As she fanned, she gazed at the flower beds with a sense of accomplishment. They looked neat and the plants, hardy.

Thirst motivated her to give up her venture. She bent to retrieve the trowel and gardening fork, then slipped off her canvas gloves and headed toward the house. As she stepped onto the veranda, her mother opened the door. "Would you like a lemonade?"

"Thanks. That sounds good." Susan set the tools on the porch edge and sank into a wicker chair, setting her hat on the table.

In a moment, her mother came outside with two glasses. "You've worked hard. Thank you." She sat beside Susan in another wicker chair.

"You're welcome." She took a needed sip of the tart drink as she pondered her next move.

"I see he's back," her mother said.

Her mother seemed unable to speak Justin's name. "Yes, for a while."

"Then you've talked with him?"

Her mother had set her up, and she'd fallen for it. "Yes, he called me over to talk about the house, and what he's going to do."

Her mother's frown deepened. "And what's that?"

"Libby's will restricts the sale of Rose Arbor. He either has to live there or give it to the historical society."

"Really?" Her mother looked as if she couldn't believe Libby had made stipulations. "What about Caroline? Did Libby leave her out of the will?"

"I don't know about that. She may have left her something. Money or jewelry. We didn't discuss that."

Her mother seemed to ponder the possibility.

"Georgia offered to come down from Natchez and give Justin an estimate on what she thinks it will cost to turn the property into a bed and breakfast."

"Your friend Georgia?"

"Yes, I asked her, and she volunteered." Here I go. Her admission had opened the door and it was too late to shut it. She delved into her meek supply of courage to tell her mother what she intended to do. "I've offered to help him until I find a full-time position."

"You what?" Her mother's back straightened, and the expression on her face made her appear that the lemonade had been non-sweetened.

"Mother, please understand. I've prayed about this. I've read scripture. I believe that God's directing me."

"So, you think God's directing you to spend time with the man who ruined your life?"

Through the years, her mother's anger knifed her over and over. Yet the hurt reflected in her mother's eyes nearly undid Susan. "I ruined my own life. He didn't rape me, remember? I gave myself to him. You can't blame Justin."

"But I can, Susan."

"Please let it go. Help me to let it go. Please understand I've already suffered the consequence of my past. I've repented, as God is my witness, and don't regret the promise I've made to remain chaste before marriage."

Her mother released a ragged breath. "But what about your career. You need permanent work? Are you still looking?"

"Yes, but Justin's offered to pay me. I'd rather not, but he insists."

"At least he has a brain in his head."

That's more than I can say for you. Susan finished her mother's thought. "I wanted you to understand so that there are no surprises. After I talk with Justin today, I'll call Georgia and invite her down."

"I haven't seen Georgia for years."

Susan sat a moment weighing her mother's comment. Did that mean she approved?

♥

Justin paced the gallery floor, checking his watch and wondering about Susan's decision. She'd startled him last night. Spoiled? He couldn't believe she'd called him spoiled. Yet as he thought, he did focus too much on his own needs and not enough on others.

He plopped into a wicker chair, eyeing the fresh rosebud in the vase. He'd tossed a dead one out when he'd returned two days earlier, and now another had appeared. He'd thought Susan had placed them there, but now he wasn't certain.

The family legend came to mind, but he shook his head at his meandering thoughts. He didn't believe in ghosts any more than Susan, and he'd never heard of one who left roses.

While he gazed at the flower, a thump on the gallery made him turn to the steps. Susan appeared, her dark hair waving around her shoulders as it did so long ago. The summer sun had left its mark, and tinges of red glistened before she stepped into the shadow of the gallery roof.

"I thought you weren't coming."

"I always keep my promises."

"I knew that." He motioned for her to sit, amazed at the anticipation that charged through him.

"I'll help you, Justin, but only until I find work."

Only until she found work. He needed to be grateful. "Thanks. Without you I wouldn't know where to begin."

"Did you call an inspector?"

"He'll be here tomorrow morning. I can't imagine he'll find anything serious."

"I agree, but it's best to check."

She crossed her leg, and her trim ankle peeked from beneath her beige pants. His stare traveled upward and riveted to her steady gaze.

"How long will you be in town?" she asked.

"A week, at least. Maybe two."

"I'll call Georgia and see if she can come next weekend before you go back. That only leaves a week to inventory the grounds for furniture. The attic, for one."

"We can check the other wing and the outbuilding. I haven't been in them for years."

"Once we know what we have, Georgia's up on the value of antiques and should give you a good estimate how much you'll still need to spend on furnishings."

"You're amazing, Susan." He reached across the short distance and touched her arm, then pulled back, remembering his promise.

She looked at him with questioning eyes, as if she'd drifted off in some kind of a dream. "You're welcome."

His mind lingered with the touch of Susan's soft skin beneath his hands. Too familiar to be safe.

"Justin?"

He saw Susan's concerned expression and managed to refocus. "Only thinking. It's nothing."

She gave him a curious look. "When do you want to begin?"

Chapter Eight

Susan's arm prickled with the pressure of Justin's touch. She rose, walked to the edge of the gallery and rested her hands on the railing, to remove herself from the closeness.

"When do you want to begin?"

"We only have a few days." She gazed toward the outbuilding.

"Then how about now?" Justin rose. "Come see."

He passed her and took the gallery steps to the grass. "Let's check the newer wing while it's light."

Surprised at his eagerness, she followed him to the two-storied building, anxious to see what was inside. Susan waited while he tried the keys dangling from a ring. When he found the correct one, he pushed open the door. It grated along the wooden floor, but he forced it open. "Warped," he said, waving away the dust particles that filled the air when he stepped inside.

Susan stood on the threshold gazing inside at the white sheets like hulking ghosts posed around the room.

Justin had crossed the room and lifted the dust cover from a giant object in the corner, and Susan's spirit lifted. "That's an armoire, Justin." She sprang across the room. "Look at the inlaid wood. It's beautiful." She drew her fingers along the smooth rosewood design. "We could use this in one of the guest rooms."

She turned, gazing at the simplicity of the room's design—plain white walls, simple lines—nothing to give a sense of luxury. "This must have been the servants' wing."

"I think it was," he said, more intent on nosing behind another cloth drapery.

The dust flew in the air, and when she inhaled, her nose tickled. She closed her eyes and sneezed.

"God bless you," Justin said, brushing the dust from his hands on his pant leg. "I hope you don't have allergies."

She grinned. At this point, she didn't care if she did as her excitement grew. "Look. It's part of a tester bed." She stepped closer and studied the headboard and posts. "Or maybe a half tester. I can't tell if the upper beams are there for the canopy or not, but it's a find. We need two beds in the other wing. This is one of them."

She studied the cabriole legs and posts, amazed that the wonderful antiques were stored instead of filling the empty bedrooms on the gallery, her excitement growing. "Let's keep looking. The more we find the less I have to purchase."

They moved to the next room, then the next, each time finding a treasure or two—a tufted Queen Anne settee, a horse-back shaped rocker that needed new upholstery, a Duncan Phyfe pedestal table, and two matching fireside chairs. Each find charged her with enthusiasm for the job.

"Oh, Justin, I can't believe this." She clasped his arm. "Such treasures here." She felt his muscle flex beneath her hand and regretted her action. It had been far too familiar. She wanted to keep their relationship business. Yet their friendship rolled across her like the sweet scent of old roses.

Susan noticed his questioning look. She tried to pull away, but Justin grasped her arm and drew her around to face him. He slipped his palms to her shoulders and drew her into an embrace. "You're the treasure, Susan. How can I thank you for stepping in to help me?"

His whisper sent frissons along her neck and down her arms. She curled her shoulder in reaction, and he released her, drawing back to look into her eyes. "I mean what I said. You could have distrusted me, but you didn't. I know you're doing this as much for Aunt Libby as for me, but I don't care. You've put yourself out to help." He lowered his gaze and his jaw tensed. "Besides Aunt Libby, you're the only one—"

He dropped his hands, then shoved one in his pocket and stepped away. "I don't need to be sappy. I just want you to know how much I appreciate this."

He turned and headed toward the door. "I suppose this is enough for one day."

You're the only one— The only one what? She followed him back to the gallery, feeling giddy yet confused. She wanted to get away, yet wanted to stay. The feeling of Justin's body close to hers had sent her pulse skittering. Foolish, she knew. Justin had only meant a sincere thank you, but her imagination raced, wondering what she'd done so special and wanting to do something again that would—

Temptation. Repentance. The words charged through her. Her mother had cautioned her about tempting herself, and she hadn't listened. Susan thought a mature woman could control her emotions, but maybe she couldn't. Pressed close to Justin, she had drawn in his scent—the fragrance of a spring rain and subtle spices like cassia.

"What's wrong?" Justin studied her face when they reached the gallery.

"Nothing. Nothing at all. I'll get my notes together when I get home. Tomorrow, maybe, we can check the attic if you'd like." She studied his eyes hoping he looked as excited as she felt.

He averted her gaze. "The inspector will be here tomorrow. You're welcome to do it alone though."

Her jaw drooped, but she managed to compose herself. "I'll do that." The disappointed feeling sent her a warning signal. "I need to get home, Justin. I want to call Georgia and see when she'll be coming."

She took a step backward, to fend off the longing she had to touch him. "We had a good day today with all the finds."

"We did." But a bewildered look rose on his face. "Then I'll see you tomorrow."

"Tomorrow." The word hit as it did Scarlet O'Hara. *After all, tomorrow is another day.*

♥

Justin pulled into the driveway of his mother's house and stepped out. Before approaching the porch, he stopped a moment and scanned the familiar surroundings. His gaze drifted to the Spanish moss dripping from the live oaks and the tight buds of the crape myrtles. In another week, they would be in full bloom, their pink, white and purple blossoms brightening the landscape.

The crape myrtles sent his mind racing to Susan. She reminded him of a flower—in her youth a bud that held great promise and now a full bouquet of womanhood. She'd matured even more beautifully than she'd been as a naive girl. Today she displayed a range of emotion and talents, a fervor that he'd never dreamed possible from the young woman whose gaze never left Libby.

Justin stopped beside the front door, facing his own reality. Going inside meant leaving the sunshine and stepping into the shadows. He put his finger on the bell and pushed, waiting for Clovis to answer.

When the door opened, Clovis' face brightened to a smile. "Mista Justin, *bon jour*."

"*Très bien*, Clovis." Justin nodded at the older gentleman.

"It's so good to lay mah eyes on you again." Clovis swung his hand toward an open doorway. "Yo momma's in da lib'ary waitin' fo' ya."

"Thanks. It's always good to see you, too." Justin smiled at the long-time servant, then drew in a lengthy breath and strode through the doorway.

"Justin," Caroline said from a wingback chair near the grand piano.

He had never heard anyone in the house play the instrument except an occasional guest, and he often wondered why they owned such a lovely instrument.

"Mother," he said, sinking in a matching wingback across from her. He'd learned long ago outward affection wasn't appreciated. "How are you?"

"The same." Her hands clasped the chair arms, and he watched her fingers twitch against the upholstery. "I wondered when you'd find time to come by again."

"I've been busy. I'm sorry."

"Busy with Rose Arbor, I suppose."

Her expression told him what he already knew. Although she'd denied being upset over Libby's will, he suspected differently. "Yes, I've made some decisions."

"What's your decision?" She straightened, allowing her grip to fall away from the arm rest and drop to her lap. "Have you decided to give it to the historic society?"

"No."

Her cold eyes looked back at him with curiosity. "So, what will you do?"

He avoided her question for the moment, although he knew she would bring him back to it. "I've deposited the check from Aunt Libby's estate into your account, Mother. I'll go over that with you while I'm here today."

"Thank you." She looked away a moment, and then returned to the question. "So, then what is your plan for the plantation?"

He took a moment to settle his thoughts and then explained Susan's idea. Her expression told him what she thought.

"A bed and breakfast? How can you run a business in Devereaux and another in Baton Rouge?"

"I'll need help."

"I should say. Was this your idea? I'm surprised."

He could no longer bear the charade, and he gave her the details.

"Susan? You mean the little flighty thing from the servants' quarters."

"Susan Boyd. The Boyds weren't servants, Mother. You recall much of the surrounding acres of Rose Arbor were sold even when you were a girl. Susan's parents bought the house and farmed the land."

"I hadn't meant to imply she was a servant. I know she was a farmer's daughter."

Her imperious manner grinded against Justin's patience. Why argue? "She has a degree in art history and was employed as a curator at the museum in Baton Rouge until she came home. From what she tells me, she'd worked to restore antebellum homes in Baton Rouge. I think she's quite capable."

His mother's eyes glazed with solidness. "Just be careful, Justin."

He drew back at her comment. "What?"

"You know how the poor will do anything to marry a wealthy man."

Justin snorted. "First, sorry to disappoint you, but I'm not a wealthy man, and second, Susan has no interest in me as a husband." The comment struck him in the core of his belly.

He tossed off the feeling. It was pride. No one wanted to be rejected.

He realized he'd always needed an upper hand, a sense of control, knowing who he was and where he was headed. Maybe he was spoiled, but that wasn't his reason for not marrying.

His gaze drifted to the brocade sofa and weighty draperies of the library. The house had tried to oppress him, but it hadn't succeeded. He'd come a long way from the withdrawn boy to a man who owned a business, made sensible decisions, and earned a rather good income. In this time of his life, he wouldn't put himself in jeopardy of a rejection.

"Lunch is in da dinin' room."

Justin turned toward the doorway and saw Rèmi's smiling face aimed at him.

"Did you set a place for Justin?" Caroline asked.

"Yesum. Always a plate for our boy."

Rèmi backed away as his mother muttered something beneath her breath.

Justin rose and helped Caroline from her chair. She moved ahead of him, her head tilted upward as if she were checking the ceiling for cobwebs.

When they entered the dining room, Justin felt overpowered by his surroundings. The decor seemed burdened with large furniture and dark walls. Yet he wondered if Susan had been beside him would he have noticed.

Justin pulled out his mother's chair, and after she was settled, he sat adjacent to her. His own weighted thoughts dragged him as low as the oriental carpet beneath his feet.

The butler's door swung open, and the aroma of Rèmi's spicy jambalaya filled the room. She smiled as she entered carrying two tureens in her spindly fingers. Justin didn't need to check the first dish. Its scent had given it away, but he eyed the second that held boiled greens.

Rèmi bent toward his ear as she lowered the bowls. "I got praline pie waitin' fo' ya."

"You always remember," he said, giving her hand a pat as she passed.

Justin had suspected the family servants had pitied him. Clovis had often tried to make him smile, and Rèmi filled his stomach with his favorite foods when she could. Though Caroline usually set the weekly menu, Rèmi would sometimes sneak him a special treat without her being aware.

As he watched his mother's drawn face, guilt settled over him. He'd become heir to his mother's girlhood home while she had received only a substantial gift of money—one thing she didn't need.

He spooned the jambalaya onto his plate and a helping of greens, and then paused. The pinched look on his mother's face, he was certain, reflected her wounded feelings over Libby's will, and he believed his mother had rights to some of the family treasures.

He lowered his fork. "Mother, would you like to come to Rose Arbor and choose some of the Taylor heirlooms to bring home? They belong to you more than to me."

Her head shot upward, and she eyed him with a piercing gaze. "Libby left the plantation and contents to you, and rightly so." Her coloring faded, and she lowered her head. "I want no part of it. I don't care to set foot in Rose Arbor."

Her look disquieted Justin. "But I only—"

She lifted her hand. "That's all we will say on the matter."

♥

Susan waved at Justin as he spoke with the inspector, then made her way to the attic stairs. She opened the door and climbed the creaking staircase. At the top, she paused to let her eyes adjust to the gloom. One octagonal window at the far end let in shreds of light where its sunny pattern lit the wide plank flooring.

As she moved through the furniture covers, dust fairies rose from the floor and drifted past. Near the window, she paused, scanning the attic nooks and feeling crushed by the low ceilings and somberness that surrounded her.

Yet, her heart thudded, knowing beneath the white shrouds more lovely antiques had been sitting for years, waiting to be rediscovered. She shifted to one and tugged off the covering. Beneath she found a roll-top desk. Holding her breath, she pushed back the tambour-cover. Nothing had been stored inside, and she released the air from her lungs.

What had she expected? Old letters? Saved greeting cards? Bills for rendered services long past? She shook her head at her imagination and moved on.

Beneath the next dust cover appeared a chaise longue supported by lion-paw feet and covered with bright upholstery in a blooming rhododendron design. She couldn't wait for Georgia to see it this coming weekend. She studied the piece accessing that it was a true antique and not a reproduction.

Next, she uncovered a cheval mirror with only a spattering of patina. Leaning against a wall, she found a lovely folding screen with petit-point panels, and farther on, a Seth Thomas mantle clock with ornate leaf carvings. The piece would be perfect for the formal parlor or perhaps one of the bedroom fireplaces. She couldn't help but grin, knowing Georgia would be thrilled seeing her finds.

Her nose twitching from the dust, she turned, scanning the attic one more time. In the darkest corner, more white sheeting caught her eye. When she moved closer and removed the dust cover, a washstand table with its decorative towel rod appeared from beneath, and sitting beside it, she found a commode set—basin, pitcher, and soap dish in a blue and rose floral pattern. Too perfect. Her heart gave a skip of pleasure as she listed her finds in the notebook.

When she looked up, something behind the table caught her eye. She moved the washstand aside and knelt next to the mahogany chest. Dust covered the deep-hued wood, and she swept it away with her hand and admired the marquetry pattern on top, then wiped the grit onto her jeans.

Not wanting to be disappointed as she was with the roll-top desk, she inched the lid upward. Inside she saw old movie magazines from the fifties and a wonderful antique photo album with its satin and velvet lid—items representing decades. Susan opened the album and gazed at the sepia photographs and tintypes, faded with time. Faces of the Taylors, she presumed, in an era she would never know.

She shifted the items from one side of the chest to the other, peering into its depth and knowing she could spend days going through the memorabilia. Near the bottom, she found a small wooden crate and stacked inside where notebooks. Her breath hitched. Journals, some with a lock and key like a diary.

Her hand trembled as she lifted one, opened to the first page and squinted in the gloom. Her pulse skipped. The handwriting looked like Libby's. She checked the date on the first page. January, 1951. She lowered her gaze to the bottom of the first page. She sucked in a breath when she saw Libby's signature.

Libby's diaries. As her excitement heightened, an edge of concern ruined the pleasure. Her thoughts flew back to the journal she'd found in Libby's room filled with regret and prayers for forgiveness. The journal had confused her. Would she find more of the same here?

She carried the book across the room to the sunlight and sat on the dusty floor, afraid to read, yet afraid not to. She drew in a breath and lowered her eyes.

Dear Diary, Today is January 1,1951. My friend Rosalie gave me this journal for Christmas, and so today I begin. My first diary, the first of a new year, and the first time I will write down my private thoughts. Maybe my secret thoughts.

Libby

She lowered the diary, her emotions tangled between eager curiosity and edginess. Libby may have written something she wanted no one to know. These were her private thoughts. She'd said it herself. But then she'd only been eleven, nearly twelve. What secrets would a young girl have?

She flipped through the pages and scanned entries that caught her eye, grinning at Libby's comments and feeling relieved she saw nothing secret, nothing that seemed noteworthy. Her entries were a young girl's scattered thoughts about friends, music, school, and life...and her not-so-good relationship with her sister Caroline.

"Dear Libby, you left us with a little bit of yourself." She caressed the cover. "Thank you."

Turning pages, a new one caught her attention.

October 7, 1951

Dear Diary,

I tried my best, but Caroline threw a hissy fit when I offered to fix her makeup for the high school Homecoming Dance. Everyone's going but not Caroline. She said she has schoolwork, but I know the truth. No one asked her.

When I'm in high school, I won't miss a party or dance. How can a person waste the best years of her life doing homework? Daddy says I probably won't make it to high school if I don't get my grades up. I'm passing, but he wants me to get As. I figure Bs and Cs are fine for my plans. I want to get married to someone as handsome as a movie star, like Gig Young or maybe Marlon Brando.

Libby

Susan chuckled, washed in her own nostalgia. She turned the book over in her hand and rubbed the cover. She longed to delve inside the others, but she felt a little guilty. Maybe she should check with Justin first. The diaries belonged to him. He should be the one to read them.

With the thought nudging her action, she forced herself to rise and replace the diary where she'd found it. She would tell Justin and see what he wanted to do.

She gave a last lingering look at the small wooden carton, picked up her notebook from the washstand and headed down the stairs, having one nagging question answered about the journal she'd found in her room. Writing her thoughts had not been something new for Libby.

When she reached the hallway, Susan listened for voices but heard none. She eyed her watch, surprised she'd been in the attic over an hour. The time had flown. She wandered into the kitchen, then to the gallery and spotted Justin with the inspector standing on the side steps near about where the inspector had parked his van.

Instead of bothering them, she wandered down the center steps into the backyard and headed toward the large outbuilding, a storage shed, she figured, though she'd never been inside. When she reached the door, she spotted a padlock.

So much for pirooting inside, she thought as she turned. When she gazed ahead, Justin was striding across the grass toward her.

"How did it go?" she called, trying to read the results from his expression. "Did everything pass inspection?"

♥

Hearing Susan's voice, Justin's stomach knotted when he looked up, seeing her in the afternoon sunlight. "Everything meets code—foundation, electrical, plumbing. No problem." He sent her a smile, admiring her dark hair glinting with red highlights. Her eyes sparkled with excitement as they had done yesterday when they'd discovered so many antiques in the two-story wing. When he reached her, he fought the desire to brush strands of hair from her flushed cheek.

"That's wonderful news."

He grinned and, unable to contain himself, chucked her chin. "It is." He pulled his gaze from her sparkling eyes and noticed the notebook in her hand. "What did you find in the attic? Anything worthwhile?"

Her hand shot out, and she clutched his arm. "You won't believe what I found. So many great things." He watched as she eyed her notes, then listened as she listed the items she'd found stored on the third floor.

"That's a relief. The more we find the less—"

"You have to buy." She let out a knowing chuckle.

"Not me, Susan. Us. I'd have no idea what would be a good buy and what wouldn't. You're my guide here. When it comes to antiques, I'm like a northerner who doesn't know a thing about grits."

She grinned, then swatted at him. "You don't give yourself credit, Justin."

Though teasing, a look appeared on her face he couldn't read. "We'll see, *cher*." He'd let the word slip, but she didn't seem to notice, and he felt better saying the endearment he'd been feeling.

Her look brightened. "Oh, I didn't tell you." She clapped her hands like a child watching a circus parade. "The best find was a cassone filled with some real treasures."

"Cassone?"

She chuckled. "You don't know what it is? It's a hope chest."

"A hope chest?"

"They called it a marriage chest years ago. Women stored their dowry in it—embroidery work, tatting, handmade linens—things to take into their new homes after the wedding."

"So, you found linens?"

"No." Her gaze darted away for a moment as if she were unsure of herself. "Among other things, I found Libby's diaries."

"Diaries. You mean those little books girls write in?"

"Yes. I saw her first entries from 1951. I thought you'd want to see them. Read them, maybe."

"What would I want to do reading old diaries." He shook his head, not wanting to delve into Libby's past. Not wanting to be hurt if she'd written something unpleasant about him. "Just leave them there or toss them."

"Toss them? I couldn't, Justin. They're Libby's, and she's kept them all of these—"

"Then let them be. I don't want to read them."

She looked away as if surprised at his attitude. "I'm sorry I asked."

He didn't respond. Too much had happened in Libby's life with his mother's near alienation of Libby and Libby's doting on him that caused undo problems. Why would he want to take a chance on reading something that would scar him again?

Yet, Susan's disappointment stuck in his thoughts. He motioned toward the outbuilding. "Do you want to look inside?" He figured it was a good way to change the subject.

She lifted her downcast eyes and shrugged. "If you have time."

He pulled out the ring of keys, found the correct one, turned the lock and pulled open the heavy door. The scent of decaying wood and mildew mingling with earth and time sailed from the shed. The sunlight penetrated the dark interior, lighting the tools that stood inside the doorway.

Rusted gardening tools—an old cultivator, a pony plow, shovels and hoes—had been propped against the barren studs. Barrels and bushel baskets stood in a heap. He scanned the outbuilding. "I think we're out of luck."

Susan looked at him but didn't seem to listen. She walked ahead of him into the shadows, then knelt and rose again, holding a floral-design banquet lamp. "There's another just like this." She sent him a wry look as if poking fun at him for what he'd just said.

He walked around the plow and a rickety set of shelves and looked into the wooden crate at the antique globe lamps. "They're in good condition."

"Perfect."

With a more positive attitude, Justin made a slow turn and spotted a fireplace screen leaning against the back corner. He pulled it out and watched Susan's face brighten.

"That's lovely. Very special," she said. As she stepped toward him, her eyes shifted beyond his shoulder. He followed her gaze.

She hurried past him and picked up something from another crate, then turned. "What is this doing in here?" She held it out to him. "A Wedgewood vase. This has to be from the eighteenth century."

Eighteenth Century. Where had all the valuable pieces come from? He wished now he could talk with Libby again and ask her more about the Taylor family. This time he would listen. But it was too late. Libby and all her wonderful memories were gone.

Susan clutched the vase against her. “I’d like to bring these things inside if you don’t mind. We can put them in one of the empty gallery rooms.”

He nodded and lifted the crate with the two lamps and propped it against his hip, then reached for the Wedgewood vase. His fingers clasped around Susan’s, and heat rolled up his arm. His gaze captured hers, and they stood a moment in the shadowed light, riveted by a connection they’d tried to forget, but never could.

Chapter Nine

Susan sat across from her mother at the dinner table. She'd avoided her mother's dour expression as much as she could rather than be overcome with her judgment. They ate, their silence dotted with sparse conversation. Susan preferred silence to the bitterness in her mother's tone.

Susan had prayed about it and asked God's help. She'd thought her mother had accepted her work at Rose Arbor, but now she questioned if her association with the manor and Justin went against God's will. The joy she felt finding the lovely antiques and the friendly moments with Justin seemed to outweigh her question. How could it be wrong?

"You're spending a lot of time next door," Margaret said, her voice jarring the silence.

With her pulse kicking through her veins, she looked at her mother's pinched face. "Georgia's coming tomorrow so I wanted to locate whatever furniture I can find in the manor. We need to know what we have to work with."

Her mother didn't respond but turned her attention to her po'boy.

The roast beef seemed tough, and Susan chewed it, swallowing and feeling a lump in her stomach. She had to eat or her mother would make some kind of snide comment that she'd rather eat with Justin, which was true. Guilt riddled Susan and took away the last of her appetite.

"Once we get Georgia's ideas and form a plan, Justin will be returning to Baton Rouge."

The tension lessened in her mother's face. "I don't understand why you're not looking for a real job, Susan. You can't play house with Justin for the rest of your life."

Her biting words sank into Susan's wounded spirit. The constant barbs pierced Susan's longing to heal their relationship. "For now, this is better than no job at all. Justin's paying me and I'm still looking for a permanent position. I've found jobs, Mother, but I wanted something that I know I'll love. If you want me to leave town, maybe I can find what I'm looking for outside of Devereaux. "

"I wasn't suggesting you leave. I was only—"

Susan waited, but she didn't finish the sentence, and Susan didn't ask, fearing it would lead to angry words. Most of the time, they had both tolerated the situation. Most of their conversation dealt with general topics like the weather or something her mother heard on TV.

After she forced down all she could manage, Susan excused herself. She tossed away the bulk of her po'boy, rinsed off her plate, and put it in the dishwasher. As if they had a mind of their own, her feet headed back to Rose Arbor.

When she arrived, Justin's car was gone, and as she paused by the door to find the key he'd given her, she noticed another rose bud in the slender vase. Each rose she saw there touched her, and no matter what Justin said, she knew he had picked it as a reminder of his promise.

Susan slipped the key into the lock and stepped inside. She stood in the wide foyer, breathing in the fresh scent of lemon polish mingled with Libby's potpourri.

She wandered through the empty rooms, listening to the silence, and when she returned to the foyer, the upstairs rooms beckoned her. She wandered along the hallway, peeking into the rooms, smelling the peculiar scent of old wood and the past.

Near the end of the hall, Susan stood in front of the attic door. Justin had said he didn't want to read Libby's diaries, but he hadn't said she couldn't. What would it hurt?

Even the question sent guilt down her back. The journals were Libby's private thoughts even though she'd shared so many stories about her youth with Susan. All teens had secret thoughts at one time or another.

Susan knew because she had them.

She placed her hand on the doorknob, feeling out of control as if her life hinged on Libby's. It made no sense, except to recapture her own teen years.

A mirror hung above a half table in the hallway between two bedroom doors. She glanced at her image, noting the soft lines around her mouth, the furrow between her brows. The mirror told her the truth. Though her mind flew back so easily to her teen years, she had past those years a long time ago.

She stood a moment gathering her senses. The diaries were no big deal. They gave her a fun insight into the fifties. Susan yanked at the knob and pulled open the door.

Her feet scuffed on the wooden steps as she climbed, and at the top, she went directly to the diaries. She'd take one home perhaps and then tell Justin how fun they were to read.

She grasped the diary and headed toward the light. Even after her rationalization, she still felt guilty, but that didn't stop her. She opened the diary and began to read. The entries were the same, but offered her a delightful view of life in the fifties—the music, the artists, the movie stars, and the drive-in restaurants and movies. The next entry caught her interest.

April 27, 1952

Dear Diary, Today is my fourteenth birthday. Daddy gave me my first bottle of perfume. It's called Blue Waltz. Caroline's moping around the house, because I'm getting all the attention. Every time she passes by, she reminds me she's nearly seventeen. Well, bust my drawers, I said to her, but Momma overheard me and now I'm in trouble all because of Caroline.

Why can't she be like the other girls. Daddy said I could have three friends over for a pajama party tonight, but now Momma said I couldn't until I apologize to Caroline. I'd rather eat dirt.

Happy birthday to me!

Libby

Bust your drawers. She hadn't heard that phrase in years. Susan grinned and lowered the journal. She could picture the scene and almost hear Libby challenge Caroline.

Her gaze fell to the next page, like a good novel, anxious to know what happened next.

April 28, 1952

Dear Diary, Okay, I broke my promise. No matter how hard I coaxed, Momma wouldn't give in, so I had to say I was sorry to bratty Caroline. She gloated, but I didn't care, I had my pajama party.

My friends Jeanette, Clara, and Dorie Mae came over, and everyone brought their 45s. I put my record player on the gallery, and we drank sweet tea and pretended it was mint juleps. We sang all our favorites—Too Young by Nat King Cole and How High the Moon by Les Paul and Mary Ford. Momma shushed us when we sang Mocking Bird Hill because she said Caroline couldn't do her homework. Yuk. She's such a cry baby.

But we were so embarrassed. We were jumping around like monkeys in the yard listening to Debbie Reynolds sing Abba Daba Honeymoon and singing at the top of our lungs, and I almost died. Lonnie LaMott and Tommy Bengard were hiding behind the oak tree, watching us. When Momma saw, she made us come in.

We stayed up all night eating chips and talking. I think Lonnie LaMott is cute, but I'm looking for someone with a future. Momma says love is nice, but security is better. I'm not so sure about that.

Libby

Susan chuckled at Libby's honesty. Perhaps Libby had been wiser than most teens with her awareness. Susan remembered having overnights with her girl friends. They'd done the same—eaten potato chips, looked at movie magazines, fixed each other's hair and gabbed all night long until her mother knocked on the door to remind them that other people were trying to sleep.

She stared at the page. Caroline had no interest in dating or marriage and from what she'd read, Libby had a flirtatious nature and loved the attention. How did it happen that Caroline married Adam Robard and Libby remained single?

Susan had never met Justin's mother, and she tried to picture the woman, but she could only create an image from Libby's diaries.

She brushed a strand of hair from her neck and heard the sound of a door slam below. Her heart jumped, and she felt guilty pirooting through Libby's diaries.

After replacing the diary in the chest, she hurried down the stairs to the kitchen. "Where've you been?" She heard no response, but she received the answer when she stepped into the room and saw Justin putting up groceries.

"There you are." He faced her with a bag of salad greens in his hand. "I went up town, and on the way back, I noticed an estate sale sign. We should go see."

"But Georgia's coming tomorrow. Should we wait?"

He looked disappointed and crossed the room to shove the salad bag into the crisper drawer. "I suppose. I'm only afraid we might miss out on the best deals."

"You're right. Let's take a look."

His frown lessened. "I heard from Rod, and I'm afraid I'll have to go back to Baton Rouge Saturday afternoon."

"Really." She tried to sound casual.

"I need Sunday to review a proposal. We have a meeting Monday morning. At least, I'll be back here to meet Georgia."

Though disappointed, she managed a pleasant expression. "I'll keep working while you're gone."

"Thanks. It'll only be a couple of days, I hope." He returned to the refrigerator. "Are you hungry?"

"No, I had lunch at home."

He delved into the meat drawer and pulled out some meat slices, slapped them on bread with butter, and sat at the table. "I'll just have this, and we can go."

She pulled out a chair and joined him. Some days she felt relaxed with Justin as if time hadn't changed a thing, but other times a barricade seemed to fall between them. Today was that day.

She could see in his eyes he was thinking, and she so longed to be part of his thoughts, to know where his mind sailed when that familiar look glazed his eyes.

She cleared her throat. "I want to talk with someone about brochures for Rose Arbor. We'll need promotion if you want people to know about the B & B. You'll need a website. That's very important, and hopefully we can hyperlink with the Chamber of Commerce site."

His distant look faded. "So soon. We're not ready for anything yet."

"No, but people begin planning vacations in advance. A web site announcing the grand opening of a new antebellum bed and breakfast will catch people's interest. Once we get an idea what we have to do—and I don't think too much—we can open on a small scale and then add the gallery rooms as they're ready."

A look of panic filled his face. "I didn't realize we were moving so quickly."

She stopped herself and drew in a breath. "I thought you wanted to get everything in order and open."

"I do, Susan. I'm sorry I sounded abrupt. This business is so new to me, and I'm worried about your getting things ready and then leaving for a new job. I'll be like an undersized catfish tossed back into the Mississippi for a bigger catch." He reached out and grasped her hand. "I'm not certain the bed and breakfast will be successful without your enthusiasm."

Despite the tension, the warmth of his touch caressed her skin, and she grinned at his analogy. "Don't worry, Justin. I won't drop you like a hot potato. You'll have someone to run Rose Arbor who knows as much or more than I do. I promise."

The comment had dragged from her throat. She wished it could be her. She longed to be part of the business, But she faced reality. *Lead me not into temptation*. The more time she spent with Justin the more difficult it would be to let go.

A brooding look washed over him again, and she longed to know what triggered those moments when he sat beside her but seemed so far away.

He jerked out of his reverie, rose, and brushed the crumbs from his lap. "Ready? Or isn't this a good time?"

"It's a good time."

For better or worse, Justin. Being with you has become good time.

♥

As Justin drove, he listened to Susan read the list of furnishings they still needed for the manor. He'd begun to note pride in her voice as she talked about the plantation house. He understood her earlier skepticism, and he suspected their past was the motivation.

His own memory never changed, and he could never repair the damage he had done to their relationship. If he would ever consider marriage, Susan would be a perfect wife. He'd always looked at her in a special way—not just her closeness to Libby—but because of who Susan was. She helped him find pleasure in life. She made him smile and helped him imagine. Imagination had never been his gift. Reality was what he'd been taught—ethics, career, social standing.

He could only see his life following his father's path. His father had spent most waking hours away from Robard Hall. When he was there, he seemed only the shadow of the man Justin figured he must be away from the manor's gloom.

He'd heard his father laugh one time when he'd dropped him off at Aunt Libby's, and it had startled him. Libby could make anyone laugh with her wonderful amazing spirit.

"So, what do you think?"

Susan's voice jolted him from his reverie, and he had to apologize and admit he hadn't heard her.

"Well, I'm not going over it all again."

"Let's just see what they have. If we see something special, we'll consider it—if the price is right." The price. He'd taken a long look at his finances, then asked himself why he had taken a chance with Susan's harebrained scheme. Harebrained? It was better than any he'd come up with.

They sat in silence the last few blocks. Susan seemed hurt by his distraction, and he wished it hadn't happened. Her excitement over every trinket she found at Rose Arbor amazed him, and he wanted to show his appreciation somehow, but the more he showed her that he cared, the more real his feelings grew.

"This is it," he said, pulling along the shoulder of the road. "The property is on a bayou of the Mississippi River." He turned off the ignition and slid from the car, then hurried around it and opened Susan's door.

"Thank you," she said, stepping to the ground and moving off ahead of him.

"Susan."

She slowed and glanced over her shoulder. Justin caught up with her and clasped her arm. "Look, I'm really sorry. My mind just got tangled in thought. I don't like it any more than you do."

Her look softened, and he felt her arm relax beneath his hand. "You were thinking of Libby."

"Yes." Among other things, he added to himself. "Let's start fresh. Okay?"

She nodded, and he sensed she meant it.

Once inside the house, Susan headed straight toward a dresser. He followed in the wake of her enthusiasm.

"It's walnut. Look at the intricate carvings." She darted in another direction. "And a matching bed table." She rubbed her hand along the wooden design. "Justin, this is a must. It's beautiful."

Justin eyed the price tag, letting his mental computer ring in the amount. He hoped the owners would barter.

Some rooms held nothing of interest, others held promise, and within the hour, they'd purchased the dresser and bed table, another washstand that Susan called a commode table, and a vanity table including a mirror and matching bench.

"We'll deliver," the seller told Justin as he bartered for price.

"Delivery and ten percent discount?"

"Yes sir, that's agreeable."

Justin wrote the check, wondering how many more he would have to write before Susan had enough furnishings.

"Thank you," the man said, as Justin handed him the check. "And you're welcome to walk the grounds. It's a lovely day, and you and your wife might enjoy the gardens."

Justin opened his mouth to correct the man, but he closed it. He'd never see the man again, and refuting it seemed to make more of it than he wanted to deal with at the moment. "Thank you. We might do that."

Susan looked flushed as he guided her outside and into the fresh air. "I'm sorry, Justin. He embarrassed you."

"It wasn't your doing, and it's not a problem." Justin grasped her arm and turned her to face him. "I'd never be ashamed of that, Susan. If I were the marrying kind, I'd—" He stopped himself and let the comment slide, figuring he'd do more damage to continue.

He kept his hand on her arm as they followed the sidewalk to the parking area where he stopped and looked toward the back of the house. "I'd thought we'd drop by my mother's when we leave here, but would you like to walk down to the bayou first?"

"Visit your mother?"

"I want to see how she's feeling, and I thought you might like to meet her." He lowered his gaze to her feet to check her footwear. She'd worn solid walking shoes. "The bayou first?"

"That would be nice," she said, not looking into his eyes.

He wondered if she had reservations meeting his mother or if she were just surprised. He linked his arm in hers as they stepped back to the sidewalk that led behind the house. He heard Susan's intake of breath when they reached the gardens. Colorful crape myrtles were in full bloom, the violets and reds in contrast to the sky. Below them, camellias grew, their coral reds and whites, splotches of color against the greenery. The scent of rich earth and sweetness of jasmine filled the air. Below the trees, azaleas still blossomed, and between the plants, roses weighed the boughs.

"It's like a fantasy." Susan's face glowed in the brilliant light.

"It's the early spring rain. This boggy earth holds in the moisture. It's good for the plants."

He'd released her arm as they viewed the array of color, but she grasped his arm again with a naturalness that took him back to the time when their friendship left no turning back from the power of emotions.

"Let's walk closer to the bank," she said.

His muscles tensed as they strode along the grassy slope to the river, and when the ground felt spongy beneath his feet, Justin grasped Susan's arm to help her over the pliant earth to the water's edge.

"It's wet here, Susan. We'd better stop."

She paused as he'd suggested.

Taller grass grew along the bank, and though he doubted an alligator had traveled so far, he gave a nearby log scrutiny to make sure.

As he watched, the log appeared to move, and he yanked Susan toward him. Disbelieving, he let out cry. "It's a—" But his anxiety turned to laughter.

"What is it?" Susan asked, her eyes as wide as a harvest moon.

"It's a turtle." He pointed to the creature, lumbering along the log until it tumbled to the earth.

The heat bore down on the sedge-strewn bank, and Justin felt the moisture penetrate his shoes. "We'd better go back," he said.

Susan tilted her head to the sunlight, giving him a grin and then took a step closer to the log and the turtle who lolled beside it. When she neared the creature, her scream pierced the air.

Justin's heart flew to his throat as he bounded toward her.

She opened her arms and threw them around his neck, her feet attempting to climb his legs. "What is it?" He yelled, trying to keep his balance with Susan digging her shoes into his shin.

"A snake." Her voice quaked her fear.

He swung her into his arms, then looked where she'd seen the reptile. When he located the coil of dark skin, its mouth spread open displaying the white interior, Justin caught his breath and stepped back.

"It's a water moccasin," he said, trying to sound calm while his own alarm told him to move away as fast as he could. "Cottonmouth. The bank must have recently flooded."

"It's poisonous," she whispered, still clinging to his neck.

"It is." Justin became aware of her small frame captured in his arms, the fragrance of her perfume, the feel of her arms around his neck, her breath against his skin. After stepping away, he paused a moment, enjoying the closeness and hating to set her down.

He didn't. He strode through the marshy grass until he felt solid ground beneath his feet and smelled the sweetness of the surrounding gardens—yet nothing as sweet as the flower he held in his arms.

"You can put me down now," Susan said, releasing her hold.

He lowered his arm, letting her feet swing to the earth and then let go. The emptiness washed over him with more emotion than seeing the snake. What was he doing? He had to stop before he lost control all together.

Susan's gaze captured his, and once more, he read so much in her eyes.

♥

Susan looked from the broad foyer toward the parlor where the servant, Clovis, had indicated Justin would find his mother.

The man led the way and rapped on the doorframe. "Mista Justin is here, Ma'am," he said, then motioned for them to enter.

When he headed across the room to his mother, Susan stopped at the door and looked toward the wiry woman sitting in a wingback chair at a small desk. Her gray hair neatly framed her face, her gray eyes looked sunken and dim as if they rarely saw the light even though sunshine spread across the lush carpet.

Justin turned and beckoned to Susan. "Mother, this is Susan Boyd. I don't know if you've been introduced."

She placed the papers she'd been holding on the desk. "We've never met formally. You're the farmer's daughter," she said, with little more than a glance.

Justin's expression looked frantic. "Mother, I told you—"

Susan gave a faint shake of her head and stepped forward extending her hand. "That's right, Mrs. Robard. I lived next door to Libby as a girl."

Catherine accepted her hand with a brief touch, then placed her knotted fingers in her lap.

"I told mother about your career in Baton Rouge," Justin said, as if trying to remind his mother she'd moved past the farmer's daughter title.

Susan didn't let the comment throw her. She was the daughter of an honest farmer who'd worked hard for a living. Looking at Catherine's well-groomed hands, she wondered if the woman had worked a day in her life.

"So, Justin, why the surprise visit?" Catherine's back remained stiff against the chair back.

The strain between them seemed evident to Susan, and she watched Justin withdraw as she'd seen him do so often.

"We were at an estate sale not too far from here, and I wanted to see how you're feeling."

"I'm perfectly fine, thank you."

A rap came from behind them, and Susan turned toward the sound. A middle-aged woman stood at the door, her eyes aimed toward Justin. "Y'all like some refreshment?" Though she addressed the question to Catherine, her gentle eyes settled on Justin.

Catherine drew up her shoulders. "Would you—"

Justin ignored his mother's attempt to respond. "We won't be staying, Rèmi, but thank you."

Susan's gaze volleyed like a tennis match as she watched Justin's reaction, then his mother's, then Rèmi's.

"Good to see you, Mista' Justin," the woman said, backing through the doorway.

Catherine watched the servant leave. "Are you still throwing money away on this plan to save the homestead?" She shifted her gaze to Justin.

"Throwing money away?" He shook his head. "No. I think it will be interesting, Mother, and a good investment. Can you imagine how nice it will be to share Libby's charming home plantation with visitors."

"Libby." She shook her head. "Libby lived in a fantasy world much of the time."

Susan had to agree that Libby did love fantasy. She'd seen Libby's drama demonstrated in her diaries, yet Libby had more substance than Catherine gave her credit. "I think a blend of reality and fantasy makes life interesting."

Catherine arched a brow. "Really."

"Susan means life should combine expectation with adventure." He glanced at Susan as if validating his definition.

"Life is reality," Susan said, "but I believe we should have dreams and hopes, too. Even the Bible tells us to have hope."

"The Bible says, 'When I was a child, I talked like a child, I thought like a child, I reasoned like a child. When I became a man, I put childish ways behind me.' Libby was never able to do that."

Susan glanced at Justin, trying to imagine why his mother would say such a thing, but Justin had again retreated into himself.

"Would you care to sit?" Catherine asked.

Susan thought escaping was more to her liking. She eyed Justin who awakened from his thoughts.

"I think we'll be going, Mother, but I'd like to show Susan the garden,"

"The garden is lovely." His mother's voice had muted to an agreeable tone.

"Goodbye, Mother. Please take care of yourself." He caught Susan's arm and turned her toward the doorway.

Susan mumbled a goodbye as they exited.

"I'm sorry," he whispered when they reached the foyer.

"It's okay." Susan saw the discomfort in his eyes.

"It's not okay." He held up a finger. "I want to speak with Rèmi before we leave. She'll tell me the truth about my mother's health."

Susan watched him leave through a doorway, wondering if this was the life as a child. If so, she could understand his inability to value marriage and his appreciation for Libby's single life.

And his inclination for distraction—Susan guessed Justin used it to get away from the tension and confusion that home life had to offer.

If this was wealth and status, it wasn't worth it. She'd been happy as a farmer's child. The problems that arose came later when she'd gone against her morals, when she'd disappointed her parents and herself.

The bitterness she'd witnessed between Justin and his mother comforted her in a strange way. She'd thought she and her mother had problems. Today their relationship hadn't seemed so bad. She needed to hang on to that awareness.

Chapter 10

Susan spent the morning anticipating Georgia's arrival, but Georgia hadn't been the center of her thoughts. Although the image of the cottonmouth sent chills down her back, more so had been the icy feelings when she thought of Justin's mother. She pushed the vision aside and clung to the memory of Justin's arms around her on the banks of the bayou.

She'd spent the evening in prayer, asking the Lord for guidance. She fought against her feelings. She felt resentment for Justin's mother, and worse the growing attachment she had for Justin. If she didn't act upon it, if she controlled the longing to nestle in Justin's arms and to feel his lips on hers, could it be a sin? How could loving be wrong?

The commandments said to lust after a neighbor's wife, servant or cattle was a sin, but Justin was a single man. The question wavered in her mind until she felt weary. Lead me not into temptation. She'd prayed those words so many times. She felt confident that she could control her actions. Only her thoughts seemed out of control.

As the questions pressed against her mind, she heard a car pull into the side driveway, and the heaviness lifted from her spirit. Georgia. She rose from the sofa and hurried to the back veranda to greet her.

Georgia's grin met her as she opened the car door. "Susan." She slid out and opened her arms.

Susan raced into her embrace. Now she would have someone to talk with, someone to toss around her ideas, and, she hoped, someone to validate her longing to read Libby's journals.

"I'm so glad you came, and I can't wait for you to see what we found."

"I remember the house." She swung her gaze in that direction. "It looks like Tara."

Susan nodded. "Wait until you see the antiques we found."

Georgia opened her back door and pulled out an overnight bag.

"Is that it?"

"I'm only stayin' 'til Sunday afternoon."

Susan gave her a poke. "I know. I'm just so happy to see you. I wish you could stay for weeks. I've been lonely for some real girl talk. It's been too long."

"Bless your heart," Georgia said, wrapping an arm around her back. "I can use some of that myself."

They giggled like schoolgirls heading up the stairs, and Susan didn't care how old she was. She and Georgia had been so close when she lived in Natchez.

"What I'd like," Georgia said, as she followed Susan inside, "is to have you move back to Natchez. You won't have a problem job-hunting there."

Move back to Natchez. Susan kept her smile, but the idea gave her pangs of regret. Natchez had been her prison, her Elba Island, her place of exile until she'd met Georgia when she'd overcome the trauma. Georgia had made life easier there, and Susan would never forget their friendship.

"I can't, Georgia. Not now. I just came back, and the relationship with my mother is still shaky."

"I never understood that, Susan. She's always been so nice to me."

Bitterness charged through Susan. "She likes you."

Georgia's face marched through a variety of expressions until she smiled. "Oh, you," she said, giving her arm a shake. "You're always pullin' my leg."

Susan managed to grin and kept the truth hidden.

Inside, Georgia looked around the living room, then peeked into the kitchen. "Where's your momma?"

"She's at a ladies circle at church. Let's get your bags into my room."

Georgia's brow flickered as if she didn't quite understand, then followed Susan down the hallway to her room. When they stepped inside, Georgia looked at the small room, then at Susan.

"If you're wondering, you're not sleeping with me in that little bed. We don't have a guest room, so I'll use the sofa." She smoothed the bed and gestured to a chair. "The linens are clean, and you can put your case on the chair, or I can clear a drawer."

"The chair is fine, Susan, but I could have stayed at an inn. I don't expect you to give up your bed."

"Shush. It's pure honey to have you here. I'd sleep on the floor."

Georgia shook her head but didn't argue. She set her bag on the chair and opened the latch. "I'd like to hang these two items and everything else is just fine."

Susan slid her clothes together on the rack, and Georgia hung a skirt and flowery blouse. "I thought I'd wear this to church." She turned and searched Susan's face. "That is if you go to church."

"I do." Susan grinned. "God and I are on speaking terms."

Georgia chuckled again, then clapped her hands together. "Now, when can I see that lovely plantation house again, and this time meet the mysterious Justin Robard?"

The look on her face sent the first inkling of concern coursing through Susan. She pushed a smile onto her face, not sure what she was worried about. "Come see." She beckoned Georgia to follow.

Georgia chattered about her drive from Natchez and about Rose Arbor. She'd met Libby on an occasional visit to Devereaux but never Justin. Susan had avoided talking about him when she lived in Natchez. Just saying his name had rent her heart.

Georgia paused when they passed the large oak and stopped, folding her arms and looking across the grass to the house. "It's a lovely place. It's just the kind of spot for a bed and breakfast. Can you picture the guests having afternoon tea on the gallery and walking through the flowers or sitting in the rose arbor?"

Susan looked at it with Georgia's eyes, seeing the visitors enjoy the traditions of a manor house. Yet more so, she tried to remove her desire to hold the house against her chest so no one else could share it. Strangers wandering through the rooms might destroy her private memories, those wonderful days before she'd made her tragic mistake with Justin.

She drew in a breath trying to control the unwanted feelings that worried her. "Let's go inside."

♥

Justin heard voices on the gallery and stood just inside the screen door, watching Susan who stood at the far end of the wing with a woman. Though he'd heard about Georgia, he'd never met her. Susan thought her friend had hung the stars in the sky, but then Susan admired most everyone but herself. He'd learned that in the past month, and it bothered him. She had so much to give, so many talents, but something had beaten her down and taken away her ability to see herself with others' eyes.

Justin also had a stake in Georgia's ability. He'd hoped she would be candid and knowledgeable about the property. He needed that now while big decisions were hanging like a catfish fighting against the line.

He pushed open the screen door and stepped onto the gallery. Both women looked his way. Susan gave him a wave, and Georgia sent him a broad smile.

"Justin," Susan said, picking up her stride, "this is my friend Georgia."

"Well now," Georgia said, extending her hand toward him, "I'm certainly glad to make your acquaintance."

He bit his cheek to avoid chuckling at her obvious flirting. "I've heard nice things about you, Georgia. Susan thinks a lot of you."

"The feeling is mutual," she said, giving Susan a one-arm hug. "I've been inside your home once or twice many years ago, but I've never seen the gallery bedrooms. The location will be excellent for a bed and breakfast." She gestured toward the outside rooms. "Along here, no stairs to climb. Privacy."

"Would you like to look inside?"

She chuckled. "I guess my little hint worked." She gave him a wink. "I'm dyin' to see the rooms."

Justin reciprocated by leading them back to the gallery bedrooms and opening the doors. He stayed back, letting the women go inside and piroot.

When Georgia saw some of the antiques they'd found, she let out a squeal like a stuck pig. Justin chuckled at her excitement over a few old pieces of furniture.

He returned inside, still hearing their voices, jabbering about the house, and he could only hope that Georgia's knowledge and Susan's wisdom would give him a solid plan.

Justin sank onto a kitchen chair as the future struck him. Susan had given him an idea and was bringing it to life, but what about next year or the next. He would need competent staff to run the house while he drove back and forth on weekends to oversee the place. He felt totally inadequate, and he didn't like the feeling.

He knew electronics. He could deal with technical data and theorems, but he had never been a people person. Susan was. If he could afford to keep her here, he'd be grateful, but the position could offer her no advancement. A bed and breakfast would probably be seasonal. How could he ask her to stay?

Georgia's animated voice drew nearer, and in a moment, Susan gave a rap on the door. "Justin?"

"Y'all come in." He pulled himself from the chair to welcome them.

Susan held the door for Georgia, trailing her inside.

"This is a lovely home, Justin. I can understand why you can't bear to let it go." Georgia pivoted as she looked around the kitchen. "This room has been modernized."

"Rose Arbor was my aunt's family plantation, but it was also her home. She enjoyed living with conveniences."

"Don't we all." Georgia gave him one of those looks he'd seen so often at the firm.

He noticed Susan's frown and wondered what she was thinking.

"Come see the parlor." He beckoned them to follow. He led the way, and when they came through the arch, he motioned them to sit.

Susan selected her spot on the settee, and Georgia took the chair he often chose. Instead, he settled beside Susan.

"Tell me about yourself," Justin said.

Georgia studied him a minute. "I'm a single woman. I come and go as I please."

He'd already deduced she was single. "You'll stay through the weekend?"

"I'll leave Sunday afternoon. I have to be back to work on Monday." She glanced at Susan, then turned back to him. "Bless her heart, Susan has given up her bed for me? I feel I'm infringing on her generosity."

Susan waved her hand as if trying to stop her. "It's not a problem. I told you, Georgia."

Justin took a quick look to catch Susan's expression. Her voice rang with a touch of aggravation as if they'd already discussed it and Susan had thought it was settled. She's been irritated at him enough times to recognize her tone.

"I know, Suga', but I'd willingly to sleep on the floor."

"Ladies," Justin said, knowing he had the solution, "there's no need for anyone to sleep on the floor. I have a rash of empty rooms here. Georgia, why don't you sleep in one of the furnished bedrooms on the gallery? I'm sure we can find linens. You'd be welcome, and the rooms are private."

"Well now, how kind of you, Justin. I'd never thought of that."

Her smile held a toying look, and it struck him that she had thought of it.

"Thank you," she said. "I'll accept your generous offer."

Susan shot Justin a look to let him know what he already knew. He'd fallen into Georgia's trap.

♥

As they headed back home, Susan's back prickled with irritation. Why hadn't she thought to ask Justin if she could stay at the plantation. Then Georgia wouldn't have come up with the idea first. She'd seen her flirting and had been disconcerted.

But why? Why wouldn't Georgia flirt with Justin. He was handsome, single, and charming. Only when they were alone and at odds did she see his darker side—the private side she couldn't understand.

"You're so quiet," Georgia said. "Suga', did I hurt your feelings?" She wrapped her arm around Susan's shoulders. "It's not that I don't appreciate your hospitality, but I just couldn't bear to know you weren't sleeping well while I slept in your bed. This is the answer."

"It's fine," Susan said. "I'm glad Justin invited you. I'd love to stay there sometime, just to have the experience."

"Why now, you should just ask. Justin likes you a lot."

She couldn't respond, and she was saved by her mother pulling into the driveway. "Momma's home," she said, praying her mother would keep the feelings she had about her private.

When they stepped inside, southern charm had won out over personal wills.

"Georgia," Margaret said, rising and opening her arms, "it's so nice to see you again. You look lovely."

"Thank you, Mrs. Boyd. It's always nice to visit."

Susan listened while her mother carried on polite conversation with Georgia. Once or twice, Susan read a subtle dig woven within her mother's dialogue, but she suspected Georgia hadn't picked up on it.

Georgia had never understood her relationship with her mother because she'd never witnessed it, and mostly, because she didn't know the facts. Though Georgia had asked Susan about it a few times, she'd finally accepted her general comments, and the discussion had ended.

After dinner, she and Georgia settled in her room to talk before Georgia left for Rose Arbor. That fact tightened in Susan's chest.

"You saw the furniture and other items I found in the shed. Tomorrow, I'll show you what's in the attic.

"You found some gems in the shed. I'd guess the fireplace screen is from the late seventeen hundreds. It appears in perfect condition."

"And the lamps. I love those."

Georgia's gaze drifted, and Susan sensed she wasn't thinking about the bed and breakfast.

"You never told me much about Justin, except that he was Libby's nephew. Are you blind, girl?"

"Blind?"

"You know what I mean."

"We're old friends, Georgia. That's all." Heat crept from her chest and up her neck. She willed it away, but it rose on its own determination.

"If I were living in town, I'd latch on to that dream man. What a hunk."

"You don't know him, Georgia. He's handsome, but Justin has a side not many people see."

Georgia leaned closer, a wry smile curving her lips. "Really? He seemed all charm to me."

Susan swallowed "Like I said—"

Georgia arched an eyebrow. "He has a side most people don't see. But you're one of them that has. So give, Susan. What's up? Your cheeks are the color of the roses in the arbor. What's going on between y'all."

"Nothing. Really."

"Suga', you can't fool Georgia."

Susan drew in a deep breath, struggling with how much to say. She had to protect herself, and she wanted to protect Justin—protect him mainly from Georgia. The thought mortified her.

"I had a crush on him when we were teens. He went off to college. I moved to Natchez, finished high school and went on to college. I never saw Justin after that. It's nothing."

"Yes, it is. Why didn't you tell me?"

"I can't tell you something that isn't."

"You can fool yourself, Susan, but you can't fool me. I wish I'd known. I was flirting with him the whole time we were there."

"I know."

"And that's why you were so quiet coming home." Georgia shook her head. "Mercy, I'm as dim as a five-watt bulb. I'm so sorry."

"Please, it's nothing. I-I don't know. I think so much of Justin, but he frustrates me, too." She wished she'd kept her mouth closed.

"Frustrates you?"

"He's so confusing. One minute he's conversing, the next he's staring off into space with those stormy eyes. Libby meant the world to him, and his only affection came from her. Justin grew up in a wealthy home. His father worked all the time, and his momma was cold as a cadaver from what I can gather."

Georgia flinched at her description.

"I mean his mother didn't give him attention, but Libby did. She spoiled him, but it was out of love." Her memory triggered an added thought. "Libby seemed to love everyone."

"She was charming the few times I met her, and so sincere."

Susan's pulse tripped. "By the by, I'm glad we got talking on this. I need your opinion."

Once again, Georgia's interest had been piqued. "About Justin?"

"No. Libby." Susan uncurled her legs from beneath her and stretched.

Georgia looked curious. “So, tell me.”

“I found Libby’s diaries in the attic.

“Her diaries? She’d been keeping a journal?” She rose and ambled her way to Susan’s chair and sat on the arm. “Tell me.”

“They’re from her teen years.” Susan swallowed back finding the one in her bedroom. That journal wasn’t for anyone to see. “I read a few entries, but I didn’t think it was right to read them all without Justin’s permission. I feel like they are his.”

“And he forbade you?”

“No. He said he didn’t want to read them, and I should toss them.” Her pulse gave another kick. “I can’t do that.”

She leaned forward. “But he didn’t say you couldn’t read them.” Her conspiring smile said it all.

“I know, but I’m afraid if I do ask if he minds, he’ll say not to.”

“Don’t ask and read them if you want. You don’t have to tell Justin.”

Susan still struggled. “But I feel guilty.”

“Don’t. You won’t find one commandment that says you can’t read old diaries. You can’t gossip about them or use them to hurt someone, but you can read them.”

“I suppose I’m making a big ruckus out of this. The ones I looked at is from 1951 and 52.”

“The fifties. That was a great time in history. All that rock and roll.” She chuckled, rising and giving her hips a playful swivel before ambling across the rug and plopping back into the chair. “You’ve probably already heard most of it anyways. You said she told you yards of stories about her teen years.”

“I loved to hear about the fifties. It was a time of innocence, not like the seventies and eighties when drugs and sex became so important. She talked about hayrides and ice-skating parties. Sock hops and her favorite movie stars. She made those days come to life.”

“Then read the journals, Susan. What difference will it make?”

♥

“So, what do you think?” Susan asked Saturday afternoon after she and Georgia had moved all of the furniture into the center of the attic.

“Perfect as Granny’s pecan pie,” Georgia said, admiring the upholstery of the chaise lounge.

"I know. I couldn't believe what I'd found." She held the best for last and lifted the lid on the marriage chest. "And see here." She bent to retrieve one of the diaries. "Here it is. Libby's first." She handed the diary to Georgia.

Georgia opened the book and read the first page, then flipped the leaves, her eyes scanning the pages. "You'll have fun, reading these." She closed the book and knelt beside the trunk. "How many are there?"

"A heap of them in that box."

Georgia opened one that looked more like a journal and scanned the pages. "She stopped writing in it daily. See."

Susan peered at the ledger, noting Libby's entries had jumped from April 14, 1968 to July 4. "She used it more to journal, I think." Her heart skipped when she saw references to Justin's mother. Intrigued, she longed to read further, but she'd wait until another day when she was alone.

"You must read them," Georgia said.

"I know."

Susan heard Justin clear his throat and she gasped, letting the journal fall from her hands into the chest. She closed the lid as guilt flooded over her.

"Having a good time?" Justin asked.

"We are." She gestured to the furnishings they'd gathered. "We need to get these downstairs."

Justin eyed the collection. "We'll need help on that. I'll contact someone when it's time."

He stood at the head of the stairway, studying her, and Susan feared she'd offended him.

"Is something wrong?" She kept her shaking hands at her sides. She felt silly reacting so dramatically over showing Georgia Libby's diaries.

"Not at all. I thought I'd make y'all dinner since you've worked so hard today. It's the least I can do."

"That's so kind of you," Georgia said. "I'd love that."

Susan released a ragged breath. "Thanks. That would be nice." She looked around the attic, then motioned toward Justin. "I think we're done up here."

"Then come down and get some fresh air while I cook."

He turned and descended the stairs as they followed. At the bottom,

Susan paused. "I'll be with you in a minute. I want to wash my hands. I'll be there directly."

Georgia followed Justin into the kitchen, and Susan slipped into the bathroom and turned the lock. She leaned her back against the door and sucked in a full breath. Why did she feel so guilty about the silly diaries?

And now Georgia had opened doors that Susan didn't want opened. Georgia stopped flirting with Justin because she'd realized Susan had feelings for him. Did Justin know? She'd tried so hard to hide the longing that grew stronger every day.

Could she ever forget those earlier years? She pulled her back from the door and rested her hands on the sink. Could she ever look at Justin with fresh eyes? Why couldn't she let those memories fade and see him in the light of the present?

Concern trickled through her—a possibility that had never entered her mind before. Was she looking for atonement? She could never offer herself to another man, not with her past hanging over her head. But if she found love with Justin again, did she think that would erase her sin or make things right? The weighty thought pressed on her until she wanted to cry.

Lord, please. Don't let me think that way. I know I've been forgiven. I know I can't make up for my sin. You gave your life and covered my sin with love. Please, help me to accept that.

Muddled in thought, she washed her hands and rinsed her face, then patted it dry and looked at herself in the mirror. She looked the same, but she prayed she had changed inwardly with her prayer.

When she joined Georgia, she and Justin were in the kitchen working on dinner. Justin hovered over a large steaming pot while Georgia peeled potatoes. She grinned when she saw a pile of corn on the cob.

"You're making crawfish boil," Susan said. "I'll shuck the corn."

Justin looked at her over his shoulder. "It'll be a picnic."

She grinned and set to the task of pulling the husks from the cob and cleaning away the strands of golden hair. When she carried the ears to the pot, Justin dropped them in and the scent of spices rose with the steam.

Perspiration beaded Justin's forehead, and he wiped it away with a paper towel and motioned toward the gallery. "Let's get some air while this stews."

Susan grabbed her notebook from the dining room table where they had been working earlier.

They sat on the gallery, drinking sweet tea and talking about what they still needed for the bed and breakfast until dinner was ready.

They ate with their hands, on newspaper spread out on a large table on the gallery. The savory meat pulled from the little mudbugs, and she grabbed napkin after napkin to wipe the juice from her fingers.

At the end of the meal, Justin rose and pushed his chair beneath the table. "I'm sorry to hurry off. Remember, I told you I need to get back to Baton Rouge tonight. I have my luggage in the car already. I should be back mid-week. Probably Wednesday."

Susan's chest tightened. She'd forgotten.

"You have a key, Susan. Do you mind cleaning up the mess here? I don't want to rush y'all." He gestured to the table.

"Not at all. The boil was wonderful." She forced a lighthearted tone to her voice.

Georgia stood. "It was, Justin. Just delicious."

Justin nodded his thanks. "You can lock up for me." He turned and extended his hand to Georgia. "It was nice meeting you. Thanks for all you've done for us."

For us. Us. Justin and her. Susan and Justin. She felt like a love-sick teen writing a boy's name with hers in her notebook.

Justin gave a final wave and headed inside, and in a few moments, he returned, called his goodbye and bounded down the sidesteps. She heard his car door slam followed by the rev of the engine, and the car pulling away.

"You're in love," Georgia said.

Susan felt her jaw slack. "I'm what?"

"In love. How long has this been going on?"

"I'm not in love. I admire Justin. My heart goes out to him having lost one of the most important people in his life."

"It's more than that, Susan. Why fight it?"

"I'm not fighting anything."

Georgia shook her head. "It's your life, but I don't understand why you can't admit your feelings. He admires you. Let him know how you feel."

He admires you. Susan realized that, but love was different. He'd loved her once. Or had he? "Why open myself for hurt, Georgia?"

"Hurt? He's moody maybe—although I haven't seen it. But he's not spiteful."

"Spiteful? No. Never."

"Then I'd make a move, but it's your life, Suga'."

Georgia and her speculating were getting on Susan's nerves. "Picture the headline, Georgia. Little Farm Girl Moons Over Wealthy Businessman from Prominent Family. How does that sound?"

"It sounds stupid." She rose and wrapped her arms around Susan's shoulders. "Bless your heart, Susan, you've missed the point. Love has no boundaries. Justin has a good head on his shoulders. He's looking at you with the eyes of a man who holds you in admiration. Admiration can slip into love with the blink of an eye."

Love has no boundaries. If Georgia only knew, the barricade Susan had to hurdle.

Georgia gave her shoulder a shake "Just blink your eyes, Susan, and see what happens."

Chapter Eleven

Susan unwound her legs from beneath her on the settee, leaned back and eyed her watch. She'd been certain Justin would arrive home today. He'd said mid-week, probably Wednesday. She'd been nervous about bringing down the diaries, worrying about what Justin would think, but she decided to admit she was reading them. She'd feel much better by being honest. So far, she'd found nothing except Libby's delightful personality bubbling from the pages.

She slipped deeper into the settee, anxious to find a sofa for the other parlor. Then she could really stretch out.

She opened the diary and glanced at Libby's thoughts. Through the summer of 1952, boys had become even more important to Libby. She'd spent the summer mooning over one young man after another or going to the soda fountain with girlfriends and drinking malted milks.

Susan focused on the next entry and laughed.

August 2, 1952

Dear Diary,

School's about to begin, and I'll be glad. Summer gets boring especially when it's so hot and muggy. Since we got a television set, all Daddy talks about is politics—President

Truman this and President Truman that. Then he goes on about the Korean War. All I want to do is stay in my room with a fan and read books or listen to the radio. I just love Tony Bennet singing Because of You.

I wish Daddy would let me have boys over. He said I was too young. He keeps reminding me that Caroline doesn't have boys over. Well that's because Caroline doesn't want to have any boys over. She says she doesn't want to date and get married. All she does is read and play the piano. Daddy said I should take up an instrument. Not me. I can't sit still that long. Maybe if I bug Caroline, she'll fix herself up a little and get a date. Then she'll open the door for me.

I know. No such luck.

Libby

Susan's smile faded as dusky shadows stretched over the gallery. Disappointment replaced her grin. By now she guessed Justin wouldn't be back tonight after all. She closed the diary, lifted her glass, and carried both inside.

While Justin had been gone, she'd accomplished a number of things. She'd made a list of the furnishings she still needed and had picked up paint samples at the paint shop. Staying authentic was important, and she wanted to use colors that were common in the antebellum homes. She'd looked at fabric to re-upholster the horse-back shaped rocker. She'd settled on a brocade that looked authentic for the time period and heavy enough cloth to wear well.

She'd checked with the city offices and collected the forms she needed for the bed and breakfast license, and had talked with the clerk at the Office of Cultural Preservation in Baton Rogue to obtain the rules for renovation and restoration of homes on the National Register. Still so much had to be done, but she'd made a good beginning.

Instead of returning home, Susan settled in the parlor and turned on the light, then focused her attention on the diary. She skimmed the pages but when something captured her attention, she became an avid reader.

October 10 1952

Dear Diary,

"I'm yours." I love that song by Eddie Fisher, and they

played it in the barn after the hayride tonight. And we sang Jambalaya by Jo Stafford, laughing at the part about a crawfish pie and a filet gumbo. I had so much fun, except for Caroline who kept her eagle eye on me.

Daddy let me go to the church's youth group hayride only if Caroline came along. She threw a hissy fit when Momma told her she had to go. She sat like a lump on the wagon while we all sang songs—Breaking Up Is Hard to Do and Matilda by Cookie and the Cupcakes. And when Tommy Bengard and I sneaked away for a minute, he kissed me on the lips. I thought I would die.

I was so excited. I'm fourteen and had never been kissed!!! But afterward, all I could do was pray that Caroline didn't see and tell Daddy.

Libby

Susan smiled at Libby's entry, then paused a moment, recalling her own first kiss. She'd been sixteen; Libby, fourteen. Libby would have certainly won the prize if first kisses had been a contest.

Justin's face centered in her thoughts—no longer the young Justin, but the man she knew now. She pictured his wide-set stormy eyes, his classic nose, firm jaw, and the deep cleft in his chin that winked when he smiled. Susan wished he would smile more often.

Oh, Justin, if only... the impossible thought faded, and Susan focused on the journal.

November 17, 1952

Dear Diary,

Tomorrow is Caroline's birthday. She's seventeen. I don't even want to celebrate it. I'm still angry at her for telling Daddy about Tommy and me at the hayride. She'd seen us. I know the kiss was too good to be true.

But I'm still grinning because I overheard Momma tell her that if she didn't start dating, she'd wind up an old maid. Momma's old-fashioned phrases make me laugh. I think they've invited Daddy's business partner Mr. Robard's son for dinner. The young man's name is Adam. I can't wait to see him. I bet

he's a square and uglier than sin.
Libby

Adam Robard. So, the fathers' must have collaborated so that Adam and Caroline met. Susan had read stories of business partners wanting to keep a business strong by arranging marriages, but that was in the old days, or in fiction, not in real life. She glanced at the next entry and smiled when she read Libby's first sentence.

November 18, 1952
Dear Diary,
Wow! Was I wrong. Adam Robard is handsome. I can't believe his parents made him come here for dinner. He seemed so nice, and we laughed and talked, except for Caroline. I hate to say it, but I felt sorry for her tonight. She looked as nervous as a cat in a room full of rocking chairs.

Adam was so polite. He held out Caroline's chair at dinner. I know it's a sin, but I'd wished it was my birthday. Momma gave me the eye when I was too talkative, but I couldn't help it. Adam has beautiful eyes, and when he smiles, they seem to twinkle like the diamonds on Mrs. Robard's fingers. I've never seen the likes of diamonds that big.

After they left, I heard Momma say Mrs. Robard's diamonds looked pretentious. I think I know what that means. It must come from the word pretend. So, she meant they were fake. Fake or not, they were sparkling like the sun on the morning dew.

I wish I could help Caroline be more relaxed. She's not an outgoing person. I never could understand why. I'm certainly talkative.
Libby

Questions arose again. Why the push to bring Caroline and Adam together? If Adam were as handsome as Libby said—although that was coming from a hormonal teenager—then Susan figured Adam wouldn't need his father's help in meeting a young woman.

Susan scanned the rest of the year, but nothing caught her eye. Adam Robard was never mentioned again. Yet Susan knew he had to return into the picture since he and Caroline did marry, eventually.

♥

Justin threw his bag into the car and headed back to Devereaux. He was getting a late start, but it had taken that long to finish his business.

He'd picked up the telephone to call Susan so many times in the past days, but he'd stopped himself. He had nothing to say, except to hear her voice. He couldn't believe how much he missed her voice and her smile. He felt whole for the first time in years since he'd been spending time at Rose Arbor.

Was it the manor or Susan that made him feel different? He'd asked himself numerous times, but he always came up with the same result. A little of both. He'd spent the happiest part of his youth at the plantation house with Aunt Libby and later with Susan, and once again, they were there together—except for Libby—but he'd begun to accept that.

Libby had enjoyed a full life even though she'd died too young. Justin often wondered, with such a lust for life, why Libby hadn't married. He guessed it was the same reason he hadn't. Life seemed to be easier as a single person. Marriage didn't guarantee much of anything from what he'd seen growing up.

Some people thrived in marriage. He thought about his partner Rod. The man doted on his wife and child even though he worked long hours. When he was home, Justin knew they did things together. He often talked about games he'd played with his son and places they'd gone, and the way he talked about his wife sometimes filled Justin with a mixture of envy and confusion. He could never be sure his life would be as fulfilled as Rod's. Justin had grown up on Robard turf. Life had been different.

Because of that difference, he needed to guard himself with Susan. They were both vulnerable in a way, both involved in a major life change—his losing Libby, Susan leaving her career, and both finding themselves back in Devereaux. The situation left them hot-wired for trouble. No matter how lovely, no matter how she pleased him, Justin knew marriage wasn't for him. He had too many issues to resolve, too many attitudes to change. Yet when he thought of her, his chest tightened, and he wondered if he could be wrong.

Could he give it a try? Would Susan even want him?

He drew in a lengthy breath, fighting his wavering thoughts. He turned on his headlights as the sun sank below the horizon.

He pictured the plantation house surrounded by towering oaks, the Federal architecture with its columned portico, the balcony running the length of the building, its black shutters and fanlight front door that welcomed so many people. Calling Rose Arbor home seemed so easy.

Headlights flashed past in the southbound lanes, and he squinted to fend off the glare. The frown brought his mother to mind. Why had she been so rude to Susan, and why had she refused visiting Rose Arbor to select some mementos? He longed to know why she resented Aunt Libby.

Often, he wondered how they could have been sisters, stemming from the same parents and yet be so different. Even as a boy he'd known his mother and Libby were like two magnetic poles, pulling in opposite directions. Libby drew him to her, and his mother pushed him away.

An old ache settled inside him, and he snapped on the radio and turned up the volume. Loud music might drive out the memories.

He left the highway and turned down the road leading to Rose Arbor. When he pulled into the parking space, he lifted his bag from the trunk and walked up the side stairs of the gallery to the dark house. It reminded him of the night he'd sat outside, unable to open the door. Outside the kitchen, he made out the shape of the glass vase and, in it, a rose. He smiled, seeing the blossom. The rose had become a game Susan had been playing with him.

He jiggled his keys, locating the one he needed, slipped it into the lock, and turned it. The door clicked open. He reached up to snap on the light and entered the kitchen. He took a moment to let his eyes adjust to the brightness, then headed for the doorway into the dining room, but he came to a stop when he saw a note propped against the coffeepot.

He held the paper running his finger over the neat, feminine script—every I dotted and every comma in the right place. He slipped the note into his pocket and kept his fingers wrapped around the paper as he headed for the bedroom. He couldn't believe how much Susan invaded his life.

♥

Susan opened her eyes and saw a streak of light glinting along the edge of her window shade. She brushed the sleep from her eyes and rose on one elbow to read the clock. Six. It was too early to get up and face her mother. She'd come home with such hope after seeing Justin's mother, but she'd been met with tolerant acceptance.

She plumped her pillow and scooted herself into a semi-seated position, then pulled Libby's diary from her bed table drawer.

Last night she'd been intrigued and had read halfway through 1953. The tension between Libby and Caroline leaped from the page. They were so different.

Adam Robard's name did reappear early in 1953. He'd called Caroline to ask her out, but she'd refused again. Her father had been furious. Libby said he told Caroline it was time she grew up.

Susan grinned, thinking he should have said that to Libby. She was more than ready.

Susan opened the diary where she'd left off and began to read.

August 14, 1953

Dear Diary,

Today the house seemed as quiet as a tomb. We just heard that Adam Robard is engaged. Momma and Daddy's plan failed, and poor Caroline will never hear the end of it.

I don't know why they insist Caroline get married. Today girls can almost support themselves if they have skills. I'm studying business classes because I'd like to become a travel agent, and that's about the best classes I can think of. My next favorite is an airline stewardess. Daddy says no way will I be traipsing all over the U.S. in an airplane, but it sounds glamorous to me. I might even fall in love with a pilot.

Libby

Susan turned the page and skimmed the entries. Libby had become a sophomore when school started that year and won the election as class secretary. Libby seemed happy that Caroline had graduated the past June and had entered Louisiana State University.

November 18, 1953

Dear Diary,

Caroline turned eighteen today and is definitely an old maid like Daddy said. She came home from LSU and said she's not going back. You should have heard Daddy carrying on like the world had come to an end.

I can't wait to be an adult. I'm fifteen and that seems adult enough for me, but Momma said to be one you have to act like one. How can I when they won't let me do anything?

I didn't tell them when I went to Clara's to spend the night we went to Walgreen's for a soda, and we met Tommy and Lonnie there. Tommy flirted and said I was the prettiest girl in Devereaux. He kept singing No Other Love Have I in my ear. I like Tommy, but he's not my dream man.

Libby

Dream man. Libby's comment made her chuckle. Yet she had to face it. She'd had a dream man for years. Justin. If God truly guided her life, for what purpose had the Lord brought Justin and her together again?

Susan leaned back, picturing the Libby she knew and surprised how in a strange way she looked a little like Catherine, except Libby always smiled. Their outlook was the difference. Both women were slender with straight backs, heads held high, but Libby's head turned toward people, her broad smile welcomed everyone. Catherine seemed evasive and arrogant. Yet Libby, too, had the gray eyes, except hers had a twinkle in them.

Letting her visions fade, she returned to the diary, and when she'd finished the one from 1953, she slid it back onto her nightstand and slipped her legs over the edge of the bed. She could hear her mother up and probably preparing breakfast, so she rose and headed to the bathroom to shower. Before she left the room, she dropped the diary into her shoulder bag. She wanted to avoid her mother's curious eyes.

After she'd showered and dressed, Susan followed the sweet scent and entered the kitchen.

"I made griddle cakes." Her mother turned toward her and set a platter on the table.

Susan noticed the bright blueberries peeking from the cakes. "These are my favorite."

"I know."

"This was thoughtful. Thank you."

"Welcome." Her mother poured coffee into their cups, returned the carafe to the brewer and sat.

Susan eyed her, aware that she was apologizing in her own way. She poured on syrup and pushed her fork into the fluffy dough, cutting off a hunk. She slipped the treat into her mouth and licked her lips. "They're good, Momma," she said, using the name she'd called her mother before the tension.

"Thank you."

The room became silent with only the sounds of their forks hitting the plates, the tink of the coffee cup against the saucer, and an occasional birdcall that came through the window.

Finally, her mother laid her fork on top of her plate and shifted in her chair, and Susan knew another something would be said.

"Are you still looking for full-time work?"

"I'm checking the want ads every day, but right now Rose Arbor is a full-time job. While Justin's been gone, I've gotten a lot done. I think he'll be surprised."

"He's been gone again?"

"Yes. For a few days. He won't be staying in town often. He has his business in Baton Rouge."

"He's not moving into Rose Arbor?"

"No. Justin'll have a room at the house when he stays in Devereaux."

Her mother nodded as if Susan's response had satisfied her, and she gave her own sigh of relief. If they could at least talk without the digs and innuendos, she was certain their relationship would improve. It all had to do with... With what? She rose and rinsed her plate under the tap as she thought.

Trust. It had to do with trust. God wanted people to trust each other out of love. Susan knew that, but it was difficult to love. Trusting meant having confidence in someone, and she had lost her confidence in her parents' love when they sent her away, because they'd lost confidence in her.

But God gave people second chances. Secrets couldn't be hidden from God, and He still loved her. Although it had taken time, she'd finally figured that out. She recalled her talk with Pastor Ralph about patience and forgiveness, and she realized her bitterness had remained.

She continued to feel abandoned.

Susan had almost memorized two verses from Psalms 90 she thought of each morning. They had become her litany. *You have set our iniquities before you, our secret sins in the light of your presence. Satisfy us in the morning with your unfailing love, that we may sing for joy and be glad all our days*. Though she said the prayer, she wondered if she truly exercised the request. Could she ever reach her mother with unfailing love?

The question clung in her thoughts when she returned to the bedroom for her handbag. She paused to repeat the prayer, and then returned to the kitchen. Her mother was rinsing the dishes, and she stepped beside her.

"I'm going to work, Momma. You know where I am." Susan leaned over and kissed her mother's cheek.

She didn't look back, but she knew her mother had stopped rinsing dishes, and she guessed she was watching her as she opened the door to leave.

Chapter 12

Justin heard the kitchen door close. He folded the morning paper and laid it on the coffee table, then picked up his mug and headed for the kitchen. The excitement he felt astounded him. He recalled similar feelings so many years ago, hearing Susan's voice at the door when she'd come to visit Libby.

"Good morning," he said, managing to sound casual.

"Hi. What time did you get in?"

"Late last night. Thanks for the note."

She looked a little uneasy. "I thought you'd be in yesterday—but earlier."

"That's what I'd planned, but the deal took longer than I expected. I should be here for a few days, barring any crises in Baton Rouge."

Finally, she dropped her handbag on a chair, then stood as if weighing her thoughts.

Justin studied her and suspected her problem. "You're tired. I'm working you too hard."

"You weren't here so you can't blame yourself. I stayed late last night."

Had she stayed waiting for him? The possibility dropped through his belly like a fast elevator ride. He shifted behind her and raised his hand, letting his palms relax on her shoulders. "You look stressed."

He felt her tense for a moment and recalled his earlier thoughts about avoiding Susan. That had been his intention, so why did he persist in deluding himself about his feelings. He loved the feel of her flesh beneath his hands, and he plied his fingers into the knotted cords of her shoulders and then up her neck.

His fingers touched the chain of her locket, and its closure had shifted to the side. Justin pulled it around and centered it at her neck, feeling a deep longing to kiss the white skin beneath her hair. He let his fingers linger there a moment before he pressed his thumbs into the softness and massaged away the tension.

Susan didn't resist. Instead she rolled her head from side to side and released a soft groan of pleasure. "That feels wonderful. Thanks."

He didn't want to tempt himself any more than he had already, and he didn't want to frighten Susan, so he gave her shoulders one last squeeze and let his hands drop, but the locket stayed in his mind. "That's the locket Aunt Libby gave you."

"Yes," she said, fondling the pendant.

"Does it open?"

She touched the pendant. "You mean to hold photographs?"

He nodded.

"Yes. They're the same as the day Libby gave it to me."

"May I see?"

She looked uncomfortable, but she pulled the tiny latch and opened the round charm. When he looked at the photographs, his chest tightened.

"It's Libby and you." Her gaze captured his.

"I see that."

"I thought it was very touching. She loved you so much, Justin."

He could only nod, strangled by emotion. He pushed the two sides together until the pendant snapped closed, then let it drop against her neck. He covered his ragged breath. "What are your plans for today?"

Her eyes still looked glazed and heavy-lidded, he assumed from the massage, and it took her a moment to respond. When she did, he followed her into the dining room where she'd left her notes. They sat in the wooden chairs while she reviewed her conversations with the Historic Preservation office in Baton Rouge and the city about the license.

"I checked on building codes, Justin, and we're fine with that. Once we're set up, we need a fire inspection, but that's only a formality. The business won't require a food service license if we serve fewer than five guests, and if we serve continental, we don't need a license at all, so we'll have to decide."

He couldn't help but admire the professional way she'd handled the business. Would he have thought of all the details? He was certain he wouldn't have.

"We'll need to register the business name once we decide. We have to contact the Secretary of State office for that."

We. He loved the sound of the word. We have to do this, and we need to do that.

"You've done so much the past week, Susan." His amazement grew. "Thanks."

"That's what you hired me for."

She smiled, but the thought didn't set well. Hired seems so cold. When she'd finally agreed, she'd taken the job with more enthusiasm and commitment than he'd expected.

Susan rose and stacked the documents into a pile. "Why are you grinning?" She paused with a curious look.

"Just thinking."

"You should do that more often."

"What? Think?" He rose to pick up one of her notes that had slipped to the floor.

"No." She chuckled. "Smile. It looks so good on you."

He lay the paper on the table, unable to stop himself. "You look good all the time, Susan." He placed his palm against her hand, then raised it up her arm and drew her to his side.

Her face filled with confusion, then expectation, then wonder. As if she read his mind, she tilted her lips upward in agreement, and he lost himself. He pulled her into a full embrace. His lips met hers with such pleasure his knees weakened. How long had he waited, yearning to kiss her again, remembering the sweetness, the yielding that had undone him.

Like melted wax, the present mellowed into the past. He felt her heart beating against his as it had so many summers ago. A ragged sigh rolled through her, and then she eased back, a flush glowing on her cheeks.

"We can't do this, Justin."

Her words felt like a slap, and he dropped his arms and stepped back. "I'm sorry. I didn't mean to offend you."

"You didn't offend me, but it's dangerous. It's—"

"We're adults now, Susan. We're not silly kids, playing at romance."

"You're right. We're adults who know where kisses can lead."

"Then you admit you're attracted to me." He studied her face, hoping to see the truth.

"Yes, I am."

Her answer surprised him. He'd expected denial or an argument, but she'd given in with no fight. "Then why can't we—"

"I'm working for you now. Years have passed. Time—"

"Time changes things." He'd known where she was heading.

"We're not the same people we were then. We've both hardened. We have our own lives."

"I'm not proposing, Susan. I'm just..." What was he saying?

He watched her expression sink to dejection.

"I didn't mean it that way." He touched her cheek, and she pulled away. "I'm only suggesting if we enjoy each other's company and have fun together, then let's enjoy the relationship. We've been hiding behind our real feelings since we saw each other the night you came back."

He winced, having revealed too much.

"But our relationship is different, Justin. We went too far in our youth."

He was startled by the sorrow in her eyes. He excused this indiscretion. They'd both been willing, but this morning he saw that it had hurt her even more than he'd realized.

"What will stop us now?"

Her question weighted his chest. "Our good sense." But did he have any?

"Lead us not into temptation."

"I can control my actions now."

Her head drooped, and she shook it slowly not making eye contract.

"*Cher*, forgive me. You're a beautiful woman. You're special. I admire you. What can I say? I shouldn't have kissed you."

♥

Susan raised her eyes and saw the desperation in his face. She'd been as much at fault this time as he had. She'd sensed he wanted to kiss her, and she'd wanted him to. How could she explain her fear without telling him what had happened years earlier?

"I won't kiss you again, *Cher*. Please. I won't do anything you don't want me to. Let's be friends like we have been."

His eyes pleaded, and she couldn't look away. Her stomach knotted with her longing to let temptation win, but she knew better now. "We're working together, and I don't want this to come between us, Justin. I just don't think it should happen again."

"And it won't. I promise."

His promise struck her like a knife, but that's what she'd asked for. "Thank you."

He looked so tense, and to ease the strain she went to him and wrapped her arms around his shoulders. He stood a moment as if a robot, then raised his arms and drew her into an embrace. "I'll never hurt you, Susan," he whispered in her hair. "I treated you so badly. I let my desire do my thinking."

"So did I," she whispered back.

They stood together, his arms around her, her knees weak. She wanted to tell him why she'd been so hurt, why she feared loving him. She relaxed her arms, and he let go and stepped back.

"So, what do we do now? Where do we go from here?"

She didn't know how to answer. "You mean about the house?"

He chucked her chin. "About us?"

Where do we go from here? The phrase wended through her "Let's wait and see. We're both dealing with so much. I'm here. You're here. We have a past and a present. That's enough for now."

He gazed past her for a moment, then brushed her cheek. "You know best." His focus shifted and he gestured to the room. "So, what's our plan of action?"

"Clean and paint. I have color samples. We want to be authentic."

"I'll expect nothing, but authenticity."

He was trying to be lighthearted, and she was touched by his effort. She would have loved to talk about a future, but for now, they needed to sort out their lives, and if they had a future, she would have to tell him about the baby. She feared how he would react.

Susan managed to let her thoughts slide. He was trying to be cheery, and she needed to do the same. "Yesterday a woman in the paint store had on white shoes. She must be an out-of-towner. I wanted to explain to her that a real southern woman never wears white shoes before Memorial Day."

Justin grinned. "Is that white shoe rule in the Bible?"

They both had a needed laugh.

♥

Susan dropped her purse on the bed. After she slipped off her shoes, she grabbed her robe and hurried to the bathroom. In the mirror, she could see the paint spatters in her hair, and she hoped a good washing would get rid of it. She'd covered herself with turpentine, but paint had a way of finding every nook and cranny to hide in.

Steam rose from the bathtub, and she stepped inside and slipped beneath the showerhead, letting the water wash over her aches and pains. Painting had never been a favorite task, but she'd decided to do some of it, although tonight, after five days of painting, Justin had convinced her that they needed to hire a painter for the rest of the rooms that needed it.

The gallery bedroom looked bright and fresh with paint, but they'd decided that washing the walls of some of the rooms would be easier since the paint remained in perfect condition. She'd enjoyed cleaning with Justin at her side the past week, but each night when she came home, she'd fallen asleep before she could read more than a few scattered pages of Libby's diary.

The hot water beat against her back and eased her aches, though not the one in her heart. Even after a week she could still feel the pressure of Justin's mouth against hers, his arms holding her close.

Susan wet her hair and poured shampoo into her hands. She loved the fruity fragrance as she worked the lather through her hair. The water streamed over her like a cleansing of her soul. She'd done the right thing by suggesting the kisses end.

Justin had made it clear, in fact, that he had no desire to take their relationship any deeper than friendship. That was for the best, and she wished she could convince her mother of that—tell her how much good sense she'd had last week.

But as she thought about her good sense, the ache returned. She wanted so much more. She wanted to be a wife and mother, and her youthful actions had made a mess of that. Or had it? Maybe in today's world it wouldn't mean anything to anyone but her. Still, it did. It meant a great deal to her.

She rinsed her hair, turned off the tap, and reached past the shower curtain to find her towel. The nubby fabric tingled against her body as she dried, then she stepped out onto the mat and wrapped the towel around her hair to keep it from dripping.

She slipped into her pajamas and buttoned the top. Steam on the mirror blocked her view, and she left it there. She jammed her feet into her slippers and opened the door.

The room's warmth followed her into the cooler air of the hallway. She crossed the hall and slipped inside her room where she tousled the towel over her hair, then hung it across the chair back. Clean and ready to relax, she opened her handbag and delved for Libby's diary.

Though she considered telling Justin about the contents—thinking he'd enjoy getting a glimpse of Libby's younger days—no time seemed appropriate, and then she feared he would insist she dispose of the books.

She snuggled between the sheets and opened the diary.

May 10,1954

Dear Diary,

I'm part of an experiment. I'm not sure I like it, but our school was selected to test the Salk polio vaccine. Some city in Texas had the most cases in the whole country. I've been praying that I don't get it. I suppose it's better to be an experiment than to get no protection at all. The TV's calling polio an epidemic.

School will be out soon, and I'll officially be a junior. One more year after that, and I'm free. At least I'm sixteen now and an official adult, and I'm allowed to date. Glad they don't know I've been seeing Tommy Bengard on the sly. Daddy says an adult is actually eighteen, but, give me a break, I feel like an adult now.

One of my favorite things about this year is Rock and Roll. Bill Haley and the Comets are neat. I hope Rock and Roll is here to stay. Momma says the music hurts her ears, but I love it.

Libby

Susan fondled her locket, wondering if Libby's sixteenth year served her better than hers had. Justin filled her mind again, along with guilt.

She skimmed the next pages, smiling often at Libby's delightful monologue, until a name jumped from the page.

August 2, 1954

Dear Diary,

I nearly fell through the floor. Daddy came home from work and said Adam Robard had ended his engagement. I could almost see Daddy rubbing his hands together, making more plans. I still don't understand that, but I don't think it's right at all.

Caroline nearly had a cow when she heard, and as much as she drives me crazy, I feel sorry for her. I hope they don't push it again. She seems happy working at the bank as a teller.

I've been hurrying home from school so I can see American Band Stand. It's so fun to see all my favorite singers. My friend Clara said her father's going to let her go to Shreveport next fall to see the Louisiana Hayride radio show at the Municipal Auditorium. Everyone listens to it on the radio. I'm going to ask Daddy if I can go, too. At least I'm old enough now so they won't make Caroline go with me.

Libby

Louisiana Hayride. That brought back her own memories. She had gone there when she was fifteen. She remembered telling Justin about it when she'd been visiting Libby. He called it girl stuff. He said guys didn't scream and act like nuts over some singer like Carl Perkins or Eddie Fisher. Remembering made her smile. It seemed so long ago.

So many things seemed long ago, except Justin's kiss, and more than his kiss, her response. She'd wanted the kiss. She admitted that, and it all seemed so silly now when she thought about it. She was a mature adult who still had the mind of a teenager when she was with Justin. She felt as giddy and naive as she had years earlier.

Last week she'd fallen right into his kiss. She hadn't held back but had clung to him. Her knees had weakened. Her pulse had kicked into high speed, heart thundering. All the romantic clichés that she found embarrassing.

She still pictured Justin's startled face when she'd said never again.

She'd done the right thing. Women were supposed to be strong. They had to guard their morals. Men were excused for their behavior, but women had to bear the brunt of the sin.

Another thought smacked her. Was Justin only toying with her? He'd said as blatantly as a man could that his offer hadn't been a proposal. So, what had it been? An offer to make out like teenagers in the back of a car and then pass it off as friendship? That's not what God commanded, and it's not what she wanted.

Questions flooded her. What had made Justin the man he was? Why had the family pushed Caroline into a relationship with Adam? Why had Libby remained single?

How would Justin respond if she asked him questions about his parents? He rarely spoke of them, and when he did, she noticed he seemed to tense up. After reading the diary, she knew the questions would drive her mad until she found the answer.

Chapter Thirteen

Justin stood on the gallery watching the wall-washers pack up their gear. In two weeks, the walls had been painted and the others washed. Rose Arbor had been spit-and-polished.

A car door slammed, and he turned his attention to the side steps. Dressed in a loose-fitting top and pants, Susan met his eye as she bounced up the stairs and gave him a wave. She paused and drew in a lengthy breath. "Soap and paint. I love that smell." She grinned and plopped into a wicker chair, spreading out some papers on a table. "What do you think?"

He eyed the table and realized she'd brought home brochure designs. But he couldn't pull his gaze from her glowing face, even brighter than the newly painted walls. He pulled out a chair and sat beside her, breathing in the subtle fragrance of fruit and flowers.

She spread her long fingers over the brochures, then slid them his way. "Here are some of the designs. We'll need to hire a photographer to take some pictures of the grounds and rooms."

He looked at the brochure while his thoughts ran rampant. When his mind persisted, he stopped. "Susan, you amaze me."

A puzzled expression settled over her. "Why?"

"You have tremendous business sense with all of this as well as a creative talent that I'd never expected."

"You thought I'd always be an addled teenager?"

Her comment made him chuckle. "Not that exactly, but you have to admit, you were a dreamer. I just never thought—"

"I'm still a dreamer, Justin. That's where the creativity comes from."

"But you have finesse and savvy. Wisdom and charm."

She touched his arm. "What are you doing?" She cocked her head. "You're trying to set me up for something. Lure me in to—"

He pressed his hand against hers. "No. I'm being honest for once."

She studied his face as if making sure he was being honest. "Thanks, then," she said, apparently satisfied that he wasn't trying to manipulate her to do something she didn't want. Her distrust disappointed him.

He slid the samples in front of him and gazed at the options, finding some more appealing than others, but his thoughts kept slipping back to Susan.

"You remind me of aunt Libby sometimes." He shifted his gaze from the pamphlets to her face. "She didn't have business sense that I know of, but you have her spirit."

Susan's face distorted with emotion. "I sometimes think about the comparison, too. She was far more outspoken than I am. She had a confidence that I don't have." She gave a sad grin. "I may have once when I was younger, but not anymore."

A deep sadness marred her face, and he longed to know why. "I don't remember what you liked to do when you were younger. I don't remember your talking about school or friends. Tell me about those days."

"Not much to tell," she said.

"I'd like to hear the 'not much to tell' anyways."

A faint grin softened the tenseness of her face. "I liked school, and I was a pretty good student."

"Were you popular?"

"I wasn't queen of homecoming, but I was class vice president. I had to oversee the class activities."

"Like what?" He watched her animation as she forgot whatever had saddened her.

"The class float for the homecoming parade, our class parties, the candy sale. It was a fund raiser. I can't remember everything." She gave him a silly smile. "Why do you care?"

"I don't know. I just want to know more about you."

She looked down at the table and moved a couple of the brochures around, running her finger over the slippery paper. "I've wanted to know things about you."

He felt his stomach knot, and now he wished he hadn't started the conversation. "I don't like to talk about myself."

"I don't either, but I did."

He gathered his thoughts. "My dad worked long hours. My mom ran the house. I went to school, then college. That's about—"

"Don't tell me that's it." She shook her head. "I want details."

"I went to a boy's school."

"For rich kids?"

Her tone wasn't biting but it had an edge.

"Yes, and it wasn't nearly as fun as public school, I'm sure."

"I wouldn't know." She looked away as if too aware of their differences in social status, and it bothered him.

"I belonged to the electronics club and played soccer. That's about it. I didn't live near the other students, so life was quiet at home."

"What did you do at home?"

He flinched with the memory. "I read, built a radio. My best friends were Rèmi and Clovis."

"The servants?"

"Sad isn't it?"

"No. I think it's kind of nice. I noticed that they both had a special connection with you."

"I'm irresistible." He managed a grin to cover the depth of his sadness.

She shook her head. "That's what you say." She learned forward. "You and Libby had a wonderful bond."

"We did. It's difficult to explain what she meant to me. Sometimes she seemed to almost read my mind. I'd come there upset or sad about something, even lonely, and Libby seemed to have the answer."

Susan's eyes widened with such deep interest, he felt compelled to open his heart, a heart he'd rarely opened for anyone. "This may sound silly, but I watched my schoolmate's parents attend school functions, and I listened to them talk about birthday parties. I never had a birthday party. Nothing like that for me."

"Justin, that can't be true." Her disbelief was softened by tears pooling on her lashes.

"It's true. I was given every expensive toy you can name and the attention of a nanny when I was a boy, but all I really wanted was an expression of my parents' love—a hug, a caress, anything."

Susan rested her hand over his. The warmth radiated up his arm and was touched by her empathy, yet embarrassed by his foolish misery.

"I should have gotten over that long ago, I know."

"I don't think so, Justin. As frustrated as I've been with my parents, they've been there in their own way, but I knew I was loved."

They grew silent a moment, and Susan lifted her hand from his and drew it through her hair. She looked at him and then away, and he sensed she had more to say.

"Tell me about your mother and Libby," she said.

Her request twisted the knot already settled in his stomach. "What about them?" He eyed her, wondering where the question had come from.

"Were they close these past years? I don't remember Libby talking much about her family."

"They were never close from what I know." His own question niggled him again. Why wouldn't his mother come to Rose Arbor for a few of the family heirlooms?

Susan nodded. "They were different. Personality I mean."

She'd made a statement and not asked a question. Uneasiness crept up Justin's back like frissons. "Yes, very different, but how do you know that?"

Her face reddened, and he knew he'd put her on the spot.

"I read a little of Libby's diaries, that's all," she said.

Diaries. Why hadn't he insisted she throw them out? He stopped himself. Was he being rash? Most teenagers wouldn't write anything that they didn't want nosy parents to read, and he'd guessed, his grandfather had been loving but firm.

"I'm sorry, Justin. You didn't tell me not to look at them. You said you didn't want to."

He looked at her, noting the bewildered sadness in her eyes. "I know I didn't. It's just that—"

"You'd enjoy them, Justin. They make me laugh. Libby was so high-spirited. She brings the fifties to life with her stories. I feel closer to her reading them. She's still alive in those journals."

Justin searched her eyes. "Why does Libby mean so much to you?"

Susan winced at his question. "I don't know. I suppose for the same reason she meant so much to you. She loved life. She made everything seem fun, even though sometimes I saw a distant sadness in her eyes. She loved me unconditionally. Her love was different than I had at home. My parents loved me because I was their daughter. Libby loved me because I was me. Do you understand?"

His chest tightened, and the knot in his stomach moved to his throat. He'd been close to Libby for the same reason. "Yes," was all he managed to say. He couldn't tell Susan the tense relationship he had at home. Rèmi and Clovis showed more love to him than either parent.

When he looked up, Susan was studying him. He spread the brochures out in front of him again and picked up one that had a nice layout. "Should we get back to the brochures?"

♥

October 15, 1954

Dear Diary,

I can't wait!!! Tomorrow I'm going with Clara to Shreveport to the Louisiana Hayride. I've been listening to the program on the radio, but I can't wait to be there in person. I don't know who's appearing, but I don't care.

I nearly dropped my teeth when Caroline agreed to go to the movies with Adam Robard. He's really neat. He finished college and works at Taylor Robard Distributors. Daddy said he's a good worker and a good catch for Caroline. Daddy can say that again. If I had my dibs, I'd love to go to the movies.

Tomorrow night I'll be in Shreveport. I wanted to get a poodle skirt to wear tomorrow, but Momma said it's a waste of money. Seems like everything I want to do is a waste of something. I did get some new 45 records. My favorite is Mr. Sandman by the Cordettes. I walk around singing about Mr. Sandman bringing me a dream. The words should be dreamboat.

Someone like Troy Donahue.
Libby

Susan chuckled, remembering those days when she'd become aware of boys, even before she'd met Justin.

October 16, 1954
Dear Diary,
I'm in love. We had so much fun in Shreveport. We ate at a place called Shrimp Boats, and then we went to the Municipal Auditorium. The program was good, but at nine o'clock when they had the newcomers sing, that's when I fell in love. His name is Elvis Presley. He just made a record, and he sang, "That's All right, Mama" and "Blue Moon of Kentucky." I'd never heard it sung that way before. He wiggled his hips and legs like I've never seen. The older people don't like him that much, but all of us teenagers clapped our hands until they hurt. All the way home, we talked about him. He beats out Tommy Bengard even though he has a ducktail haircut now which is kinda cute.
Caroline has another date with Adam. He's taking her to a country club or something. I can't help but laugh. Caroline needs some lessons from Emily Post in being social.
Libby

Susan lowered the diary. Another date with Adam. Libby had always made Caroline sound dull and studious, but maybe that was just Libby. As she'd noticed when she met Caroline, the woman could have been very attractive with a quiet kind of charm that Libby didn't appreciate.

Susan wondered what it would be like to have a sister. Would they have gotten along? A sister would have given her someone to talk with, someone who might have cautioned her about getting herself in trouble. She'd never been able to talk to her mother about things like that. But Susan knew better. She would have done anything for Justin.

From the gallery, Susan heard the sounds of the moving men bringing furniture into the wing bedrooms. She'd tagged all the large pieces and gave them floor plans for where each piece should go. Last she checked, they had been following her instructions.

She sipped her sweet tea, shifted her attention to the diary, and scanned the rest of 1954. She had so many more things to do and so little time to read, but Libby's entries had become like a page-turner novel for her. She hated to put the books down.

She thought about putting the diaries away. It seemed a boring way to spend Memorial day. While everyone was at picnics, she sat alone with the movers who'd been willing to fit the job into their holiday. She eyed the stack of diaries beside her, figuring, at least, they helped time to pass. Once the furniture was in place her work would begin in earnest.

Susan picked up the next journal and turned her focus back to Libby's world. She'd begun to skim pages looking for events and information that captured her interest since the diaries were taking too long to read. More were stored in the chest, and she couldn't wait to get to the later years. She wondered if Libby had ever mentioned her.

June 12, 1955

Dear Diary,

My mouth is hanging open a foot. Caroline is engaged!!!!! Adam asked her tonight. Momma and Daddy are going crazy. Caroline almost looked pretty when she talked about how he proposed. He knelt down on his knee just like in the movies. Someday someone will do that for me, too!!!

Tonight I've found that dream man in a movie, one of the best movies in the whole world. Rebel Without A Cause. James Dean just melted my heart he's so handsome. He has that pouty look like Elvis with those deep eyes. Whew! I can hardly breathe thinking of him.

And now Caroline has something else to gloat about. I can't believe Adam proposed!!!

Libby

Susan scanned the next entries, glazed over more of Libby's comments about her father's attitude toward President Eisenhower's policies and his thoughts on Churchill's resignation. She talked about her summer reading, and finally school's opening. 1955 had been Libby's junior year of high school.

September 30, 1955

Dear Diary,

I've spent the last hour in my room crying. When I got home from the church's youth group, I heard that James Dean was killed in a car accident. He was so young and so talented. I can't believe he's gone. He only made three movies.

Momma is mad at me because I'm crying. She said I'm making an idol out of him, but I'm not. On Good Friday, I always cry, thinking of Jesus dying on the cross for my sins. I'm not comparing James Dean to Jesus. I just meant that shocking deaths make me cry.

Adam was here when I got home, and he was so sweet. He gave me a hug and said he understood how upset I was about James Dean. No one else understands. I stood in Adam's arms a long time, smelling his aftershave and realizing how lucky Caroline is. I wonder if she realizes it.

Libby

She read a few more of Libby's entries: her favorite movies and how much she loved Bill Haley and the Comets' *Rock Around the Clock*. She had heard the song many times. Who would have known it would become a classic.

November 16, 1955

Dear Diary,

Tonight I was so thrilled. Caroline asked me to be the maid of honor at her wedding next June. Adam said I was his favorite sister-in-law. Adam is so fun. I wish Caroline seemed more fun for him. They always talk so serious, but with me, he teases and jokes.

Daddy's paying for the whole wedding, and he'll have to pay for my dress, too. Caroline said her color theme would be yellow and white. She's wearing white naturally, so I get to wear yellow. I like yellow okay. It looks good with my dark hair. Caroline won't look good in white. She's too pale, but I guess that's what brides wear. Momma said it means they're chaste. That's really important to Momma and Daddy.

Libby

Chaste. Susan's chest tightened knowing that chastity had been important to her mother and dad, too. She'd broken their hearts. The day she had to tell her mother she was pregnant barraged her thoughts.

A thud jarred her memory, and she felt gratefulness for the reprieve from those difficult memories. She set the diary on the table and ambled outside. The movers had been working for two hours, and she figured they should be finished soon. She could hear noises coming from a room in the single story wing, and she headed there to check on their progress.

When she came into the doorway, she watched them attach the last cross piece onto the tester bed. She gazed around the room, seeing most everything in place. "Y'all nearly finished?"

The man that seemed to be the supervisor gave her a nod. "We're jus' about done here, Ma'am. You want to eyeball the rooms and make sure everything's how you want it?"

She agreed and wandered back to the other two rooms where they'd placed the furniture. Everything looked in order. The rooms still needed her loving touch—the lamps, art pieces, bric-a-brac, and linens, but the worst was done.

She strode from the last room and met the supervisor coming out the door. "Everything looks fine. If you leave your bill, Mr. Robard will be back in a few days and he'll mail you a check."

"He prepaid. We're all set, Ma'am," he said, tipping his cap. "We'll load up our dollies and be out of your way."

"Thanks so much." She backed away, eager to get back to the diaries. "Y'all drive careful now."

He nodded, and she returned to her spot on the settee and opened the diary again. She cringed, knowing she had plenty to do besides reading them. She and Justin had selected a brochure, and she needed to get the rooms ready so the photographer could take pictures of the house and grounds. She'd priced getting a website and needed to talk that over with Justin.

She missed Justin. The house seemed lonelier when he wasn't there, and this morning when she arrived, she'd been startled to see a fresh rose in the vase on the gallery. The flower gave her the jitters, and despite her Christian upbringing, she took a long look at the bedroom that was supposed to be haunted. Her reasoning and Christianity spurned the idea, but curiosity made her wonder. She'd thought Justin had been playing games with her, but now she knew that couldn't be it. A frisson rolled down her spine.

Dispelling the strange feeling, she lowered her gaze to the diary and skimmed the entries.

June 11, 1956

Dear Diary,

Tonight was the wedding rehearsal dinner. It's exciting but sad. As much as Caroline drives me crazy, I'll miss her. Especially Adam. He's been so nice to me. Today he gave me a present. I couldn't believe it. It was a beautiful locket that opens with a place to put two pictures. I thought about putting one of him on one side and Caroline on the other, but I haven't decided.

Momma was so excited, and Adam's parents were there, too. They're different from us. They seem richer. I don't know why, because Mr. Robard and Daddy own the same business. Maybe Mrs. Robard handles the money better.

Libby

Susan lifted her head and heard the mover's truck pull away. She should get to work, but she couldn't stop now.

June 12, 1956

Dear Diary,

The wedding was beautiful. Even Caroline looked very pretty in her wedding dress. She's not so bad when she wears makeup and fixes her hair. I loved my yellow dress. The bridesmaids and me carried yellow daisies and white roses with ivy. Caroline carried white roses and some other little white flower. I wore the locket that Adam gave me.

Daddy let me invite Claude Beauvoir. We had so much fun except I was supposed to sit at the bride's table. I sat there when I had to, but most of the time, I just had a great time sitting wherever I wanted.

Caroline and Adam stood wrapped in each other arms during "Love Me Tender." It wasn't long ago I thought I was in love with Elvis Presley. I'm over him now, although I will admit he's still sexy. He's got those pouty lips like James Dean.

I almost died when Adam invited me to dance. Caroline is so lucky. When they played "My Prayer," Adam sang the words in my ear. He really has a nice voice, and when he sang the part about my prayer is a rapture in blue, he changed the word to yellow. It didn't rhyme, but it was so sweet.

Before he left, he told me I was his favorite sister-in-law. I laughed and then he kissed me right on the mouth. I thought I'd fall through the floor. His lips are so soft. Much softer than Wade's. Caroline, you're a lucky dog.

Libby

Susan sat a moment and tried to understand Adam Robard. She didn't know the man, but the little she'd heard from Justin, his father wasn't the same man Susan had come to know in the diaries. Captivated by Libby's story, Susan continued to read the pages, some brief, some more lengthy until something new entered the picture.

December 8, 1956

Dear Diary,

I'm so excited. I know one of my Christmas presents. Adam called to ask permission and Daddy said yes. Adam and Caroline are taking me to Shreveport next Sunday to see Elvis Presley. He's appearing at the Youth Building at the Fair Grounds. It's the biggest place in the city for a concert. Adam asked me what I wanted for Christmas, and I told him I'd give anything to see Elvis again, now that he's so famous.

Momma wasn't real happy because we'll have to spend the night in Shreveport, and I'll miss school on Monday. She talked to Caroline later, and I overheard Caroline's upset. She doesn't want to sit through "a bunch of rock and roll screeching." That's what she called it, but we're going according to Adam. I can't wait!!!

Libby

Susan leafed the pages, anxious to read about the following Sunday.

December 17, 1956

Dear Diary,

I'm in a hotel in Shreveport with Caroline and Adam. I'm sleeping on a sofa bed. The concert was a blast!! No one can sing like Elvis. He'll be one of the biggest singers in the world, I bet.

Caroline didn't go to the concert. She stayed at the hotel. She's such a party-pooper. Adam and I had so much fun. After we were inside, we heard people saying that a pink Cadillac had a police escort to the concert, and when the crowd mobbed Elvis, it wasn't him at all. He'd sneaked in the back. I'm glad it wasn't me waiting out there. Adam said we're too smart. I heard people say they were going to catch him going out.

Elvis sang every one of his songs. Adam and I stood up and clapped our hands, bouncing to the music. He acted like he was having as much fun as I was. He's so neat. When Elvis left the stage. Everyone dashed for the doors, but the show wasn't over yet, so the announcer came over the PA and said, "Young people, Elvis has left the building. He's already in his car and gone."

I'm glad we stayed put.

I'm sort of miserable now, because I know Caroline is mad at Adam. She's giving him her usual look that means she's not happy. I don't know how he puts up with her. What was the attraction anyways? But I'm still happy we went to see Elvis. It was the best Christmas present ever.

Libby

Susan realized she wasn't the only one asking the question. What was the attraction anyways?

♥

"Hold the picture frame while I mark a spot for the nail." Justin looked over his shoulder at Susan.

She turned away and rearranged the dresser scarf. "I'm really pleased with the way things look. I hope you are." She stood back and eyed the newly decorated gallery guestroom.

Justin smiled at her over his shoulder. "I'll be even happier when you hold this frame."

She poked him in the side, and when he flinched, the picture shifted.

"Thanks," he said, tickling her back.

Susan dodged away and fled to the far side of the room.

He lifted the hammer, his nostrils flaring like they did when he got angry, but she saw the sparkle in his eyes. "If you want this picture hung, you'd better get over here."

She inched her way back, keeping an eye on his hands, one occupied holding the frame in place and the other clutching the hammer. While she held the artwork, he made a tiny dot with a pencil, then moved the frame to pound in the nail. When he finished, she hung the landscape and stepped back.

"I love how the colors pull the room together. See the blues and greens. They're in the canopy fabric and the same shades are in the rug."

Justin stood back, an inquisitive grin on his face. "For someone who's so up on color and style, I've often wondered why you wear such baggy clothing."

She looked down at her oversize knit top, surprised he'd noticed what she wore and startled that he asked the question. "Do I look like a bag lady?"

"No. You look like an attractive woman trying to hide beneath a tent."

"What difference does it make?"

His head jerked back as if she'd slapped him. "Would you throw a drape over the Pietà or the statue of David?"

"What does that have to do with me?" The look in his eyes made her nervous.

He moved closer and brushed his finger along her jaw, letting his fingers flow through her hair. "You're such a beautiful woman, Susan. You make me feel guilty."

Her knees trembled as he caressed her hair. "Guilty?" She could barely speak.

"You're trying to hide from me because of what happened between us."

The words swept over Susan. What could she say? Maybe that's why she didn't like to show her curves. She felt safer keeping her figure hidden from prying eyes.

His hands shifted from her hair to her shoulders. "That's it, isn't it?"

She didn't know, but it was possible. Why had he ruined a perfectly fun moment with his probing question.

"*Cher*." He drew her into his arms. "Please forgive me. Why am I getting serious when we're having fun? I've caused you to distrust me. Forgive me."

She leaned against his chest, fighting the tears that pushed behind her eyes. Why couldn't he let her forget? "I've never blamed you, Justin, so there's nothing to forgive."

He tilted his head downward to look into her eyes. "How can you say that? I was two years older. I knew better."

"So did I, but—" She stopped herself, smothering her face into his shoulder.

"But?" He reached up and tilted her head toward his.

"But I didn't care."

"*Mon Cher*," he whispered into her hair.

His voice sounded so soft she wasn't certain she really heard him. She felt him tremble against her, and her heart ached, knowing that each had their burdens and secrets. She knew hers, but Justin had his own as dark as hers. She saw it in his stormy eyes.

She and Justin seemed like two ships tossed by stormy seas, never sailing close enough to hear the other's distress signal.

He drew back and held her away from him. "Susan, we really need to talk."

Chapter Fourteen

Justin's mind spun as he steered Susan toward the only chair in the room. When she was seated, her eyes searched his, and he settled on the edge of the bed, having no idea why he's said they needed to talk. He had things to say, but was this the time or the situation?

His feelings were strong, and he'd weighed them over and over, trying to understand them and trying to make sense of his life.

"What is it?" Susan's forehead furrowed.

"I don't know," He felt out of control. "Being with you has almost unleashed me. I can't pretend that I don't care about you, Susan. I know I made you the promise, but I can't handle it anymore. I feel as if I'm playing a game with you." His pulse surged, and he felt overwhelmed.

"I know, Justin. I understand."

"I don't think the past should rule us now. We're fond of—" He stopped himself. "That's playing games again. We're more than fond of each other. I think you feel the same." As his gaze lowered to her full lips, his heart gave a kick.

He watched her expression shift from discomfort to confusion.

"This is a big step for me, Susan. A huge step. I know there are things you don't understand about me. I don't understand them either." His stomach knotted.

"I want to understand you, Justin. So often it seems you go on a mental vacation. Your body's here, but your mind is many miles away."

He winced, washed in self-pity. "Affection doesn't come easy for me, but now..." Now what? He drew in a breath. "I don't want anyone's pity."

Susan shook her head. "I would never pity you. I don't know why you would say that."

"I didn't grow up around affection. It's as if life had burned out of my parents' relationship. No one hugged me." He thought back. "Except Rèmi and Clovis, they treated me as if I were their son. They cared."

"But what about—"

"How could I forget," he said, addled Susan's questioning eyes. "And Aunt Libby. She was the one who salvaged some of my best qualities. She loved me unconditionally."

Guilt washed over him, knowing he'd done his parents a disservice. "Don't think I'm not grateful. My parents took good care of me. I had expensive clothes, a good education, the best of everything, but not the things that are important."

A different look came over her, and she lowered her gaze, her dark lashes accentuating her pale skin. "What is important to you, Justin?"

What is important? He hardly knew anymore. "I've blocked all that. I've avoided getting involved with people. I've kept my troubles private until now. I put my energies in my business. My father was like that."

"But not always."

His head jerked upward involuntarily. "What do you mean?" He studied her expression and knew. "Those diaries."

She nodded. "He was fun-loving. He joked and laughed. He sang. He bought Libby special gifts. He even took her to an Elvis concert in Shreveport despite your mother's protests. Can you believe it? That's not the father that you talk about."

His father joked and sang? He couldn't imagine. The man he knew was a shadow who appeared when the sun had set, ate a quiet dinner, and went to bed.

"I wish you would read the journals, Justin. You'd learn so much about your family. Things you don't know."

His chest tightened. Did he want to know? He felt like a child who'd learned he'd been kidnapped and raised by strangers. Now was too late to learn about a family he didn't know.

He shook his head. "I told you I don't want to read them. I wish you wouldn't."

Her eyes pleaded with him. "Please, Justin, please don't ask me not to read them. It's such a pleasure. They're like a gripping novel. Libby is such a character. Her thoughts about life and people, her—?"

"Read them, but I don't want to hear about them, Susan. I can't handle any more confusion in my life than I already have."

She rose, slipped beside him on the edge of the mattress, and clasped his arm. "I'm sorry. I shouldn't have said anything. But I thought you might understand your parents better if you did."

Sitting so close to her, Justin could smell her fragrance like sweet lemons. He looked at her tapering fingers, then at his own knotted on his lap. Her earlier question shot into his mind. He knew what he wanted. He wanted to hold her, run his fingers through her long, dark curls, feel his lips against her full mouth.

"What are you thinking?" Her query touched him as soft as a Louisiana breeze.

"About your question. What's important to me."

"I know what's important to me," she said.

He turned his eyes to hers and read her answer.

"You, Justin." Her whisper swept through him. She moved her hand along his arm, then ran her finger along the nape of his neck while she rested her cheek against his shoulder.

He did what he'd longed to do. He moved his free arm upward, drawing his palm along her cheek and caressing her lips. She kissed his fingers, and his heart swelled, filling his chest with warmth.

She raised her head, her gaze locked with his, and he gave his fingers permission to tangle in her hair. Her dark lashes lowered and brushed her cheek, then lifted pulling him into the deep blue depths. When he was able to look away from the eddies of her eyes, he saw her lips part.

Be gentle, he told himself, and from her look, he realized she felt as vulnerable as he did. He lowered his mouth with a soft caress. Her full lower lip moved against his as he languished in her gift. He forced himself to release the kiss and moved his mouth to her cheek, her eyes, her nose with all the tenderness he could summon.

When he eased back, Susan opened her eyes.

When their gaze met again, he read so much in her eyes. "Slowly, Susan. If you're willing, we'll move slowly and see what surprises God has for us."

She looked puzzled, and he understood. He'd never talked about God much. He'd fought the Lord most of his life, but he'd grown closer to God through Susan's faithfulness.

"Do you pray, Justin?"

Did he pray? "Not in any formal way, but I do talk to someone in my head, and the only One that makes sense is God." He tried to smile. "Unless I'm totally crazy."

She gave him a sad grin. "Would you go to church with me some Sunday? I want my mother to know a different Justin than she thinks she knows."

"She doesn't like me, and I doubt if going to church will change that."

"She thinks you and Libby held me captive." Her eyes grazed the room as if in thought, then they widened. "I've never thought about that much, but I suppose if I were a mother and my child would rather spend time with the neighbors, I'd feel hurt and defensive, too. I'm afraid I never treated my mother well. She's not demonstrative either. She's more old-fashioned. I couldn't talk with her about things like some girls could. Libby made it easy."

"Easy for a girl." He recalled how much he longed to talk with a man, a man who'd understand the new feelings he'd felt, the yearning that drove him to distraction. "If I'd had a man to talk with, I might have understood what feelings were normal for a teenage boy."

"I didn't realize boys had those questions."

He gave her the first easy smile he'd felt since they'd begun to talk. "You didn't know much about boys."

She closed her eyes and moved her head slowly. "I was in the dark."

He took her hands in his. "Are you willing? Slow and easy?"

She lowered her gaze and thought a moment. "Very slow and very easy."

He squeezed her hand, knowing he couldn't ask for more.

♥

"Clarissa called about the *cushon de lei*," Margaret said as Susan walked into the house.

"I thought she'd forgotten about inviting us."

"Not us. You."

Susan let go of the door handle and dropped her purse on a kitchen chair. "Momma, I'm sure she meant both of us."

"I don't really care to go, Susan. It's younger people. Anyways I've been feeling tired the past few days."

She studied her mother's face and realized she looked peaked. "You're not feeling well?"

"I said I'm tired. Not sick."

"But you don't look well. I'd like you to call the doctor."

"I'd like a lot of things that don't happen. I'm fine."

Her comment had been the first real dig in the past week. She let it roll past her. "Tomorrow if you're still feeling tired, we'll call the doctor."

Her mother didn't say anymore, so she took it as an acceptance. "Is there anything to eat?"

Margaret's eyes widened. "I thought you'd eaten next door."

"No. I went to town to pick up some things I needed and the brochures for the bed and breakfast." She pulled one from her handbag. "I have a large box in the car. Would you like to see one?"

Her mother's eyes turned cold for a moment, but she didn't say anything and held out her hand for the sample. She glanced through the pages and handed it back. "You've done a lot of work."

"I have. The gallery rooms needed the most attention. We—I hired wall-washers to do the rest that didn't need painting."

Although she'd been disappointed that Justin hadn't gone to church with her, the more she thought about it, she was puzzled about her mother's possible reaction. She might have been rude. She decided it would be only right to prepare her mother first before inviting Justin into their lives—if that was even possible.

Her mother waved her hand toward the refrigerator. "There's some fried chicken and salad if you want."

Susan wanted. She headed for the refrigerator and pulled out a drumstick and a bowl of salad, then sat at the table where Margaret was working on a crossword puzzle.

"What's the name of the island where Napoleon was exiled?"

"Does it start with E?"

Her mother nodded.

"E-L-B-A. Elba." She watched her mother fit in the letters and give her a quick grin. The feeling seemed so nice—the two of them talking like people who didn't dislike each other.

Quiet settled over them as her mother concentrated on the crossword, and while she ate, she reviewed the past week since she and Justin had come to their agreement. The time had been wonderful. They'd avoided conversation about what happened years earlier and spent the time working on Rose Arbor.

The rooms where nearly ready, the Chamber of Commerce had linked their new website to theirs, and now she had the brochures. Justin still needed to hire staff—kitchen help to prepare the breakfasts, a housekeeper, and... she faltered realizing she was at the crossroads of a decision. Would she agree to stay or should she leave?

If she stayed at Rose Arbor, she had no guarantee of a future with Justin. He'd mentioned more than once he wasn't the marrying kind. He'd even said if he were, she would be first on his list. The comment didn't make her feel any better.

Did she want to settle for a relationship that led nowhere? But what choice did she have? If she met a man and formed a relationship, she would have to confess what had happened. The promiscuity seemed bad enough. The pregnancy had been bitter. And her son. The thought brought tears to her eyes. She hadn't had the heart to tell Justin. She didn't want his pity any more than he wanted hers. She could never tell him, and that always left a barrier between them.

Sometimes she thought about talking with Pastor Ralph again. He'd suspected something deeper troubled her. What would he think? What would he say? Did he have an answer to make telling him worthwhile? She suspected he wouldn't.

Her throat tightened with each thought, and she forced herself to finish the salad and chicken. When she rose to put up the dishes, her mother glanced at her.

"Don't forget to call Clarissa before it's too late," her mother said.

Clarissa. She'd forgotten. "Thanks. I will."

She eyed the kitchen phone, then decided to call from her cell phone in the privacy of her room. She grabbed her handbag and drink, then left her mother with the puzzle.

Inside her bedroom, she dug out her cell phone along with one of Libby's journals. They'd begun to get scanty, and days passed without an entry. After graduation she'd stopped writing Dear Diary and her signature and only jotted down her thoughts.

Life had changed for Libby in her senior year. She'd spent time with Claude Beauvoir steadily, but from Libby's entries, the relationship had begun to fade. Susan suspected, Libby would hang on for her senior dance, and then poor Claude would be off to college to find a new girlfriend.

Susan placed the journal on her nightstand and opened the narrow drawer to find Clarissa's telephone number. She pulled out the calling card and shook her head. No one used social calling cards in this century except Clarissa.

Trying to think of an excuse to decline the invitation, Susan punched in Clarissa's number. Her friend's hello sounded cheery.

"This is Susan. Mom said you called." She listened while Clarissa told her about the invitation.

"You must come, and you have no excuse. It's the Fourth of July. It'll be a great party. It's couples, mainly, so I hope you'll bring along a friend. I love to keep my table settings even."

Another out-of-era tradition as her heart sank. A date? That meant she'd have to ask Justin, and she knew he would hate going.

"I don't know about bringing a guest. I'm still new in town."

"My, my. You're Momma told me you're at Rose Arbor day and night with Justin Robard." Her voice softened in collusion. "Tell me all about it."

Glad she was on the telephone, Susan grasped her wits and forced a chuckle. "You know mothers, Clarissa. They see things that aren't there. I work for Mr. Robard." Why did she say Mr. Robard? It sounded so forced. "Justin," she corrected.

Susan gave a concise explanation and hoped it would end there, but not Clarissa, bless her heart.

"You still must bring Justin along. I'm dyin' to meet him."

"I'll see if he's in town. That's all I can promise."

She finished the conversation and said goodbye, wondering why she'd agreed to go to the pig roast. She'd hoped to find an excuse, but

Clarissa had a way of throwing her off-kilter.

Wondering who else would be at the gathering, Susan prayed no one who would remember how she'd suddenly vanished from school in her junior year.

She tossed her cell phone into her purse and stretched out on the bed, hoping to get lost in Libby's story. She snapped on the bed lamp and reached for the journal. After plumping the pillow, she fingered through the pages to find where she'd left off.

May 22, 1958

I haven't dated much since I graduated and told Claude that I thought we should be free to date others. He looked startled, but I knew it was for the best. Anyways I suspect he'll be drafted. I couldn't believe when Elvis Presley had to give up his career to go into the army.

Last week, I met a nice guy while I was sitting in a restaurant near Babin Hall where I take accounting. His name is Jefferson Landry. I like his name. It sounds distinguished. He ran into me three more times during the week. I'm sure he's watching for me. He's a photographer at the studio next door. He said he wants to take my photograph. He seems very nice, and I'm planning to see where it goes.

Right now, I'm most worried about Momma. She's not feeling well, and the doctor thinks she had a slight stroke. She said it was a warning. I'm praying she'll get better soon. Daddy would be lost without her.

Libby with another boyfriend. Every time she read the journals, Susan became more bewildered how an attractive woman so eager to date and have fun ended up single. The question set her back. She'd been fun-loving in high school. She'd had an interest in numerous boys, some reciprocal and some not, and she'd always thought of marriage and family. She'd also remained single. Libby's recent journal flashed in Susan's mind. The Bible verses and the prayers set Susan on edge. Had Libby been asking forgiveness for remaining single? That didn't make sense but what did?

Susan dropped her thoughts and read further. Libby's mother had suffered a stroke, and she had another one only a month later. Libby finished her courses and spent the summer helping to care for her mother who'd lost the use of her left side. The next entry stopped Susan, cold.

October 17, 1958

I'm astounded how life changes in the blink of an eye. Momma died this morning. I've felt as if I'm walking in a fog. Daddy is so confused. We're like the blind leading the blind, but the neighbors have been wonderful. We won't have to cook for months. The house is filled with food that no one wants to eat.

Death. It happened so suddenly. Susan thought of her mother's health and prayed the Lord keep her safe. Finally, they could spend time together without digs and unkind words. She longed to see the day when she and her mother had truly forgiven each other.

October 20, 1958

Momma was buried today. My chest aches from trying to hold back my tears. I have to be strong for Daddy. He sits in the kitchen morning to night as if Momma will suddenly appear and join him at the table. I walked in on him yesterday after we'd gotten home from the visitation, and he hadn't even turned on the lights.

Since one of my college English classes, I've grown to love Emily Dickinson's poetry. Last night I picked up my volume of her works and read the one that begins: "The bustle in the house the morning after death." Her words about death wrapped around me like a shawl—so true and so difficult. 'The sweeping up the heart and putting love away we shall not want to use again until eternity."

What more could anyone say?

November 20, 1958

Caroline and Adam have been so good to Daddy. They've insisted he go there for dinner a couple times a week, although we all see he doesn't eat much. I talked with Adam about getting a job, but he tells me to wait. Daddy needs someone around, and if I'm gone all day, he thinks Daddy won't make it. I've heard of people dying from a broken heart, and I think that's what Daddy is doing.

Susan gazed at the page, feeling Libby's sorrow. She remembered losing her own father, and though they hadn't been close, she felt as if she'd lost part of herself. She'd wanted so badly to make amends, to heal the rift that had split the family in two. But it never happened, and now it was too late.

I've seen Jefferson a few times, but I'm not really interested anymore. Life changes when someone you love dies. I hope I'm changing for the better. Adam says I am.

I worry about Adam and Caroline. They don't seem suited to each other. The longer they're married, the less Adam laughs. He told me privately that he wanted to have a child, but Caroline pushes him away. I'm praying for them. Adam would make a wonderful father. He seems so different lately.

Libby's prayers had obviously been answered. Adam did have his son. Justin. But if he wanted a child so badly, why didn't he dote on him like a father should? Every page of Libby's journal confused Susan more and more.

Unhappiness changed people, Susan knew. They became bitter. She saw it on every page, even Libby seemed to change. Her quips and sassy comments had faded with time. Maybe the same had happened to Adam.

Susan knew her life had followed a similar path, and it would never end until she made the right decision. And she needed to make it now.

♥

When Justin's feet hit the gallery, the back door flew open.

"I wondered if you weren't coming today." Susan stood in the doorway, holding open the screen.

Her expression concerned him. It wasn't anger or disappointment but something deeper that he saw.

"I stopped at an employment agency. You said we're all set to go except for staff so I figured I could see if the agency had anyone listed who would meet our needs." Justin set his briefcase on a chair near the door, walked to the refrigerator and opened the door.

"How did it go?"

He'd expected her to be pleased. Instead, she only gave him a blank look.

Before he answered, he pulled out a coke and snapped open the lid. The sweet liquid rolled across his parched tongue and down his throat. He swiped the moisture away from his lips with the back of his hand and turned to face her. "I found a housekeeper and a cook who I can interview."

She blinked and waited.

"That's it?"

"Did I miss someone?"

"A groundskeeper and a hostess. You need someone to answer the phone, take reservations, run the business. You can't do that, and we haven't—"

"No, but I thought—" He thought she would be there. She'd been there for him since the plan began. The plan was hers.

"Thought what?" Her face changed when his silence lasted too long.

"I-I don't know."

"You thought I would stay here forever. I don't know what I'm going to do, Justin."

"But I thought that you... You've been doing so much I assumed that you would stay on. I suppose I've assumed too much."

"Probably."

Her confused expression reflected how he felt.

"You forgot I said I'd work until the business was ready."

His jaw ached from its tightness. "But I thought since things have changed between us that—" He searched her eyes, longing to know what had changed. "I was wrong."

Susan didn't look at him. She lowered her gaze and sank into a nearby chair. "I've given this a lot of thought. I don't know exactly what I want to do with my life. The longer I wait the more confused I get. I don't know if it's possible that I might marry someday. Probably not, but if I stay here in Devereaux, nothing will happen."

He looked at her with new eyes. He'd been selfish to think that Susan felt the same about marriage as he did.

Bewilderment flooded her face.

He tried to gather his thoughts. "I weigh my parents' happiness against Libby's freedom. I might be wrong, Susan." His chest tightened. "You've been telling me how Libby was a party girl with snappy comebacks. I never saw her that way. She was a storyteller. She talked about her girlhood and family history. She was a woman of strength and generosity. She seemed happy with her single life. I never heard any regrets from her. I always figured if it were good enough for Aunt Libby it's good enough for me. The lesser of the evils."

"Lesser of the evils." Susan shook her head with the direst expression he'd ever seen. "That seems so sad. Is that what life is? The lesser of the evils?" She rose and rested her hand on the back of the chair. "Maybe I am a foolish dreamer, but I like to think that God has a purpose for my life, and I hope it's more than running your bed and breakfast and dying alone."

Her words kicked him in the gut. He dashed from his chair and grasped her arm. "Susan, please, that's not exactly what I meant." He dropped his hand when he felt her resistance. "I don't know what I mean."

"You need to think about it, Justin. Why don't you find someone else to run the bed and breakfast? I need to make some decisions, and I'm not sure which fantasy I'll follow."

She grabbed her bag and slammed the door as she left.

He listened to her footsteps tromp along the gallery floor until they faded away. He started to rise, to go after her, but maybe she was right. He needed to think first. What did he expect of her? What did he want in his life? Emptiness washed over him. Rose Arbor without Susan seemed like a museum without artwork, a song without music, heart without blood.

He sank back into the chair and put his face in his hands. What had triggered Susan's frustration? What had he missed?

Chapter 15

"Justin," Susan rapped on the door. The house was quiet, and the moon was the only light. "Justin, can we talk."

She stood at the door, waiting. Had he gone to bed? Could he sleep? She hadn't been able to. She tried to read Libby's diaries, and the words blurred. She couldn't sleep without talking this through.

A sudden sound came from behind her, and she spun around. A shadow flashed at the end of the gallery, and then disappeared. Her heart rose to her throat. What had it been? She stood frozen, the old myth washing over her before she could shuck it away.

She listened and heard nothing but night sounds, empty sounds of life somewhere. She took a slow step toward the end of the gallery, bewildered at what she'd seen. Her heart jolted when the porch light flashed on, and she heard the lock click.

The door opened, and Justin stood on the other side of the screen, his hair disheveled, his shirt unbuttoned and hanging loose. Her gaze lowered to his muscular torso feathered with dark bristles.

"Susan?"

"Did I wake you? I'm sorry." she hurried back toward the door.

"No. I haven't slept."

"Me, neither." She searched his eyes through the screen in the shadowy foyer.

He hadn't opened the door further, and she didn't know for sure what to do. "I came to apologize."

Silence fell between them.

He pulled his fingers through his hair and looked at her.

"Is tomorrow better?" She studied his expression for an answer. "I'll come back tomorr—"

"No, it's fine." He eased open the screen door, and she stepped inside.

Justin didn't speak but turned and headed into the parlor. He motioned for her to find a seat, and he sank into a chair.

"I couldn't sleep having you upset with me. I have some thinking to do about my life, and I guess I threw a little hissy fit."

"I've been thinking, too, and you're probably right. I can't hold you back from finding the perfect position for your career. I know a woman who worked for me in Baton Rouge. She moved close to Devereaux. I'll give her a call. I think she could do this. She was a receptionist and handled appointment and details.

Susan's heart sank. She wasn't sure that's what she wanted. She'd tried to push Justin out of her mind to ease her confusion, but it only added to it. Maybe her present uneasiness was God's way of leading her. She had to have faith. "That's good, Justin." She prayed it was good.

"If she's available, she'll be perfect," he said.

He'd been playing with a button on his shirt, and as if he'd become aware of his bared chest, he began buttoning his shirt.

She grinned when she noticed he'd buttoned it cockeyed.

He glanced down, shrugged, and tried to straighten the closure.

"Justin, I felt horrible once I got home. God tells us not to let the sun go down on our anger, and I'd walked out without resolving things with you. Forgive me."

He leaned forward, his elbow on one knee and dragged his fingers through his hair with the other hand. "There's nothing to forgive. I hadn't been clear about what I meant."

"It's late, Justin." She rose. "As long as we're not angry at each other, I should go. We can talk more tomorrow." The shadowy figure rose in her thoughts. "By the by, I saw something strange outside." Frissons rose on her arms.

"Strange?"

"A sound at the end of the gallery and a shadow. It vanished so fast I missed what it was."

He looked puzzled. "I'll walk out with you."

He followed her to the foyer doorway, then held the screen. When she stepped outside the scent of roses blanketed her. The rose arbor appeared only a shadow deep in the garden. A thought struck her, and she let her gaze drop to the small vase by the door. It stood empty.

Their footsteps thudded on the wooden floor as he walked beside her past the main living quarters, then turned at the wing of bedrooms along the gallery. Outside the bedroom linked to the myth, something lay on the gallery floor.

He bent and picked it up. When he turned toward her, he held a rose in his hand. They stood a moment, gazing at the red bud—not a flower she recognized from Libby's garden. Justin shook his head and handed it to her.

She drew in the sweet fragrance and brushed the velvety pedals against her cheek.

"Let's sit in the arbor," He grasped her hand.

His touch wavered up her arm into her heart along with the heady scent of roses. Nostalgia. She would never forget those days. Her problems began here. Could they end here?

They walked through the damp grass with her hand locked in his firm grip. She felt a muscle twitch in his arm as he moved beside her, and when they reached the bench, he let go of her hand and used his shirttail to wipe moisture from the seat.

She watched the moonlight play with shadows as they sat in silence. She wondered if it had only been a passing cloud that had caused her to jump earlier. Yet the rose clutched in her fingers stirred her imagination. Tonight, she knew it hadn't been Justin who had been placing the roses there. Tonight, he'd been inside as she waited at the door, and the flower had not been there when she walked along the gallery earlier.

She placed the rose on the bench beside her and folded her hands in her lap. "Justin, can I speak openly?"

His intake of breath signaled he wanted to say no. "Sure," he said.

"We've both remained single, each for our own reasons, I realize, but your attitude about marriage saddens me. I think it's unfair of you to judge relationships based on your parents' marriage. I'm saying this for you. It has nothing to do with me."

"I'm like my father, Susan. Work is my life. I live it and breathe it."

"There's nothing wrong with that."

"Don't you think marriage should be more than that?"

She thought about what he'd said, and his comments opened the Pandora's box in her head. "My mother said something about marriage a while back that struck me. Working side by side connects people. It binds them together for better or worse. She's right. Marriage takes two people. When one doesn't participate, the other fills his life with other things more meaningful."

A locust buzzed in the distance.

"Do you understand what I mean?" She studied his face.

"You're talking about my mother."

"In a way."

"You hardly know her."

A knife twisted in her stomach. "I know, but I've—"

"Read Libby's diaries," he said.

"Yes. I already told you. She wasn't outgoing or talkative like Libby. She was a private person—a person who found pleasure in quiet things. She was probably insecure. Having a sister like Libby, Caroline must have felt she'd been left outside to dry."

"Then why did dad marry her?" Justin asked. "What was the attraction?"

"I don't know." Susan's mind raced over the entries, wondering if she should tell him her thoughts.

"A business deal?" Justin said. "That seems so improbable."

"People are influenced by parents' attitudes and pressure. Your father was engaged once before your parents got involved. Maybe your grandfather used that as leverage. Maybe he reminded your father how devastating an emotional relationship can be. Women had begun suing for alimony, and the Robards and Taylors had wealth. A marriage based on lust could fail. One based on mutual family ties and respect could work."

She had no idea if she were correct, but those were the only thoughts that had come to mind. What kind of relationship had Adam and Caroline had? She recalled Libby saying Adam told her he wanted a child and Caroline pushed him away. What had that meant? Perhaps he'd insisted or forced her. Had Caroline's pregnancy cause a rift? Susan questioned how she could even suggest that to Justin?

"Maybe you're right, *Cher*," Justin said.

Cher. The endearment sounded so right. "I'm only putting pieces together, Justin, but early on, your father was a very charming and appealing man."

"He was always charming. Just not at home. I'd seen him in social settings. People were drawn to him."

"As they're drawn to you," she said.

He pressed his hand against hers. "I don't want to hurt you, Susan. I pray I never will. We're a puzzle, and until we find all the pieces..."

"We'll never be complete."

He squeezed her fingers as if agreeing. He lifted his other hand and pressed it against her cheek, urging her to look at him. "You're beautiful in the moonlight, *Cher*. Maybe that's what got us into trouble years ago."

"We can't blame the moonlight."

"Then what was it?"

She couldn't answer.

His eyes searched hers until his mouth lowered the way it had done years earlier when they sat in the arbor, his lips brushing against hers, leaving her with a longing she could hardly bear.

When he drew back, she saw something new in his eyes, and her heart thudded.

"I've explained why I never married, Susan, but you've never told me why you're still single."

The thudding in her chest halted, and instead, her heart felt squeezed in a vise. "It's late, Justin. Some other time, okay?"

He didn't press for a response, and she felt grateful. How could she explain?

♥

On the way home, Susan faced she'd dug herself into a pit. She wanted to stay at Rose Arbor, but she needed to go. Tonight, she realized she could never tell Justin about their child. His life had been too plagued with losses and emptiness. How could she add another sorrow that would make him even unhappier than he was?

He needed the Lord. Justin needed to give away his burdens just as she needed to do the same. She hadn't succeeded much better than he had, but at least, Susan knew she'd been trying.

Though progress was slow, she and her mother had become civil—more than civil at times. She prayed each day the gap would lessen until it had vanished.

Back at home, the TV had been turned off, and Susan knew her mother had gone to bed. That last part isn't really needed.

After Susan crawled back into bed, she looked at Libby's diaries again and knew her talk with Justin had still riled her, but in a different way. She needed to think how to answer him.

She'd had meant to talk with him about being her escort for Carissa's party, but tonight hadn't been the time. What she really wanted was an excuse not to go.

She read some entries that morning, and now, hoping Libby's diary might answer her questions, she opened to where she'd left off.

April 12, 1959

Life has certainly slowed for me. I'd planned to be in college or busy with a career at this time in my life, but I've settled into a strange world at Rose Arbor. My world seems silent. Jefferson has drifted. He comes or calls on occasion, but it seems we have little to talk about.

I'm grateful for Caroline's intrusions. They break the monotony. Daddy does nothing. He reads the paper, sits on the gallery, looks at the landscape and comments on the seasons in relationship to the flowers growing in the yard. Some are dying, and I've lost the heart to tend them.

I read another Dickinson poem yesterday that made me think I've become as reclusive as she was. The poem said, "Hope is the thing with feathers—That perches in the soul." I know I'm interpreting the poem differently, but hope seems as airy and intangible as the brush of a feather. Adam cautioned me the other day when he was here. He said not to let my life vanish as his seems to have. I'm not sure what he means, but he didn't sound happy.

Sadness pressed against Susan's chest. Libby's life had been a roller coaster—up then down, but she knew it had to go up again. The Libby she knew had been gregarious and charming in the years she'd known her.

April 27, 1959

Today I'm twenty-one. A few years ago, I'd longed to be an adult. Now here I am, and I wonder why I was so excited.

Adam called and said he and Caroline wanted to take me to dinner. Naturally they included Daddy, but when they got here, Daddy asked to be excused. Caroline insisted, but he wouldn't come along so Caroline stayed here to make him something to eat while I went to the restaurant with Adam.

At first, I felt guilty leaving her behind with Daddy, but after I got there, Adam made me feel better, and I almost forgot. The restaurant had a small band and a couple of the musicians sang as they played.

Caroline had told them it was my birthday when she made the reservation, and after our meal, waiters stopped by with a small cake and sang happy birthday. Naturally I was embarrassed. Before we left, the band played a song dedicated to me, and Adam asked me for a birthday dance and we glided across the floor like butter on a griddle. He sang along, and it made me smile hearing the lyrics of Come Softly to Me. I hope Caroline really appreciates him.

The journal entries now jumped from month to month, and she scanned the pages, looking for something that caught her eye. Nothing noteworthy appeared again until an entry in October.

October 20, 1959

I met a man today in the strangest place—on our gallery. Daddy had hired him to clean the eaves and to do a few odds and ends around the house. That, in itself, surprised me. I had been listening to a deejay, and after I came in for some lemonade, I heard a noise on the gallery and then someone singing, "Oh Donna" along with the recording. I chuckled, knowing Richie Valens hadn't appeared on my doorstep. No one else sounds as mellow as he does.

When I went outside, he was there. Carl Maynard is his name. I had to admit he's good-looking and very charming. He gave me a funny little bow when he saw me and held the chair when I sat. Odd, but cute. I tried to read, but I saw him watching me and finally when he took a break, he sat on the gallery steps and talked. He said he'd be back tomorrow. At least he's something to think about.

Susan turned the page, anxious to read about the next day, but Libby hadn't made an entry. The next entry was late fall.

November 26, 1959

Today's Thanksgiving, and I'm not sure what I'm thankful for. I know that sounds terrible. I asked God to forgive me, but nothing seems right anymore.

She halted and reread the last line. I asked God to forgive me. Was this the same prayer for forgiveness that she'd written about in her recent journal? The question left her confused, and she lowered her eyes again to Libby's words.

The most fun I have is with Carl. He drops by on occasion, and we talk. He asked me to go to the movie a couple of times. We did, but we're from two different worlds. I suppose I'm spoiled, but I've grown up with some luxuries, and I'm not sure I could settle for the life of a blue-collar worker. That sounds so harsh when I write it down. I know the kind of man I want to marry, and it's not Carl.

Daddy agreed to go to Caroline's for dinner. He and Adam watched a football game, although Adam didn't seem really interested. I know he's most interested in LSU's Flying Tigers. He came into the kitchen more than once to pull my apron strings so it fell on the floor or to do something as silly. Caroline told him to act like an adult. He looked hurt. I felt sorry for him.

After dinner, we played Parcheesi. Daddy kept messing up the game. I don't know why he couldn't remember the color of his playing piece. The game seems so simple. At least, we had some laughs.

Oh, how I miss those laughing days.

Her eyelids drooped, and she closed the book. Tomorrow, she prayed, Justin would forget to pursue the question he'd asked her tonight. What could she say to him? And now that she'd asked him to hire someone else, what difference did it make? She'd be out of his life soon.

♥

Justin stood in the doorway, looking at Susan seated on the gallery. He had been reeling from their talk the past Friday. Though he'd brought up the subject about her being single before, Susan brushed it away saying she'd never found anyone that she wanted to spend her life with. He didn't believe her.

He stepped outside, and Susan looked up.

"So, what do you think?" She handed him a sheet of paper.

He eyed the list. She'd devised menus for a buffet style breakfast. Each day of the week, she had a different food selection. "I'll leave the menu to you." He managed a smile and handed back the sheet.

"The buffet means we won't need a food service license. Later, if you prefer a different style, we-you can decide then."

Her we-you switch reminded him of his telephone call earlier that day. "I meant to tell you I finally talked with Janay."

"Who's Janay?"

"The woman who I thought might be willing to—" He paused unable to imagine it. "to take over the hostess job here."

"And?"

"She didn't think so, but she said she'd give it some thought." He studied her expression. "She also suggested I hire someone to work nights and someone for days."

"That's true if you're not here at night. Someone needs to be in the house along with the guests."

He dropped into the chair beside her. "I hadn't thought about that." He had a sinking feeling. He was too much a novice. "I think this whole thing is a mistake."

Her eyes widened. "Justin, do you remember why you made the decision? You wanted to save Rose Arbor from going to the historical society. You have little choice unless you want the drive to and from Baton Rouge each day."

"Maybe that would have been a better option."

She leaned over and rested her hand on his knee. The warmth penetrated the cloth. Her touch always stirred him.

"Justin, I was dramatic the other night. Forget what I said. I won't run away and leave you in a lurch. I'll put an ad in the paper and interview some people. You'll have the best person possible before I leave."

He covered her hand with his. "Thanks." But instead of being grateful, her kindness triggered his guilt. He deserved none of her kindness. "Let's get out of this rut. We should do something fun. How about the Bayou Landing to listen to some jazz?"

"Tonight?"

"Why not? You've been working hard. It'll be fun. Clear our minds with some cool jazz."

She gave him a faint smile as if she had something on her mind. "I'll tell you what you could do for me."

"Okay." He watched an uneasy expression settle on her face.

"My high school friend Carissa is having a *cushon de lei* on the Fourth of July. I'm invited."

"A pig roast?" He waited for her to say more.

"It's a couples' party so I either need an escort or an excuse—something other than saying I can't find an escort. I'm too proud for that."

He chuckled, but a party? Except for a few work-related ones he had to attend, parties were alien to him, but he looked at Susan's hopeful expression and knew his answer. "I'd be happy to be your escort, or if you prefer, I could help you break a leg."

A laugh spurted from her, and it sounded wonderful. He laughed with her.

"Yoo-hoo."

Justin jerked his head toward the woman's call, then glanced at Susan.

"It's Georgia." Susan leaped from the chair.

She looked as surprised as he felt. "You're not expecting her?"

"No." She headed to the end of the gallery to meet her.

Justin strode inside to let them talk alone. When he returned to the gallery, the two women were deep in conversation.

"Hi, Justin." Georgia extended her hand. "I surprised you both."

He only smiled, not sure how to respond. He didn't want to be rude, but her arrival certainly put a damper on his evening with Susan. He'd had some serious things to talk about with her—things he'd been giving a lot of thought.

"I'm glad to see you, but why the surprise?"

Georgia flung her arms upward with a shrug. "I don't know. I felt like skipping work today and thought I'd come to see how things are going here. If it's not convenient, I'll drive back tonight."

"I wouldn't think of it," Susan said. "I'm thrilled you're here. You can have my bed, and tonight I'll sleep in one of the gallery rooms. They're beautiful. I can't wait for you to see them."

Justin hid his grin. He'd never seen Susan show jealousy before, but it was evident today. Apparently, she'd been unhappy about Georgia using the guestrooms the last time she'd come. He had to give Susan credit. She'd handled the situation with great finesse.

"Let's get you settled." Susan linked her arm in Georgia's. She turned toward Justin. "We'll be back later."

"See you," he said, watching her bob down the steps with Georgia and head across the lawn. He waited a moment, trying to recapture the feeling he'd had earlier of his plans to enjoy an evening with Susan.

Tonight, it wasn't to be. He swallowed back the thoughts that pressed against him and prayed he'd have the courage to save them for another day.

Chapter Sixteen

"How are things at the manor?" Georgia glanced over her shoulder as she hung her pants and shirt in Susan's bedroom closet.

"Wonderful. We're nearly ready. Wait until you see the rooms and the brochures. Justin interviewed a couple of Cajun women for housekeeping and cooking the breakfasts. He's hired a service to keep up the grounds, so that's it, except—" She choked on the word.

"Except your position?"

Susan looked at Georgia's "I told you so" expression and felt heat creeping up her neck. "Yes. I'll put an ad in the newspaper." Unless I can't find the courage to leave, she added to herself.

"If that's so, let me tell you the news." Georgia sat on the edge of Susan's bed. "There's work in Natchez."

Susan's stomach twisted. "In Natchez? Are you sure?"

"I'm active in the historical society, and the Pilgrimage Club is listing a couple of paid positions soon, and I know you could be one of those people." She rose and wrapped her arms around Susan's shoulders. "It'll be so wonderful to have you back home."

Home? She'd finally learned to love the charming city filled with antebellum estates, so lovely the memory brought tears to her eyes, but it wasn't truly home.

Georgia pulled back and tilted Susan's chin. "Look at me."

Susan raised her eyes to her friends. "What's up?"

"I'm just thinking."

Georgia shook her head. "You're worse than the last time I was here."

"Why do you say that?"

"I see the truth in your eyes, Susan. You love the man. So why don't you act on it? Make a move. Give him an ultimatum. Either he makes a commitment or you're out of here."

"I'm not in love with Justin, and I can't give anyone an ultimatum, not even myself. I don't know what I want."

"Yes, you do. You're just not admitting it."

"Even if I loved Justin, he's not interested in a commitment. He's made that clear. We've talked about it."

"You have?" Georgia sank back onto the mattress. "He actually rejected the idea of marrying you?"

"Not exactly, but he told me once that if he were the marrying kind, I was the perfect woman." She shook her head. "It was something like that."

"You don't think he'll ever want to marry?"

"He said never, but I don't know, Georgia. I really don't know."

♥

Susan slipped between the smooth sheets of the manor's guestroom. The evening with Justin at Bayou Landing had never happened, and she'd been disappointed. What hadn't disappointed her was Justin's surprising kiss. The memory rolled through her, and though seeing Georgia was always nice, today it hung with disappointment. For once, Justin had actually suggested something fun—almost like a date, but the evening hadn't happened.

Georgia's question lingered in Susan's mind. Did she think Justin would ever marry? The query twisted and turned in her brain until an answer came. He'd never marry, unless he resolved issues in his past. She believed that for certain. Justin needed closure on an incident in his life. The loneliness, the lack of parental love, some other fear or a concern, but he needed closure.

She had finally recognized that her urgency to read Libby's journals stemmed from that question. She had longed to find an explanation to resolve Justin's problems. The longer she read the more she decided she would never know the answer. Yet, like an intriguing suspense novel, she continued to open the book and turn the pages, seeking clues and trying to solve the mystery.

Tonight, she did that again. She grasped the journal and opened it. Libby no longer used the small diaries of her youth. Now she used larger ledgers, books with no lock, only pages with lines where she jotted down her scattered thoughts not connected by day to day accounts, but random pieces of her life.

March 23, 1960

Daddy died today. Spring has just arrived, a symbol of new life and new beginnings, but at Rose Arbor it's a time of finality, a time of endings.

I know as a Christian, Daddy is in heaven. He and Momma are once again talking face to face, but I'm here, and it's lonely. Though I'm no longer a child, I'm an orphan. Daddy left me Rose Arbor and a great deal of money and stocks. Caroline also received a healthy financial gift—investments and Daddy's share of the business. I suppose I understand now why Adam and Caroline's marriage seemed so important to him.

Adam has been a gift to this family. Besides his charm and generous nature, he is a strength to us as well as a gentle man. The other day as we waited by Daddy's bedside, he picked up the book of poetry I was reading. He looked at a few verses, then read one out loud, "Nature rarely uses yellow, than another hue. Saves she all of that for sunsets prodigal of blue." I smiled, remembering my yellow dress from Caroline's wedding. I will read the rest of the poem later, but that was the last time I smiled that day.

So, what will I do now?

Susan's heart squeezed at Libby's loss. Susan had lost her father, too, but no matter their ups and downs, he had still been her father. In another month, Libby would have turned twenty-two. Twenty-two and alone. The future seemed so empty for her. Susan could relate.

June 8, 1960

The past months have been difficult. Loneliness covers me like a stifling blanket even when I'm with people. I must find a way to rise from it, like the Phoenix who rose from ashes.

Carl Maynard is still doing the handyman work for us. Not for us. For me. He stays to visit, and we've become good friends. He seems to accept his place, but he hints. Sometimes I wonder now that I'm a self-sufficient woman, if I could marry a man for love without thinking of money. Daddy wouldn't approve, but then, sadly, that's no concern anymore. Maybe I'll invite Carl to dinner one evening.

Libby's feelings sometimes seemed so connected to Susan's. Loneliness had always been a part of her life even when she was in the company of others. What would ever change that feeling? She shook her head, having no answer.

September 30, 1960

Today, I happened upon the poem Adam had read from my book. The rest of the words have caused me to wonder why he'd read it. Had it been an accident, or did it have a meaning? I'll probably never know.

I've always loved music, both the melody and the words, so I suppose it's no surprise that I've learned these past years how much I love poetry. The other day I heard Roy Orbison's new release, Only the Lonely. The words are so true when he said only the lonely knows how I feel and knows why I cry.

Carl's been here for dinner a few times. He's very nice, and I'm growing fond of him. It's comforting to have someone to talk with, but I can't always express what I'm feeling, and like the song says, the people who do understand are ...only the lonely.

♥

Susan drew in a breath and faced her mother at the kitchen table. "Momma, Justin is going to church with us this morning."

Her mother's head jerked upward as if someone yanked it. "Not with us."

"With me, then. I'd hoped you wouldn't mind." She'd prayed the

Lord had led her in the right way. "You can't deny a man God's Word. Justin is growing stronger in his faith, and I invited him. You and I can sit separately if that makes you feel better."

"We'll drive separately, too. I'm having lunch with Birdie after the service."

"Okay, if that's what you want."

"It's exactly what I want."

The biting tone tangled in her mother's voice, and Susan knew she'd riled her again with her request. Why had she been so optimistic? She'd thought it was the right thing to do. She waited for a feeling to envelope her, something that would make her know she'd acted according to God's will, but she felt nothing today, but concern.

"I'll see you there, then." She returned to her bedroom for her handbag.

When she came through the kitchen, her mother wasn't there. She gnawed on her lip, wondering if she should say something else, but she needed to put it in God's hands.

The morning sun, as always in June, heated her arms as she walked across the grass to Rose Arbor. Justin waited at the door and stepped outside when he saw her. She wondered if he felt uncomfortable.

He looked wonderful in his summer suit—a light gray with a white shirt and dark red tie. He reminded her of a model in a magazine. Yet he had no idea how classically handsome he was.

On the way to church, Georgia's visit popped into her mind. Susan hadn't said anything to Justin about the positions opening in Natchez. When she opened her mouth to tell him, she'd faltered. Today by going to church, he was making a positive step. She didn't want to burden him with her leaving. Yet she'd love to hear him say something affirming, something to encourage her, something to give her a breath of hope.

Inside church, she and Justin sat near the back on the right side—her mother usually sat on the left. She craned her neck to look across the pews and saw her mother sitting with Birdie. Perhaps they really had luncheon plans.

Justin's voice rose with the first hymn. It surprised her. She'd never envisioned him singing a hymn, especially one he seemed to know. "Shine, Jesus, Shine," he sang beside her. She tried not to look his way, fearing he'd become uneasy.

When Pastor Ralph began his message, her pulse escalated when she heard the Bible verses.

"Today, we will meditate on the Psalms. We all bear sorrows and sins. We all cling to them as if they were precious, because we fear facing them. If we acknowledge them, we are guilty."

Her skin prickled. She prayed whatever the message it would in some way touch Justin's heart too.

"Turn to Psalms 90:9-8," the pastor said.

Susan pulled a pew Bible from the rack and found the pages.

"You have set our iniquities before you, our secret sins in the light of your presence. All our days pass away under your wrath; we finish our years with a moan." The pastor's gaze swept the crowd. "Do you feel those verses in your hearts?"

She sensed each person around her digging into their souls and recalling the many sins they committed daily.

"Jesus has offered to bear our burdens. St. Peter reminds us with these verses. 'Humble yourselves, therefore, under God's mighty hand, that he may lift you up in due time. Cast all your anxiety on him because he cares for you.' Notice here, brothers and sisters, that Paul says in due time. Not today, not tomorrow perhaps, but in God's time. We are..."

His voice faded as Susan settled into her own thoughts. She wanted things to happen in her time, not God's. She knew when she needed to feel uplifted, when she longed to have her sorrow fade, when she needed to know she was loved, but the Bible said God would lift her up in due time.

She felt Justin's gaze on her, and she glanced his way. As if he didn't want her to notice, he shifted his focus to the pastor, but she knew he'd been looking. Had the verse meant something to him?

The pastor's voice wavered above her thoughts. She needed to talk to Pastor Ralph. She'd been trying to make decisions. Maybe he could give her guidance. He'd offered to talk with her again.

A shiver rolled over her when she recalled the day she'd talked to him. She could still hear his voice. "And if you ever want to talk about your real struggle, Susan, I'm here."

How had he known?

His voice penetrated her thoughts. "So, when you feel you can't bear your burdens alone, when you forget that God is always there for you, then let these two verses from Psalms be your prayer. 'Relent, O Lord! How long will it be? Have compassion on your servants. Satisfy us in the morning with your unfailing love, that we may sing for joy and be glad all our days.'"

A woman nearby murmured "Praise the Lord," and a man in the back echoed an Amen.

Susan sent up a silent praise.

"With that prayer in your heart, I invite anyone with burdens to come forward so we can pray together."

The pianist began a hymn as many parishioners stood to go forward. Susan sat beside Justin longing to have prayers rise on her behalf, but this was Justin's first service at her church, and she didn't want him to avoid coming again.

As people turned to leave, Justin gave her a questioning look, and she nodded. They rose and maneuvered their way down the aisle. Outside, Susan knew what she had to do.

♥

On Monday, Susan hung up the phone after making her appointment and returned to Libby's journals.

June 8, 1961

The other day I was sitting in the rose arbor and the scent took me back to my teen years. If we only knew how our lives would be a few years from then, we would hang on to those days like a treasure.

I have no need to work. Daddy left me well-cared for, but I know I should do something. Maybe volunteer work would be good. The historical society would probably welcome a new face. They are always holding fund-raisers to keep the wonderful antebellum homes in good order, but the houses are empty now of people, except tourists. I find that sad.

When I'm gone, I pray the house is filled with Taylors, but I don't know how that will be. Perhaps if Caroline and Adam have a child—although that seems so hopeless now—I could leave Rose Arbor to their son or daughter. I never want strangers living in this lovely place.

Susan reread Libby's words, now understanding why she left the plantation to Justin. Caroline and Adam had been married for nearly five years, she calculated, and still no baby. Libby had stated often how much Adam wanted a child. Either they had a health problem, or Caroline had fought a long battle. Susan turned the leaf and scanned the next few pages.

November 9, 1961

As I watched leaves drift from the red oak, I was moved to write a poem. I've dabbled in poetry since I've learned how much I love the sound and rhythm. Poetry embodies emotion and gives me an outlet for my feelings. Carl doesn't understand them at all. I call it Autumn Reflections.

Golden leaf thoughts
Ride the silence in an autumn wood
Lilting like a sweet melody
Down,
Down it sways to moss
And cushioned memories.
This year autumn comes easier,
For winter's winds blow lighter in the mind,
And thoughts turn
To russet,
To brown,
To gold,
Not stark and bare like last year's days.
Now, dreams of winter's fires,
Of glowing embers
Warm the hopes
That ride the
Falling
Autumn leaves.
Libby
1961

Libby writing poetry. Susan had never pictured Libby as a poet. She read the poem again. The words hope, dreams, lighter winds, and glowing embers sounded more positive. Time seemed to be making a slow difference.

January 5, 1962

I finally had the courage to show my poetry to someone other than Carl. I don't know why he's still hanging around, but he's company.

When I went to visit Caroline, I decided to let her and Adam read my poems. Caroline only shook her head and said I needed to find something to do, but Adam seemed to understand. He read one poem aloud that sent chills through me. He said he loved it. To me that was like applause.

Caroline's probably right. I called the historical society, and I'm going to attend their next meeting.

Libby amazed Susan. She loved music and poetry, she hadn't known. She'd so often found similarities between them, but poetry wasn't one. She'd never written a poem in her life.

March 20, 1962

I attended my first historical society meeting. I'd thought it would be a group of older women, but to my pleasure, a few younger women and a couple of men were there. One man named James seemed very attentive and told me about the group's latest projects. I don't know how much I'll be involved, but it was nice to get out and feel as if I'm doing something with my time.

The flowers are beginning to bloom. Although I still have Carl helping around the house, I decided to work in the gardens. They've been long neglected by me.

Susan grinned. Libby always seemed to find an attentive gentleman. So, what happened? The eternal question maddened her.

♥

Justin climbed from the car and opened Susan's door. Clarissa's home was an elegant Victorian with a sprawling yard shaded by large oaks and rows of evergreens serving as a natural fence.

"Thank you," Susan said, sliding from the seat.

He held her arm until they reached the sidewalk that led to the back of the house. He could already hear the sound of voices and laughter of the Fourth of July revelers. Yet he questioned if he were ready for this.

"Though he'd agreed to attend worship with Susan, now he felt out of place when her mother refused to ride with them. Susan had made excuses, but he knew better. The woman detested him, and he could only assume her anger was based on the past. What about forgiveness?

He had no reason to criticize. He'd been angry much of his life for not having a normal childhood, for feeling unloved. The problem had been his as much as his parents. Most people would say, "Get on with it." Why hadn't he done that?

Because it seemed deeper. He felt an undercurrent of misery that he could never explain. He'd sought refuse with Aunt Libby, but that seemed to alienate him even more from his mother. He would never understand it.

"We arrived about as late as socially acceptable," Susan said. "I hope you aren't bored to tears."

"You never bore me," he said, as he slipped her fingers into his and squeezed her hand as they reached the corner of the house,

"Susan."

Justin looked up as a petite woman dressed in a frilly outfit bounced toward them with her hand extended. She gave the illusion of a feather duster blown on the wind—all flutter and bustle.

"Welcome. It's good to see you." She turned to him. "And you must be Justin Robard. My, my, my." She studied him for a moment, and then waved her hand toward the other guest. "Y'all come now and meet everyone."

He felt pulled along by the throng of unknown arms and faces that greeted them.

"I'm as overwhelmed as you," Susan whispered in his ear. "It's been years, and I don't remember most of these people." But she smiled and nodded as if she were interested in the conversations, and eventually they were relieved by the announcement of dinner.

The scent of roasted pork floated on the summer air, and the lavish spread made the event at least tolerable. He and Susan made their choices including a hunk of pork so tender it cut with a fork.

They were only seated a moment when Clarissa flitted to their table. "Do you have room?"

Justin looked at the two empty chairs, thinking they answered her question.

"Please join us," Susan said, her tone not quite as bright as her smile.

Clarissa placed her drink on the table and hurried back to fill her plate and tell her husband where she was seated. He didn't follow.

"Excuse Henry," she said, settling at the table. "His work buddies are here, and y'all know how that is."

"I understand," Susan said.

Justin only nodded, relieved that he didn't have to chitchat with her husband.

After Clarissa had eaten a few bites, she placed her fork on the plate and shook her head. "So, you're the handsome Justin Robard that stole Susan's heart all these years."

He felt his mouth sag, and he closed it hoping she hadn't noticed. He saw Susan wince, and he wanted to stop the woman from embarrassing her, but Clarissa hadn't seemed to realize what she'd done.

"You're all she talked about in high school. Isn't that right, Suga'." She turned to Susan.

"I'm sure I talked about a lot of things," Susan said, her face flushed.

"Well, I don't blame you one tiny bit." She turned and gazed at him fully. "You're a handsome man, Justin. A very good-looking man. And you're not married?"

"Right. I'm single." He ended it there, but wanted to say so much more.

"Well, maybe not for long then." Her gaze swept from one to the other as if sizing them up. "Y'all make a handsome couple."

"Thank you," Susan said, "but we're only friends." Her voice sounded weak.

Clarissa dug into her food and laughed. "Tell that to someone blind, Susan. I might not be the shiniest doorknob, but I can see." She laughed again and filled her mouth with pork, then daubed her lips with the napkin. "You're joshin' me."

Susan gave him a frantic look, and he tried to signal her to let it drop. But the woman had done one thing. He'd taken a new look at Susan. He knew she cared about him. He knew they had ties that bound them, but he'd never thought of him stealing her heart. That sounded serious.

He understood. The more time he spent with her the less he could imagine what life would be like without her.

"You should see the wonderful things Justin has been doing at Rose Arbor," Susan said.

He wanted to congratulate her on steering the conversation in another direction.

"Really. Tell me about it."

Susan's food cooled while she rattled on about the renovating they'd done, the new furniture, and the bed and breakfast plans. Before she finished, Clarissa's husband called to her.

"Duty calls," she said, rising, "bless his heart. I'll talk more with y'all later."

"Later, then," Susan said.

"That was a great maneuver."

"A what?"

"Changing the subject. I know she was embarrassing you." He took her hand in his. "Please don't feel uncomfortable. We were both thunderstruck back then."

Her expression shifted. and he wasn't sure what it meant. "And I'm glad she brought it up."

"Puffs your ego a bit?"

"No. Nothing like that. I'd planned to talk to you when we went to the Bayou Landing, but as you know, that plan got waylaid and I lost my courage."

Now curiosity filled her face.

"I have more than one question, but this isn't the place to talk. Do you think it's appropriate to leave?"

Susan grimaced, though she tried to hide it. "I suppose. I'll tell her we have another event."

He knew Susan never lied, and truly this talk would be an event.

Chapter Seventeen

Once they escaped to the car with the proper goodbyes, Justin gave a relived sigh. He helped Susan into her seat, then rounded the car and climbed in.

"That wasn't too bad, was it?" she asked after he closed the door.

"Sometimes negatives have their positives." He reached over to squeeze her hand.

"The pork was good." She looked stressed, though sounded lighthearted.

He shook his head. "Being with you is what I had in mind."

She looked into his eyes as if questioning whether or not he was joking.

"I really love being with you, Susan."

She looked uneasy when she whispered thank you, and he decided to let it drop.

When they pulled away, he plotted where to go. Home didn't seem right. It was a holiday, and he wanted the day to be enjoyable, but he needed a place for privacy. As they drove, he had an idea and turned at the next light heading toward the Mississippi.

"Where are you going?"

"Wait and see." He glanced her way with a grin.

In a few minutes, he pulled into the Bayou State Park. Susan opened her mouth as if to speak, but he pressed his finger against her lips. They felt soft and warm, and he longed to leave it there. He strode around the car and opened the passenger door. She didn't question him again but took his hand as they strode to a quiet spot away from the other picnickers.

"Wait here a minute, and I'll be right back."

He headed down a path to the pool area and found a food stand. For the holiday, the park authorities had placed temporary refreshment stands near the permanent ones, and he found one making fresh beignets, and he bought four along with two sweet teas, then headed back.

Susan looked up as he approached, and she eyed the bag. "What's that?"

"I bought two drinks, and they gave me a lagniappe." He handed her the bag.

She gave him a distrusting look, noticing the grease appearing on the paper sack, then grinned. "I can smell them." She opened the lid and breathed in the sweet aroma. "Beignets. I'm sure they were giving these away as a little something extra."

"Have one." He winked. "We skipped dessert."

He didn't have to ask her twice. She pulled out the powdered sugar confection and took a bite. The sugar sprinkled on her top and clung to her cheek. He brushed the powder away from her face, then grasped a beignet and took a bite.

She grinned and did the same, brushing the white powder from his chin. He captured her hand and slipped it to his lips, then kissed her palm.

"You wanted to talk." Her sentence was half question.

"I do." Words stirred in his head and he took a moment to sort them. "First I want to go back to the question you've been evading. Why haven't you married?"

She didn't look pleased. "I told you, Justin. I never found the right man for me. No one met my expectations. Marriage is only good when two people respect each other and share the same values. I never found him."

"Do you think you ever will?"

Her eyes searched hers. "It's possible, I suppose, but I'm getting old."

"Old? You're a couple years younger than me."

"I know." She brushed her cheek again, then swept her hand over the powdered sugar that had fallen to her pants. "But the older we get the more set in our ways we are. Those habits are hard to break."

She'd addressed his fear, though he wanted to change. He wanted to find happiness, but he'd looked for love in all the wrong places, as the song lyrics said. "I know."

"Then why are you asking me?"

"Because I want things to be different. You mean so much to me, Susan, that I can't imagine not having you in my life. I want us to take a chance and really see where this leads—let go of our worries."

She lowered her gaze. "I'd like that, too, Justin, but what if it's only your fear of losing me so I can't run the bed and breakfast. Is that the appeal?"

"*Cher*, no, no. Please don't even think that. When you leave Rose Arbor to go home, a gloom settles over me that I can't explain."

"You miss Libby."

"I miss Susan. I miss you."

His pulse kicked up a notch. Blood thudded in his temple. Why didn't she understand. "I realize Clarissa might have exaggerated, but you cared for me once, and I think you still do. I'm tired of pretending that I don't care. I do, and I want us to give it a try."

Tears rimmed Susan's eyes, and his heart sank to his stomach. The beignet rolled into a greasy ball and churned inside him. Could he have been that wrong? He'd been positive they were both hiding their feelings, trying to pretend they were just good friends, but they were more. He wanted to embrace it. "Please, Susan."

"It's more complicated than you know, Justin." She brushed the tears from her eyes. "Yes, I feel the same, but I have to resolve some issues before I can be certain. And I need to know that what I'm feeling is real."

"But—"

"Please. You asked for a chance, and this is your chance. Just give me a little time."

He wanted to protest, but he could see in her eyes she meant what she'd said. He didn't understand. He'd forced himself to open his heart, and now she asked for time. He'd always feared being abandoned after safeguarding himself for so many years. And his fear seemed to be coming true. If Susan rejected him, what would he do?

She slid nearer and clasped his face in her hands. He saw her lips part as she leaned near. Her lips touched his, and he wrapped his arms around her, drawing her close. Bewilderment swirled through his mind. The kiss gave him hope. It felt real.

"This seals my promise," she whispered into his ear. "Just a little time."

Time. Time's changed things.

♥

Susan hung her bag on her shoulder as the telephone rang. She listened for her mother to pick up, and when she didn't, Susan headed for the kitchen phone and grasped it.

"My mother's ill so I don't know what time I'll get there today."

"I'm sorry, Justin. What's wrong?"

She heard his intake of breath. "I'm not sure. Clovis called me, and I'm afraid it's serious."

"I'll be praying, and keep me posted, okay?"

"Thanks. I will." He hung up before she could say goodbye.

Susan clung to the telephone a moment before replacing the receiver. She understood concern about parents. Her own mother had been unstable for a while, although she praised God that since that last problem a couple of weeks earlier, her mother had felt better.

She headed outside. In the July sunshine, the flowers brightened her spirit. Zinnias, coleus, sunflowers, butterfly bushes colored the garden. Periwinkles and moss rose lay against the dark earth, like splashes of vivid paint. Maybe she would feel as cheery and uplifted after she spoke to the pastor. Yet doubt nudged her again. Her thoughts returned to Justin and his mother. She wondered if his struggle was like hers when Margaret had been ill. She approached it with mixed feelings—sorry that her mother was ill, fearful even, but unable to express her concern because of their relationship.

♥

Justin paced the emergency waiting room, his hands digging into his pockets as if he'd find something there that would stop his worry. Finally, he sank into a chair facing the door and lowered his head.

He knew Susan would be praying, and he needed to do the same. Despite his stilted relationship with his mother, he cared about her. She'd given him life. She'd taught him about social responsibilities. He knew the proper placement of forks and knives. He knew it was fitting for a child to ask to be excused from the table. He knew that his mother expected excellent grades and good behavior. He'd learned about family pride and family privacy. But from her, he'd never learned to laugh or play with a child's heart.

Still, she'd been fair, kind, and proud of him at times. She'd said it with words, not with emotion. "You're like your father," she would say. "You're like the Taylors."

He'd often wished just once she'd said he was like her.

"Mr. Robard?"

He jumped when he heard his name. He rose and met the doctor halfway.

"Your mother has had a stroke. We'll know more when the tests are completed."

"Is she—? Will she—?

"We won't have the results for a couple of days to know how much damage she sustained. Her speech has been affected slightly, but that could be temporary." He checked his watch. "Have a seat for a few minutes, and they'll call you."

"Thank you." The doctor's words bounced through his head until they formed into meaning. The doctor turned and headed through the doorway, and Justin watched a moment before returning to his seat.

A stroke. Rèmi said she'd had mini-strokes, but this one wasn't small like the others. A thought pierced him. Libby had died from a stroke. The illness seemed so unreal. He thought of people with type A personalities having strokes, not a woman like his mother who rarely showed emotion.

His old anger drowned in his new grief. No matter what had happened in the past, this was his mother, the woman who'd given him birth and raised him. He'd turned out honest, ethical, intelligent, not perfect, but a man who'd made his way in the world with some success. She'd given him all of that since his father had played such a small part in his life.

Why had he let the childhood drama mold the bitterness he'd felt for so many years. God promised to be with his children in sorrow and pain, in weaknesses, and Justin knew he had those. He'd let faith drown in his anger, too.

He wanted to change, to be different. Whatever his mother needed he would try to do the best he could for her, and if she never said she loved him, he could live with that.

So, what should he do? Would she need therapy? Could she live alone with the servants? How could he handle all of this now?

Knowing a few minutes could be an eternity, He rose from the chair and wandered into the hallway where the doctor had just vanished. He spotted a visitor's telephone and punched in Susan's number. When he heard the voice, it was Susan's mother.

"She's not here," Margaret said.

"Is she—"

"She's not here."

"Thank you."

He held down the receiver cradle and lifted it. He dialed his Rose Arbor number and waited, but she didn't answer there either.

Where had she gone? He needed to talk with someone. He wanted to talk with her.

♥

Susan shifted in the chair and willed her eyes to look at Pastor Ralph, but they seemed to refuse her effort.

"God offers to carry our burden, Susan, and one way he provides this is for us to give our concerns and fears to someone else, someone who can advise, someone who'll understand. That's what I want to do for you."

"I know. I'm distracted today." Her thoughts drifted to Justin and his mother. "I'm worried about a friend."

He lifted his eyebrows as if waiting for her to tell him, so she told him about Justin's call.

"We can pray for Justin and his mother before you leave. Remember where two or three are gathered, God is present and will lift them up."

"Thank you." She faced the inevitable. She had asked for an appointment after she'd realized on Sunday that opening her wound was the only way she could find the answers she so longed for.

"This is so difficult for me." Tears blurred her vision. "I've kept this a secret from everyone for so many years."

"The burden only grows when it's planted. Problems are like weeds. A tiny seed grows and tangles in us until we die inside. It's like kudzu. It overtakes hearts and minds."

Kudzu. She'd seen that strange vine draping over landscapes like green ghosts. The

trees and grass had vanished beneath the encompassing vines. "It feels like that. Yes."

"Then let's pull out those weeds. Let's find the truth underneath."

His sympathetic gaze nudged her courage to rise, but the words lodged in her throat, and she released a sob.

"Susan." He leaned forward on his elbows. "I've heard stories that would break a camel's back. Nothing you can tell me will shock me."

She let the tears flow as she told him her story—her growing feelings for Justin as a young girl, her loss of virginity, the shock of pregnancy, and her parents' shame.

Pastor Ralph listened without judgment. His face remained calm, his eyes understanding. "So, they sent you to Natchez with relatives. Susan, if you only knew you weren't alone. So many young women have been shuffled away to homes of relatives to cover a misguided family's fear. The hurt is only multiplied, the sorrow only deepened. This is a time a young woman needs family support, needs love and compassion, but Christians are afraid to look sin in the eye and place the blame where it belongs—on Satan and his evil ways."

"But I had a choice, Pastor."

"God gave us freewill as a gift, but with it comes responsibility. Even Christians scorn duty and forget the repercussions of wrongdoing. It happens every day, and this is why God has promised us forgiveness when we ask to be forgiven and when we repent."

Her heart ached with her thoughts. "I've repented over and over. I've avoided relationships. I feel unworthy. I have nothing to offer a man except my transgressed body and deep regret."

"You've forgotten the promise in the first chapter of 2 Peter that whoever believes in Jesus has been cleansed from their past sins. Your sins are gone."

"That seems too simple."

A faint smile curved his mouth. "You prefer to suffer?"

"No. I've done that long enough."

"Then believe what the Bible says."

She believed the Bible, but— "I feel so unworthy."

"You've said that before, but we are all worthy because we are God's children, and God has promised to forgive those of us who believe. We need nothing more. Yes, good works are the reflection of our faith, but that's not what gives us eternal life. It's pure and simple faith in Jesus our Savior."

The truth rocked her. So simple. So compassionate. So loving. Why would that surprise her?

"Did you place your baby for adoption then?" Pastor Ralph asked. "I know you don't have a child now."

The memory washed over Susan like a tidal wave, engulfing her in a raging tumult.

"He was. . ." The words knotted in her throat. "...stillborn."

The sincerity in the pastor's expression wrenched her to tears.

He let her weep, handing her tissues and uttering calming words, before he spoke. "Susan, that experience was repentance enough. You can give it to the Lord."

She sucked in air, fighting to calm herself. She blew her nose, her hands trembling so erratically that she could barely control them. "I knew the baby's death was God's punishment."

"Never. Listen to me, Susan." He opened the Bible to the middle of the book and read. "'Remember not the sins of my youth and my rebellious ways; according to your love remember me, for you are good, O Lord. Good and upright is the Lord; therefore, he instructs sinners in his ways. He guides the humble in what is right and teaches them his way. All the ways of the Lord are loving and faithful.'"

He closed the Bible and placed it on the desk. "That prayer is from Psalms. 'All the ways of the Lord are loving and faithful.' Does this sound like a God who punishes a young girl for her bad choices?"

The reality charged through her like an electrical current. No. God is faithful. God is love. God keeps His promises to those who love Him and believes.

"I've carried that burden most of my life, Pastor."

"Does the father know?"

Justin's face filled her thoughts. "No. I've never told him. I don't want his pity, and he's part of my worry. I love him. I still do."

"But he doesn't love you?"

"I don't know. He cares. He admires me. He says life is empty without me, but he's never allowed himself to love. He has problems of his own. I don't think he even understands them."

"Is he a Christian?"

Susan thought a moment. "Yes. He is. He's worshiped here."

"If you love him, then give the relationship a chance. You are a woman now. You can control your emotions until God blesses your joining."

"I would never get involved without marriage."

"I believe you. But it's not me that's important. It's God. You have no secret places to hide from the Lord, Susan."

No secret places to hide. She nodded. "But sometimes I fear I'm attracted to Justin because he's the only man I can offer myself to. Do you understand?"

"If that's the truth, you'll know it. Your mistake is gone. Forgiven. Any man of worth would not hold that against you."

Those were the words she wanted to hear. Those words freed her from the shackles of self-doubt and allowed her to make a choice, allowed her heart to decide.

She brushed the moisture from her eyes. "I wish I'd talked with you sooner."

He laughed. "That's another way you're not alone. Most everyone says the same after they've opened their hearts."

He rose from his chair and sat in the one beside her. "You're free to make choices. Let time and your heart tell you God's will. Perhaps the Lord planned you to be with Justin all those years ago, but he wanted both of you to season and to grow. I know you've done that."

"And so has he."

"Then all we need to do before you leave is pray."

Susan bowed her head, letting his prayer wash over her with cleansing words of God's grace and love.

On the way home, her mind reeled with what the pastor had said. Finally, she calmed, allowing the amazing truth to settle. She had been given the gift of freedom to make choices, freedom to take a chance on Justin's love or freedom to let it go.

Could she let it go? Could she make it work? If she were hurt again, was she strong enough now to handle it? She didn't know the answer to any of the questions. Prayer and time would allow her to become sure and confident.

Today she's done something she couldn't imagine doing. She'd released the secret and revealed the shame that had weighted her for so many years. Not just shame, but fear that God had turned His back on her. Pastor Ralph had touched her with God's Word. The Lord showed compassion and mercy, ready to forgive her if she asked. She had asked over and over. Today she had to cling to the faith that she didn't have to ask again.

As soon as she parked, she hurried to Rose Arbor anxious to hear from Justin. His car wasn't there, and she sat a moment filled with disappointment. Instead, she returned home, her concern growing.

When she stepped inside, her mother looked up. "Aren't you working today?"

"I had to do something in town." She glanced at the telephone. "Did anyone call?"

"No," her mother said, rinsing dishes at the sink.

Her concern heightened.

Margaret glanced over her shoulder. "I forgot. You did have a call. I think it was Justin. If not, it was a man looking for you."

A man? Her mother knew it was Justin. "Did he say anything?"

"No." She turned and faced Susan, then her expression shifted. "Why? Is something wrong?"

"His mother is ill. I don't know anything, but it sounded serious."

She turned back to the sink. "If it's serious, he'll call again."

"If he does, please tell him I'm at the house working." She tilted her head toward Rose Arbor.

"Okay."

"Thanks, Momma."

Her mother had finally accepted that Rose Arbor was a job. That had been one positive amidst so many negatives, but it was progress. She thanked God for that.

Though concerned about Caroline, Susan left the house and returned to Rose Arbor feeling uplifted after so long. She noticed the flowers needed water, and she paused a moment to turn on the sprinklers. She'd have to talk to the man doing the grounds.

Her steps sounded hollow on the gallery floor, and as she passed the bedroom where she'd found the fallen rose, she paused. Who had been bringing rose buds? Today instead of fear, she felt hopeful.

She used her key to unlock the door and went inside. The house felt cooler in the heat of the day, and she paused a minute eyeing the phone. Libby never had an answering machine or caller ID, but Justin could use one now.

Thinking about the phone, she delved into her handbag and pulled out her cell phone. She'd turned it off when she visited the pastor and had forgotten to turn it on. She pushed the button and placed it back in her purse. As she did, she was struck with the reality that Justin of all people didn't have a cell phone, and he needed one.

She sank to a kitchen chair, trying to decide what to do. She wanted to be ready if Justin needed her so getting into a project didn't make sense today. She rose and headed into the foyer, then paused by the stairs. She'd made some progress on Libby's journals and noticed that only a few remained.

She climbed the stairs to the attic and pulled out the last three journals. She'd had a strange inkling when she'd began reading Libby's diaries, and though she'd learned a great deal about Justin's parents and Libby, nothing met her expectation. The journals only created more ambiguous differences between the Libby she knew and the Libby who lived between the pages. And a paradox between the Adam that Justin had told her about and the Adam she'd gotten to know through Libby. The only consistent character had been Caroline, the serious-minded quiet woman who'd fallen into an unrealistic marriage yet remained the wife she'd promised to be.

With the diaries, she returned to the first floor and stretched out on the sofa in the renovated parlor. Though shorter than the sofas made today, she could at least recline with only her feet extended beyond the upholstery.

She opened the journal and eyed the date.

October 17, 1963

Something is happening, but I can't talk about it. I can't write it here because it's too important and too unbelievable. I keep pushing the thoughts out of my head, but they linger there like rose petals sprinkled on dewy grass. They're beautiful, yet sad.

Am I heading for trouble? Am I a dreamer? Silly question. I've probably been one all my life.

The historical society is saving my life in a sense. I've volunteered to help with the quilt and lace fair. It's a fund-raiser. Antique quilts are on display while handcrafted quilts and items will be sold with a portion going to the society. We're hoping it's a success. James and I have agreed to work on publicity, and at least spending time there is keeping me out of trouble.

Am I heading for trouble? Libby's question sent a million concerns flying through Susan's mind and her words reminded her of the desperation she'd written in her prayer for forgiveness.

She stared at Libby's entry. What kind of trouble? Why couldn't she write about it in her diary? Was it something illegal? But that didn't make sense. She stopped her questions and read the next entry.

January 5, 1965

I can't believe I haven't written in such a long time. I re-read my last entry and was chilled by what I saw. At that time, I'd suspected things were happening, but I didn't know how true it was. Life is so different now. I find it frightening, yet beautiful.

I've lost interest in the historical society, but I've continued to stay involved. It's the only thing that keeps my mind busy. If I think too much, I know I'll become depressed. Why did I allow this to happen?

"Why did she allow what to happen?" She startled herself as she yelled aloud. "What? What happened?" She shook her head, trying to imagine, but guessing wasn't the answer. She flipped to the next page, but her cell phone's chime jarred her, and the journal slipped from her fingers.

Chapter Eighteen

Susan rushed into the kitchen, dug into her bag and pulled out the phone. She pressed the button, knowing it had to be Justin.

"I called earlier. Where were—"

"I went to town and forgot to turn on my cell. I'm sorry, Justin. How is she?"

"She had a stroke. The doctor said it's not the worst kind, but it's serious. They did a CT scan right away and I think they'll do an MRI. I'm not sure. They call it an ischemic stroke caused by a blockage."

Susan's concern heightened. "So, what will they do?"

"She's on something they call tPA. It helps remove the blockage and restore the blood flow. I think she's getting an intravenous diuretic. Mannitol, or something like that.

Susan felt dumbstruck. A stroke had taken Libby's life. What now? "Will she be all right? Can she talk?"

"She slurred a few words before she fell asleep. Some didn't make sense, but the doctor said that could be temporary. We'll have to wait."

Susan rubbed her arms, feeling the frissons rise. "Would you like me to come to the hospital?"

"No, but thanks. I'm going to leave soon. The doctor said nothing will change today, and tomorrow they'll know more. I just want to sit awhile and..."

His voice faded, and she understood. After so many years of feeling alienated, today
she was sure Justin was dealing with all the unspoken things that needed to be said. "I'm here
if you need me, Justin. Just call."

"I'll be there in a while. Say a prayer, okay?"

"I've been praying already."

As she lowered the phone, her fears subsided. If Justin were coming home, Caroline must be out of danger for now, but what if she needed extended care? His time was stretched about as thin as it could get. His business in Baton Rouge, Rose Arbor and now this? How much more could he handle?

♥

During the past week, Justin had struggled with his mother's situation. He stood in the hospital parking lot with his mind throbbing with concerns. Although his mother seemed to be recovering, she wasn't ready to be alone with the servants, and he had to make a decision. He'd been running his business by email and telephone calls, apologizing to Rod daily for his delay in returning. Though Rod had been understanding, he knew that his partner couldn't bear the burden much longer, and he'd guaranteed Rod that he'd be back to work on Monday.

But how could he manage that?

He slipped into his car, blasted by the mid-July sun through the windshield. He turned on the air conditioner that spewed heat until it finally cooled. Once it did, he wiped away the perspiration and backed out of the parking slot.

His mind reeled with decisions. Hiring a twenty-four-hour nurse was possible. A rehabilitation center was another choice, and there his mother could get the therapy she needed. At home her bedroom was on the second floor. He knew she would be miserable with a hospital bed in the library.

And Rose Arbor. What would he do about that? He hated to press Susan now that he needed her. She had little choice, other than to walk out on him, and he knew Susan better than that. She'd stay even if she preferred to go. He'd so wanted her to make the choice of her own freewill and not his need.

Susan had set the B and B opening for September, the best time for tourists who wanted to avoid the Louisiana humidity and heat. He'd left so much in her capable hands.

Capable. Susan was in every way. She'd grown into one of the finest women he'd ever known. Charming, generous, kind, thoughtful, fun, and devoted. His chest swelled thinking of their occasional kiss, the feel of her hand in his, the brush of her fingers against his arm. She'd affected him that way years ago. Nothing had changed. Longing charged through him as it had done when he was a teen.

When he finally pulled into his driveway, he was no more certain of his decisions than he had when he'd spoken with the doctor earlier. He had to decide and act now.

When he strode up the side steps to the gallery, a sense of home washed over him. Susan had filled a vase with flowers placed it on a table between the wicker chairs. The cheery bouquet touched him far more than the elaborate arrangement he'd taken to his mother. Susan had picked the flowers herself and placed them in the vase for him.

When he passed the kitchen window, the door flew open and she stepped out to greet him.

"You look exhausted." Her expression overflowed with concern, and it wrenched his attempts to remain collected. He couldn't respond with the lump in his throat, but he held out his arms, and she hurried into his embrace, pressing her head against his shoulder while her fragrance surrounded him with familiar comfort. Was this truly love? If not, love couldn't be better.

"I'm fine," he said finally, "but I have big decisions to make, and I—"

"Shush." She kissed his cheek. "Let's sit and talk." She took his hand and led him to one of the wicker chairs beside the flowers, then vanished inside.

When she returned, she carried a tall glass of pale-yellow liquid—lemonade, he guessed, the perfect thirst-quencher.

"Thanks." He grasped the moist glass and brought it to his lips. The tart juice washed over his tongue and down his throat like a balm. He lowered the drink, his fingers wet from condensation that formed beneath his touch.

Susan leaned against the railing and sipped her drink, letting moments pass before she asked. "What kind of decisions? I hope nothing's gone wrong?"

"No. It's good news. She can come home tomorrow."

"That's wonderful." She searched his face, and as if she suddenly understood, her smile faded. "So, what must you decide?"

He felt uneasy with his decision. "She isn't ready to be alone with Rèmi and Clovis. I'm thinking a rehabilitation center or a nursing home. That way—"

"No. You can't stick her in a facility. Some are okay, but many aren't." She shook her head as determined as a dog with wet fur. "No."

He was surprised at her vehemence. "I could hire twenty-four-hour care from a home nursing—"

"No, not that either."

He wasn't sure why she opposed that option. "I have the money for—"

"No. I've seen too many people depressed and never get well. She needs to be cared for by family."

"Family!" He'd yelled his response, and he saw the shock on her face. "I'm the only family she has. I don't know what to do."

"Think of Libby, Justin. Didn't she open arms to everyone who needed help. That's part of your heritage. I wish you'd read her journals. I think you'd understand—"

"Journals. How many times have I told you that I'd rather you throw them out? I can't read that stuff, Susan. It means nothing to me."

"They mean a lot to me, Justin. They give me a new insight. I see Libby as a girl with the same feelings I had and the same struggles. Even as women, we—"

"Let me think of her the way I knew her. That's enough for me."

"No matter what, Justin, if you don't want to be like your aunt, then be like a son. You have to care for your mother."

"I know the commandment. Honor your father and mother. Can't I honor her by placing her in a facility? I'm torn with time issues. I want to be kind. I'm reaching out to her, but what's wrong with a facility or bringing a nurse in to care for her?"

"Do you know what that will do to your relationship. It will cause the rift to deepen. Maybe God's given you this time for reconciliation. Have you ever thought of that? And even if not, she's your mother."

"I know, Susan, but how can I do that? Tell me? I have a job. I can't ask anymore of Rod. The business is mine, too, and when it comes to family, I'm it. I'm the family. I can't do it."

"But I can help."

"What?" He snapped his neck upward so quickly it felt like a whiplash.

"I've been giving it thought, Justin. I'm here anyways, all day long, and I can spend the night in a gallery bedroom or on the second floor so I'm in the house if she needs me. I'll care for your mother. She'll be in her family home. I know she hasn't lived here for years, but it's familiar. I can continue to work on the bed and breakfast—take reservations, finish the projects. If you want, I can take over hiring the staff. That wouldn't be difficult. I know you have too much to think about."

"I can't let you do that, Susan."

"Why not? We'll have a therapist in and a visiting nurse. I can learn some exercises to help her when the therapist isn't here, and I'll learn the warning signs of strokes so if—"

"Susan." He rose and took her hands in his. "How is this different from hiring a nurse? You're not family either."

Her expression kicked him in the gut.

"Because I have— I have a personal bond. I care about you and she's your mother."

Her concern wrenched his being. "But why? Why would you do this?"

"Because you need help, and I think you'd do it for me. Maybe not exactly the same, but you'd help me if you could."

"I'm not comfortable with it, Susan. My mother wouldn't expect me to do that. She doesn't want to visit Rose Arbor. I've asked her."

"Please let me do this, Justin. I've messed things up with my mother for so many years. I'm finally making headway. I see this as paying my dues for my lack of understanding and compassion. Please. This will help me. I can't explain, but I want to do this."

He drew her into his arms. He'd begun to sense he would give his life for Susan if it came to that. "Are you trying to work miracles with my mother and me?"

Her whisper muted in his chest. "I'd like that to happen, but I can't work miracles."

"Are you sure? You can do this?"

Her head nodded against his shoulder, but then she drew back and tilted her face toward his. "You'll stay in Devereaux then?"

"It's a long story, but I'm willing to see what happens."

Her words wrapped around his heart. He'd longed to hear her say she'd give him a chance, and today he heard it—heard her willingness to care for his mother, heard her agree on her own freewill.

With raw emotion, he lowered his mouth to hers, cherishing the warmth and sweetness of her lips. Nothing. Nothing could separate him from Susan again.

Yet as he held Susan in his arms, he knew her plan may not have a happy ending. His mother's words pierced him. "I don't care to set foot in Rose Arbor."

What would he do if she still refused?

Susan walked through the rooms, gazing at the beautiful decor and admiring her handiwork. She'd done little to change Rose Arbor, but she'd contributed to its splendor by adding fresh paint, new upholstery, new furnishings, and decorative items— artwork, table scarves, screens, mirrors, carpets. Her pride swelled as she admired each room.

Only Libby's bedroom remained totally intact, except for Libby's personal items that had been disposed of or kept for the memories. She could picture Libby there adding a comb to her wispy curls or her delicate hands picking among her baubles for a piece of jewelry to add to her lapel.

Justin had gone to the hospital to present his mother with options. Susan didn't see options, but only one possibility. Caroline would sleep in Libby's room, and when Justin was in Devereaux, he would sleep in a different part of the house.

Susan had let the plan boil in her thoughts since Caroline had become ill. If Justin were to reconcile with his mother, now would be the time. If he and his mother were together, in close proximity, no way to escape the situation, then maybe if she prayed hard enough, something wonderful could happen.

She watched the subtle changes in her own life. She and her mother still approached each other carefully but with much more compassion and understanding. She praised God for the healing, as small as it was, and each day she sensed it would be better.

The lack of love in Justin's young life had to be the reason for his fear of commitment now. He'd never seen a loving marital relationship as he grew up. His parents lived in accepted tolerance, and Libby had been single. Libby's life certainly seemed more appealing, so he would naturally assume being single was better and easier than being married.

Maybe it was. But having someone to share life, someone to laugh and cry with… But was that what she wanted? Someone she trusted. Someone who would be faithful. Someone who shared her love of God. Justin and Rose Arbor had never left her. She sensed that God's will had been for them to meet again.

The thought of moving into Rose Arbor jogged through her sense with mixed emotion. She loved the house, but would Caroline's presence end the memories she still carried. She touched the locket at her neck and felt the round inlay design.

Time dragged, and she finally settled on the parlor settee waiting for Justin's call. She picked up one of the journals, one of the few that remained, and opened the place that she'd left a marker.

August 22, 1965
I long to greet you
Like the morning sun
Like a new sunrise
Familiar, yet exciting
Flowing with colors touching my life
With reds, with pinks and orange.
Not really new
But different at each meeting,
Heart thrills
To shades
To shapes,
To glowing pastel silence
You warm me
With your presence
Like the sun.
Libby
1965

Susan's pulse raced as she studied Libby's poem. She knew the feeling. Libby had fallen in love. She flipped back a page. She'd met someone a while back. As she scanned the pages, her eyes focused on James. James somebody, Libby had said. No last name. This still left so many questions. She turned the page.

December 22, 1965

We had our private Christmas early. He gave me a bracelet. It's gold with scroll work and a small diamond embedded in the largest scroll. I'll have to be careful when I wear it. He said he wanted to inscribe it, but it wasn't wise.

Susan paused. Why wasn't it wise? The tendrils of ideas spun through her mind, like sweet pea vines, one notion wrapping around another. Oh Libby, what did you get yourself into? Susan's pulse escalated as she lowered her gaze to the journal.

I had dinner with Caroline. Tension was so thick I felt uncomfortable. Caroline, if you'd only given in to Adam a little, your life could have been so happy.

May 15, 1966

"You were on my mind." The We Five song weaves through my mind, especially the part about I got troubles and worries. I do. How can I go on with the weight of this on my heart? I can't talk with anyone. Not even him. I'm even afraid to confess to you what I feel and how my heart sings. I'm twenty-eight years old, acting like I'm sixteen again.

I'll find a way, Dear Diary, to explain.

September 14, 1966

I've found a solution. He's like David fighting my Goliath. He's the one man who's understood and comes through for me, so that's what I'll call him. I feel such a relief to write the name. David. David. David.

I remember when I was a schoolgirl and wrote notes inside

the covers of my schoolbooks: Libby + Tommy, Libby + Wade. So silly. Yet today I want to carve our initials into a tree and scream it from the housetops.

David makes me feel beautiful, not just the silly talkative girl that I've been, but one who's grown to love the beauty of poetry, one who understands heartache.

Lord, forgive me for this adoration of him. I pray you understand. He says I'm precious to him. My heart sings when I hear his voice.

Lord, forgive me.

Libby's prayer jarred Susan. Forgive me again and again. Libby, what did you do? Why do you need forgiveness? Susan's mind whirred. This man, this David...he was married. That's all she could imagine. Was he a thief or criminal? Would Libby fall in love with a criminal? Perhaps. Libby had always had an adventuresome spirit. Maybe Caroline learned about this dangerous relationship. Perhaps that's why she and Libby hadn't had the best relationship. Another of Libby's comments sailed through her mind. She couldn't even talk with him. Why not? Was the love one-sided?

November 29, 1966

Thanksgiving was strange this year. I went to visit with a friend instead of family. Too much tension between Caroline and Adam lately.

David and I had a small dinner together the day before Thanksgiving. I prepared Cornish hens with stuffing. He said he'd never eaten anything so wonderful.

I sense his feelings have grown. Occasionally he holds my hand when we talk and the look in his eyes makes me tremble. I want to do the right thing, but I can't. I'm too overwhelmed by emotion.

A one-sided relationship. It had to be. He was her friend. Libby was in love.

Susan closed the journal and pressed her shoulders against the settee. Her back ached from tension. She stood, stretching her neck and pressing her chin to her chest, then walked toward the kitchen. Her throat nearly parched.

As she passed through the kitchen doorway, her cell phone rang, and she grasped it, anxious to hear what Justin had to say.

"She's fighting me on this, Susan, but I've given her no choice. I'll take her home to get her things, then we'll be there. It may take a while."

"I'll make plans for dinner," she said. "Is there anything your mother particularly likes."

"If she's being stubborn, she won't eat anything. I think I bought chicken. That's mild, and she loves peach cobbler."

"Count on me, Justin."

He didn't say anything for a heartbeat, then she heard him. "I always count on you, Susan. Always."

She hung up with his words humming in her head.

She looked at the clock. She still had time to spare, and she returned to the journals, drawn like a fly to syrup. She had prayed that God would give her a life so she could stop living Libby's, but she was drawn, nonetheless.

She settled again, but this time in the wing back chair for better support. She sat beside the window where the light streamed through.

February 4, 1967

David decided he shouldn't see me anymore. I'm lost. I feel as if the bottom has fallen out of my world. I know this is God's punishment. I've been wrong to feel so strongly about him, but I can't help the path my heart has taken.

Before things get too out of hand, I must get control. Logic tells me David is doing the right thing, but I'm fighting reason and allowing my heart to dictate. I need to pray that God give me strength.

Susan's heart broke for Libby, yet she sensed David had again been David who slew Libby's Goliath. If she were treading in Asp-filled water, then she needed to find dry land, she needed to cling to a firm foundation, and asking God to help her was it.

The bracelet slipped into Libby's thoughts, and she rose and hurried into Libby's bedroom. She stood a moment, letting her gaze drift around the room. What had Justin done with Libby's jewelry box? She was certain he hadn't gotten rid of it. She walked deeper into the room and noticed a box on the top of the armoire.

She crossed the room and lifted it down, then set it on the bed and opened the lid. She moved her finger through the baubles until she spotted a circular bangle with whorls of design around its half inch gold width. A small diamond studded the largest curlicue. She looked inside the hoop. No inscription. She replaced the bracelet into the box and returned it to the top of the armoire.

What difference did it make? It only made it all too real, too sad.

October 2, 1967

I haven't had the heart to write. I'm trying to keep active at the historical society, but James doesn't attend as often as before so it's different. Boring. I've begun reading poetry again and picked up my volume of Emily Dickinson's poetry, but it's too sad. Her sorrow seems so akin to mine.

I cannot live with you—
It would be life—
And life is over there—
Behind the shelf.

Dickinson has said what I feel as if my life were a book or plate sitting on a shelf waiting for someone to find me and appreciate what I have to offer. I hate self-pity. Where is my faith?

Her tears blurred Libby's words. Self-pity had been horrible, and she recalled being saturated with it. She'd finally overcome it, and so had Libby. The Libby she knew had pulled herself from the doldrums. She'd found life exciting once more.

Susan's thoughts shifted to Justin and his mother, then to her relationship with her own mother. She bowed her head asking God for strength.

♥

"You're what?" Margaret's face paled.

"It's only temporary, Momma, until Justin's mother can go home."

She straightened, her look questioning. "She's coming to Rose

Arbor? I've rarely seen her there."

"I know." Susan watched color return to her mother's face.

"And you think this is wise?"

Susan gapped at her "For me to be there or for Justin's mother to be there?"

An uneasy grin settled on her face. "Both, I suppose."

"I made you and God a promise, Momma, and I won't break that. I won't do anything to make you ashamed of me again."

"Oh, Susan." Her mother's voice broke as she said her name. "I hate to call it shame. I was hurt and angry at Justin. Your father and I were heartbroken that you had to go through the pain of having a child without a husband. We didn't know what to do. We sent you away as much for you as for ourselves."

Susan rose and wrapped her arms around her mother. The closest she'd been to her except for the kiss on her mother's cheek one day that had even surprised Susan. "I understand now, but I felt so wounded. So scared. So ashamed, and I felt as if you and Daddy turned your backs on me when I needed you so badly. I felt so alone."

"We did wrong."

"No, Momma. There was no right in that situation. If you want to sing, you must pay the piper as you've said to me so often. If only young girls learned the sorrow before they made the mistake."

Her mother gave her shoulder a pat. "You've done the best you could. I'm proud of your college education. You've grown into a lovely woman, but I can't help but blame Justin. If not for him, you would have been married and had children..." Her voice faded as she stepped back.

"It's the past. Let's not hang on to it, and I don't want Justin to either. I'm praying that by spending time together, he and his mother will ease some of the tension between them."

Her mother raised her hand and placed her palm against Susan's cheek. "I'm sorry for all the added sorrow you've had. And please don't blame your daddy."

"I don't blame either one of you, Momma. I blame myself. You raised me right, and I stumbled."

Her mother brushed tears from her eyes. "I still blame myself, Susan. Everyday."

Chapter Nineteen

Justin helped his mother through the front door since the veranda had less steps than the gallery. She leaned against her walker, her back rounded, her face with a slight sneer, perhaps from the stroke, perhaps not. Despite his reservations, he ached, seeing her this way.

He brightened when he saw Susan standing in the dining room archway. “Hello, Mrs. Boyd.”

“Susan,” Catherine said with only a cursory glance.

“You’ll use the bedroom on the first floor.” Justin aimed her toward Libby’s room, though he witnessed her resistance.

“I don’t want—”

“You can’t make it up the stairs, and it’s foolish for you to be out in the guestrooms. You’re staying here, closer to everything. I’ll bring your luggage in a minute.”

Caroline mumbled under her breath, but let him guide her through the doorway. She gazed around the room, a moment. “I remember the cheval mirror. It was my mother’s.”

“Would you like to take it back to Robard Hall when you go home?”

“No. It belongs here.”

She sank to the edge of the mattress, her eyes rheumy with tears. He felt relieved her garbled speech had improved to almost normal, but one leg dragged throwing her off balance.

"Are you tired, Mother?"

"I want to go home. Where's Rèmi and Clovis?"

"I can have Rèmi come over for part of the day if you want. I'll be here, and when I'm not, Susan will be here, and the hospital has arranged for a therapist and a nurse to visit. The more you work at getting well, the quicker you'll go home."

She released a deep sigh, and he felt a wave of grief for his mother's lack of independence. She was a proud woman, and he knew being beholden to others wouldn't make her happy.

"It's stuffy in here, Mother. Would you like to sit on the gallery?"

"I suppose." Her tone had a hint of resentment.

He set the walker in front of her, then helped her maneuver through the foyer and out the door. She settled into a wicker chair that faced the yard.

He smelled food drifting from inside and thought about talking with Susan privately. "I'll be right back in a minute." He headed through the kitchen entrance.

Susan stood over the stove preparing a chicken dish, and he could smell the fragrance of peaches coming from the oven. "Cobbler?"

She nodded.

"I'm sorry for Mother's abruptness, Susan. I hope you have patience." While she sautéed the chicken, he stood behind her and rested his hand on her shoulders.

"I can handle it, Justin." She placed the spatula on a spoon rest and turned toward him. "How about you?"

Her question hadn't been what he'd expected. "I don't know. I usually put a chip on my shoulder as soon as—"

"Then knock it off, Justin." She grinned. "In more ways than one. Let me handle my side, and you work at finding peace with your mother."

"Peace? Sometimes it seems so hopeless." He shook his head.

"You're familiar with the Bible. Follow the Lord's example. Love, mercy, forgiveness. I know it's difficult. I've made only a few strides at home, but it's an improvement."

"What did your mother say about your moving in here?"

"She understood. We had a good talk, like two people having a real conversation. I think the worst is over for us."

"You've never told me why you and your mother haven't gotten along."

She turned away and busied herself with the chicken. She didn't respond, but added a sprinkle of flour, then orange juice to make a citrus sauce. Finally, she glanced his way. "Some other time."

"Today."

She eyed him over her shoulder. "Today?"

"I want to understand. I know this has something to do with me. I know because of how she treats me."

He noticed Susan's hand tremble.

"That's why they sent you away." He moved beside her to see her face. "Because she knew about us. Is that right?"

Tension covered her face, and he noticed her hand tremble. "Yes."

"Is that all?"

"Later," she said. "This isn't a good time."

He gave up. She was right. Now wasn't the best time, but this is the most he'd gotten from her.

"Tell your mother we'll be eating in a few minutes," Susan said.

Though the aroma had aroused his hunger, at that moment, he had lost interest in food.

♥

Susan slid beneath the fresh sheets on the second floor of Rose Arbor. She and Justin had little time alone, so she'd been able to avoid his earlier question. If she were going to have a relationship with Justin, she would have to tell him the truth that she never thought she could. She had no idea how she would find the courage.

Seeing Caroline's puckered expression for the rest of the evening had given her a good picture of what Justin's life had been. Perhaps it had been the stroke, but Caroline had a way of phrasing things that was cutting.

Susan had tried to understand. Caroline apparently lacked self-worth. She'd been under the glare of Libby's outgoing personality for so many years, she'd taken a backseat. The resentment still seemed evident, and Susan figured being in Libby's house only reminded Caroline more of Justin's love for his aunt and Caroline's inability to offer the same kind of love to her son.

The situation seemed sadder than Susan had imagined.

Slipping away early had been part of her plan. She'd nearly gotten through the stack of diaries and wanted to finish them. She wanted them off her mind.

Tomorrow she had her first full day with Caroline in the house, and she anticipated how they would fare together. Justin would leave for Baton Rouge in the afternoon for a day, and Susan faced that her work had just begun. She picked up Libby's journal and paused to pray, asking God to give her the right words so she could become a catalyst for healing between Justin and his mother.

Though she prayed, she questioned her sanity. How could she change something that had taken years and years to develop? The answer didn't come, but hope rose. She and her mother were making progress, step by step. Justin and his mother could do the same.

She plumped her pillow, then opened the journal.

December 31, 1967

Today a miracle happened. David called. He said he couldn't end the year without speaking from his heart. He said he loves me. My heart is in my throat, and though his words were what I longed to hear, I can't stop crying. It's too impossible. It's like grasping for the moon, even worse.

He said he would try to drop by for a few minutes tonight before he left for his obligations. I resent being his secret, but that's what I am. I knew it when this first began. But the Lord knows, I tried to fight it. I'm just too weak, and it all breaks my heart.

Susan flipped the page, her pulse racing.

January 1, 1968

David came as he promised. We spent an hour together. He kissed me like I've never been kissed. What are we doing? Why can't we just move on with our lives and stop this useless relationship. We can go nowhere. We're lost.

Lost? It's sin. We can call it nothing else. But doesn't God put love in our hearts. It's the Lord who rules the universe and causes things to happen. This can't be part of His plan, but it feels so right. This is the first day of a new year, and I've begun the year with the man I love, and it's a sin.

Susan's palms grew moist as she gripped the journal. The unthinkable rose in her thoughts. No, it couldn't be what it seemed. She didn't want to believe it. Her hands trembled as she reread Libby's entry. She knew about blaming God. She'd tried to do it herself, but it all came around to her. She'd been to blame, and so had Libby. Wishful thinking wouldn't change the truth.

April 5, 1968

I feel lost when David isn't here. I feel afraid when he is. I'm like a ladybug caught in a spider's web, and I created the web myself.

I pray over and over, and I know I must repent to be forgiven, but I can't. I can't stop the feelings that fill me, and my heart longs to make him happy, but how can I do that?

She closed the journal and took a deep breath. What had Libby gotten herself into? How did she get herself out? The more Susan read the more entangled she became. She had so often saw parallels to Libby's life, but if she was correct, Libby's problem had been more dire.

With sleep weighing her eyes, she glanced at the clock. Just a little more. She wanted to get Libby out of the clutches of the sin she'd gotten herself into. She wanted to hear Libby's faith-filled repentance.

May 3, 1968

I can't see how Caroline's marriage can last. I'm so involved in my own feelings I can't sort out what she's thinking. I don't know what I'm thinking.

Sometimes I can't sleep at night. I rise and sit on the gallery, listening to the katydids buzz their evening song. The sound makes me feel lonely. I smell the roses, and I long to be that youthful girl again who could look at God and feel forgiven.

July 4, 1968

I spent the day with Caroline and Adam at a community picnic. The day stressed me. I sat in a chair, trying to listen to the conversation, but my thoughts were miles away. Adam is so kind to Caroline, even though I know he isn't happy. He and Caroline are sleeping in separate rooms. I can't imagine a situation like that.

Adam's told me more than once he felt if they'd had a child that might have knit them together. Yet, I've heard others say that doesn't work. A failed relationship can't be mended by adding a new problem, and children do add stress. I pray with such mixed emotion.

Susan fought to keep her eyes open, but she lost the battle. In the middle of the night, she woke and placed the journal on the bed stand and turned off the light.

♥

When Susan came through the doorway, her mother clicked off the television. "Decided you'd come for a visit?"

"I need a few things, and..." She paused, knowing she had another reason for coming home. "I've been doing a lot of thinking since we talked."

Her mother's face furrowed into deep lines. "Thinking about what?"

"Us. Family."

"There isn't much us when you're not here most of the time, but I'm trying to understand."

"I really appreciate that, Momma." She knelt beside her mother's chair and touched her hand. "I've been learning a lot of things about troubled families, and I'm so grateful we've been able to talk about ours."

"Families have problems. It's part of life."

Susan rose from her haunches and edged a chair closer to her mother's. She felt hot tears pool in her eyes, and she'd never allowed her mother to see her cry. "I'm over at Rose Arbor, seeing hurt and sadness, day in and day out. No matter what Justin does, he can't get a truly kind word from his mother. I've prayed for them, and I've come to realize my life has been much better than that."

Her mother looked perplexed. "We talked about this a few days ago."

"But it's horrible to see it every day. I knew he had problems. His pride didn't let it show. Maybe we weren't rich, and we didn't have as much as Justin in material things when I was a kid, but we had more, because we had love."

Her mother's hand touch hers, and she grasped her mother's thin fingers, fingers that had helped plow a field and plant seeds, had shucked corn and canned vegetables, and had scrubbed floors on her knees.

"Momma, I want you to know that money and luxuries don't make happy families. They can make people arrogant and less willing to deal with issues than we do."

Her mother's eyes filled with emotion.

She swallowed, blocking the words she wanted to say about Caroline's hurtful comments.

"Is Caroline that difficult?"

"It's a strange kind of difficult. She's silent and abrupt. So bitter."

"I figure she's angry at what Justin has done, too?"

"I don't think she knows about that. Nor cares. It's something else. It has to do with Libby and Caroline's sense of worth. She's lacking the faith that let would let her know a child of God has worth beyond measure. Jesus said, if God worries about each sparrow that falls and counts the hairs on our heads, how much more are we worth. I wish she realized that, but I'm afraid it's too late."

Margaret squeezed her daughter's hand. "It's never too late, Susan. We've dallied a long time, but you see, it's never too late."

Susan rose and kissed her mother's cheek. Her skin felt cool and dry. "I need to get back, but I've been thinking about something else. We shouldn't have pride in things that we can see and touch, but only pride for what is in our heart—our faith, our love, and our blessings."

Her mother brushed more tears from her eyes. "I'll pray you can make a difference over there, Susan. If you don't, it's not for trying. You're a brave Christian woman."

"Thanks, Momma. That's the nicest thing you could say."

"And never forget, I love you."

Her words filled Susan's heart with relief and joy. "I love you, too."

♥

Susan sat on the gallery but could still hear Justin and his mother through the open window. She walked into the dusky garden, soothed by the scent of roses, but when she returned, it hadn't stopped. She tried to concentrate on something other than their conversation, but she couldn't.

For the past week since Caroline had been at Rose Arbor, she and Justin had made no real progress to reconcile. Yes, they were spending more time together now that he had returned from Baton Rouge, but the time certainly wasn't quality.

"You should have donated Rose Arbor to the historical society." Caroline voice sailed through the open window. "The place is too filled with ghosts."

"You don't believe in that myth, do you?" Justin's voice lifted in surprise.

"I didn't mean the Rose Arbor ghost. I meant ghosts. Memories, images, the past. I don't like it here."

"I do, and I wanted to keep the house. I would think Rose Arbor would mean something to you. It's your childhood home and—"

"It's Libby's home," Caroline said. "That's what you're clinging to." Bitterness rasped through her voice.

"I'm sorry that I loved your sister, Mother. I wish you would have. I wish you'd seen—"

"I saw enough, Justin. Enough for a hundred years." Her voice became almost menacing. "You don't know the woman who I knew. You've made Libby a god."

"I haven't made Libby anything but a loving aunt who made me feel welcome, which is more than I felt at home."

Susan cringed hearing Justin's words through the window. Why had he said that? It only deepened the wound.

Silence hung like a guillotine, and Susan waited for the blade to drop.

"I'm sorry we didn't make you feel welcome, Justin. I tried."

Caroline's voice had softened to a whisper, and Susan could visualize the hurt in Caroline's eyes from the sound of her voice.

"Perhaps you did," Justin said. "I didn't feel it, but then maybe I wasn't looking hard enough."

Lord, please keep this going. Susan lifted her eyes heavenward. *Let them soften and let their hurt vanish.*

"I realize Aunt Libby was your sister. You had childhood issues that—"

"We had adult issues, Justin. You don't know the side of your aunt that I do. She wasn't perfect. Far from it. She had her selfish side, a hurtful side. That's all I'm going to say. I'll leave you with your good memories."

He didn't respond, and Susan's mind flew back to the diaries, putting pieces together, pieces of the puzzle she didn't want to see as the picture formed in her mind's eye.

"Tell me what she did," Justin said finally. "Let me hear about the hurtful side."

"It will do no good now. I've said too much. Let's end this here. I'm sorry that I wasn't a good parent."

"You were a good parent." He silenced for a moment. "You weren't a loving parent. You never kissed me or—"

"You were a boy. It's improper to lavish affection on a son."

"Oh, Mother, it's not improper. Even boys need to be certain they're loved. They need to learn that it's okay to express feelings, to hug, to kiss, to cry. I never learned that from anyone but Aunt Libby and..."

His voice trailed off, and Susan held her breath, fearing he would say and Susan.

"I know. Rèmi and Clovis spoiled you. They didn't know that I was aware of the special treats they gave you. I knew, but I didn't stop them. They adored you."

"You knew?"

"Yes. It's their way. They're happy people, and I let them enjoy lavishing their attention even though I knew it spoiled you."

"Mother, it made me feel worthy. It didn't spoil me."

"You were always worthy, Justin. I've always been proud of you. I admire and respect you. You're like your father in many ways, but you learned things from me, too. You have pride and morals. I taught you that. You're charming and a hard worker with a quick mind. That came from your father."

And Adam could be playful and tender, Susan rebutted Caroline's claim. He learned that from Libby.

"I never knew you respected and admired me."

"I did, and I do."

The silence returned again, and Susan wished she could walk back into the moonlight again or go to her room and read the journals, but they would hear her if she moved outside the window, and Caroline might think she'd been eavesdropping. She winced, knowing she had been.

"I wish I knew you better," Justin said. "You always surprise me."

"You know enough. I have flaws. I'm not perfect."

Justin chuckled for the first time. "None of us are perfect, Mother."

Susan heard the chair creak and saw from his shadow that Justin had risen.

"I know you're tired. Can I help you to bed?"

"Yes, thank you. I am weary."

Susan waited while they moved away from the parlor toward Libby's bedroom. When they vanished, she rose and slipped up the staircase to her room.

Alone, she pondered what she'd heard. The weight of their words blended with Libby's journal. Perhaps she'd made a mistake reading it. Maybe she'd learned too much about Libby—a side Justin would never want to know.

She slipped into her nightclothes and slid between the sheets, then grasped one of the last two journals she'd found in the attic. If there were more, she didn't know where they would be.

October 6, 1968

I was surprised when Carl came to the door to talk after so long a time. We'd drifted, and he'd stopped working for me. I hired a college boy who's attending the community college. He's doing fine, but not as thorough as Carl.

Carl said he'd been seeing someone, but they'd split, and he missed talking with me. He's a nice man, but my life has drifted so far from the woman I was to the woman I am now that I can hardly relate to him anymore. I avoid talking about David. David's a secret. He's a phantom. I so wish it could be different, but it never will be.

Susan reread the last phrase of the entry. *He's a phantom.* She had never even considered it, but could David be an imaginary friend—

someone Libby created to fulfill her dreams of having someone? She shook her head. Impossible. Yet. Libby had a broad imagination. She shared her stories with the flair of a storyteller, and Susan often suspected she brightened them a little, made them even more exciting than they were, especially now that she'd read the diary.

Or could time turn the events of the past into something more dramatic and more memorable? She thought back to her own youth. Were the experiences of her life more dynamic now than they were then? She tried to delve into her thoughts but was no longer sure what was fact and what was fact with a twist.

January 28, 1969

Carl asked me to go to dinner. I accepted, but I made it clear we were only friends. He agreed. I haven't been out in a long time. I seem to live within these four walls except for church, necessary shopping, an occasional historical society meeting, and visiting Caroline. That seems a dull life for a chaste woman of thirty-one.

David wasn't happy to hear about the dinner with Carl, but I asked him what I'm supposed to do. He looked so depressed it broke my heart. I apologized and kissed him—always the sweetest kisses that make me weak. How can I be so sorrowful and happy at the same time?

Susan released a breath. Chaste. Libby had called herself chaste. Relief swept over her. If David were a real person, and her instinct told her he was, she'd so feared from what she'd read that Libby had lost herself in this impossible relationship. The secretive nature of it still sent concern skittering over her.

June 14, 1969

David is trying to be more attentive. He brought me a beautiful bouquet of flowers last night, and we sat on the sofa lost in each other's arms and talking about if things had been different. But they weren't, and they will never be. I'm facing the truth more and more. Our relationship has mellowed into a comfortable bond, but when reality smacks me between the eyes, it's far from comfortable.

February 19, 1970

I'm losing control. Our kisses are more urgent. We know better. We agreed this was our special friendship, but it's grown into something so deep it hurts. I fear where this will lead, and I fear the hurt that will be as a result. This can't go on forever, and when it ends, where will I be in this wonderful mess?

April 20, 1970

I never dreamed that love could be so warm and fresh even when it's familiar. Our love cries split the air, and I know and understand so many things I never knew before. I wish I could say it all, Dear Diary, but I'm a grown woman who should have known this before. I didn't. It's all so new, so bonding, so uniting.

Though we both felt horrible afterward, we laughed and hugged and shared so much. I have never known such feelings in my life until now.

Susan sat paralyzed staring at the page. Libby's life had made a turn, a turn that could change her life forever. Startled by what she'd read, Susan sat a moment thinking of how she'd played with fire and had paid the price. What price would Libby pay?

Chapter 20

"Who are those people?" Caroline asked.

Susan's neck pivoted to the doorway where Caroline stood supported by her walker. "I'm interviewing staff for the bed and breakfast."

"You are?"

Her tone sent a message Susan couldn't question. How could a farmer's daughter have the ability to interview for a position? "Yes. Justin's been too busy, and we open the bed and breakfast September first."

"What do you mean we open the bed and breakfast?"

"As of now, I'm in charge."

"You? I would certainly think Justin could find a professional."

Her gaze penetrated Susan's like a knife, and Susan remained calm. "I am a professional. I thought Justin told you."

"What do you know, my dear, about social amenities and proprieties?"

"Mrs. Robard, my education prepared me for many things that my family didn't have the wherewithal to enjoy. Being raised in an affluent home doesn't always give a person tact and friendliness that it takes to run a cozy bed and breakfast. Justin has faith that I can do the job."

Her face twisted with obvious irritation. "I don't like the tone of your voice, Susan."

"And I didn't like the tone of yours, but that doesn't mean that we can't talk." She held back her frustration and patted the chair next to hers at the dining room table. "Why don't you sit here so we can?"

"Talk? Talk about what?"

"About a lot of things."

"I don't think so." Caroline attempted to shift her walker so she could turn away.

Susan rose and moved beside her. "Please. I'd like to talk with you."

Caroline studied her for a lengthy time before finally giving in and making her way to the chair.

When she was seated, Susan joined her. "You can help me make some decisions."

Caroline's head lifted as if Susan had piqued her interest. "What decisions?"

"I've interviewed two women for the breakfast cook's position. The woman will also do some cleaning in the kitchen and dining room area. One woman was raised in Texas, but she's lived in Louisiana for a few years. The other is a native Louisianan, a Cajun woman. I'd value your opinion on which would be best for Rose Arbor."

"Did they have similar backgrounds in cooking? References?"

"Yes."

"Then the Cajun woman. She'll work hard, cook excellent food, and be a pleasure to work with. They are happy people, and you'll want that."

"Thank you. I appreciate your input." Susan had already made her decision, but Caroline's validation did two things—gave Susan certainty and pleased Caroline.

"You're welcome. Do you have a housekeeper?"

"Here's the resume of the woman I interviewed yesterday."

Caroline studied the document. "Check her references. Otherwise she seems a good choice."

"I'll do that."

Susan stacked the documents into a pile and drew in a breath, wondering what she could say to Caroline to make things better.

Caroline's fingers trembled as she folded them in front of her. "Thank you for asking."

"I respect your opinion. Justin does, too." She wasn't sure about that, but she assumed he did. "He'd often talked about your ability to run a well-organized house."

She looked at Susan with question in her eyes. "I didn't know he talked about home."

Susan tried to come up with another positive comment, but Caroline didn't leave her time.

"What is your relationship with Justin?"

The question startled her. "I work for him right now."

"And that's all?"

"We've been friends a long time. I used to visit Libby, and I got to know Justin when we were teens."

"He spoke of you," Caroline said.

"Of me?"

She nodded. "When I'd ask what he had done at Rose Arbor, he'd mention you. I wondered if your relationship had been more than casual friends."

Susan choked on the question and struggled for a response.

The doorbell rang breaking the silence. "It's the therapist, I suppose," Susan rose to answer the door.

Relief spread over her when she let the therapist in and left Caroline in his hands. She darted up the staircase to her room, wondering if Caroline would ask the question again. The answer should be simple. She could have said, we enjoy each other's company, or Libby kept us busy with her stories or anything, but the guilty memories that filled her thoughts. She had been drawn back to the scent of roses and moonlight where she and Justin had hidden beneath the arbor.

Today she'd witnessed Caroline's need to feel purposeful, her need to be appreciated. Adam had not appreciated her, apparently. Maybe he'd tried, but her quiet, undemonstrative way had caused him to alienate himself. She'd been unwilling to have a child so perhaps he forced her which had truly been their undoing. She could only guess, but from Libby's diaries, Adam seemed a more dynamic man, a man who made Libby laugh and who had found pleasure in life.

Susan planned to use her free hour to read the journals. When she'd finished them, she knew she would feel a sense of loss, like a person who completes a wonderful novel and wishes the story to go on and on, like a person who longs to know what happens next in the lives of the characters who seemed as real as the people in the next room. She grasped the journal and stretched out on the bed.

June 15, 1970

We're taking too many chances. David visits me too often, not that I don't want him here, but I'm afraid someone will notice, and our lives will never be the same. He holds me in his arms and tells me his dreams. I feel like a foolish schoolgirl singing to the Carpenter's popular song, "Close To You." David has become the center of my world. The years have flown, and I've dedicated my life to him.

Caroline asks why I've never shown interest in marriage. I can't explain it to her. I make excuses just as she makes excuses why she doesn't want children. Life is so confusing. Sometimes the weight of my actions pushes me into the ground. Will God forgive me?

September 7, 1970

I haven't stopped crying for days. I don't know what to do. I'm expecting a child, and I haven't told David. What will he do? What will we do? I fell on my knees and prayed God help me. Why didn't I do that long ago before this happened.

Susan smothered her sobs. The situation was too real, too painful, too awful. Libby had been her mentor all those years, the woman she admired the most, the person she knew would be most disappointed if she knew about her and Justin's sin, but this news changed that. Libby would have understood and would have felt her sorrow.

She closed her eyes, letting the tears flow. She'd kept her emotions intact for too many years. She'd fought the moisture that rose to her eyes and the sorrow that filled her heart. If she could only be a lesson to the world, if from her ache others could learn the truth—now Libby's truth as well.

She rolled on her back allowing the healing tears to roll freely down her cheeks. Shame had stopped her from allowing God's love and mercy to take away the pain. It was time. Libby had overcome her sorrow somehow. Susan wanted the answer. How did Libby seem so positive and cheerful when she carried the same burden?

September 10, 1970

I have been stung to the core. David wants an abortion. I may be a sinner, but I could never do that. This tiny shape growing within me is a life. I am hurt to the depth of my being. I never thought my David, who fought Goliath, would suggest such an unthinkable thing.

September 12, 1970

David cried in my arms and begged my forgiveness. He said later he'd thought about what he'd said and knew he had been horribly wrong. We clung together like two lost souls, searching for an answer that only God can provide. We have sinned, and we must find a way to make this right.

Frissons rose down Susan's spine, speculating what Libby might have done to right her wrong.

October 15, 1970

As much as it hurts and as deep as my sorrow, I know that I have done the right thing. Caroline has agreed to take my child as her own. She will announce her pregnancy, and she and Adam will go on a trip at the time of birth and come back with a baby. It's the only way. At least, Adam will have his child.

What will I have? Peace of mind and a gift to Adam.

Susan couldn't take her eyes from the page. Caroline had agreed to take her child. Her child? That had to be Justin? Caroline only had one child. That meant Libby was Justin's mother, not Caroline. Susan's pulse charged through her with the burden of what she'd learned. She felt faint and covered her face with her hands. Why hadn't she thrown the journals away? Why hadn't she let them collect dust in the attic.

"Dear Lord," she whispered, "are my suspicions right? Heavenly father help me understand, and if I'm right, what do I do now?

Her suspicion knifed her heart. She'd begun to suspect David had been the name Caroline used for Adam? With this new information, the whole puzzle fell into place. Caroline's bitterness and lack of affection, Justin's special love for Libby, Libby's devotion to Justin, Adam's avoidance of family life. Caroline and Adam had kept their marriage intact to protect Libby and raise Justin. Caroline's sacrifice washed over Susan like a tidal wave, knocking her to the ground.

Her heart thundered, realizing how she and Libby had walked a similar path that hurt so many innocent people. The news could make a tremendous difference in Justin's relationship with his mother, but how could she tell him? *Lord, what am I to do now that I've meddled? Father, help me do what is right and best.*

♥

"How did it go?" Justin stood above her, Libby's features etched in his, a connection she'd never made before.

Susan grasped the arms of the wicker rocker to calm herself. "Fine. The therapy went well." Her hands trembled against the rocker. "Your mother's making good progress. Her therapist said another week or even less, and she'll be ready to go home."

"I'm sure she was relieved to hear that."

"On one hand, yes."

"What does that mean?"

"I think she enjoys spending time with you even though it doesn't always seem that way."

He glanced toward the window and lowered his voice. "Where is she?"

"She took a nap. Therapy always tires her."

He came closer and settled into a chair nearby. "I have a difficult time accepting that."

"I had a good talk with her today, Justin. I had those three interviews to decide about, and I asked her opinion. I was pleased to see how she reacted."

"You asked her opinion?" He narrowed his eyes. "About who to hire, you mean?"

"Yes. She looked at the resumes, and we agreed on the cook. I called the housekeeper's references and got a positive response. That's what she suggested, although I would have done that anyways."

He studied her so long she felt uneasy.

"Your mother appreciated being asked and thanked me. I think letting her see that you value her opinion will make a difference. I'm beginning to understand her—" Susan felt the stir of emotion rising in her chest. "To understand her better. She can't help herself, Justin. Just trust me on this."

"Why are you so certain?" He eyed her suspiciously. "Aunt Libby's diaries again?"

"Yes. I see the relationships and the personalities. It's complex, but I understand."

"And you think I should read them."

His comment punched her in the solar plexus. "No, I realize you don't want to do that. It's not a good idea."

She wished she wouldn't have added the last comment because Justin's gaze probed hers as if he didn't understand.

"What did you read?"

"Just about relationships and—" Susan choked on the words. And what? And who your real mother is. How could she say it? Should she? Susan needed God's help on this one. She glanced at her watch. "I imagine your mother's awake by now."

Justin rose and leaned above her. "Thanks for trying to include her. It's more than I've done. I guess I need to learn from you."

"Maybe a little."

He bent lower and pressed his lips to hers. They lingered a moment, then drew back and kissed her forehead, then lowered his mouth again and deepened the kiss.

Her body trembled not only from the kiss, but from the secret she carried in her heart. When he drew back, she tried to smile.

"We can't do this very often with my mother here."

"It won't be long," she said, knowing by then something had to happen. She couldn't stay here with the secret burning in her. She must tell him or leave.

♥

That evening Susan sat in her room at Rose Arbor. She'd read the last entry in Libby's journals.

November 2, 1970

The decision has been made. I'm going away to Europe for

three months, but really, I'll be near Shreveport at a home for women like me. I don't know what will happen, but when I come back to Rose Arbor, I'll build a new life, one without David and without my child.

The loss of those two loves is worse than the death of my parents—worse than anything I can imagine, but what I have gained is forgiveness, just as it says in Colossians 1:13-14 God has taken me out of the darkness of sin and has brought me to His Son who loves me and has redeemed me from my sins.

I'm so sorry for what I've done. I've promised God I will learn to smile again and to follow His will. I'm not sure why I went astray, but like the lost sheep or the Prodigal son, the Lord welcomed me back to His fold. I'll learn to live the lie and allow Adam to have his child and Caroline to be the mother she should have been all along.

Once again, Emily Dickinson has said it better than I can. I haven't read her poetry for a long time, but I did today in sadness.

Remorse—is a memory—awake—
Her parties all astir—
A presence of departed acts—
At window and at door—

Remorse. Memories. Loneliness covers me. I place my hand on my belly and know that beneath my palm is a life made from love, but a love that should have never been. Dickinson says at the end of the poem,

Remorse is clueless, the disease
Not even God can heal—

What more can I say? Dickinson has said it all.

Susan closed the cover as if saying goodbye to an old friend. The journals had been part of her life for the past two months. They were difficult to let go. She slipped the last book into the bed stand drawer until she could return it to the attic.

In its place, she lifted out the Bible and clutched it to her. Since she'd learned Libby's secret, she'd been searching for an answer to her unending question. What was God's will?

Footsteps sounded below her on the gallery, and she wondered if Justin had been as sleepless as she had. She looked at the clock. It was one in the morning. She slipped her feet to the floor and snapped off the light before peering through the window.

A shadow stretched along the floor and vanished off the end of the gallery near the bedrooms. She saw a motion inside Justin's room. The light was still on, and he appeared to be moving inside. The intruder hadn't been Justin, and if not, then who was he?

Instead of going down, she sat on the bed and stretched out. She turned the page to the next chapter in First Corinthians. St. Paul's words struck her, saying that God's children had been entrusted with the secret things of God and those who'd been given a trust must prove faithful.

The secret things of God. But these weren't God's secrets they were human's secrets. Was this what God wanted her to do—to keep her secret?

Susan's heart lifted when she read the thirteenth verse. *Love does not delight in evil but rejoices with the truth. It always protects, always trusts, always hopes, always perseveres.*

She lowered the Bible to her bed and closed her eyes. She had asked herself over and over if she should tell Justin the truth. Would it protect him or harm him? She believed with her whole heart it would protect him. He'd never understood his parents. If he knew the truth, it would open his eyes and, she prayed, his heart.

She plumped her pillow and picked up the Bible. "Lord," she said aloud, "help me know what to do."

Lowering her gaze, she realized pages had flipped of their own accord while the Bible lay on her bed. She lowered her gaze to a verse in Second Corinthians. *We have renounced secret and shameful ways.* She raced through the scripture, her heart pounding. She feared she'd read the next verse out of context, but the message seemed clear. *By setting forth the truth plainly we commend ourselves to everyman's conscience in the sight of God.* These were God's words. Was this the answer to her question?

Chapter Twenty-One

In the middle of breakfast, Susan's cell phone jarred her. She excused herself to Caroline and located her phone. Georgia's voice poured from the line. "It's time to decide, Susan. There's one opening left here, and I think you'd love working with the pilgrimage organization in Natchez."

Susan gaped at the phone. "I-I don't know, Georgia. Now I'm more confused than ever." She wanted to tell her what she'd learned about Libby, but the truth was Justin's, not hers to tell.

"Have you decided to work for Justin permanently? Or is something more serious going on between you two?"

Her voice rang with hope, and Susan struggled with her response. "We've taken a few positive steps, but nothing permanent. Right now, I'm caring for his mother. She had a stroke."

"I'm sorry to hear that, but that's not a career, Susan."

"I know. It's just that—"

"It's your decision, and if you think something good can come of this with Justin, then go for it, but I know this position in Natchez won't last long, and I'd hate for you to change your mind next week. I'm sure it'll be gone."

"It's difficult right now."

"I'd just hoped maybe..."

Susan heard disappointment in her voice, and she understood. "I'm not saying no, Georgia, but I need to give this more thought, and it's only fair I talk to Justin. I don't want to leave him in a bad spot. The bed and breakfast opens in another month. We have bookings and—"

"I understand. I really do. I knew things were a bit touchy when I was there, and—"

"I've made some great strides with my mother. That's a positive."

"That's wonderful. Now just take care of yourself."

"I will, and I'll call in a day or two. I promise."

When she hung up, she stared at the cell phone.

She spent the next day, tossing Georgia's offer back and forth in her mind. Had the call been God's will to get her away from Rose Arbor? Or wasn't it God's will at all, but coincidence?

Coincidence seemed too simple or perhaps too complex. She couldn't decide just as she couldn't decide what she should do. Her heart wanted to stay. She wanted to tell Justin about the journals and then have him thank her, because it answered all of the questions he'd brooded about for years.

But would he say thank you? If she left, then maybe he would learn the answer on his own. That didn't ring true. Justin was two years older than she—thirty-five and had never learned the truth. Caroline wasn't likely to tell him now, and Susan felt he would never read the journals on his own.

Her stomach churned as a decision struck her. She looked at the clock. Justin should arrive soon. He'd left Thursday morning to work in Baton Rouge, but he'd promised to return Friday night.

Caroline had begun sewing on a crewel project Susan had purchased. She'd never done much needlework, but the therapist recommended keeping her hands busy to work on coordination. The piece looked lovely and could be framed or could be used to upholster a footstool. Seeing Caroline at work pleased her.

"How's it going?" Susan stepped into the parlor. "Can I get you anything."

"No, I'm fine. I enjoyed the tea."

"Good." Susan picked up the cup and saucer. "I'm preparing dinner. Justin should be here, soon." She hoped.

Caroline lifted her eyes from the stitches and gazed at her. "Is something wrong?"

"No."

"You seem unsettled today. I feel it."

Before reading the journals, Susan had never thought that Caroline would care about anyone's feelings. Now her attitude had softened. "A friend of mine called to tell me about a job in Natchez. She wants me to come there."

"And you don't want go?"

"I'm undecided. I—"

"I suppose you don't want to disappoint Justin."

"That's part of it."

"Susan, being a good friend is important, but I've learned something in my old age. Don't let someone else's needs totally overshadow your own. Think of yourself, too."

"I will. Thank you." She backed away, startled at the truth she heard in Caroline's words. Two days ago, the words may have been only a cryptic comment Susan wouldn't have understood. Today it held a deeper meaning.

When she set the cup and saucer into the sink, she paused while the thought rang in her ears, but the comment faded when she heard Justin's footsteps on the stairs.

The door opened, and he stepped inside with a lovely bouquet of flowers.

She hoped she could cover her unbridled emotion. "That's nice," she said. "For your mother?"

He looked sheepish. "They're for you, but—"

"They're for your mother." Though touched by the gift, she was giving it away.

He set the flowers on the table and took her into his arms. "Thank you. I wasn't thinking. I could have bought two bouquets."

"I'll enjoy them from afar."

His lips touched hers, and as always, she reeled at his touch. She loved him. She no longer questioned why or how. She only knew the truth. She didn't love him for any other reason except the one she knew in her heart. He was the man of her dreams, as Libby had once said.

"Take them to her. She's in the parlor, and I'll put dinner on the table."

She longed to follow him to watch his mother's expression. Instead she focused on the meal, and only went in the parlor when she knew they'd had time to talk.

"Look at the lovely bouquet." Caroline held them cradled in her arm.

"Would you like me to put the flowers in water?" Susan stepped closer.

"Please." She held them out with her shaky grip. "Thank you."

Susan nodded and took the bouquet, trying to catch a glimpse of Justin's face, but she returned to the kitchen and found the proper size vase and went to work arranging them.

The flowers reminded her of the rose she'd found in the vase that morning. One day she would learn the story of that mysterious rose.

The arrangement looked lovely in the crystal vase, and Susan carried it back into the parlor when she called them to dinner. In the past days, Justin and his mother's voices were not as loud as they had been when she first arrived. Though the evidence of strain remained, it had eased.

If only he knew the truth. *Truth*. The word stabbed her.

Caroline excused herself after dinner, saying she was tired and would rest a while. Sometimes Susan guessed she was uncomfortable around her and Justin and only used that as an excuse.

The heat of the day had cooled slightly as the sun sank lower in the sky, and she took a glass of sweet tea and headed onto the gallery. Her thoughts were heavy as she took the steps into the yard and wended her way to the garden.

The arbor looked inviting since it was made cooler by the shade. The roses seemed to thrive in the Louisiana sun. They were the old roses, bred to withstand the heat, and she realized she, too, had been bred to withstand many things, but lately she'd become tired of the burden.

She sank onto the shaded bench, took a sip of the sweet drink and set it beside her. In moments an elongated shadow fell outside the arbor and seemed to move closer. Soon Justin appeared in the sunshine, looking in at her. He lowered his head to avoid the thorny blossoms and sat beside her.

"A difficult day?" he asked

"A little."

"My mother?"

"No. We're getting along fine."

"I'm glad." His mouth curved to a grin. "You work miracles in all of us, Susan. I brought you the flowers today to let you know how much you mean to me. You've changed my life, and I'm sure you realize my feelings have grown so deeply for you. I have a hard time saying what I feel, but I hope you know."

"I know," she said, realizing if she opened Pandora's box, she would change his life forever. "But you have to know that I don't work miracles. Only God does that, and to perceive a miracle, you have to see the change and trust that it's the Lord's work."

"I feel God's work in me, but I'm still dubious. I cherish you, Susan, with all my heart, but I fear making a commitment. I've told myself for so many years, a relationship with me would fail, that I'm too much like my parents to give life a chance."

No, Susan cried inside. You are like your mother who loved life.

"I want you more than I can bear, but—"

He quieted and drew her into his arms and lowered his mouth to hers. The fragrance of roses and the surroundings overwhelmed her. She longed for the day when Justin would say he loved her and wanted to spend his life with her, but it would never happen.

"What's wrong?" He released his grip. "You pulled away."

"I didn't mean to." She hugged her arms around herself, feeling a chill course through her. "I have something on my mind, I guess."

"Something about my mother?"

"No. I told you we're getting along fine."

"Me?"

She hesitated.

"The diaries?"

She felt as if she would vomit.

He grasped her arms. "It's those diaries. I asked you to forget them. I wanted you to—" His grip tightened, and concern filled his face. "What is it, Susan? What's wrong."

She shook her head, wishing she could erase what had happened, but as long as she lived in Devereaux, seeing Justin day after day, she couldn't forget. She couldn't bear the burden of knowing what she'd learned.

"Tell me," he demanded. "If she said something about me, then tell me."

"She loved you, Justin."

"That wouldn't upset you. Tell me."

Love does not delight in evil but rejoices with the truth. God's Word in First Corinthians filled her mind. "I'm sorry this came up, Justin. Please, just forget it."

"How can I forget it? You look as if you'd seen a ghost."

She had in a way, the ghost of the past. "Read the journals yourself. It would be better."

"I'm not going to let this die now, Susan. It's up in the air, so let it fall. Tell me."

She dragged in a breath that seared her lungs. Why had she opened her mouth? "Justin, let me preface this with the good news."

"Good news?"

"What I learned from Libby's journals will answer all your questions. You won't wonder anymore why your life was different."

"You can tell me that?" His face filled with mocking doubt.

"Yes."

"That simple?"

"It's not simple, and I'm not making light of it. It's tearing me apart."

"Say it, Susan." His eyes narrowed, and his words hissed at her.

Bile rose up her throat like fire. "Caroline is not your mother," she whispered.

"What are you saying?" He grasped her shoulders. "I was adopted?"

She shook her head.

"Then who was my mother?"

A knot tightened in Susan's throat.

"Tell me, Susan. Tell me. Who is my mother?"

Susan looked into Justin's desperate eyes. "Libby."

"Aunt Libby?" He rose like a rocket and spun away from her, then pivoted back, his eyes ablaze. "My Aunt Libby?"

"Yes."

He reeled, and Susan reached for him.

"Do I have a father?" His voice rose. "Do you know who my father is?"

She nodded. "It's Adam, Justin. He's your real father."

"Aunt Libby and my father?"

Fire shot from his eyes. "I asked you not to read the journals. I told you they should be thrown away."

"But Justin, I thought—"

"Get away from me. Leave me alone. You've done enough."

Susan rose, darted into the house, grabbed her belongings and left without looking back. Her feet sank into the grass as she tore past the oak tree, heading for the back door—to the farmer's house where she was born.

Why had she gotten involved? Is this what God wanted? She'd meant to save him not ruin his life, but she'd done that, she feared, with her meddling.

She had no choice. Natchez had a possible position for her, and she needed to get out of Devereaux. She'd accomplished her purpose in coming home by making amends with her mother. Now she could leave with a clear conscience.

She'd been sent to Natchez once to get away from Justin's grasp. This time she would make the move herself.

♥

Justin dashed into the house, checked on his mother and said he had to leave.

She looked startled but didn't speak. He knew she'd seen Susan race from the house. He eyed her for a moment, tangled in Susan's words. His aunt had been his mother; his mother, his aunt. His world had turned upside down in the fraction of a second.

Confusion tore through him as he backed from his parking space and raced away. He had no idea where he was going but soon found himself headed toward Baton Rouge. He passed a police car at the side of the road and eased his foot off the gas pedal, letting the car slow until he'd reached the speed limit.

He'd told Susan to forget the journals. He wanted no part of them. Anger seethed through him, yet at whom? Susan for telling him? His mother and father for the lie? Aunt Libby for loving him without telling him the truth?

As he drove, things fell into place, he remembered the innuendos he'd heard through the years—things he never understood and didn't want to. Now they stood out in his mind like the hairs on the back of his neck when he'd heard Susan's words.

Why had she read the diaries? Why hadn't she listened? He'd realized that she had been enjoying them, hearing about Libby's youth and delving into the fifties and sixties—times of innocence and Rock and Roll. The seventies brought flower children, communes, drugs and wildness into society, but not the lack of standards in his family, Aunt Libby's innocence? Why had Libby allowed herself to get involved with his father. Had his mother been distant all her life? If so, why had his father married her?

Questions darted through his mind, questions only Susan could answer or the journals. As he pondered the truth, he saw his mother in a new light. Caroline had been the victim of a scandalous relationship. She'd agreed to raise her sister and husband's child as if he were her own, yet facing daily the living awareness of their sin. He'd been the constant reminder. Why had his mother been willing? Was it to save face? To save her marriage? To protect Libby? To try to make a wrong a right?

He would never know unless he faced his mother, but could he? She would never forgive Susan for her interference, and he'd loved Susan...until this. He still loved her, but she'd hurt him with this shattering news.

He let his mind sail back to his years with Libby, and as the miles rolled past so did the memories. She'd nurtured him, guided him, loved him without asking for anything. He's spent as much time as possible with her because she opened her arms and her heart to him without question. Now he understood.

He pulled into his parking slot at his condo in Baton Rouge. He sat a moment before he pushed open the door and slipped out of the car. The air smelled damp and hot. Rain, he guessed. Inside he looked out his window and saw the Mississippi churning past in the distance. Old Man River. Tote that barge. Lift that bale.

His life had been easy compared to those who'd worked the docks. His parents had given him a life of luxuries. *Oh, Lord, what should I do? What have I done*? He'd told Susan to leave, to get away from him. The look on her face turned his stomach. Why hadn't he waited a moment to consider her logic? She hadn't told him this to hurt him. He'd watched her struggling to avoid saying it, but he'd demanded that she tell him. She had, and he'd treated her as if she'd done something wrong.

"Forgive me, Susan," he said aloud. "I'm a wreck. A deeply confused, hurting foolish man who's blamed this on you."

But now what could he do? He staggered to a chair, overwhelmed by the information and by what he'd done. He'd left his mother alone at Rose Arbor, and he'd sent Susan away. He reached for the telephone on the lamp table, then pulled back his hand. He couldn't call Susan now and expect her to forgive him. He needed to speak with her, to fall on his knees and beg her mercy.

She'd not only given him love, but she'd given him his faith—weak as it was, it was growing daily. He'd needed to put his trust in God, and he'd begun to do that with Susan's example.

She'd mentioned that she and her mother had made headway. Had he even scraped the wounds that were there with his mother? Now that he knew the truth, maybe they could truly move forward. God willing, he could have a real relationship with the woman who dedicated her life to raise him as her son.

♥

"I don't understand why you're leaving," Margaret said early the next morning from the doorway of Susan's bedroom.

"I have to go, Momma. Georgia says there's a position available in Natchez, and I hate to pass it up. Justin will survive without me, and you and I have finally come to an understanding. We can't go anywhere but up now."

Concern filled her mother's eyes. "Have I done something?"

She dropped her garment on the bed and wrapped her arms around her mother's shoulders. "You've done nothing. I promise."

"Did he? Did Justin try something again?"

"Justin did nothing like that. This is my decision. I decided last tonight."

"Caroline said something to you. I never understood her."

"My decision has nothing to do with Caroline." She released her mother's shoulders and returned to the closet, pulling out her clothing. "In fact, I'd appreciate it if you'd call her after I leave and tell her I had to go out of town."

"You don't want to tell her. What about Justin?"

"I'd rather you call." She opened a drawer, grabbed her belongings and stuffed them into the bag. "I need to do this, and I promise if I don't like the work I'll come back home."

Her hands trembled as she folded her last garment into the case, then slipped her Bible along the edge.

Her mother stepped forward and placed her hand on the book. "Are you reading the Bible?"

"Yes."

"I started reading scripture again, too. I'm ashamed that I neglected it for so many years, angry at God, I suppose."

"And at me." She gave her mother a wry grin.

"And at you." She let her fingers drop from the Bible and folded her hands in front of her. "But not anymore. I'm over that now."

"I'm glad, Momma." She leaned closer and kissed her mother's cheek, then pressed her hand over the spot she'd kissed. "You and Daddy had a difficult life, but you stuck together and did your best to raise me with morals and faith. I failed you back then. I let emotions undo my good sense. Not anymore. Don't worry about that."

"I'm not worried. I've watched you these past months, and I see the truth." She pressed her hand over Susan's. "Have you told him, Susan?"

"Justin?"

"Yes. Have you told him he had a son?"

She shook her head, a lump forming in her throat. "No."

"Why?"

"Because I never saw a reason." And when I did see a reason it was too late.

Her mother shook her head. "He deserves to know, I think."

"It will only upset him, and there's nothing he can do about it now."

"I suppose unless—"

Susan read her mind. "No unless, Momma. Those are dreams, and I'm not living in dreams anymore. Only reality." She paused as a thought struck. "Promise you won't tell Justin where I've gone."

Margaret shook her head and lowered her hand. "I can't do that."

"Please, Momma."

Her mother gave a faint nod.

Susan backed away and closed the lid on her bag. "I'm leaving a lot of things here. You're not that far from Natchez, and I'll come to visit so if I need anything else, I can always pick it up then."

"It's nice to hear you say that."

She embraced her mother, then lifted her bag and walked through the doorway.

Her mother snapped the light switch, and the glow vanished behind her.

She didn't look back. She gave a wave over her shoulder. "I love you, Momma," she said and stepped outside, allowing her tears to roll freely down her cheeks.

Once again Natchez would become her sanctuary.

Chapter Twenty-two

The sunlight sneaked between the blinds, and Justin sat bolt upright in bed. He took a moment to realize where he was—Baton Rouge. All that had occurred since the day before covered him like a raging river, then the memory swept him away.

He slipped his feet to the floor, stretched his arms, and rubbed his fists into his eyes before reading the clock. Six in the morning. He needed to get home.

He showered while the coffeemaker brewed the caffeine he needed to face the day. He dressed and drank down the black coffee, then locked his door and headed back to Devereaux.

He'd struggled with how he could apologize and ask for forgiveness. Would Susan accept his apology or would he have to beg? He wouldn't blame her.

And his mother? What could he say? How could he tell her he knew the dark secret she had kept all those years?

He pulled into the driveway of Rose Arbor at seven-thirty. He'd made good time so early in the morning. The sun had risen in pastel shades of orange and gold as he drove, and he couldn't help but think of the glow on Susan's face when she looked at him. But yesterday's fiasco reared up like a tiger, slashing its claws at the image and shredding it into sadness.

He crept across the gallery to the kitchen door, not wanting to frighten his mother. He hoped Susan had come back to see that she was safe. He'd been foolish to leave as he had.

The house was quiet when he entered, and he put on the coffeepot, wondering if Susan

had returned last night. He saw his mother's bedroom door still closed, so he climbed the stairs.

His heart dropped when he saw the empty room Susan had used. He stepped inside, breathing deeply to capture her scent. He sat on the edge of the bed and ran his hand over the pillow. He'd been horrible to her.

Curious if she'd left things behind, he opened the nightstand drawer. Inside, he spotted Libby's journal. His chest felt hollow when he touched the book, but he pulled it out and stared at it for a moment before opening to the middle.

He scanned the entries, seeing that Libby had been in love with someone. The words jarred him, seeming so unbelievable. He turned pages, scanning the entries until his gaze settle on one of the shocking paragraphs. Libby was expecting. His pulse hammered in his ears, and he closed the book, then slid it back into the drawer. Maybe another time, but not today.

When he came down the stairs, his mother's door was open, and he saw her sitting at the vanity in her robe, combing her hair.

"I thought you were gone." She paused with the brush suspended.

"I came back." His palms began to perspire, knowing he had to talk with her about what he'd learned.

"You had an argument with Susan?"

"No. I was angry at her. She went home, but I need to talk with her."

"She's gone." His mother set the brush on the vanity and grasped her walker and the edge of the table to help her rise.

"Gone?" He searched her face. "Gone where?"

"I don't know. Her mother called and said Susan had asked her to call and say she had to go out of town."

Justin's heart stood still. He lowered his head, staring at the ground and trying to make sense out of what had happened. Why had she gone away? Why so soon? He had to talk with her.

"I've made some coffee, Mother. Let's sit in the parlor. I need to talk with you about something important."

She rested her weight on the walker, her eyes searching his. "Talk?"

"I'll get your coffee."

"A little cream and sugar, please," she said finally.

He moved to help her, but she waved him away. "I'm doing fine, Justin. Really. In fact, I'm about ready to return home. I think it's time."

He wouldn't agree with her now about that. They had more important things to discuss. As his mother headed for the parlor, he continued to the kitchen and returned with the drinks.

Caroline took the cup from the saucer he'd placed beside her and took a careful sip, then replaced it. "You have something serious to talk about."

"Yes. Very serious."

She didn't say anything, and her gaze didn't veer.

He dug deep for courage and for the right words. "Did you know Aunt Libby kept a diary?"

"When she was a girl, she always wrote in it. I peeked a couple of times."

"She kept journals later. Actually, for many years."

Her mother's brow wrinkled. "I didn't know that." Stress sounded in her voice. "Have you read them?"

"No, but Susan did. She was so thrilled to read about Libby's teen years, then later about her life as she grew older."

"Oh." For the first time, she broke her direct gaze and lowered her eyes. "Is that why Susan left?"

"She left because I told her to get out. I'm sorry now, but I was startled."

His mother's voice softened. "She told you something she'd read."

"She didn't do it to cause trouble. She did it because she thought I would understand things about my life better. Instead I was angry."

"At her or me?"

"At life. At you and Dad. At Aunt Libby. At Susan. At myself. At God. I didn't want to know the truth, not because it made me unhappy, but it seemed impossible, but now that I look back, Mother, it makes so much sense."

"I'm sorry, Justin. I thought it was best you never knew. I wish—"

"Please, Mother, don't wish Susan hadn't told me, because telling me makes all the difference in the world. You've become my hero. You sacrificed your life so you could protect Dad and Aunt Libby."

"It was pride, too, Justin, but yes, I had to do it for them. I'd cheated your father out of something he wanted so badly. A child. That's all he ever asked of me. He gave me everything, and only asked for one thing I didn't give him. I don't know why. Fear that I wouldn't be a good mother. Fear I wasn't worthy to be a mother, and I was right, I'm afraid."

"You're wrong. You accepted motherhood under a shocking and horrible circumstance. You didn't give yourself the chance." He rose and knelt beside her chair. "You'll always be my mother. Libby was my aunt. That will never change. I love you both for the roles you played in my life, and I'm sorry that the chasm between us had to happen."

"I'm sorry, too, Justin. I wanted to be a good mother, but every day—"

"Every day you had to be reminded of what your husband and sister had done. I'm sorry Dad hurt you like that. He may have had his reasons, and your marriage may not have been the best, but you tried. You stuck it out. That's more than most people would have done under the circumstances." He rose and kissed her cheek, and for the first time in his life, he saw his mother's tears.

He sat in silence awhile, adjusting to the news they shared and accepting the reality.

"What will you do now?" she asked.

"About us?"

"No. Susan."

"I need to find her. I've been so afraid to marry, afraid I would mess up her life and not be a good husband. I'm not worried anymore. I love her, but I've never been able to tell her."

"Then find her, Justin." She lifted her cup and took another sip, then replaced it on the saucer. "I know we still have much to talk about, but now, I'm ready to go home. You have things to do, and I'm sure Rèmi and Clovis will be waiting for me.

"They don't know, do they?" He studied her face for the truth.

"No, but I think they'll enjoy seeing the difference in both of us when you come to visit."

"And so will we." He smiled, and she smiled back.

♥

"You're upset," Georgia said, standing in the doorway of her guestroom. "Maybe this was a mistake."

Susan looked up from her unpacking, praying tears wouldn't pervade her eyes again. "It's the only thing I could do. Nothing will change in Devereaux."

"But I thought you and your mother—"

"Yes." She opened a drawer, "Momma and I are doing much better. I think we finally came to an understanding. I'm talking about Justin and me."

"You really fell for him, didn't you?"

"Yes, but this time it's worse." She remembered the pregnancy and rethought her statement. "It's not worse, but it's more hurtful this time. I'm older and, I thought, wiser, but that proved false. I let my heart go as easily as a helium balloon. It soared off into his gray eyes."

Georgia moved closer and sat on the edge of the bed. "Then why did you leave?"

"He told me to."

"He what?"

"It's a long story, and I'm not ready to talk about it now."

Georgia rose and wrapped her arms around Susan. "You know, Susan, harsh words aren't always the heart speaking. Do you think you should have waited? I know I tempted you with this job, but that was selfish. I want you to be happy, and I'm not sure it'll happen here."

"I have to give it a try, and thanks for letting me stay with you on such short notice."

"You're always welcome, and I'm sorry I can't be with you here tonight. I have a date."

"A date. Wonderful. Anything serious?"

Georgia shrugged. "Not now, but it could be. He's a really nice man. We only met a few weeks ago. Time will tell."

"I'm happy for you. Go have a good time. I need to get my resume together and set up an appointment for the job interview."

"I think you'll love it. You'd be working with promotion for the Pilgrimage plus involved with the staff who'll work in the houses."

Susan closed her suitcase and slid it to the floor. "I've always admired the antebellum homes in Natchez. I'd love to work inside them."

"You'll have your chance if you take the position."

"If I'm offered the position."

Georgia grinned. "I have no doubt."

♥

Justin pulled into the driveway and walked up the gallery steps. The house seemed lonely without Susan and his mother. He was supposed to open the bed and breakfast in another month, and though Susan had hired some staff, he was missing the most important person—Susan. No one could replace her at Rose Arbor or in his heart.

He wandered up the staircase and returned to the room Susan had used. The fresh paint, the new quilt and pillow, the shining surfaces—everything spoke to him of her touch. He sat on the edge of the bed and ran his hand over the mattress, picturing her lying there at night while he slept in the gallery bedroom.

Curiosity roused him to pull open the drawer again and pull out the journal. He checked the first date in the book—1970. He'd been born in 1971. He slipped off his shoes and reclined on the bed, burying his nose in the pillow a moment, longing for the familiar fragrance of Susan's shampoo.

He turned again to the journal, releasing a ragged sigh. Guilt charged through him as he opened the cover. Yet knowing the information in this volume had changed his life, he felt requited.

He scanned the opening pages. Libby wrote about David someone. That wasn't his father. Why had Susan assumed the man his aunt called David had been his father? He became more intent as he read Libby's words—I've lost control, we should know better, we're taking chances, and then, Justin read the final blow. Libby had become pregnant.

David? Why had Libby called his father David? To protect him? But why had Susan presumed this? He wanted an explanation.

His fist smacked the soft mattress, a useless gesture and about as useless as his desire to talk with Susan. Where had she gone?

He turned his focus back to the journal, tearing through the pages as Libby's entries jumped weeks at a time. His gaze settled on an October entry. *Caroline has agreed to take my child as her own.* A rush of blood raced to his head as his vision blurred.

Startled, he lowered the journal and breathed deeply, fighting the white flashes behind his eyes. He needed to regain control of himself. He waited a moment to calm his throbbing pulse, then opened the journal again.

A trip to Europe had been part of the cover-up plan. He read Libby's heartache, knowing she would live her life without David and her child. Her child—Justin. It seemed so unreal, like a movie he'd watched that captured his emotion.

His chest tightened as the November entry jarred him. *I will learn to live the lie and allow Adam to have his child and Caroline to be the mother she should have been all along.* The words struck him as proof. He understood why Susan had made her assumption—no longer a guess but reality. His mother had validated it.

He read to the end, Libby's last entry—the Emily Dickinson poem on remorse. His stomach knotted, imagining the sorrow his aunt had felt giving up her child and the man she loved. But she'd realized that with the loss and her repentance came forgiveness. She had reconciled with God as he had just done.

But Justin knew he had the opportunity for another reconciliation. He'd wronged Susan years ago by taking her virginity so lightly, and he'd gone off to college not realizing the repercussion of his action. He'd thought of her often. He sensed that Susan had avoided relationships from that point on. He'd ruined her life.

He owed her more than that, not as a payback, but because he truly loved her. Understanding his past, eased his fears. Libby had loved life. She had been a good role model and would have been a wonderful mother had she had the chance, but she'd given up the opportunity to save his mother and father's reputation and marriage. He'd always considered theirs a weak relationship, a poor marriage, but realizing the strength it had taken them to stay together and to make their vows work, despite all the setbacks, gave him new hope. He couldn't let love slip through his fingers so easily.

He slipped the journal back into the drawer, and as he did, a scratching sound came from inside. He withdrew the journal and reached inside. His fingers grasped a chain. When he pulled it out, his heart stopped.

Susan's locket.

She always wore the locket, and his spirit weighted knowing the meaning of her leaving it behind.

He ran his finger over the etched face, then snapped the latch, and when he opened the pendant, a small round photo fell from its frame and slipped to the floor.

He reached down and retrieved it. The picture was the one of him that he'd seen the day Susan had shown it to him. Opening the pendant again to replace it, his pulse skipped. Within the same frame, he saw his father's photo from years earlier. His picture had covered it.

He held the locket in his hand, fighting the emotion that rattled through him, seeing another validation of his father and aunt's relationship. He managed to calm himself, then maneuvered his photograph where it had been lodged and snapped the cover.

The locket belonged to Susan, no matter what happened between them. His determination grew. He would give it back to her, and he prayed she would accept the love he had to give. He slipped the chain into his pocket with a prayer.

Justin rose from the bed. Sitting there was passive. He needed to act. Where would she go? The first thought was Susan's friend Georgia. Had she gone back to Natchez where she'd lived for so long, or would she have gone back to Baton Rouge?

Having no idea, he did what was logical. She had a cell phone. He grasped the phone and called her number. When it rang, his heart flew to his throat. But she didn't answer. It rang again. Again. Again. He feared she had blocked his number. So now what?

Georgia. He would call her, but how? He'd never heard her last name. He remembered she worked for an organization that had to do with the historical homes in Natchez, but that information would be too vague to locate her. The only person who could answer his question was Susan's mother.

He headed for the telephone and punched in the number he'd come to know by heart. When he heard Margaret's voice, he sent up a prayer.

"This is Justin, Mrs. Boyd. I'm trying to locate—"

"Susan's gone."

"I know, but I need to speak with her. Could you—"

"I can't help you."

Justin stared at the mouthpiece without speaking. He heard a click, then silence until the dial tone clicked in. He slammed his fist against the wall, his knuckles stinging from the impact. He shook his throbbing hand, checked the wall for damage and, seeing none, hung up the phone.

He needed to get a grip. Anger wouldn't solve the problem, nor would force. He'd keep trying.

He sat at the table, his mind reeling. His mother? Had Susan said something to her? His hope rose as he returned to the phone. They'd spent time together before Susan left. Had she mentioned anything?

With his knuckles throbbing, he picked up the receiver and pressed in his mother's number. Clovis answered and he waited for his mother to get on the line.

Clovis' and Rèmi's faces hung in his thoughts when he'd taken his mother home. They'd greeted him with bright smiles and affection that he'd enjoyed as a boy. They'd been faithful and recalling that his mother had known about their special treats and hadn't stopped them. It warmed his heart.

When Caroline answered, he asked his question.

"I don't recall her mentioning anything, Justin. I didn't talk to her when she left. She had her mother call me."

"I meant earlier in the day. Anything?"

"No. She seemed busy with her own projects. I'm sorry."

He thanked her and hung up, then recalled the notes Susan had kept for the bed and breakfast. Had she jotted down Georgia's telephone number when she'd called her? He searched around the kitchen, then in the dining room and found a folder of her plans in a drawer of the buffet.

He sank into a chair and opened the folder. He went through each piece—her list of furnishings, a copy of the brochure, the web site info, bills from purchases, resumes of the people she'd interviewed with notes on the ones she'd hired. No reference to Georgia.

His head ached, and he lowered it and rested his forehead on the pile of documents. What would he do now? The answer seemed easy. He prayed.

When the telephone rang, his head jolted upward, and he raced to it, praying the caller was Susan—even her mother. Instead he heard his mother's voice.

"I've been thinking about what you asked, and I remember now that Susan had seemed distraught and I asked her if she had a problem. She said a friend had called to tell her about a job opening in Natchez."

Natchez. He'd been right.

"She wasn't sure she wanted to pursue it, because she'd made a commitment to you." She faltered for a moment. "I'm sorry, Justin, but I told her not to give up on her dream to make others happy."

He realized the impact of that statement. His mother had done that. "I wondered if she might have gone to Natchez. She spent a number of years there before moving to Baton Rouge."

"Did she mention her friends name? I'm sure it's Georgia, but I don't know the last name."

"I'm positive she didn't. I went over the conversation in my head, so I had it right."

"Thanks. At least I know she's in Natchez."

He hung up and stared at the phone again. Margaret Boyd was his key, but she'd rejected him once. Wouldn't she do the same again?

♥

Susan shifted the telephone to the other ear. "I just wanted to tell you I had a job interview on Monday, Momma, and it looks good."

"It's what you want?"

No. She wanted a life with Justin. She wanted Rose Arbor. "I think it'll be fine. I'd work with people involving the Pilgrimage tours in the spring and fall. Many tourists stay in Natchez and visit the homes. It's really exciting."

"I'm glad, then."

Her mother's voice sounded strained. "Is something wrong, Momma? Aren't you feeling well?" She realized she'd been so wrapped up in her problems, she had forgotten about her mother's illness.

"I'm fine. Don't worry about me."

Susan hesitated, yet sensed her mother had something on her mind. "Is something bothering you?"

"Justin's called three times since you've been gone."

Justin. Her pulse skipped. "What did he say?"

"He wants your telephone number. He knows you're in Natchez and suspects you blocked his number."

How did he know that? She pushed her thoughts back, wondering if she'd ever mentioned Georgia's offer. She didn't think she had. "Did you tell him?"

"No. His mother remembered you had a job offer there."

Caroline. Caroline, who once referred to her as a farmer's daughter had been helping Justin find her. Her joy vanished as the heartache grew.

"But, I wanted to give him the number, Susan. Will you let me tell him where you are?"

"It's best that you don't."

"If you're sure, Susan. He's very determined. He asked me about Georgia's last name and if I knew where she worked."

He was trying to locate her through Georgia. Justin could be overbearing when he had his mind set on something. "You did the right thing. Don't involve Georgia. This is between Justin and me."

After she promised her mother she would call again soon, she hung up the phone, feeling lonelier than she'd ever felt in her life…even worse than when she'd originally come to Natchez.

When she arrived, she'd felt hurt and betrayed, not lonely, and by the time loneliness had set in, she had felt more empty than anything.

God's words rose in her mind. Forgive so that the Lord can forgive you. The hurt seemed too fresh to deal with now. If Justin wanted to find her, he would. That would be God's will and not hers.

When she returned to the living room, Georgia pulled the recliner handle and sat upright. "How is she?"

"Good, but—"

Georgia's expression shifted to concern. "What?"

Susan sank onto the sofa. "Justin's looking for me. He can't remember your last name. He's called my mother, but she won't tell him without my permission."

"Did you give it?"

"No. I don't know what to do, Georgia."

"Before you accept the position, you'd better decide." Her expression changed as she rose and sat beside Susan. "You don't have to tell me, but something big is going on between you and Justin. I suspected you had a deeper connection with him than you let on. If it's that important, Susan, you need to resolve it before it's too late."

Susan lowered her head, surprised that Georgia had been aware of what she'd tried to hide. She nodded. "I've struggled with something for years, and being back with Justin has only made it more complicated."

"I'll listen if you want to tell me. I love you, Susan. You're a good friend. Whatever you tell me is between us."

Justin's situation is what Susan longed to talk about, but that was his. Could she tell Georgia about her own trials. If she were truly forgiven, shc should be able to. She drew in a ragged breath.

"I learned some things about Justin's family that caused the rift over the weekend. Some important things that I'm not comfortable talking about, not now, but maybe someday with Justin's permission."

"I'd rather not know until Justin's ready," Georgia said.

"I thought I could change him. I thought what I learned could calm the stormy look that opened my heart to him as a girl and love him without reservation. But only God can work that kind of miracle. I should have known."

"God expects us to do our best dealing with problems. Don't beat yourself up."

"I know. Still, I'd hoped. But you're right, Georgia. Justin and I had a past."

Georgia held her hands while Susan told her story, the sad, horrible story she hadn't spoken above a whisper to anyone but her parents and Pastor Ralph.

Georgia didn't blanch. She listened with sorrow on her face and love in her eyes. Tears flowed down Susan's cheeks as she told about her stillborn child and her feeling that not only her family, but God had abandoned her.

Georgia released her hands and placed her arms around Susan's body holding her close, rocking back and forth as a mother would her child, and when her tears were spent, Susan realized the gift that had occurred. The weight of her secret had once again been lifted from her shoulders.

If only she could tell Justin, then let Jesus carry her burden.

Chapter Twenty-three

Justin strode across the grass and stepped onto the Boyd's veranda. He'd called numerous times and got nothing. A week had passed, and he prayed that face-to-face Margaret would relent. He had no doubt she knew about his relationship with Susan and that had been the cause of her anger. He'd always wondered why it had dragged on so long. He could only guess her parents had blamed him for Susan remaining single.

And rightly so.

But he needed to ask her forgiveness, just as the Lord told him to do. Forgive as the Father forgives you.

When he rapped on the door, he heard nothing. The house seemed quiet, and he wondered if she'd gone out. The car stood in the driveway, but someone may have picked her up for a church circle. Susan mentioned she liked to lunch with the ladies and often went to circle meetings.

He rapped again and waited, then overwrought with disappointment, he stepped from the veranda. But the door opened, and he swung around facing Margaret. She stood inside looking at him with unwelcome eyes.

"Please, may I speak with you for just a minute. I—"

"It's not my place to tell you where Susan is." She gripped the door as if he might try to jerk it from her hands.

"I know where she is. I only need a phone number, but that's not the only reason I came."

Her eyebrows lifted, and she cocked her head.

"I came to ask your forgiveness."

"Forgiveness." She took a step backward as if unsure what to make of him.

"I know you're aware of what happened between Susan and me so many years ago, and I can only guess that's why you hate me so much. I'm sorry for anything I've done to hurt Susan or your family. I only want to ask your forgiveness."

Margaret came closer to the screen and rested her arm against the doorjamb. She didn't speak for an eternity, and he waited for her verdict.

"I told Susan I wouldn't give you the phone number, Justin, but I think this is important. You only know half of the hurt she went through, and maybe it's time you know the full story."

Her words sounded ominous, and fear coiled up his back like a snake waiting to strike. "What is it?"

She pushed the door open and stepped back. "Come inside."

He hesitated. He'd never set foot inside Susan's home in all the years he'd known her.

Margaret led him into her living room with flowery print upholstery and pale-yellow walls. Pictures hung around the room, and the stone mantel held family photos that tugged at his emotion. Susan's photograph stood on one end, the same way she looked at the time he'd left for college.

She motioned to a chair, and he lowered himself into it while she sat across from him.

"Perhaps Susan has done you a disservice, and I think you'll understand more if I tell you. I pray she won't hate me for this."

Frissons tingled along his arms, and his hands felt numb as he clenched them in his lap.

She began her story, and Justin listened, his throat in his mouth when he realized where the story was going. When he could remain quiet no longer, he held up his hand to stop her.

"Pregnant?" The word rushed over him like ice water. "Susan was pregnant?"

"Yes. We were heartsick."

"And that's why she went to Natchez."

"Yes, we had family there. They're gone now, but back then I had an elderly cousin who agreed she could stay with them."

"And the baby?" His heart pounded so loudly he could barely hear his own voice.

Margaret didn't answer.

"Where's the baby?"

She lowered her head, looking at her vein-gnarled hands clutched in her lap. "He was stillborn."

A sob came from Justin's throat. Stillborn. He. A son. Stillborn. His heart hammered against his chest until he thought it would break through. He covered his eyes, feeling the tears flow through his fingers. Susan had endured the grief alone in Natchez. She'd suffered for his sin. She'd unselfishly carried the burden to protect him.

"Justin." Margaret's soft voice forced him to lift his head. His sight was blurred, and he brushed away the moisture before he could get her in focus.

"I'm sorry. I know it's difficult."

"I love her, Mrs. Boyd. She's the best thing that ever happened to me. I need to tell her that and—" He paused to swallow back his emotion. "—and to tell her how sorry I am for what she went through—all of you. You could have dragged me through hot coals."

"And ourselves, too." Her head lowered as she spoke. "We thought we were saving Susan from all the gossip."

Margaret rose, crossed to a small desk by the window, and came back with a piece of paper. He looked at the numbers she'd scrawled.

"She's at Georgia's. That's her address and phone number. I'd recommend you call first."

He clutched the paper as he rose. "Thank you. Thank you from the bottom of my heart."

She crossed to him and wrapped her fingers over his hand. "I'll pray for you. I'll pray for you and Susan."

♥

"I think I'll enjoy the work," Susan said. "I was startled when he offered to let me spend a couple days with the staff before I make up my mind. Everyone has been very nice, and I've had a chance to see how things work."

"But you don't sound enthusiastic," Georgia said, wiping the last of the dinner dishes.

"I have a week to decide. He invited me back next week whenever I want." Susan's thoughts strayed until she managed to get them back on track. "I don't want to take advantage of these people. I'm struggling, Georgia."

"You said Justin's trying to get in touch. Let him. Then you can make a wiser decision."

"I know."

"You'll have to call him."

"I could tell Momma to give him the number if he asks again."

The telephone's jingle stopped the conversation. Georgia picked it up, said hello, then turned toward Susan and pointed at the phone. "It's for you."

"My mother?"

Georgia shook her head. "It's Justin." She handed her the telephone, then left the kitchen, leaving Susan alone.

Susan's chest tightened as she sank into a chair. "How did you get my number?"

"Your mother."

His answer knocked her backward. "My mother? I'm surprised."

"So was I, but she gave it to me without my asking."

That made no sense, but he sounded like he meant it.

"I need to talk with you, Susan. In person. Not on the phone. Can I come to Natchez tomorrow?"

Sunday. Could she bare to see him and let him go again. "I don't know if that's a good idea, Justin. I think you told me all I needed to hear when—"

"I'm sorry for that. It was ignorant and unfounded. You told me the truth. I'd asked for it. Demanded it. I've spoken with my mother. I know the truth, and we've made great strides in the past days. I owe it to you."

"I'm glad, Justin. That's what I wanted to hear."

"I know. I understand why you told me. I read the last journal myself. I saw what you saw. I understood what I read. I have questions, but that's not important now. I have more important things to talk about."

"I'm sorry I left you in a lurch with the bed and breakfast. I'd recommend—"

"Susan, please." He released a puff of air. "This isn't about that."

His voice barked over the phone, and she drew back the receiver until he silenced.

"Don't raise your voice to me, Justin. I thought you'd called about—"

"I called about us. I don't care a dime about the business. I'll give up Rose Arbor if I must, but I can't give up you."

"Please, Justin. I don't know if I can trust you anymore."

"Don't say that, Susan. Please, believe me. Just let me talk with you. Give me an hour. A half-hour."

"What's made the difference? I'm trying to start a new life here. It's a good job, and I need to find peace of mind."

"I want your forgiveness." His voice faded so soft she barely heard him.

"I forgive you, if that's what you want. I've never held anything against you, Justin."

He began to speak, but his voice cracked. "I don't mean for this incidence. I'm talking about the past."

The past. He'd talked to her mother. Susan froze as icy reality streamed over her. He knew.

"You talked with my mother. She told you." Anger burned within her at her mother's disclosure, yet in a heartbeat the flame turned to embers, then ash. Now he knew. That guilt had ended. He knew, and yet he'd called.

"Let's talk in person, Susan, not on the phone. This is not a thing to talk about when we're miles apart. I'll come tonight."

Pity. He felt guilt and pity. If he hadn't been able to fully love her before, then he only responded now out of regret and sympathy. She didn't want it. "I don't think so, Justin. It's over and done with. It was years ago. I never held you at fault. It was my own actions as much as yours. You're forgiven."

"Susan. If you'd only told me. If you'd only— Don't do this, I'm begging you. "

"I'm sorry, Justin. This is really for the best. You understand my problem and know more about your own. I understand yours. We need to get on with our lives. I appreciate your call, but I'm staying here. Please don't come. I don't want to see you."

"Susan, listen, I—"

She lowered the telephone to the cradle and wept.

♥

Justin thrashed between the sheets, plumped his pillow and buried his face in the soft down. He'd looked at the clock only minutes earlier. It was three in the morning, and he couldn't sleep.

Susan had sent him into doldrums of despair. She wouldn't listen, and he'd spent the night praying that God intervene. He'd sat beside the telephone waiting for her to call back and agree to see him. The phone remained silent.

He turned again, finally shoved back the sheet and slipped his legs to the floor. He sat a moment on the edge of the mattress while his future lay like cold sod in his mind. Nothing. His life was nothing without Susan. He'd wronged her, and he'd hurt her, but he'd also repented. What more could he do?

The moonlight spilled through a crevice in the shade, and he rose. He arched his back, stretching it to relieve the pain that settled there with the weight of his thoughts. He looked around the room, Libby's bedroom once, then his mother's, but tonight his.

Perhaps that had been his mistake. He should have slept in the gallery guestroom where he'd been the past weeks while his mother had been with him. He passed through the parlor and picked up Libby's Bible, then stepped onto the gallery and made his way to the guestroom.

Inside, he stood on familiar ground. He sank into a chair beside a table and opened the Bible. He'd been reading verses from First Corinthians and flipped pages until he'd located where he'd left off.

His eyes burned from lack of sleep and blurred as he tried to read the small print. His focus settled on the thirteenth chapter. Love is patient, love is kind. He hadn't been patient, but he'd tried to be kind. He'd wanted to follow God's will and repent. He'd wanted to make amends.

He lowered his eyes again. Love is not self-seeking, it is not easily angered, it keeps no record of wrongs. *Lord, I've kept a record of my wrongs. Susan is innocent, but I have been angry. Angry at myself and at her*. He read on. Love rejoices with the truth. It always protects, always trusts, always hopes, always perseveres.

Susan had meant to protect him in so many ways. What had he done for her? His gaze lowered to the scripture. Love never fails.

Lord, if this is true, if love never fails then I'll put my trust in you.

He closed the Bible and stretched out on the bed while the verse repeated in his head.

Startled, he jolted upward in bed. He took a moment to acclimate himself. A sound on the gallery jarred him, and he sat up. Is that what had wakened him?

His heart pumped as he rose and peeked through the small gap between the shade and the window frame. Had Susan come back? A shadowy figure moved along the gallery toward the kitchen door, stopped a moment, then headed back. From the shape, he knew it wasn't Susan, and though disappointed, adrenaline spurred him to the door.

He flung it open as the intruder passed. "What are you doing?"

The sun hadn't risen, but in the half-lit dawn, he saw the face of a frightened elderly man, white hair and blue eyes as wide as a full moon. "I'm sorry," he said. "I-I—" He flung his hand toward the kitchen door. "I don't sleep well, and sometimes I used to bring a rose for Libby to surprise her."

Justin searched the man's face, his eyes willed with sincerity. "So, it's you who's been bringing the roses."

"Yes. I know she's gone, but..."

His voice faded, yet Justin heard the sorrow.

He glanced down at his pajamas, motioned for the gentleman to wait, then reached for his robe. "Would you like to come in for some coffee?"

"I didn't mean to wake you. I tried to be quiet not to bother anyone."

"I haven't slept well myself. Please," he said again, "come in."

The man nodded and followed him to the door, then into the kitchen. Justin put on a pot of coffee while the gentleman waited and then steered him into the parlor. After they'd been seated, Justin asked the question that had piqued his curiosity. "Who are you?"

"My name's Arthur LaPlante. Libby and I have been friends for the past twenty-years or so."

"Twenty years?"

He nodded. "I live a couple streets over. I liked to walk, and we met on one of my morning jaunts. Libby was a lovely woman."

"You were just neighbors, then?"

"Neighbors, yes, but more companions. Getting old is lonely."

A deep sorrow rocked Justin.

"I would have married her if she'd have me, but she said it was better to be friends."

"And you've been bringing flowers here since she died?"

"I always brought Libby flowers. She loved them. She would laugh and call me the family ghost." He gestured toward the room off the gallery. "She told me about the family myth. She thought it was amusing that I sneaked the rose over in the wee hours of the morning. I loved to hear her laugh."

"So did I," He remembered Libby's lilting voice.

"You're one of her relatives, I suppose. Is it Justin?" he asked.

"I'm Justin, yes. I'm..." He paused, letting the thought roll through his mind. "I'm her nephew. Her sister's son."

"She loved you. She often talked about you. She left Rose Arbor to you, I know."

"She did."

"And you can't sell it."

"That's right." He eyed the man wondering if he'd given her the idea.

"She told me. I told her it was a hard stipulation to add to a will, and she said you'd understand."

Justin nodded. He did, especially now.

The scent of coffee drifted into the room, and Justin rose and went for the drinks. He stood in the silence thinking about Libby and Susan—two of the most important women in his life. As he thought about all that he'd learned, he saw how their lives had paralleled in a unique, yet sad way, and he'd been part of both.

He needed patience. Arthur seemed to have it. He'd stuck by Libby without any promise of commitment, yet loved her with his heart, but lately his patience hadn't faired so well. Patience was a gift of the Spirit. He closed his eyes a moment, thinking about God's will and his own. He prayed they would mesh, yet he would have to accept whatever came to be.

He forced his eyes wider though sleep weighted them and read the clock. He wanted to go to church in the morning. He needed to go, because today he planned to put his problem in God's hands, but before that, he had another job to do.

He poured coffee into the cups, picturing the elderly gentleman who sat in the parlor. The awareness filled him with gratefulness, knowing Libby had not been alone all these years as he'd thought. Just like her, he realized now, she'd had another secret friend to keep her company.

Libby's life had been filled with secrets. Justin suspected most everyone's did.

Chapter Twenty-four

Before church, Justin had sent Susan flowers with a simple message that said, "Love is patient." He figured she'd understand. The day had dragged on as if unending. He sat in the parlor, listening to the tick-tock of the clock.

The house creaked in the quiet. He should have gone back to Baton Rouge, but he couldn't. His heart was here at Rose Arbor. He'd learn to travel back and forth or sell his share of the business. He had to do something. He'd realized these past days that his life had been bound within these walls. Libby and Susan. Their faces glowed in his memory, and he could only pray that God would give him strength to face whatever happened.

He stood and wandered through the house, looking at Susan's handiwork. Everything was ready for the bed and breakfast except the most important job of hostess. To him a hostess should embody the spirit of Rose Arbor, a hostess should love the house as much as he did. Who could do the job better than Susan?

Who could complete him more than Susan?

As he stood in the dining room, he heard a sound on the gallery. Arthur, he figured, although it was probably too early for one of his mid-night walks. Perhaps he'd made a new friend.

He walked to the door and pulled it open. He peered through the screen but saw nothing. He opened the door and glanced at the vase where a new bud had been placed.

Justin smiled. Arthur would continue his visits, bringing a rose. He stepped onto the gallery, breathing in the sweetness of the night. He sank into the rocker, recalling the night he'd sat there trying to find the courage to go inside after Libby's funeral. That day had seemed so final, so empty, until Susan had appeared. A deep sigh escaped him, and he closed his tired eyes, praying tonight he could sleep.

He rocked a moment until something stirred him to open his eyes. Frissons prickled along his spine, and he rose, narrowing his eyes to look across the moonlit garden. When he saw her shadow, his pulse skipped before it galloped as he stepped from the gallery onto the dewy grass.

♥

Her heart thundering, Susan stood near the arbor and brushed tears from her eyes. She'd arrived, then struggled to find the courage to go to the door. The bouquet of flowers Justin had sent her filled her thoughts. Two dozen roses of every hue with three simple words on the card. Love is patient.

Her hard heart had softened, and at that moment, she knew that her prayers had been answered. God had touched her life in the most beautiful way. She'd made peace with her mother. Her meddling had brought peace to Justin's weighty spirit. And today, the Lord had blessed her with her own peace of mind by washing her in forgiveness.

"Susan."

Justin's soft voice touched her ear like a welcomed breeze.

"Justin. I'm sorry."

He drew her into his arms and pressed his finger against her lips. "No more sorrys. No more apologies. No more secrets. This is all I need." He pressed his palm against her cheek and brushed it with his feathery touch. "Finally, we've come full circle." He gave a slight toss of his head. "Is the rose from you?"

She nodded, feeling her heart would burst as she thought back. "I was wrong, Justin. Time doesn't change things. It's a healer. It's a gift."

"You're the gift. You brought me to life, Susan. You gave me love when I thought I wasn't worthy. You gave me hope when I felt lost. You gave me your all."

This time she pressed her finger against his mouth. "It's what was meant to be, Justin. It began so long ago, and tonight is another beginning."

"On the same kind of night." He drew her closer, his heart thundering against hers. "I took part of you that night, and tonight I'm giving it back. It's been part of me, and now we can be one forever, Susan. I love you. Please don't ever leave me. I promise to be here for you in sickness and health. I promise to be a good father to our children. I promise to love you until death...and even afterward."

He reached into his pocket and pulled out something that glinted in the moonlight. He caught her shoulder and turned her away from him, then reached around her. She saw the glint again as it fell against her neck. The locket. He was clasping the locket.

His words washed over her like a healing balm. The sense of wholeness, of completeness filled her heart and soul. When he'd finished, she turned back and rapped her arms around his neck. "I love you, too, Justin. I have forever."

His mouth found hers—tender, yet promising; gentle yet powerful. He eased back and kissed her eyes and the tip of her nose, then sought her mouth again, and she knew that the secret places of her heart had opened, love had filled the empty space, and she would never let it go.

♥

Six Years Later

"This is such a lovely house," the woman said. "And such amazing history."

"Do you find it difficult to raise two children with tourists coming and going?"

Susan chuckled. "Not at all. They love the guests, and it's a wonderful place for children to grow up. We have a special sense of family here."

"Momma, can I pick some roses?"

Susan turned and looked at her four-year-old son. "Wait until I can help you, Taylor. For now, please keep an eye on Libby."

Hearing her name, two-year-old Libby rose on wobbly legs and headed for her mother.

"Come here, Suga'," Susan said.

"She's beautiful." The woman smiled at the toddler. "And such a pretty name."

"She's named after my husband's aunt who owned the plantation. She was an amazing woman. She loved this place so dearly."

The woman chucked Libby's cheek, then looked at Susan, "I'd guess this house has so many secrets it could tell."

"You wouldn't believe how many."

Hearing Justin's voice, Susan's heart lurched as he stepped behind her. He wrapped his arm around her shoulders, and as always, she felt lost in his embrace. She loved him more each day and still felt like a schoolgirl in his arms. "This is my husband, Justin Robard."

"Nice to meet you," the man said, shaking Justin's hand. "I'm looking forward to spending a couple days at your charming bed and breakfast."

"We're glad to have you," Justin said.

"Tell us about the bedroom on the gallery," the woman said, motioning toward the one-story wing. "I've read in a little book I bought in town that it's haunted. Do you really believe in ghosts?"

Susan grinned at Justin before she turned to the woman, "No, we're Christians and don't believe in ghosts, but I have a wonderful story to tell y'all about a rose that appeared so many nights beside the kitchen door."

The woman drew closer and followed Susan toward the gallery. "A rose?"

"Yes, a fresh rose in the small vase you see beside the door."

"Please. I'd love to hear about it."

"Well, the story goes this way..."

~~~
~~~

Recipe: New Orleans Beignets

The French style donuts are popular in many places but are found especially in New Orleans Louisiana. Café Du Monde is where I've had them. They are delicious and worth the time making them.

Ingredients

- 1/4 ounce package active dry yeast
- 1/4 cup warm water (110° to 115°)
- 1 cup evaporated milk
- 1/2 cup cooking oil
- 1/4 cup sugar
- 1 large egg
- 4-1/2 cups self-rising flour
- Oil for frying
- Confectioners' sugar

Directions

- In a large bowl, dissolve yeast in warm water. Add milk, oil, sugar, egg and 2 cups flour. Beat until smooth. Stir in enough remaining flour to form a soft dough (dough will be sticky). Do not knead. Cover and refrigerate overnight.
- Remove from refrigerator. Punch dough down. Turn onto a floured surface and roll into a 16x12-in. rectangle. Cut into 2-in. squares or triangles.
- In an electric skillet or deep-fat fryer, heat oil to 375°. Fry squares/triangles, a few at a time, until golden brown on both sides. Drain on paper towels. Roll warm beignets in confectioners' sugar.

- **About Gail**
- Best-selling and award-winning novelist, Gail Gaymer Martin is the author of contemporary romance and romantic suspense with 87 published novels and over five million books sold. Her novels have won numerous national awards, including: the ACFW Carol Award, RT Reviewer's Choice Award and Booksellers Best. Gail is the author of Writer Digest's *Writing the Christian Romance***.** She is a founder of American Christian Fiction Writers and a member of Advanced Speakers and Writers. Gail is a keynote speaker at churches, civic and business organizations and a workshop presenter at conferences across the U.S. She lives with husband Bob in Sedona, AZ. Contact her by mail at: PO Box 20054, Sedona, AZ 86341 or on her website or social media.
- Website:www.gailgaymermartin.com
- Facebook:www.facebook.com/gail.g.martin.3
- Twitter:http://twitter.com/GailGMartin
- GoodReads: http://bit.ly/1e8Gt6D
- LinkedIn: www.linkedin.com/in/gailgaymermartin
- **Gail's Books from Winged Publication**
- **Novels - *Reissues***

- Dreaming of Castles 2014
- Out On A Limb 2016
- Over Her Head 2017
- Love Comes To Butterfly Tree Inn 2017
- A Love Unforeseen 2017
- Loving Treasures
- Loving Hearts
- Loving Ways
- Loving Care
- Loving Promises
- Loving Kisses
- Loving Arms
- Teacher's Pet (Former: Dad in Training)
-
- **Novels - New**
- Treasures Of Her Heart 2014
- Romance By Design 2015
- Mackinac Island Christmas 2017
- Love in the Air 2018
-
- **Novellas Reissues**
- An Open Door
- Apples Of His Eye
- Better To See You
- Once A Stranger
- Then Came Darkness
- To Keep Me Warm
- True Riches
- Yuletide Treasures
-
- **Novellas - New**
- Lattes and Love Songs 2015
- Apple Blossom Daze 2016
- A Trip To Remember 2016
- A Tucumcari Christmas 2016
- Poppy Fields and You, 2017
- Love Comes to Butterfly Tree Inn 2017
- Tumbling Into Love 2017
- Lost In Red Rock Country 2017

- Autumn's Fresh Beginnings 2017
-
- **Collections**
- Christmas Potpourri
- Forget Me Not Romances #1
- Forget Me Not Romances #2
- Love Blooms In The Here & Now
- Mocha Marriage
- Romance Across the Globe
- Romance On The Run
- Seven Mysterious Ladies
- With This Ring
- A Kiss is Still a Kiss
- Get Your Kiss On Route 66
- Valentine Matchmakers

Made in the USA
Monee, IL
08 September 2019